FERRY TO HONG KONG

Ferry To Hong Kong

By

Brian W. Lewis

FERRY TO HONG KONG
A ROMANTIC ADVENTURE

This book is a work of fiction.

Any resemblance to persons living, dead, or otherwise engaged is purely co-incidental.

Please put 10p into the pot, times are hard!

My thanks to John Williams for his sound advice during the writing of this book.

Sincere apologies to my cat 'Tiger' who endured an amount of verbal 'ear ache' on less than perfect 'litter'ary days!

BRIAN. W. LEWIS
(ARTIST & WRITER OF NO FIXED ABODE)

CHAPTER 1

It was the year 1959, and springtime in England. The trees and hedgerows were starting to bear new greenery and the land was waking from its frosty sleep, the long winter was over.

Steve Galway stared out of the 3rd class railway carriage window.

He was surprised by how clean it was and the fact that the 3rd had been newly painted.

He was alone in the small compartment, and the sliding door was firmly closed, shutting out a small amount of the 'clickety clack' noise created by the carriage wheels on the track. Possibly more passengers would arrive as the journey progressed, as it was a slow 'stopping' train and people would come and go.

He looked up at the woven material luggage rack and his holdall. He hoped that he had packed everything he needed. Before long he would be in army uniform anyway, and casual slacks and sweaters would soon be a thing of the past whilst he was in training, which would last for about eight weeks. He loosened his neck-tie, unbuttoned the top of his white shirt, ran his fingers through his brown wavy hair, and relaxed on the green upholstered bench seat.

Steve had just reached his eighteenth year, and was travelling from his home in Somerset to enlist in the British Army at a training camp near Aldershot in Hampshire. He had been aware for some time that he would be required to carry out some type of military service at the age of eighteen, or National Service as it was generally known.

He had given the matter some thought for many months. Leaving the safety and security of home for the first time was a big step to take, and not one to be taken lightly! He had the choice of joining either the British Army, the Royal Air Force or the Royal Navy.

In his mind he had contemplated the three possibilities. The air force, he had read somewhere, was actually formed by transferring officers and men from the army's 'Corp of Royal Engineers'. The officers became pilots and the other ranks became responsible for the aircrafts' superstructure and engines. The air force, in its initial stage, was called the Royal Flying Corp (R.F.C.), changing to the Royal Air Force at a later date.

Steve dismissed the idea of the R.A.F. because of the type of hats they wore and the colour of the uniform.

He realised that it was a strange basis to form an important decision on, but then many major changes in a person's life are decided by a whim, or other people's thoughts and actions, such as Adolf Hitler in 1939!

The Royal Navy did have a certain allure. It would be an interesting and free way to see many parts of the world. But the thought of weeks, and possibly months cooped up on a ship made him feel quite claustrophobic, and he wasn't too sure about sea-sickness.

The army therefore, became his first and only choice. He also decided that rather than simply carrying out the two-year service as required by law, he would 'sign on' for six years and become a professional soldier. After a long discussion with the recruiting officer, he had the relevant papers and received the Queen's shilling.

The train slowly wound its way through the green countryside, and Steve decided to recount his early days in Somerset. He closed his eyes to concentrate his thoughts. The memories of his boyhood raced through his mind like a river in full flood as he travelled back in time.

Early memories of Somerset.

Steve, although born in Lancashire had been raised by his aunt in Somerset, having left Lancashire at the age of two.

He had no recollection of his parents, and had asked his Aunt Maude about them on many occasions. She had merely said that there had been 'problems', and that she would explain more fully to him when he was older and better able to understand the circumstances surrounding the marriage. She did say that one day his parents had divorced and that his mother had emigrated to Canada with a 'friend'!

The situation troubled Steve much during his early formative years, but as time went by his feelings of insecurity lessened, and he gradually accepted the circumstances and came to terms with life.

Aunt Maude had no children of her own, having lost her husband in the early stages of the war after only a few weeks of marriage. She had, therefore, accepted Steve as her own and was more of a mother to him than an aunt. Maude didn't spoil him, but made sure that he wanted for very little. He enjoyed school and found it easy to mix with other children, even though he was an only child with no brother or sister to interact with.

Aunt Maude encouraged him to engage in all kinds of sport. It was essential, she said, for his teenage development, with his mind and body being of equal importance. She always made certain he was presentably clothed but 'drilled' it into him that he should learn to take care of himself. On one occasion when he came home with a bleeding nose, he had complained tearfully the school bully hit him over a quarrel as to who owned a particular conker. Maude looked at him sympathetically, wiped the tears from his face with a flannel, and told him to go back to school and do the same thing to the bully. She taught him many such similar lessons over the next few years, and although at first he thought them to be harsh, he gradually understood their meaning, and the lessons were to hold him in good stead as his life evolved. Steve considered that if Aunt Maude had been fortunate enough to have her own children she would have made a very good mother.

He thought to himself, *What a pity that wars have to destroy people's lives so tragically, it's so cruel.* A second, more sobering thought entered his mind, and he said to himself, *Here I am enlisting into an army, and I will be carrying a weapon capable of destroying my fellow man! Still,* he concluded, *everyone must be able to defend themselves and their own territory that is nature's way!* He moved his thoughts on to other things, still feeling slightly guilty.

Through school Steve developed a keenness for sport, and was encouraged to do so by Aunt Maude. She made certain that his football kit was washed and ironed every week to a high standard, even though it would quickly be muddied in the wet winter months, after just ten minutes of hectic schoolboy football. Steve wasn't overly keen on cricket during the summer months; it was far too slow a game to be enjoyable. He preferred the rough and tumble of soccer and rugby football, but tried to enter into the spirit of the very English game, and was picked to play for the village youth team. Aunt Maude did make some very good cucumber sandwiches for the team, so cricket had its own compensations!

It was part of the school's curriculum that every pupil was given the opportunity to learn how to swim. Steve took full advantage of the fact, once again encouraged by an enthusiastic Aunt Maude, who was once herself a junior school champion. Once a week he and his class would be taken to the local council run indoor swimming baths where they were taught the rudiments of the breaststroke and 'Australian' crawl by one of the school's qualified teachers. As with many youngsters Steve was quick to learn and although he enjoyed school it was a chance to get away from the dreaded maths lessons.

He would arrive home after swimming, smelling strongly of chlorine. Aunt Maude would immediately strip him, place him a hot bath and shampoo his hair vigorously. Later she would make some cheese and pickled onion sandwiches, followed by a hot drink, usually 'Bourn-vital', before going to bed.

Aunt Maude was renowned locally for her cheese and pickled onion sandwiches, and in particular her home-made pickled onions. She would always buy the best Spanish onions from a Frenchman who came around the village regularly. Strings of onions dangled from his heavily laden bicycle, and he had come to know Maude well. He appreciated her obvious knowledge of onions, and always saved the best strings for her. She would study them closely, squeeze them and feel the weight. Weight was a very important factor, she explained to Steve one day when he had volunteered to carry the strings of onions into the house. Aunt Maude was a very prolific pickler of onions! Steve could never understand why a Frenchman should be selling 'Spanish onions'.

The many strings of onions were certainly very weighty, and Steve, as muscular as he was becoming, struggled to carry the ungainly strings into the house. He felt sorry for the Frenchman's bicycle!

Maude had learnt the pickling recipe from an ageing aunt. It had been passed down to her from one generation to another, always by word of mouth, and nothing had ever been written down. Maude's aunt had made her swear on the Bible never to divulge the secret recipe to anyone until it was absolutely necessary! Aunt Maude, being a God fearing woman had gladly agreed, and in turn made certain that she wrote nothing down, but memorised it in the same way that a child would by repetition and practice.

The annual church fete was the ideal stage for Maude to display her pickles, and they were always a great success. The fete was always held in aid of the church restoration fund. The church itself was centuries old and constantly in need of repair. It was, naturally, the centre of the local community and people always gave freely. The fete stalls, mainly collapsible wooden tables, were strategically dotted around the church grounds, and when covered with all kinds of bright welcoming tablecloths made a pleasant scene. Bunting was brought out from the church hall and draped over the surrounding trees which provided natural shade when the weather became too hot.

Many of the stalls were run by members of the local Women's Institute, so home-made jams, honey, and a variety of cakes were plentiful. Other stalls sold all kinds of arts and crafts. It wasn't until the fetes occurred that one realised, and appreciated how talented and clever the local people were.

The time it took to prepare and produce all the foods and articles must have been quite considerable, and was clearly the culmination of many months of work.

Steve always enjoyed the fete, and it gave him a chance to meet girls from the local community, and also those from the 'all girls' school which was about five miles away. He was gradually becoming more interested in the 'Fair Sex', and to his amazement football was slipping into second place!

The ladies of the Women's Institute often tried to enrol Aunt Maude into their ranks at fete time, but she was never tempted to join, and preferred to stay independent. She considered that if she was to become a member she would be pressurised in some way to divulge her secret recipe to them, probably during some W.I. ancient ritual after they had all partaken of several 'Brandy Snaps'. It was a thought that sent a shiver down her spine, as she was only human, after all was said and done.

The vicar himself, a pleasant and 'Godly' a man as he was, had quite often tried to prise the secret recipe from Maude. However, Maude's lips were sealed, and she was certain that the vicar had been put up to it by his wife who was very jealous of Maude's pickling accomplishments! But only in an ecclesiastical way of course! During one very hot summer's fete, when the nagging from his wife had become unbearable, the vicar resorted to bribery and blackmail. He said to Maude that he was certain the Lord would appreciate the spreading of the recipe amongst the local parishioners, and likened it to the feeding of the five thousand!

Maude, however, was quite unmoved. She said that when it was time for her to meet the Lord, she would hand the secret recipe over in person, and not before. Steve had often asked Aunt Maude about divulging the contents of the recipe, but after several negative attempts he concluded that if she wouldn't tell the 'Good Lord', what chance did he have, a mere mortal?

Life was fairly slow and relaxed in Somerset, and Steve continued with his schooling at a leisurely pace. He was keen to learn, but did not take education overly seriously, and enjoyed sport more than mathematics.

Like many young boys he developed an interest in railways and steam engines. He was not the 'train spotting' type though and couldn't understand why they found an interest in collecting locomotive engine numbers. But steam locomotives had a certain fascination, and he spent many an hour at the local railway station watching all the comings and goings. It was cheap entertainment, having only to purchase a platform ticket for a penny.

The sight of a working engine, with most of its working parts visible was enchanting, and the smell of hot oil mixed with steam was like a perfume to many a young boy of his age.

The road system in Somerset was not good, and many of the roads were no more than wide country lanes. The railways were therefore still a reliable proposition and always busy. As well as many passengers much commercial goods were transported, and most passenger trains had two or three goods wagons connected to the rear end. Fish and meat was carried and off-loaded by using cumbersome platform trolleys and sack trucks. Small lorries and vans would then take the goods to their eventual destinations.

Once a month a special train carrying sheep would arrive at the station. The sheep 'hopped' onto the platform, and once the leader of the flock had been pointed in the right direction of the station exit, the rest would follow. Steve always thought that they looked contented and happy, as if they were coming home from an enjoyable day's outing, and were looking forward to a welcome evening meal. They would walk out onto the main street and be shepherded to whichever local farm they were destined for.

The surrounding farmland was ideal for both cattle and sheep. The meadows were fairly flat and the grass rich and plentiful. Several rivers ran through the area, providing natural irrigation and fertility, a green and pleasant land indeed.

Steve, when in his early teens, often toyed with the idea of working on the land. It was a healthy outdoor life and he had spoken to Aunt Maude many times about it. But after much discussion they always came to the same conclusion, that the money simply wasn't good enough to provide a comfortable living. The work prospects in Steve's part of Somerset were not good, and many young people were moving away to find better jobs. It was a situation that caused the vicar and local dignitaries concern. The village was becoming smaller by the year, and relevant government subsidies were being reduced accordingly. If the situation continued, the village would die! It was a problem they all had to face up to, and Steve was no exception. But his future was partly pre-ordained by the War Department.

Steve had talked on several occasions to the engine crews at the railway station whilst they were preparing their locomotive for work. They were not optimistic when Steve asked about railway work and engine crew in particular. The work was hard, and the hours long and disruptive to any kind of social life. An important factor for any young man!

The prospect of compulsory military service at the age of eighteen was not far down the road, and a constant reminder about the future. In a way he was quite looking forward to it. At least the decision had been made for him, and it was a solid fact to work on.

CHAPTER 2

MEMORIES (CONT'D.)

Shortly before his sixteenth birthday Steve completed his school education. He had been a 'Good Average' student not excelling in any particular subject, but always in the 'upper' half of the class.

After some searching he started work at a small local family run business which manufactured electric lighting fittings, wall lights and small decorative chandeliers. He could look forward to two years of civilian employment before embarking on some type of military service. Providing all went well at the local factory he would have a steady financial income for the first time in his life. He could never repay Aunt Maude's love and caring for him, but at least he was now able to help with the monthly bills that never ceased to appear through the letter box. Sometimes financial assistance was more welcome than 'Hearts and Flowers'!

The electrical company employed two dozen people, and although only a minor company the order books were never empty. The workforce was content and happy. Steve came to learn different skills, working with wood, metal and electrical equipment. The owner of the company, a jovial man, well beyond his pensionable age, would wander around the factory giving words of encouragement, and was always eager to enter into conversation. He enjoyed recalling his previous experiences in life, which were many. He seemed to regard the factory as his hobby and used it to pass time to occupy his later years. The Production Manager was a very different 'kettle of fish'! A much younger man who demanded a day's work for a day's pay!

The factory's wood machinist was a middle-aged man named George Robertshaw. George had been a prisoner of the Japanese in Burma during the Second World War. His face was gaunt from years of malnutrition and his skin a pale yellow. He had suffered tortures under his captors, and he would probably never recover. Steve, although curious was reticent to ask questions about his horrendous experience, but George spoke freely about his captivity, and appeared to show no malice or revenge towards the Japanese. To Steve it was a strange attitude to take. After suffering such torture, wasn't it a natural reaction to feel hatred against your enemy? Although unaware of it at the time, Steve was to undergo a similar experience at the hands of a foreign captor in the future!

The small factory was only a twenty-minute cycle ride from home. Therefore, transport was not a problem, and from time to time in good weather he would walk to and from work. He enjoyed the fresh air after a hard day's work in the pleasant but fairly 'stuffy' factory. Aunt Maude always had a cooked meal ready for him when he arrived home, and there was always her special cheese and pickled onion sandwiches available for snacks before bedtime.

Steve was a very adaptable person and made the transition from school to a work environment quite easily. Although he missed some of his school pals, he soon made new friends at the factory, and also during the weekend village dances.

The social dances were held in the church hall, and rightly considered to be an important part of village social life. Apart from the weekly dance, the only other entertainment was the small cinema and a Wednesday evening game of Bingo. The dances, being held in the church hall were always 'overseen' by the vicar and his fairly strict wife, who ensured that no untoward frivolity took place between the male and female participants.

Steve learnt the basic dance steps to the waltz and quickstep, and having gone through the ritual of asking a girl to dance, the budding Astaires and Ginger Rogers' would cavort to the strict tempo music of Victor Sylvester. When the evening became 'racy', the couples danced to Edmundo Ros and his 'Latin American' band. A certain amount of quickstep improvisation was required to appreciate the samba rhythm, but most people simply relaxed and enjoyed the evening.

The recorded music, mostly L.P's (long players), were played on a sturdy Radiogram which had been donated by a local dignitary for the wellbeing of the community. The machine was housed in a beautiful four feet high walnut cabinet, and was a piece of expensive furniture in itself. The Radiogram was always operated by the church curator, for, as the vicar pointed out, he was the only one technically qualified to control the highly intricate machine! In reality, the vicar did not want every Tom, Dick or Harry tinkering with what was after all, an expensive piece of equipment, and a very important part of the smooth running of the church hall! The vicar, if nothing else, was a good diplomat.

Halfway through the evening the vicar called an interval to allow the overworked Radiogram to cool down. At this point some of the teenage boys would retreat to the village pub in order to gain a certain amount of 'Dutch' courage for the second half of the dance, and to ask his dancing partner if she would allow him to escort her home after the dance.

Many a romance was either started or lost by the seductive tone of these few words. During the 'cooling down' interval, the girls would retire to the powder room. The evening was a chance to dress up, and of course meet a boy! Street corner courting was frowned upon! After several weekends of Victor Sylvester, Steve met a girl called Joy. She was a fresh faced girl who enjoyed sport, and a certain amount of outdoor life. They were immediately compatible, both able to freely converse about athletics, football, and nature. Joy's father was the local builder and Steve knew of him when he had carried out some work for Aunt Maude, modernising her somewhat antiquated kitchen. He was a reasonably 'well-off' man, a rugged outdoor man, with a jovial nature, and a good sense of humour.

Steve and Joy dated tentatively, slowly getting to know each other. There was not a great deal to do in the village, but the surrounding area was perfect for long, leisurely, walks. They both enjoyed the countryside, and each other's company.

After several weeks Steve was invited to meet Joy's parents. It was a 'big' day for both Steve and Joy and they were equally nervous. After the normal introductions Steve was able to converse with Joy's father freely, talking about sport, and after a 'tour' of the garden, they discussed the self-made fish pond, which was obviously the builder's pride and joy.

Joy's mother, on the other hand was somewhat stern, and introvert. When she learnt of Steve's unfortunate background, she became suspicious of him, and after a while, openly hostile.

Joy had left the 'all girls' school at much the same age as Steve had left school, and had started work at the ladies' hairdresser on the High Street. She was six months into a three-year apprenticeship, and unlike Steve, did not have to plan for military service in the near future. Perhaps the time would come when women and men were treated equally, but it seemed a strange idea! Most people considered that a woman's place was in the home.

Joy always carried the slightly perfumed fragrance of hair setting lotion in her clothes. It was not an unpleasant aroma, and one Steve quickly became used to. It was like an elixir to him, and a pleasant change to the raw odours of the factory floor. Joy was a fairly outward going, athletic person, and she and Steve complemented each other in many ways. She taught him to play tennis at the local club, where she had become a junior member through the influence of her well known builder father. Joy's mother had 'rubber stamped' the move, saying it was a good 'step up' the social ladder.

Saturday evenings were usually spent at the village dance, or the tiny cinema. Occasionally they would visit a larger, more modern cinema in a nearby town, which boasted a massive 'Wurlitzer' organ for interval music, and popcorn, a recent innovation from America. A half hour bus ride was required, but they regarded the journey as part of the evening out, and the bus service was quite punctual and reliable.

At the cinema they would watch Doris Day in the latest musical or Errol Flynn swashbuckling his way through a story of pirates in the Caribbean. Bag after bag of popcorn was consumed as the film unfolded, interlaced with the occasional vanilla ice cream. On the third visit to the cinema Steve 'accidentally' dropped an almost empty bag of popcorn onto the floor. He reached down, retrieved the bag, and as he brought up his hand, gently touched and stroked Joy's knee before placing the popcorn back on his lap. She took his hand and stroked it, and placed it back on her knee! During the bus ride home they discussed the merits of the film, and to some extent popcorn! After the bus journey Steve walked Joy home and they kissed goodnight at the garden gate. They had kissed politely before, but tonight there was a pleasant warmth on their lips. A fire had been ignited!

Elvis Presley and his films were very popular, and like many teenage girls, was Joy's favourite film star. Her mother on the other hand did not approve of Elvis, or his films. She was openly pleased when he was called upon to carry out military service in Germany. She remarked caustically "Perhaps that will put an end to his disgusting public pelvis gyrating!" The journalists of the newspaper world had aptly named the star 'Elvis the Pelvis'.

A Presley film was due to be shown at the town cinema, and Steve and Joy made a date to go on the Saturday, without announcing the fact to Joy's mother. In a cheeky way they felt like two schoolchildren disobeying an overly strict teacher. They took the early evening bus as usual, and when they arrived people were already queuing at the cinema. Such was Elvis Presley's popularity, despite the bigoted attitude of people like Joy's mother.

They queued for over an hour, eventually bought their tickets, and were ushered to their welcome seats; an hour can be a long time when waiting for Elvis. After a short recital of the 'Wurlitzer', the organist waved his arm to the audience, and disappeared into the darkness of the orchestra pit. The film started and Steve and Joy opened their bags of popcorn feeling quite American and 'with it'!

The film was entertaining, and well worth queuing for. Elvis had a 'college boy' innocence about him that teenage girls enjoyed. Presley seemed to be able to please girls and boys alike. Perhaps the boys saw him as a model, and someone to emulate?

Steve and Joy held hands and sat as closely together as the individual seats would allow. Joy's hands were soft and smooth from working at the hairdressers. She was wearing a sensuous perfume that she had bought from 'Le Boutique' on the High Street, next door to 'Boots' the chemist. Coupled together with the normal fragrance of hair solution that she always carried, it made a powerful aroma, which Steve found totally intoxicating!

They looked at each other in the semi-darkness and their cheeks touched, as if in a kiss. Joy's naturally long eyelashes 'flicked' at Steve's cheek and he squeezed her hand in reply. They shared their first passionate kiss in the darkness of the cinema. Gradually they came oblivious to the film, and Elvis 'gyrated' alone. They were two young people, discovering love for the first time, and simply being together.

Over the next three months they spent many such times together. But Steve's visits to Joy's home became less frequent, basically because of her mother's attitude towards him. It was obvious that Joy's home life was being made unpleasant by the two young lovers' relationship, and her mother was not the type to change her ways.

From time to time Steve invited Joy to his aunt's pleasant home. Aunt Maude had come to know Joy from her two-weekly visits to the High Street hairdresser. It had come as a pleasing surprise to her when Joy had mentioned Steve's name in conversation one day.

All three spent happy evenings together, and when the weather was fine enjoyed cheese and pickled onion sandwiches in the tranquillity of Aunt Maude's back garden. At the end of wonderful evenings, knowing they had shared a friendly experience, they would say goodnight to Aunt Maude, and Steve would slowly walk Joy to her home.

On his reflective return home Steve's thoughts would turn to Joy's mother, and how different she was to Aunt Maude. He was certain there was a lesson in life to be learnt from it all, but he couldn't pin it down.

The situation with Joy's mother did not change, and reluctantly Steve and Joy decided to stop seeing each other.

One evening they took a quiet stroll around the village, and then Steve walked Joy to her home. They kissed by the garden gate and out of sight from her mother. Joy then turned quickly, and ran into the house.

Steve walked home, very much alone and a feeling of emptiness inside him. He was very quiet for the next few days, and Aunt Maude sensed that something was wrong. She eventually persuaded him to talk, and he poured out his feelings to her. Aunt Maude listened to him patiently, without saying a word. There was a time to talk and a time to listen! Afterwards, Steve felt better and was able to breathe more freely again. Maude made some extra special cheese and pickled onion sandwiches, and they sat on the sofa and both enjoyed them. They continued to talk about Joy, her parents, and life in general. On reflection, Steve could understand why the jovial husband spent most of his time away from the house working!

After a while, Joy met and married a local solicitor, and they set up home in a detached house situated on the outskirts of the village. The well-appointed house was set in half an acre of ground and had a large ornate gazebo in the spacious front garden. Joy's mother was delighted with the 'liaison', and practically insisted that they should have at least two Corgis as pets. As a leading light in the Women's Institute she never ceased to update the members on her daughter's marriage, and the ever increasing balance at the local bank!

Steve, a fairly good looking and outward going boy, did not dwell on the situation for too long, and was soon dating another girl. They went to the cinema together, and before long the popcorn was flowing freely once more!

The time arrived for Steve to commence his military service. He took a few days holiday which were due to him from the lighting company, said goodbye to the workmates he had spent many happy hours with, and prepared himself for leaving Somerset, and the parental protection of Aunt Maude.

On the morning he was to leave home he woke with a slight headache. He had not slept well, his mind taken up with thoughts of the coming day. His canvas holdall had been packed, so there had been little to do apart from come to terms with the situation and make himself ready for the journey.

Steve and Aunt Maude had shared breakfast together. They had talked about the weather and other idle matters, but they were both aware it was an important day for both. Aunt Maude had made him some 'special' sandwiches and had also bought him a large bag of 'Mackintoshes' assorted chocolates. No expense was spared where Aunt Maude's little treats were concerned! Steve had thanked her and put the sandwiches and sweets into his holdall.

They finished breakfast and as planned, prepared to say goodbye at home. Maude didn't like saying goodbye at bus or railways stations. It reminded her of saying farewell to her husband, and Steve fully understood. After the emotional turmoil of saying goodbye to Joy he wasn't too keen on farewells himself.

When the moment came Steve had said goodbye to Aunt Maude. Trying to hide her emotions she had made him promise to clean his teeth every day, and to write regularly. He had said that he would, and in a sudden moment of emotion that was foreign to both of them, they had hugged each other. With tears in their eyes, Steve had walked away, not knowing when he would return. He had stepped out onto the street, and realised that the world awaited him. In that moment he had decided to grasp it with both hands.

He had strode down the street with a purposeful step, turning momentarily to wave to Aunt Maude who was stood at her garden gate. She had waved a hand, and he had seen the look of love in her eyes. His step had faltered, but he had turned, and continued his journey to the railway station.

Steve had entered the station and walked into the ticket office. The booking clerk had been sat behind his desk. He had looked up and vaguely acknowledged Steve's arrival. Steve had a 'nodding' acquaintance with the clerk through purchasing many platform tickets in the past. The clerk though, was somewhat aloof and regarded anybody who dared to enter his office with suspicion, as if his tickets were only to be sold to people whom he personally approved of. He had a certain bureaucratic nature, and regarded himself to be somewhat above the menials who chose to enter his domain.

Steve had fished around in his jacket pocket and removed the travel warrant supplied by the army to cover the cost of travelling to the training camp in Hampshire. He had handed it to the clerk who had studied it carefully before making out a ticket. The clerk had looked up, handed Steve his warrant together with his ticket and said, "Joining the army then?"

"Yes," replied Steve.

"You'll be sorry," replied the clerk.

Steve had chosen to ignore the remark, smiled and nodded to the clerk and left the booking office. He had walked out onto the platform, put his holdall down, and stretched his arms.

The station was fairly busy, people, mostly in twos and threes had been dotted along the platform, awaiting the train. The Station Master had been busy tending his geraniums that were in full blossom in his office window boxes, and a porter had been leaning on a large pair of sack trucks, hoping they would not be required when the train arrived. He had been complying with railway regulations, but at the same time was aware that he was the local union shop steward and had certain 'Stalinist' beliefs to adhere to! A fair day's work for a fair day's pay had not been in his book of words.

Steve had plenty of time before the train's arrival time and had decided to walk to the siding and talk to the locomotive crew who were preparing their engine for the forthcoming shift. He had built up a friendship with the local crew and could talk freely with them. He knew the fireman by first name, and they shared a mug of stewed tea together. The fireman, five years senior to Steve, had already served his compulsory two years National Service and had given Steve good advice about army life, his favourite piece being 'never volunteer'! The railway firemen that Steve had encountered were usually wiry men in their twenties. The nature of the work ensured that no excess weight was put on, and although they were always covered in coal dust, which seemed to eat into their skin, they all looked fit and healthy. The drivers, on the other hand, tended to be in their forties or fifties, and often sported a slight 'beer belly'. Although any work concerning steam engines was far from easy, they could at least sit down to their work for some of the time. They of course carried full responsibility for the locomotive, and a fairly portly appearance gave them an air of importance. It was quite normal for a passenger, having completed his journey safely, to walk along the platform and thank the driver personally for a safe journey.

Steve's train had come into sight. He had quickly shaken hands with the fireman and driver and boarded the train with the other passengers. The Station Master had momentarily looked up at the train, glanced at his pocket watch, and then continued tending his geraniums. The train had 'puffed' its way out of the station, steam and smoke spiralling gently into the cloudless sky.

The train jerked to a sudden halt at a station, and Steve was brought back to the present day, and reality, as if waking from a dream.

He was eighteen years of age. It was the end of an era, and hopefully the beginning of a new one.

The compartment door slid open, and a young woman entered!

CHAPTER 3

Steve glanced up as the girl entered the compartment; she was smartly dressed in a matching dark green skirt and jacket, and carried an expensive looking weekend case. No cheap holdalls for her, Steve thought to himself.

Steve pretended to be reading the newspaper he had bought earlier on his way to the station. The young woman placed her weekend case on the rack above the seats, smoothed her skirt, and sat nearly opposite Steve. She glanced at her watch, looked momentarily out of the window and settled herself on the carriage bench seat.

Steve looked at her and she smiled briefly. She was a little older than he, Steve thought, perhaps twenty or twenty-two. She was slim and fairly good looking, with dark brown shoulder length hair that went well with her dark green suit. Everything about her suggested good taste and up-bringing. As a matter of course he glared at her hands and saw that there were no rings on her slim fingers!

He returned to his newspaper, realising that he had been staring at her. The girl undid a shoulder bag that she had been carrying, placed it on the seat beside her and took out a fairly thick paperback book. She looked at Steve briefly, noticed that he was reading his paper, opened her book at a marker, made herself more comfortable and proceeded to read.

She had noticed that he was reading a good quality newspaper. Her own natural female inquisitiveness 'clicked' in and she began to ask questions in her mind about the good looking man opposite. She looked up at Steve's holdall on the rack.

Perhaps he is a sailor, she mused. *But his face doesn't have the rugged features of a skin buffeted by salty wind and rain.* He had the clear, fresh faced complexion of a person who enjoyed sport and the outdoors. She looked up at the holdall again, her questions fuelling her curiosity. *The holdall looks almost like a soldier's kit-bag.*

She told herself not to be so nosey and said to herself, *I must have inherited the trait from Mother; Dad would never be that inquisitive!* She concentrated on her book, but as an afterthought glanced down at Steve's black shoes. *They are nicely polished*, she said to herself.

The carriage bench seats were designed for practicality rather than comfort. The train stopped at every station and Steve began to wish he could have taken a faster non-stopping train. But he was tied by regulations and instructions on the travel warrant issued by the War Office.

Perhaps they are trying to save money, he said to himself.

The young woman became deeply engrossed in her book. Steve shifted relentlessly on his seat, and decided to do the daily crossword in his newspaper, and he glanced out of the carriage window whilst trying to work out the clues. Aunt Maude had purchased a newspaper most days of the week, and it had almost become a habit for them to study the clues together. Maude said it was good for his education, and it also helped to keep her own mind active and informed.

The train slowly wound its way through the countryside. Green field after green field appeared, surrounded by neat well-kept hedges. The grass was a lush green, the beneficial effect of rain and sun. Cows and sheep grazed contentedly, oblivious to the noisy steam train that was intruding into their privacy. Trees dotted the landscape, mostly sturdy oak and elm, almost fully leafed now and enjoying the benefits of the rich soil. Birds fluttered above the trees.

They're probably making nests, Steve thought. Like Joy, he appreciated nature, and never ceased to wonder at it. He thought about Joy for a second or two then moved on.

The countryside was beautiful and unspoiled. It was as if the train was passing through a fairy-tale land.

This pleasant land, he said to himself. *I wonder if I will be posted abroad after training? I will miss this greenery if I am.* He grinned to himself and thought, *We don't really appreciate something until we are in danger of losing it. Just like Aunt Maude's cheese and pickled onion sandwiches!* He chuckled quietly to himself about it whilst staring down at the crossword, completely forgetting momentarily that he was not alone in the compartment.

Steve lifted his eyes and found that the girl was staring at him quizzically. He quickly lifted the newspaper and pretended to be reading. After a while he continuously peered over the top of his paper, the young woman had returned to reading her book, but had a smile on her face.

Steve returned to watching the scenery fly by. The train seemed to be going up an incline, and smoke and steam wafted past the window. The engine was obviously working harder, and he could imagine the fireman, sweat pouring from his forehead, tending to the locomotive boiler, and wishing they were going downhill instead. His coal filled shovel would provide the 'fire-box' with much fuel before the journey was over.

The driver, sat on his fixed wooden 'flip-down' seat, would be opening the speed regulator more and more to compensate for the gradient, and the engine would be croaking and groaning under the stress.

Steve returned to his crossword. One of the clues was something to do with ironing clothes, and it reminded him of Aunt Maude's obsession for ironing clothes. She would even iron dish cloths and fold and press them before carefully stacking them neatly in the cupboard. Steve, being a man, or nearly of age, could not understand such neatness. Some of her ways had 'rubbed' off onto Steve though, and he hoped they would help in the life he was about to embark on. His shoes were always smart and polished, his hair, fairly neatly combed and kept to a conservative length. Steve finished half of the crossword in between scribbling doodles on the unprinted edge of the paper. Somebody had told him that the doodles could be translated as a person's character, but to him they just looked like a mixed up mess.

He glanced across at the girl; her eyes were slowly closing. A minute later she fell asleep and the book fell from her hand and landed with a soft thud on the carriage floor. The girl awoke, startled by the noise. Steve leant down, picked up the book and smilingly handed it back to her.

"Thanks," she said, "I must have drifted off." Steve said it was possibly the constant humming noise of the carriage wheels. "I had a late night," she explained.

Apparently, she had been to stay with friends for the weekend at a place called Brockenhurst in the New Forest. Steve said he didn't know the place, but it sounded very nice, with cattle and forest ponies being allowed to roam the streets freely.

Grateful for the break in the monotonous journey, Steve took his holdall from the rack and withdrew the bags of sweets and sandwiches Aunt Maude had packed for him. He opened the paper bag of sweets and offered them to the girl. She looked at him for a second and reached out a hand and picked a sweet from the bag.

"These look nice," she said.

Steve explained that they were Mackintoshes Assortment, bought by his Aunt Maude. The girl, recognising quality, moved along her seat to be opposite him. She had mentally 'sized' him up and felt okay about it. Anybody who ate Mackintoshes Assortment must be all right she concluded!

They talked idly about the weather and other matters of no real importance, as strangers normally do. Eventually, after several more 'Assortments', Steve explained that he was on his way to join the army at a training camp near Aldershot in Hampshire. The conversation started to flow and they both became more at ease; the sweets had broken the ice.

The young woman was in the early years of studying to be a doctor, but it was apparently a long process, taking six or seven years of study.

She said to Steve, "I do envy you being able to join the army. We girls never have the opportunity for any adventures. The world will be your oyster," she said. "I sometimes wish I had been born a boy."

Steve offered her a cheese and pickled onion sandwich, explaining that they had been made by his Aunt Maude in Somerset. The girl declined the offer, saying that they looked very nice but that it would spoil a meal she was to have later.

"I would like another sweet though," she added and thanked him after selecting one from the bag. As she was taking the sweet from the paper bag in his hand their fingers momentarily touched and they looked at each other. They both realised the importance of the moment, but said nothing.

The girl looked out of the carriage window, and recognising the scenery said to Steve, "Well this is my stop coming up, so I will say goodbye."

Steve stood up and handed down her weekend case from the rack above. She thanked him, and they both said goodbye. Steve felt awkward, thinking he should have said more, but not knowing what. The girl opened the sliding door and disappeared down the corridor. Steve shut the door and returned to his seat by the window.

The train slowly came to a halt, the brakes making a slight screeching noise as the brake blocks were applied to the rims of the wheels. There were dozens of people waiting to board the train and Steve stood up trying to catch a glimpse of the girl leaving the station, but she was nowhere to be seen.

The people on the platform milled around, some looking for empty compartments, others grappling with suitcases or saying goodbye to friends before boarding the train. Steve was disappointed at not seeing the girl, and silently cursed the people for being there and spoiling his moment. He sat down on his seat, shook his newspaper as if in a gesture of defiance, and fiddled anxiously with his pen.

Suddenly the girl appeared at the window. She pressed the palm of her hand against the glass, and he saw that on her hand she had written, 'Lorraine 253729'. Steve quickly wrote down the number on the edge of the newspaper. He had no need to write the name; he knew that he would never forget it. He smiled through the window at her, pointing to his paper confirming he had the number. She blew him a kiss from her outstretched hand, laughed, and turning, melted in to the milling crowd. He quickly stood up, but she had disappeared into the depths of darkest Hampshire. He had only been away from Somerset a short while, but he somehow knew that his 'worldly' adventure had just begun!

CHAPTER 4

Steve sank down onto the carriage seat, suddenly exhausted from the encounter. *How wonderful*, he thought, *how strangely wonderful. Could it be that we are destined to meet again?* He thought about the young woman that he had just met. He was far too young to believe in 'Destiny' or 'Fate' but he felt the seeds were being sewn.

He withdrew a cheese and pickled onion sandwich from his holdall, took a large bite, and stared into space. Steve was oblivious to his surroundings for the next five minutes, but the train had left the station and was continuing its journey.

White smoke followed from the engine as it built momentum after leaving the station. The white smoke wafted past the window, and Steve watched it with interest. It meant that the locomotive fireman was using the coal fuel to its maximum efficiency and the boiler had reached its optimum temperature. Aunt Maude likened the white smoke to that of the Vatican in Rome, saying the same thing happened when a new Pope was elected. Perhaps there were similarities to be drawn between the Catholic Church and sturdy steam engines; they were both certainly very powerful. He finished his sandwich and followed it with a Mackintosh for 'afters'. His thoughts returned to the girl and he decided to phone her as soon as possible.

The compartment door slid open and a uniformed ticket inspector stood in the doorway. He asked for Steve's ticket, and Steve delved into his jacket inside pocket and handed him the ticket together with his army travel warrant. The inspector studied both, the warrant at some length. Steve looked at the inspector; his uniform was a perfect fit and smartly pressed. He wore a black peaked cap with the words 'Southern Railway' neatly embroidered on the hat band. He had a military bearing about him, Steve thought.

The inspector, satisfied that all was in order, handed the papers back and said, "Joining the army then?"

"Yes," replied Steve.

"You'll regret it," said the inspector and continued, "I was in the Signals myself during the war, North Africa. I was a Desert Rat!" He grinned, touched his cap in farewell and left the compartment, closing the sliding door positively behind him.

Steve smiled to himself; he had been correct about the inspector's military bearing. He carefully returned the tickets to his pocket and at the same time tore the girl's name and phone number from the newspaper, putting it safely with the tickets. As he did so he said to himself, "Beautiful name, Lorraine!"

The train continued on its painfully slow journey. It was early evening now, and Steve would normally be feeling hungry, but Aunt Maude's sandwiches and the occasional Mackintosh Assortment had fortified him.

Eventually the train reached Steve's destination. He gathered his belongings together and left the train. It had been a slow but eventful journey, he thought to himself as he made his way to the station exit. He withdrew the all-important warrant and ticket from his pocket. The paper was quite crumpled now from use, and he smoothed it as best he could. He joined the other travellers who were waiting to leave and handed the warrant to the ticket collector when it was his turn. He noticed that, whereas the inspector on the train was smart and precise, the platform ticket collector was very different. He was a frail looking man with large ears that basically stopped his railway hat from falling over his eyes. His complexion was sallow, but he did sport a clipped moustache which, although grey, gave him a certain amount of dignity.

The ticket collector studied Steve's warrant for a second and handed it back to him. He had seen many army travel warrants before.

"Joining the army then?" he said.

"Yes," replied Steve.

"You'll regret it," said the collector with a sour look on his face.

Steve looked at him and chose to ignore the remark.

Steve glanced at the large platform clock. The enamelled Roman numerals registered five o'clock, and as he looked at the dial the minute hand clicked over, reminding him that his arrival at the training camp was imminent, and unstoppable. He began to feel a sensation of 'cold feet', but shrugged it off and continued on his way.

He left the station and entered the busy street, stopped a passer-by and asked directions to the bus station. It was only a short walk away, through an arcade and onto an open area that provided parking space for the buses. A small office was situated on the edge of the bus park, a pre-fabricated cabin that sorely required a coat of paint. Steve made his way towards it. There were several single-decked buses parked, and he needed to know times of departure and route numbers.

He entered the tiny office where a middle-aged, fairly plump woman was sat behind a small serving counter. She sat knitting what appeared to be a very colourful scarf.

"Can I help you?" she asked without interrupting her knitting work.

Steve asked the necessary questions and she gave him the information he required, and he thanked her and left the office. The woman had not looked up, or faltered with her obviously important knitting rhythm during the whole encounter! As he left the office Steve said to himself, "If the wooden needles go any faster they will catch fire!"

After making his enquiries he found the correct bus, climbed on board and found a window seat. The bus was only partially full. The other passengers were mostly middle- aged women, chatting amongst themselves and clutching full shopping bags having spent a pleasant day visiting the shops, and now returning home to prepare meals for their husbands and families.

The bus driver duly arrived. He was a very portly man of average height, his massive girth, which was kept in order by a strong brown leather belt had been acquired by years of bus driving, physical inactivity and pints of the local brew. The driver adjusted his belt, looked down the aisle of the bus and asked to see tickets.

Steve fished in his pocket and withdrew his travel warrant. The driver studied it with interest, handed it back to Steve and said, "Joining the army then?"

Steve replied, "Yes."

"You'll regret it," the driver said, and moved on down the bus to inspect more tickets.

Steve thought to himself, *If anybody else asks me that question I will not be responsible for my actions!*

The driver completed his ticket inspection, and satisfied that all was in order, returned to the front of the bus. He eased himself into his seat, half of the steering wheel disappearing into his stomach. He checked all of the switches and knobs on his dashboard as if he was in charge of a Boeing aircraft! With the pre-flight checks successfully completed he pressed the engine 'Start' button. The bus shook from the sudden vibration from the diesel engine, and the windows rattled in their mahogany frames.

The driver looked into his rear view mirror and then selected first gear, which provoked a loud, disturbing, crunching noise from beneath the floorboards. The driver obviously felt this was quite normal and began to whistle a light-hearted tune. It sounded like a melody from 'Brigadoon' to Steve. The driver released the handbrake and the journey commenced.

The bus stopped every half mile or so, and passengers, clutching their shopping bags, thanked the driver before leaving, asking if his wife and family were well. The driver knew most of them by first name, and he cheerfully, wished them goodbye. He was clearly more than just a bus driver to the community, and as new passengers boarded the bus he welcomed them with a cheery smile and the occasional piece of suitable humour.

After several more stops, a middle-aged man boarded the bus and sat in the vacant seat next to Steve. He was neatly dressed and carried what appeared to be the local newspaper. He turned the pages with a look of half interest on his face; he was not interested in the scenery as the bus trundled from stop to stop. He had seen it many times before.

The bus was leaving the built-up area now, and heading more into the countryside. The bus' gearbox wheels continued to suffer under the heavy hands of the driver. Steve wondered how long it would be before the much abused gearbox collapsed onto the road.

Steve decided to take advantage of the man's local knowledge, and asked him which stop to take for the army training corp. The man said he would point out the correct stop, but there was some way to go he said. Steve whiled away the time by studying the passing scenery. It was much like Somerset, but hilly and the ground seemed to be chalky, unlike the reddish soil that Steve was used to. His mind kept 'darting' back to the girl on the train and their fleeting meeting. He suddenly realised that he would be confined to camp for the first six weeks of his training, and wondered whether she would wait that long. He would phone as soon as possible and explain the situation. For some reason he had a burning desire to see her again.

After several more stops the man next to him gave instructions on when to leave the bus. The man was very precise, and Steve wondered if he was an accountant or of some other profession that required meticulous thought.

The man prepared to leave his seat, his own stop imminent. He turned to Steve and said, "Joining the army then?"

Steve said, "Yes," and waited with gritted teeth for the obvious second line.

Instead the man said, "Good luck then, enjoy the army." He shook Steve's hand and left the bus.

The bus moved on with a crunching of gear wheels. Steve, having had his faith in human nature restored, withdrew one of Aunt Maude's cheese and pickled onion sandwiches and enjoyed a welcome snack. The bus came to his allotted stop and he quickly gathered his belongings together and left the bus. As he did so, he thanked the driver who in return nodded back in reply with a half-smile on his face. Steve was a stranger in these parts.

The bus continued on its journey, the driver having subjected the gearbox to more torture selecting first gear. Steve wondered which would collapse first, the gearbox or the driver with his massive girth!

The training camp entrance was only fifty yards from the bus stop. The camp was surrounded by a five-foot-high privet hedge and Steve peered over the top to survey as much as he could. He saw row upon row of single storey wood constructed buildings, all painted black, with sloping roofs covered in black bitumen. Each building had a small annexe.

They're probably washing facilities and toilets, thought Steve.

He considered that each building could accommodate fifteen to twenty men. In front of every wooden building were a fire extinguisher and two fire buckets filled with sand. The extinguishers and buckets were painted bright red, and surrounded by a squared white line which looked freshly painted. The whole place had an air of discipline about it. A group of recruits were being drilled by an instructor who shouted commands as he marched behind the men. Steve said to himself, "There will be no messing about in there, this is no holiday camp!"

He flexed his shoulders which were stiff from the journey, picked up his luggage and strode to the camp entrance. A large wooden sign heralded: - MORVAL BARRACKS. 3RD INFANTRY TRAINING REGIMENT. Underneath someone had cheekily written in white chalk, BRING YOUR OWN SANDWICHES. The powers that be in the camp had obviously not seen it yet, when they did it would be removed in quick time. Steve looked at it, smiled, and admired the writer's sense of humour. He wondered if it had been the work of a disgruntled recruit.

Aunt Maude's culinary expertise would be much in demand here, he thought to himself.

He took the last cheese and pickled onion sandwich from his holdall and celebrated his arrival at the training camp, his home for the next six weeks! So far so good, he concluded.

CHAPTER 5

A rugged steel barrier spanned the entrance to the barracks. It was painted red and white in sections along its length, and a smartly uniformed soldier was stood in front of it on guard duty. His boots shone from hours of polishing with 'Cherry Blossom' and his khaki battle dress had been meticulously pressed before starting the duty. A less than faultless inspection by the orderly sergeant would have resulted in a charge of slovenly misconduct, and incurred extra duties! He carried a gleaming, highly polished rifle, held at the 'slope' position, and sporting a crisp green shoulder strap for use in 'active' conditions. The rifle looked extremely lethal, and not something to be challenged under any circumstances.

Steve handed his papers of enlistment, and his crumpled travel warrant that he had carefully carried, to the guard.

The soldier looked at them briefly and said, "Welcome to Hell," a half-smile on his face.

Steve waited for the 'You'll regret it line', but the guard said nothing more. Perhaps 'Hell' was sufficient. The guard pointed to a single storey building thirty yards away and told Steve to report to the orderly corporal.

"Thanks," Steve said to the guard as he looked at the gleaming rifle, and as he walked away he wondered if the gun was loaded.

Steve looked at his new surroundings. There was an air of cold military discipline in the atmosphere and he suddenly felt ill at ease, and lonely. He flexed his shoulders and moved on.

The building the guard had described was the regiment's administrative office, and Steve found the orderly corporal sat behind a desk, surrounded by an array of papers and folders, all with official War Office stamps on them. Behind him was a large notice board, also covered with sheets of official papers, arranged in what seemed to be a haphazard way. But there was no doubt the corporal had a system, and knew the location of every sheet!

The corporal was a professional soldier, and had the medal ribbons to prove it, but at the same time had all the traits of an efficient clerk. He was very neat and smart in appearance, and his hair was well-groomed with not a strand out of place. But there was a toughness about him not to be ignored!

Steve handed him the papers and warrant. The corporal efficiently stamped them several times and countersigned them with a fountain pen that was probably his own property and official insignia; no army issue pens for him! He was a cut above!

After the official papers had been dealt with and filed accordingly, the corporal told Steve to report to a certain barrack room, to pick himself a bed and bed space, and secure his belongings in a locker which would be in the 'bed space'! It was all totally foreign to Steve, but he said, "Okay, thanks."

The corporal said with a half-smile, "You call me 'Corporal', is that understood?"

"Yes, Corporal," replied Steve. The foundations of discipline had been set!

The corporal, having established his seniority continued, "The cookhouse is closed until 7am tomorrow for breakfast. If you want something to eat or drink the N.A.A.F.I. will be open until 10pm," and he gave Steve instructions on how to find the building.

Steve had never heard of an N.A.A.F.I., but assumed it was a type of cafe, serving tea and snacks. He was later to learn that N.A.A.F.I. stood for Navy, Army and Air Force Institute, an organisation designed to supply extra catering and other services to the armed forces. Steve was to appreciate how important the organisation was as his military service progressed. The army marches on its stomach, as somebody once said.

As he left the administrative office he began to feel thirsty. Aunt Maude's sandwiches had sustained him as far as food was concerned, but his throat felt dry. He decided to search for his allotted barrack room, and then the mysterious N.A.A.F.I. The barrack rooms were identical, in straight rows. A number and letter defined them. Steve's barrack was 2B, almost in the middle of the spacious camp. He cautiously opened the door to find several other new recruits, still in their civilian clothes, chatting amongst themselves, their luggage and belongings laid on the beds they had picked for themselves. It seemed to be a 'first come first served' situation, and the corner beds had been 'commandeered' for a certain amount of 'privacy'. As Steve entered, the new recruits turned and said a brief hello before returning to their conversation.

Steve returned their greetings and picked a vacant bed space near a window. The barrack room was Spartan to say the least and he looked around to survey his new environment. The wooden walls were bare and the windows curtain-less. There was no false ceiling and the roof rafters could be clearly seen. There were twenty beds, ten on each side of the room, together with their six-foot-high steel locker.

In the centre of the long barrack room a cast iron coke burning heater took pride of place, a chimney going straight up through the apex of the roof. There was a six-foot-long wooden trestle table in the centre of the room, the bare wooden top highly scrubbed as if it was a butcher's chopping board. Four wooden chairs, also highly cleaned, surrounded the table. Steve thought to himself, *Twenty men and only four seats, we could end up playing musical chairs.*

The bed he had chosen included two grey blankets, two white sheets and pillow cases, plus pillows all neatly folded on top of the mattress. Steve pushed his hand into the flimsy mattress and could feel the springs below. "Maybe it will be good for my back," he said, self-reassuringly!

Steve put his belongings on the bed and made conversation with two other recruits who had picked beds near his. The two men had 'signed on' for three years, and like Steve had decided that they would become professional soldiers, as opposed to the National Servicemen who were conscripted by law and had no choice in the matter.

One of the men was a Yorkshireman from a town called Dewsbury. Although they weren't aware of it at the time, all three men were to become firm friends and experience many adventures together. After talking for fifteen minutes they all felt thirsty and decided to find the N.A.A.F.I. and see what it had to offer in the way of food, and more importantly drink. As they left the barrack room Steve noticed a large blank 'pin' board, as yet totally bare. *Not for long*, he thought to himself.

The N.A.A.F.I. building was exactly the same design as the barrack rooms, the interior simply being adapted to act as a cafeteria with a serving counter at one end. Bare wooden trestle tables and wooden collapsible chairs were spaced around the room, making it a functional but very Spartan atmosphere.

Steve and his new found comrades entered and were immediately aware of dense cigarette smoke and the strong aroma of beer and hot steak and kidney pies. The room was full of recruits some in uniform others still in civilian clothes. The former was obviously the 'old guard' who had been through the first weeks of training, and who looked upon the men in civilian clothes as the 'new boys' and not to be unduly spoken to!

Steve looked around him and noticed that the windows did at least have curtains, which gave the N.A.A.F.I. a degree of homeliness. But the curtains had 'yellowed' from the effects of cigarette smoke, and probably had not been washed for years.

Aunt Maude would have made short work of them, Steve thought. They would have gone straight into the dustbin! He made his way to the serving counter and ordered a pint of beer and a steak pie. There wasn't a great selection to be had, but he was certain that the beer and pie would go down well.

There were four women serving behind the counter, three of them were in their mid-forties thought Steve, probably servicemen's wives trying to earn a little extra money. The fourth woman was much younger, a blonde haired woman with too much make-up on her face. She was obviously in her element flirting with the young recruits. From time to time she would disappear into a back room, to emerge a few minutes later with freshly combed hair and seemingly more make-up on.

The other women behind the counter did not approve of her, and looked down their noses when she passed. Steve wondered if they belonged to the Women's Institute and felt a sudden kinship with the blonde. Steve paid for his beer and pie at the till and looked around for the other men from his barrack room. They had found a free table and were all sitting together, looking somewhat bewildered and out of place. Steve made his way to the table trying not to spill his beer in the process of weaving his way through the crowd of men. He sat down and mixed in with the general conversation. There were no formal introductions you simply sat down, said hello and took it from there.

Steve sat next to a man from the Rhondda valley. The Welshman smiled and said, "Just call me Taff!"

They shook hands and a bond was formed. Taff had a cheerful face, and was an immediately likeable character. He had been a coal miner, but decided to join the army, hoping to find a healthier outdoor life. Steve noticed that he said "isn't it" after almost every sentence, a strange but interesting part of Welsh conversation.

They drank more beer and continued to get to know each other. They came from all walks of life; some were National Servicemen with two years to serve, whilst others had 'signed on' for three, six, or more years.

When the N.A.A.F.I. closed its doors at 10.00pm the new recruits found their way through the darkness to the barrack room 2B. Steve noticed that a sheet of paper had been pinned to the board. They were to parade outside the barrack room at 08.00 for roll call and issue of kit. They were all feeling tired from their journeys, as some had travelled hundreds of miles. After making up their beds they retired to them, and within minutes were all asleep.

CHAPTER 6

The next morning Steve decided to forego the breakfast and make himself presentable for the parade at 08.00. He had slept fairly well, albeit in strange surroundings and on a wafer thin mattress. He was not feeling hungry, the steak and kidney pie in the N.A.F.F.I. had been very sustaining and he looked forward to more in the future, pleasantly washed down with a pint of beer.

At five minutes to eight they all left the barrack room and stood in small groups on the road.

At precisely 08.00 a corporal marched around the corner of the building, official clip board in hand. He told them to 'form up' in three ranks, which they did with some confusion; they were still very much civilians, the only conformity in the past had been to queue for a bus!

The corporal, standing in front of them, looked at his watch made a note on his clip-board, looked up at them and cleared his throat. "My name is Corporal Entwhistle," he said, "I will be in charge of you for the next six weeks. You will address me as 'Corporal'!"

Steve, who was in the front rank, looked at the corporal. He was about 45 years of age and probably coming to the end of his army career. He was a slim man, thin faced, and sported a clipped military moustache. His khaki uniform was neatly pressed and he wore four medal ribbons on his tunic.

The corporal cleared his throat again and said, "Answer your name as I call it out."

They each called out "Here, Corporal," as they heard their name. The Yorkshireman from Dewsbury, whom Steve had briefly met the day before, had the surname of McGeary. The corporal read down the list quickly and mispronounced McGeary's name as Megeary! McGeary, or 'Mac' as he became known to his platoon said, "It's McGeary, Corporal, not Megeary."

The corporal, taken aback that a recruit should question him, looked at his clip-board, and decided to take offensive action. "Look," he said to Mac, "if I want to call you 'Megeary', I will call you 'Megeary'. Is that understood?"

"Yes, Corporal," said Mac gritting his teeth. Mac was not used to being subservient to anybody. The corporal flexed his shoulders, cleared his throat and moved on. There were a few quiet smiles in the ranks! It was not in an N.C.O.s (non-commissioned officer) manual to say sorry. To apologise would mean loss of face, and therefore, loss of control. If an N.C.O. was giving orders on a parade ground and made a mistake, it was simply rectified by the words of command, "As you were!"

Corporal Entwhistle marched the men to the regimental clothing and kit store. He tried to ignore their shambling gait and poor posture. That would all be changed by hours of drill on the parade ground, which was to begin before long.

They filed into the store. A long serving counter stretched the length of the store, and two private soldiers stood in readiness behind it. Stacks of kit had already been assembled, and were either marked 'Large' or 'Small'. There were no in between sizes. As each recruit approached the counter he was quickly 'sized' up and either given a 'Small' or 'Large' pack. When it came to foot wear the counter staff were a little more specific.

Mac McGeary stepped up to the counter and the serving private said, "What size?"

"Don't know," replied Mac.

The private leant over the counter, glanced briefly at Mac's feet, turned and selected a monstrous pair of black boots from the rack. He slammed them down on the counter and said sternly to Mac, "Move on."

They returned to the barrack room individually, struggling to carry all the equipment they had acquired. Steve staggered through the barrack room door and dropped his kit on the bed. It was all raw with newness, just as he was, and it would take some time before the creases were ironed out of all of them. The khaki battle dress uniform was very basic in design, and made for rugged use. Shirts and underclothes were also of Spartan design, but were easily washed and ironed when necessary. Each man was issued with what the army termed as a 'housewife, for the use of'. This was in fact an envelope shaped cotton bag, containing darning wool, cotton thread, needles and a thimble, designed for the repair of socks and the sewing on of buttons. Most of the recruits had never repaired a sock in their lives, but they would have to learn, and quickly. There was no sending worn socks back home to mother. With weeks of 'square bashing' and forced marches ahead, the woollen socks would wear quickly, and some of the initial repair work turned out to be less than exemplary.

Steve had two steel mess tins for preparing food in the 'field' and a jackknife also to be used when away from camp. He opened the four-inch blade and read 'Made in Sheffield' on the gleaming steel. If required, the knife could be used for self-defence, or equally an aggressive purpose. The latter was to be the case before long!

Every piece of kit had to be marked or stamped with the recruit's allotted army identification number, and suitable tools were passed around the room for this purpose. Steve's number was 23659265, eight digits that he was to use almost every day of his military career. They would become embedded in his mind, never to be forgotten.

The next day was Sunday, a so-called 'rest' day. The recruits spent the day becoming acquainted with their kit and generally cleaning the barrack room ready for inspection on Monday morning. The room was fairly easy to clean because of its Spartan design, and each man was responsible for his own bed space. But the standard of cleanliness was high, and not a speck of dust was allowed.

'Taff' had taken the bed space next to Steve's, and in the evening they decided to take a stroll around the camp. As recruits they were not allowed to leave the camp area, and this would be the rule for six weeks until basic training was completed. But in the evening a quiet walk and relaxation was welcome.

The Welshman talked about South Wales and the small town of Cowbridge where he was born and raised. He was an avid rugby fan, and the talk soon turned to sport as they made their way around the camp. Sport was always a compatible talking point. Politics and religion always seemed a touchy subject, and Steve, although having his own thoughts and opinions on the matters, usually tried to steer clear of them when talking to relative strangers. A time for deeper discussion would come when the men came to know each other and their ways.

The camp was quiet in the evening and the spring air pleasant. The regular training staff had all 'retreated' for the night and the recruits could relax a little. Most of the training staff were married men, and lived in the married quarters on the outskirts of the camp.

They continued their walk and passed the N.A.A.F.I. which was unusually quiet and weaved their way around the barrack rooms where the noise was also subdued. Sunday seemed to have a calming effect on people.

Steve told Taff about Somerset, his Aunt Maude, Joy, and lastly Lorraine, the girl he had recently met on the train.

Taff said, "She sounds all right, boyo, you want to follow that one up!"

Steve said that he intended to and hoped there was a public phone box on the camp. They had not seen one so far, but the camp area was large and they kept looking for the traditional red box. As they walked slowly back to the barrack, without discovering a phone, Taff explained that he had known a girl back in his home town, but she didn't like rugby, so that was that!

They found the barrack room 2B where most of the recruits had already taken to their beds. The sound of light snoring came from Mac's bed, so one of the men nudged the bed with his foot and Mac turned over in his sleep, scratched his nose and the snoring stopped.

Steve smiled at Taff and said, "There's a cure for everything." They went to their beds, and before falling asleep Steve thought about Aunt Maude and Somerset. He would buy a writing pad the next day and tell her that he was all right. She wasn't an overly worrying woman, but she would be concerned, and quite rightly inquisitive.

In the morning he went to the cookhouse clutching his newly acquired knife, fork, spoon and enamelled steel drinking mug, all part of his issued kit. The breakfast was wholesome, if not exactly gourmet standard.

They all dressed in their uniforms for the first time, trying to look as presentable as possible. They looked at each other, and certain humorous remarks were passed. The 'Keystone Cops' came to Steve's mind. They presented themselves for the parade outside the barrack room.

Corporal Entwhistle arrived at exactly 08.00, and after calling the roll, still referring to Mac as 'Megeary', he inspected them briefly. He ordered the men with the most ill-fitting uniforms to report to the regimental tailor the following day, but first they had a more pressing matter to attend to.

They were ordered to report to the regimental barber, six men at a time. Steve went with five other recruits, and they marched in twos as required by training camp regulations around the perimeter of the massive ground. The barber's 'emporium' was on the opposite side of the vast square. Nobody was allowed onto the 'hallowed' ground without the consent of the regimental sergeant major, and woe betide anybody who disobeyed the rule! In the past, one recruit who had dared to take a short cut and defy the R.S.M.'s law spent four hours on his hands and knees 'sweeping' the parade ground with his own personal toothbrush.

The six arrived at the barber's shop, entered and sat on the collapsible wooden chairs provided for waiting customers. The barber, a civilian, with neat straight black hair and a white workmanlike jacket, looked up from his newspaper and beckoned one of the recruits to sit in his chair. He deftly wrapped a white sheet around his unsuspecting customer and carefully tucked it into the shirt collar. The others looked on with interest.

The barber picked up an electric cutter, blew into the shaving head and commenced to cut the recruit's hair. He started at the base of the neck and ended at the forehead! He used the cutter in much the same way as a sheep shearer would, and Steve had a sudden urge to ask him if he came from Australia. The unsuspecting recruit was left with approximately half an inch of hair, the neck and back of the head completely bare.

The barber had finished the job in two minutes flat. He removed the white sheet, flicked it in a professional manner, and beckoned the next recruit to sit. Once again the same procedure was followed and the recruit left the barber's shop cautiously feeling the back of his head. Steve had flashing visions of the film 'Sweeney Todd'.

The next man to sit in the barber's chair was a Liverpudlian named Docherty. He was a confident lad and had a jaunty air about him. Docherty was quickly establishing himself as the barrack room's comedian. He removed a sheet of glossy paper from his tunic. It was a page from a fashion magazine and showed an advert for 'Brylcream' hair dressing and a well-dressed young man sporting a smart hairstyle. It was known as a D.A. (Duck's Anatomy) and was the height of fashion for young men.

Docherty showed the picture to the barber and asked him if he "could do something like that?" The barber glanced at the sheet of paper, smiled slightly and nodded in the affirmative, without saying a word. Docherty, having felt that he had conveyed his instructions well, relaxed and leant back in the barber's chair. The barber draped his white sheet around Docherty and carefully tucked it in. He picked up his electric cutter, blew into it twice, tapped it with his forefinger, and gave Docherty exactly the same treatment that he had given the other recruits, only this time it took one and a half minutes, not two.

The barber removed the dust sheet and shook it vigorously in front of Docherty who sneezed as pieces of his hair went up his nose. Docherty's hair lay on the floor in great chunks, held together by 'Brylcream'. He stood up, looked into the large wall mirror, and his jaw dropped. He turned to the barber who nodded and smiled as if Docherty had just thanked him and handed over a sizeable tip. Docherty was speechless and staggered out of the 'salon' feeling giddy and light-headed.

The barber expertly shook his white sheet again before saying loudly, "Next!"

They all eventually returned to the barrack room, looking decidedly different to when they left. One of the men, a well-spoken smooth talker who had studied law before 'dropping out' of college, said what the barber had just perpetrated was strictly illegal, and in a court of law the whole episode could be construed as an act of 'Barberism'. Steve laughed and thought that the 'Lawyer', as he came to be known as, had missed his vocation, and should have persevered with his studies instead of joining the army for three years. He was a born academic and orator, and would have been a boon to the legal profession.

Steve thought to himself, *At least he has a sense of humour, whether a lawyer or not!* He went to the washroom to rinse away the particles of hair, ran his hand over the back of his neck, and felt decidedly chilly.

CHAPTER 7

The next day began at 6.00am with the training corporal smartly swinging open the barrack room door, shouting "Wakey wakey," and then picking up the nearest steel studded army boot and hurling it down the centre of the room, where it clanged into the cast iron coke burning central heater. It was a far cry from the wakening's in Somerset. Basic training had begun; the short honeymoon was over!

The next three weeks were taken up with more early morning boot hurling, physical training, basic weapon training, lectures on camouflage and other field training. These activities were interspersed with hours of drill on the R.S.M.'s parade ground. Drill, drill, and more drill! The recruits' feet were not used to such prolonged harsh treatment. The black leather army boots were unforgiving, and the men all suffered blisters. Tins of talcum powder were purchased from the N.A.A.F.I. shop, and used liberally on socks and boots. Gradually the soles of their feet began to harden, and the solid army boots were broken in.

The recruits slowly became fitter and tougher, and actually started to enjoy the arduous training. Even the cynical National Servicemen, on the whole, stopped complaining and entered into the spirit of things.

One exception was a National Serviceman called Prendergast. He was from East Dulwich in London, and from the day he first entered the training camp he had decided to devise a method of extricating himself from what he called, "This ruddy den of iniquity." He considered that if he could convince the powers that be that he was partially insane and therefore not military material, he would be returned to civilian life without further ado.

His first ploy was to wear his black beret back to front on parade, the cap badge at the back of his head, therefore defaming the regiment. This only resulted in him being awarded extra cookhouse and guard duties, but he felt that he had made a start in his campaign.

A recruit who had completed his basic training and was awaiting posting to another unit was assigned to barrack room 2B with the task of teaching the new recruits how to prepare their newly acquired kit. The webbing, which consisted of web belt, ankle gaiters, ammunition pouches and straps, all had to be firstly scrubbed with water and a stiff brush. When dry, a coating of green 'Blanco' paste was applied with a damp cloth. The 'Blanco', purchased from the N.A.A.F.I. shop in powder form was mixed with cold water before being applied to the webbing. It was a very messy job that required some skill and patience to obtain a uniform finish.

'Cherry Blossom' black boot polish, 'Brasso' for polishing cap badges and buttons plus other accessories were also purchased from the N.A.A.F.I. shop which did a roaring trade with their captive clientele. New black leather army boots were always difficult to break in. The leather on the toecaps was rough and dimpled and before any polish could be applied, had to be smoothed using either a steel spoon handle or the plastic handle of a toothbrush. Once this had been achieved after several hours of work, black boot polish could be melted onto the toecap using the flame from a candle, once again purchased from the N.A.A.F.I. shop. Gradually, over days and weeks a highly polished toecap was obtained on the recruits' 'best boots', used for duties such as official parades and guard duty. A second pair of boots for everyday use was not as critical, but still had to be very presentable.

Steve regarded the kit preparation simply as part of the job, and a chore that had to be done. The National Servicemen, on the other hand, regarded it as a waste of time, especially Prendergast whose mind was totally on 'civvy street' and how to get back there.

Another 'square peg' in a round hole was a National Serviceman named Charlie Strong. Charlie was a hypochondriac and regularly, at least three times a week, reported sick, only to be sent back by the Medical Officer (MO) with two 'Aspirin' and a 'chit' for the training corporal, stating 'This man requires extra physical training'! Charlie therefore spent more time in the gymnasium than in the M.O.'s waiting room! A clever ploy by the overworked doctor.

The food in the camp cookhouse was nourishing but somewhat bland and tasteless. Fried chips were on the menu every day, with pork sausages and fried eggs. The cookhouse corporal, whose job it was to prepare the menus and oversee the cooking had a very limited culinary vocabulary. He had an obsession with meat balls, and included them on the menu every day. Steve had grown used to Aunt Maude's fairly sophisticated way of cooking, and army food was difficult to adjust to. The song, 'Ma I miss your apple pie,' played in his head whenever it was cookhouse time. After one heavy onslaught of the corporal's meat balls, Charlie Strong entered the barrack room clutching a large bottle of medicine, labelled simply 'DIGESTION'. The liquid was coloured bright pink and looked revolting, but Charlie insisted it was the only known remedy to the cookhouse corporal's meat balls!

One of the recruits, who always looked pale and drawn said, "There's nothing wrong with the meat balls, I eat them all the time."

They all looked at each other with grim faces, and Steve decided to put meat balls on his suspect list!

Being confined to the training camp for one and a half months was frustrating for the recruits, especially those who had enjoyed a full social life in 'civvy street'. The N.A.A.F.I. therefore became the centre of social life on the camp. The only other outlet on the camp was a small cinema, run by the A.K.C. (Army Kinema Corp). But the films were old and the projector was prone to breaking down halfway through the film, adding to the men's frustration. Because of those pent-up feelings the odd fight tended to break out in the N.A.A.F.I. but order was soon restored by the Regimental Police who were always present in the guardroom. The men, having vented their emotions soon returned to normal beer drinking and steak pie eating!

The conversation in the N.A.A.F.I. was always lively, there being such a diverse collection of men involved. The conversation naturally came around to girls, love and sex! The blonde at the serving counter was the only young woman in the camp, and therefore quickly became the centre of the men's attention.

None of the recruits knew her name and after several pints of beer and deliberation decided to call her the 'Blonde Bombshell', or B.B. for short. Over more pints of brew, they discussed the possibilities of whether she might have a regular boyfriend or not. They came to the conclusion that because she spent so much time at work in the N.A.A.F.I. it was likely that she didn't have a 'Beau', and was therefore a free spirit, and open to offers of a social nature.

After the men had consumed several more beers and steak pies the 'Blonde Bombshell's' curly locks of hair became even more inviting and irresistible. The talk at the table began to centre on how B.B., and her inviting body and blonde hair might possibly be wooed. They discussed the merits of bunches of flowers, boxes of chocolate and exotic perfume, but then somebody realised that such items were not available on the camp anyway.

Mac, who was a man of the world having spent many riotous weekends in

Dewsbury said, "What we must do, is use the simple method of charm and wit as a few well-chosen words can mean more than flowers or chocolates."

Mac was the most sexually experienced of the recruits, and the others listened with interest to his theories on courtship. The situation with B.B., he said, reminded him of a barmaid he once knew in Dewsbury, a relationship which resulted in many hours of social activity, and the odd free pint of 'Yorkshire Best Bitter'. He continued to expand on his theory of courtship and the raw recruits listened intently. The 'Lawyer' licked the tip of his pencil and feverishly took notes on a pad he always carried, underlining the parts he felt to be more important.

The N.A.A.F.I. doors suddenly burst open and Prendergast dressed only in his W.D. (War Department) underpants, marched to the centre of the room and announced in a loud commanding voice that the camp had just been invaded by Martians, and that everybody should report to the guardroom immediately. The recruits looked at each other, resumed their beer drinking and completely ignored him. Prendergast had just initiated phase two of his cunning withdrawal plan. He turned and left the N.A.A.F.I. as dramatically as he had entered. Steve thought to himself, *Ten out of ten for acting ability!*

Over the next three or four evenings in the N.A.A.F.I., Mac continued to expand his theories on the opposite sex and courtship. The 'Lawyer', a fairly shy person where the female gender was concerned, took more feverish notes and double underlined them! Eventually, after several more beers and steak and kidney pies, the 'Lawyer' decided to put Mac's theory to the test. He strode purposefully to the serving counter and bought another pint of beer and pie.

The 'Blonde Bombshell' was sat at the cash desk, efficiently taking money and giving change. The 'Lawyer' handed her his money and said in a voice as smooth as he could muster, "Now what's a good looking woman like you doing in a place like this?"

The 'Blonde Bombshell' looked up from the till, handed him his change and said, "Get lost!"

The 'Lawyer' turned and made his way back to the table in a daze. He sat down, took a large bite of his pie and informed Mac that his theory on courtship was deeply flawed. The recruits finished their beers and returned to barrack room 2B to re-adjust their strategy on 'wooing' B.B.

As they prepared for bed, still thinking of the opposite sex, Corporal Entwhistle entered the barrack room and stated that first thing in the morning, before breakfast, the platoon, as they had been formed into, would start assault course training. Private Strong immediately decided to report sick, and the 'Lawyer' sharpened his pencil!

The 6.00am parade arrived too soon, and they stood shivering in P.T. (Physical Training) gear outside the barrack room, and all thoughts of B.B. were put to one side. After roll call the platoon ran to the assault course, a distance of about one mile. The assault course itself was half a mile long and entailed climbing ropes, jumping six feet wide ditches, crawling through large diameter concrete pipes and clambering over high walls.

Charlie Strong complained bitterly that the M.O. had pronounced him fit for such activity, but he coped with the course very well. When Steve remarked on the fact, Charlie stated that it was due to the extra 'Linctus' and pills that he had taken in preparation for the arduous bodily and mental stress! Charlie was the perfect hypochondriac and carried a secret pouch of pills tied to his waist belt. He showed them to Steve one day. They looked like brown yeast tablets, and when they were on the assault course Charlie would pop one in his mouth every hundred yards. On one trip to the dreaded assault course he offered Steve a pill, which he accepted just to be friendly. But after taking it he felt strangely stronger and unnaturally confident. He began to wonder if they were just yeast tablets after all.

The intense physical training quickly made the newly formed platoon fitter and stronger. The aches and pains of the first weeks had gone and Steve could feel the power and strength growing in him, and it felt good. They were no longer a bunch of individuals, but part of a team with an air of self-assurance about them.

After two exhausting hours spent on the assault course the platoon would return to the barrack room, shower, and change clothes ready for a meal in the cookhouse. The main delicacy on the menu was, as always, the cookhouse corporal's meat balls. Provided they were broken in half, soaked in copious amounts of brown sauce and sprinkled with salt and pepper they were quite palatable.

A week after the B.B. 'Get Lost' incident, the platoon was sat in the N.A.A.F.I. and normal beer drinking and pie eating had resumed. At 8.30 in the evening the doors burst open and two perspiring regimental policemen entered. They asked, fairly robustly, if anybody had seen Prendergast or knew of his whereabouts. They all answered in the negative and the R.P.'s left, talking animatedly, and aggressively swinging their batons. Prendergast had initiated phase two of his exit strategy.

The wayward National Serviceman had been spotted staring through a window of the Officers' Mess, making extremely rude gestures. He was dressed only in his W.D. underpants, with his beret back to front, and the regiment's flag tied around his shoulders 'Superman' fashion. The officers could accept his rude gestures, but the desecration of their regimental flag was unforgivable! The episode resulted in Prendergast spending three days and nights in a guardroom cell on bread and water. But he was a dedicated, single minded man, and would not rest until he was back where he belonged, in Dulwich, on 'civvy street'.

When the Regimental Police had left the N.A.A.F.I. the atmosphere relaxed and normal drinking resumed. Mac, after consuming four pints of beer and two large steak and kidney pies announced he had revised his theory on courtship, and had a specific plan on how to woo the 'Blonde Bombshell'. They all put down their jars of beer and paid attention. The 'Lawyer' sceptical at first, gradually warmed to the idea, licked the tip of his pencil and took notes.

"The whole strategy," Mac said, " is to appeal directly to B.B.'s obviously very strong maternal instinct. The volunteer 'Casanova'," he continued, "will walk unsteadily to the serving counter in full view of the Blonde Bombshell. When they reach the counter they will suffer from a fainting spell, and sink slowly to the floor, moaning gently as they do so. The Blonde Bombshell will immediately lean over him and minister first aid. Therefore, the first physical barrier will have been broken down and a lasting relationship can be formed! It's all quite simple and straightforward," he concluded.

The only thing left to be done was to decide who the lucky 'Casanova' was to be. The 'Lawyer' offered to write all their names down on slips of paper from his note book. After he had carefully written the names, they were put into Steve's beret and held aloft. Mac reached up and withdrew the lucky man's name. It was Taff!

They decided to wait until later in the evening in order to catch B.B. in a receptive mood before instigating their foolproof plan. Consumption of alcohol by the N.A.A.F.I. staff was forbidden, but the men had noticed in the past that she tended to disappear into the back room from time to time, and grew more amiable with every disappearance!

Taff, after more beer, rose to his feet and staggered, quite convincingly towards the serving counter. The 'Blonde Bombshell' watched him approach with interest and smoothed her hair. At the table the platoon waited with bated breath, and Mac crossed his fingers under the table.

Taff reached the counter, gave out a low moaning noise as instructed and sank slowly to the floor. The 'Blonde Bombshell' watched the performance with interest. She turned to the washing-up sink, lifted a bowl of soapy, dirty water, and poured the bowlful directly over Taff who was lying face up on the floor.

The other members of the platoon quickly finished their beer and retreated rapidly in the direction of barrack room 2B leaving Taff at the mercy of the 'Blonde Bombshell'.

CHAPTER 8

Basic training continued at a hectic pace, from boot 'hurling' time at 6.00am until meat balls at six in the evening.

Boxing was part of the recruits' 'toughening up' process. Every Saturday morning was set aside for this robust activity. There were no exceptions allowed and even Charlie Strong was 'invited' to participate, regardless of how many times he had visited the M.O.'s waiting room for two aspirins.

The whole intake of recruits, some sixty or seventy men would march to the camp gymnasium dressed in P.T. (physical training gear), which consisted of W.D. shorts, vest and black plimsolls. A makeshift boxing ring was erected in the gym, and the proceedings were organised and overseen by the Physical Training Instructors (P.T.I.'s).

The men sat on the wooden floor of the gymnasium, surrounding the boxing ring. Half a dozen chairs were provided for the P.T.I.'s and a junior medical officer who attended in case of serious injury from a wayward left hook. The P.T.I.'s enjoyed the Saturday boxing training, some of them veteran boxers themselves, and had broken noses to prove it. One such P.T.I. was Lance Corporal 'Smoky' Funnell. 'Smoky' had seen many a regimental tournament as a middleweight, but his bouts had unfortunately resulted in him being punch-drunk, and he was destined to go no further than Corporal in his military career.

Two recruits were initially picked by the P.T.I.'s to enter the ring, and they donned the boxing gloves provided. They boxed a total of three rounds, three minutes to each round, unless one of them was carried out prematurely! The senior P.T.I., acting as referee would declare a winner and another opponent stepped into the ring to take the loser's place donning the gloves and saying a silent prayer. This procedure continued throughout the morning until every recruit had their turn in the square, uninviting ring.

When it was Steve's turn he climbed through the ropes and put the gloves on which by now were very sweaty! His opponent was much the same weight and height, and although Steve had never boxed in his life, he acquitted himself well. His success was mainly due to his previous athletic activities in civilian life. He was adjudged to be the winner after three hectic rounds of enthusiastic, if not professional 'fisticuffs'. His opponent left the ring and another recruit donned the sweaty gloves. Once again, after three competitive rounds, Steve was again declared the winner. But as his opponent left the ring he grinned at Steve and winked his eye, his day was done! Steve looked at him, and feeling his sore ribs thought to himself, *Is he a wiser man than I?*

Steve's next opponent was a tall Scotsman. His weight was about the same as Steve's, but he was a good six inches taller and had a longer arm reach. His face was tough and he had obviously survived many a pub brawl in Glasgow. Steve decided not to 'mix it' with the rugged Scot but to 'box' him from a distance. After three rounds the Scotsman was adjudged to be the winner, and Steve took off the sweaty gloves satisfied with his contribution to the morning's activity. As he left the ring the P.T.I. referee put a hand on Steve's shoulder and nodded to the other senior P.T.I. who was acting as time-keeper. Steve had just 'volunteered' for the regimental boxing team!

A certain amount of humour was allowed into the morning, strictly under the control and discretion of the senior P.T.I.'s. and a bantamweight would be matched against a heavyweight, provided they were not sworn enemies in their barrack room and a humorous interlude would follow. The spectators also lent their support with shouts of "Murder Him" or "You great bully," as they felt fit. After one or two rounds of 'clowning' the bantamweight would leap out of the ring, hotly pursued by the heavyweight chasing him around the gym, the onlookers sticking out a restricting leg to halt his progress. After everybody had enjoyed a good laugh and joke, order was restored by the P.T.I.'s and the more serious business of 'toughening up' resumed. After all the bouts were completed the makeshift ring was dismantled and the gymnasium cleaned and made ready for the next physical training session the following Monday. The men returned to their respective barrack rooms, more or less in one piece, apart from the odd bruise here and there.

Steve showered and changed. Having worked up a healthy appetite in the ring he decided to go for a meal in the cookhouse. The cookhouse corporal's meat balls were on the menu as usual, and Steve feeling in a robust mood after the boxing decided to 'take them on', feeling he was a match for the corporal's culinary flair. He was gradually becoming used to the army food, but still missed Aunt Maude's subtle sauces and delicious desserts. He attacked the meat balls over three gruelling rounds and afterwards felt he had emerged the winner!

The social life in the N.A.A.F.I. continued to be quite lively, and somebody had even taken down the drab window curtains and washed them. An iron had been smoothed over them, *But they are not up to Aunt Maude's meticulous standards*, thought Steve. *At least somebody had tried; it's the thought that counts.* He wondered if it could have been the work of the 'Blonde Bombshell', but then dismissed the idea; she was not an ironing person.

The platoon was sat at their usual table. They had come to regard it as their territory, and would be for the duration of basic training. Steve went to the serving counter to order a pint of beer and a pie. B.B. saw him approach, smoothed her hair and wetted her lips with her tongue in anticipation.

Steve picked up a pie and his beer and offered his money to B.B. who was sat at the cash till. She looked up, smiled invitingly and said, "That's all right, have the pie on the house, and pay for the beer later!"

Steve looked at her in surprise and said, "Thanks."

As he turned to walk away she said, "Do you fancy going to the pictures Saturday night?"

Steve said, "Sorry, I'm on duty Saturday."

The 'Blonde Bombshell' grabbed the pie back and threw it on the counter. She turned haughtily and disappeared into the back room. As she left Steve noticed dark roots in her blonde hair. As he made his way back to the table he said to himself, "Peroxide!"

When the N.A.A.F.I. closed, the men wandered slowly back to barrack room 2B in a fairly festive mood having consumed slightly more than the usual amount of beer. They talked about the tantalising 'Blonde Bombshell' and tried to picture her toiling over a domestic ironing board. It was like trying to visualise Mahatama Ghandi opening the batting for England at Lords!

The 'Lawyer', who was slightly more 'festive' than the others, looked up at the white painted 2B sign above the barrack room door. He assumed a dramatic Thespian stance, and announced in a loud Shakespearean voice, "2B or not 2B, that is the question! Whether it is nobler in the mind to suffer the strings and arrows of outrageous fortune, or, to take arms against a sea of troubles, and by opposing, etc., etc." he added.

Mac looked at Steve and said, "What's the silly bugger on about now?"

Steve laughed and replied, "I think he's talking about one of your ancestors, Mac, a chap called Macbeth."

Mac looked at the 'Lawyer', still in his Thespian stance, and then back at Steve, still none the wiser for his Stratford experience. The platoon went to their beds, ready for another encounter with the British Army in the morning. Some were thinking of beer, some of steak pies and B.B., and one or two about Stratford-upon-Avon.

Three weeks after the start of basic training a new recruit was posted into the platoon. He was a Scotsman named McVeigh, a short thickset man with powerful shoulders. The Scotsman who spoke with a broad Glaswegian accent was an extrovert person, and was able to mix with the entire platoon, always joking and friendly. But for some reason Steve was suspicious of the man. The ages of the other recruits ranged from eighteen to twenty-five years. But McVeigh, in Steve's estimation was at least thirty-five, maybe more. He also seemed to have little or no personal belongings, and what he did have was kept in a large brown paper carrier bag. Something was wrong with the man, Steve concluded. When Steve spoke to the other men about it they were not so questioning and passed it off lightly, but Steve remained suspicious of the man.

The army was gradually updating its basic weaponry. The old .303 bolt action, single shot rifle was being replaced by the more modern 'self-loading' rifle (SLR). The .303 had served the army well for many decades, but it was no match for the modern rifles of other armies, and had to go.

Front line units were the first to be served of course, and basic training requirements had to be content, for the time being, to train with the .303. The self-loading rifle was very different in design to the old rifle, and regardless of its efficiency, was a transitional problem on the ceremonial parade ground. R.S.M.'s were being issued with new training and drill manuals to cover the very different procedures. The younger R.S.M.'s welcomed the modernisation with enthusiasm and couldn't wait to start, but the older, senior men were not so keen on change and 'tut tutted' the idea.

Steve enjoyed the platoon's visits to the rifle ranges and soon became proficient with the .303. Cleaning the guns with 4x2 cloth and cord 'pull throughs' was not as enjoyable, but simply part of the job, like washing washing-up after a good meal. Another frustrating factor was that every cartridge case issued before the 'shoot' had to be accounted for by the range officer before anybody left the range, a procedure that could take much beer drinking time sifting through the long grass.

After a quite relaxing Sunday the platoon resumed their weapon training on the range and spent the whole day becoming accustomed to their weapons, but the .303 had a vicious recoil action and Steve's shoulder, like those of many of the other recruits, was feeling the strain. Mugs of hot coffee and 'dry rations' softened the blow, but as enjoyable as the firing was they were glad to call it a day after gun cleaning and cartridge accounting.

When they returned to camp in the early evening the rest of the platoon elected to go to the N.A.A.F.I. for the usual nutrition of beer and steak pies. But Steve, whose shoulder was aching from the constant recoil of the .303 decided to stay in the barrack room and read a book. He relaxed on his bed and lost himself in the story. Steve wasn't a big reader but found adventure stories interesting. This book was the history of an explorer who had spent most of his life climbing mountains and searching for lost civilisations in the Amazon jungle. Steve liked to read two chapters, then put the book down and mentally absorb the interesting words. He placed a bookmark on the page and closed the book. He idly lifted his head to look out of the barrack room window. The 'Blonde Bombshell' was staring at him through the window, her nose pressed up against the window pane!

As soon as B.B. realised that she had been spotted she disappeared from the window. Steve leapt off his bed, wrenching his aching shoulder as he did so and, ran out of the room. He looked around the area, but the 'Blonde Bombshell' was nowhere to be seen. He returned to the barrack room, holding his aching shoulder.

"Maybe I was seeing things," he said to himself. "The cookhouse corporal's meat balls must be stronger than I thought."

When the rest of the platoon returned from the N.A.A.F.I., Steve told them about the incident. They found it hard to believe. The barrack room areas were strictly 'out of bounds' to civilians, especially female personnel. They preferred to believe the meat balls theory.

The next day was taken up by more parade ground drill in the morning and a five-mile cross-country run in the afternoon. The platoon as a whole was now very fit and the run was no problem for the young men. But by evening they were tired, it had been a long day. They decided to go to the N.A.A.F.I. for a quick beer and pie, and then prepare for the next day before taking an early night.

At 9.30 the barrack room door crashed open and McVeigh entered, singing 'I belong to Glasgow' in a loud slurred voice; he was obviously very drunk. He staggered down the centre of the room, collided with the solid cast iron stove and kicked it violently, shouting obscenities. He flailed his arms as if he was fighting off an aggressive demon. He staggered to his bed and collapsed in a drunken stupor. Steve's suspicions about him were slowly proving to be true, and the others now agreed. They quietly discussed the idea of informing the training corporal of their suspicions, but decided that for now, they would simply 'keep an eye' on the obviously troubled Glaswegian. For the next two days the Scot was placid and jovial, but Steve felt that it was a lull before the storm.

Training continued, and a few days later Steve and some of the other men were making their way to the cookhouse around the perimeter of the parade ground, marching in twos, knife, fork, spoon and drinking mug held behind their backs as camp discipline required.

From around the corner of one of the barrack rooms Prendergast suddenly appeared. He was dressed in black gym shoes, W.D. underpants, and his black beret worn back to front in his traditional fashion. A W.D. toilet roll was taped to his beret, the open end wafting provocatively in the breeze. Prendergast was carrying a banner which stated in bold black lettering, THE TIME IS NIGH! The banner was in fact a large piece of cardboard, 'sellotaped' to the barrack room sweeping brush.

The regimental sergeant major was drilling a new intake of men on the parade ground. The R.S.M. was in his element, using his 'pacing' stick, (a large compass like piece of equipment, used to measure the correct stride of a marching soldier).

The new intake looked very smart in highly pressed uniforms and polished boots, their rifles carried at the 'slope' on the shoulder.

Steve and the other men looked on in amazement as Prendergast, holding his banner aloft, marched smartly onto the parade ground. The R.S.M. was unaware of his dramatic entrance, having his back towards Prendergast. The Dulwich man marched past the R.S.M. and directly into the ranks of the new intake who were standing to attention. Prendergast, still holding his banner high, 'nudged' the backs of the recruits as he made his way between the ranks of men. Rifles clattered to the ground as the recruits lost their balance, and the parade ground quickly became a shambles.

The R.S.M. could not believe his eyes; such things didn't happen! His knuckles turned white as he gripped his pacing stick. Prendergast marched directly in front of the R.S.M. lifting two fingers in a derogatory gesture as he did so. The R.S.M. by this time had regained some of his senses and was spluttering obscenities at Prendergast. The National Serviceman marched smartly off the parade ground, still holding his cardboard banner high. He disappeared around the corner of the barrack room from where he came. The parade ground was left in complete chaos, as was the regimental sergeant major.

Steve and the other onlookers hurried away. They were laughing uncontrollably, but did not want to be involved in the scene. Prendergast had just played his trump card, and very shortly all Hell would break loose!

The next day the R.S.M., having lost all credibility on his own parade ground, was hastily posted to another unit, hundreds of miles away. Prendergast was never seen or heard of again.

CHAPTER 9

Training was becoming more intense as the weeks went by. Instead of five-mile cross-country runs it was eight or nine miles.

The platoon continued to pay regular visits to the firing range, and whilst maintaining their standards of rifle shooting they were also instructed on the use of the B.R.E.N. gun. This was a fairly heavy machine gun, normally fired from 'prone' position. Strangely, the recoil action of the gun tended to drag the weapon forward, and not into the firer's shoulder, which allowed Steve's aching shoulder to recover.

Steve was not totally pleased that he had 'volunteered' for the regimental boxing team; it was hardly a democratic decision. But it did have its compensations. The boxing team were regarded as the 'elite', and excused all guard and other duties such as 'spud' peeling in the cookhouse, a soul destroying occupation. The team was also allowed extra food rations to build their strength for future competitions. Steve was pleased to learn, in a humorous way, that he was entitled to double helpings of the cookhouse corporals 'balls'!

In the N.A.A.F.I. the talk was about Prendergast and the parade ground incident. They discussed what might possibly have happened to him. Theories ranged from him being hung, drawn and quartered, to ten years in the French Foreign Legion. The camp seemed very quiet without Prendergast's erratic behaviour.

The 'Blonde Bombshell' still fussed with her hair and continued to change the colour of her lipstick on a daily basis. She was the sexual 'focal point' in the male dominated N.A.A.F.I. and played on the fact with enthusiasm. Taff was reticent to go to the serving counter for fear of being doused with more dirty soapy water by B.B., and Steve had to order beers and steak pies for him for several days before the drenched Welshman managed to regain his self-confidence and face the 'Blonde Bombshell' again.

The serious business of beer and pie consumption continued, and Mac, having purchased his pint of the brew and carefully placed it on the table, announced in a sober voice that the price of a pint had risen by a full five pence in the last two years. The others looked at each other, reflected on the cost of living, and drank their beer. Mac dug his hand into his trouser pocket, withdrew a handful of loose change and proceeded to meticulously count the coins on the table. Docherty watched Mac intently as Mac placed the respective half-pennies, pennies and sixpences in neat piles on the table.

Docherty grinned and said, "You Yorkshire people think too much about money, you're too frugal!"

Mac looked up sharply from his counting like a man who had suddenly been stabbed in the back. He said bluntly to Docherty, "Brass is important lad; you can't do nowt without it!"

Docherty laughed, and to emphasise his point said, "Stop playing your frugal horn."

Mac looked at Docherty as if the Liverpudlian was demented, then continued counting his coins and sipping his beer.

Taff was still smarting from the encounter with B.B. and Mac was definitely not in his good books. He was thinking of ways to 'get back' at Mac and his theories on courtship. One evening after much thought and several beers Taff said to Mac, "I'll bet you ten shillings that you can't fix up a date for yourself with B.B. before the end of training."

Mac quickly put down his half empty beer glass and looked at Taff. The thought of earning some easy money intrigued him, and would help to fill his half empty pocket. Ten shillings was a lot for a recruit to wager, but Taff felt confident.

Mac said, 'Okay, you're on."

They shook hands, both feeling they were on a certain winner. The other men at the table thought about it for a minute, and then decided to wager ten 'bob' themselves. The 'Lawyer' quickly worked out the odds on his note pad and he decided to put money down. The whole platoon, including Steve entered the fray, and Steve was appointed treasurer.

Mac solemnly finished his beer, stood, and went to the serving counter. They all looked on, fully expecting trouble from the 'Blonde Bombshell'. Mac and B.B. talked for at least five minutes before he returned to the table with a fresh pint of beer and a large steak and kidney pie. He sat down without saying a word.

"Well," said Taff, "what happened?"

Mac laughed and said, "Don't worry, there's two weeks before the end of basic training." He looked up at the roof rafters and took a bite from his pie. "Marvellous," he said to himself, "ruddy marvellous, ruddy marvellous."

Taff was mystified.

In the morning they returned to the assault course, which now had to be tackled in full battle dress. The final two weeks of training would be generally much tougher and would stretch the men's characters to the limit. The men, in the main, coped well with the assault course, but the Scotsman McVeigh struggled, mainly due to his age and generally poor physique. McVeigh had strong shoulders and arms, but little else. Steve still couldn't figure the man out, and remained deeply suspicious of him.

At lunchtime Steve walked past the N.A.A.F.I. on his way to the cookhouse. B.B. came out of the rear door having finished her shift. She caught up with Steve and said, "How do you fancy going into town with me one evening? There are some nice pubs!" He reminded her that as a recruit he was confined to the barracks. "Don't worry about that," she replied. "I know where there's a hole in the fence!" Steve declined the offer and she said peevishly, "Please yourself," and walked away.

But the 'Blonde Bombshell' was not one to be shunned easily and would continue to stalk her prey! As she walked away Steve was certain that she was accentuating the gyrations of her well-rounded posterior.

It was evening, the platoon had returned from the N.A.A.F.I. and was ready to get a good night's sleep. McVeigh had also been in the N.A.A.F.I., but drinking alone at a corner table.

The barrack room door crashed open and the Scotsman entered. He was in his usual drunken state, and rocked from side to side as he made his way down the centre of the room, mouthing obscenities as he went. He reached Taff's bed and stared drunkenly down at him, kicking the end of the bed, trying to goad a response. Taff ignored him. McVeigh grabbed the side of the bed and violently lifted it in the air, hurling Taff onto the floor.

The other recruits, incensed by what they had just witnessed, leapt out of their beds, grabbed their jackknives and opened the blades. They surrounded McVeigh, shielding Taff who was trying to recover his senses on the floor. McVeigh began flailing his arms, once again as if he was fighting a demon inside of himself. He struck one of the men a blow to the side of the head and blood started to pour from a deep gash, probably caused by a large ornate ring that McVeigh always wore.

Steve had seen enough. He grabbed a chair, lifted it high in the air and brought it down with tremendous force onto the Scotsman's head and shoulders. McVeigh sank to the floor, pole-axed.

Immediately Steve thought he had killed the man, but within seconds McVeigh's legs and arms began to tremble in nervous spasm, his head rolling from side to side. Steve looked at the chair; two of the legs had shattered from the force of the blow.

Mac ran to the guardroom and returned minutes later with the guard commander and two regimental policemen, both carrying heavy batons. They hauled McVeigh to his feet, still semi-conscious, and dragged him out of the barrack room, and took him to the guardroom where they locked him in a cell.

The orderly officer arrived, annoyed at being called away from the Officers' Mess at such an hour. He had been enjoying a few 'Gin and Tonics' with a 'lady' friend. The recruit with the gashed head was taken to the medical centre and treated by the M.O., after which he spent the rest of the night at the centre under observation for possible concussion. Taff recovered from being unceremoniously thrown out of bed and the others 'dusted' themselves off. After some talk and calming down they retired to their beds and slept as well as they could, their jackknives under their pillows.

The next day two burly military policemen arrived, one a sergeant the other a corporal. The platoon was questioned individually about the incident, and Steve gave his account of what happened and the circumstances that led up to it. Later in the day the 'Red Cops' left the camp. McVeigh was handcuffed to the corporal and carried his belongings in the brown paper carrier bag. He looked a pathetic figure as he was led away.

Three days later Corporal Entwhistle informed the platoon that McVeigh was a criminal who had escaped from jail. Somehow by deception, he had managed to enlist in the army, hoping to avoid re-capture by being posted abroad as soon as his training was completed. Corporal Entwhistle finished by adding that McVeigh had been returned to prison.

They all breathed a sigh of relief, and extra beer and pies were consumed in celebration.

The jackknives were returned to their kitbags, and they all slept soundly in their beds.

As the evenings progressed in the N.A.A.F.I., Mac continued to 'chat up' the 'Blonde Bombshell', very much with the ten shillings' wager in his mind. His courting theories seemed to work well for himself, but not other people. 'Horses for courses', Docherty concluded.

At intervals, when the other counter staff were fully occupied, B.B. invited Mac into the back room to share a quick, illicit, glass of sherry. Mac was not a sherry man, the sweet taste did not go with beer and steak pies, but it was all in the line of duty and business, and he congratulated her on the choice of beverage. B.B. said she bought the draught sherry from her local off-license, where the shop owner was a close friend. The proprietor, she said, was the only man who could insert a cork to her own personal satisfaction.

Mac looked at her, and instantly recognised a 'Cork Insertion Connoisseur'!

CHAPTER 10

The Scotsman was soon forgotten, and the normal training routine resumed. They were well into the second half of basic training, and were starting to look and feel like soldiers, from the tops of their closely cropped hair to the highly polished black boots on their much toughened feet.

It was Sunday evening and most of the National Servicemen were writing letters to home. Sunday seemed to be a time when homesickness was at its height. Steve finished his 'explorer adventure' book that he had been reading for the past two weeks when time allowed. He, Taff and the 'Lawyer' decided to go to the N.A.A.F.I. for a pint of beer or two!

They walked past the tiny camp cinema, which was showing 'Pirates of the Caribbean', starring Douglas Fairbanks Jnr. and Dorothy Lamour. The brown, varnished double doors swung open and Mac emerged, holding hands with the 'Blonde Bombshell'. They were both grinning foolishly. Mac had won his bet! The 'Blonde Bombshell' kissed Mac soundly on the cheek to emphasise the point, and at the same time trying to inject a certain amount of jealousy into the scene. But the three onlookers were more concerned about losing their ten-shilling wager than reacting to B.B.'s sexual provocations! They entered the N.A.A.F.I. in a commiserating mood, and drowned their sorrows.

The next day was 'pay parade' a weekly ritual that the men always looked forward to. The barrack room table was used as a pay desk, and the money was issued in cash by a junior officer. The 'pay parade' was organised by Corporal Entwhistle, who had been nicknamed 'Twitchy' by the platoon because of a nervous twitch he had in his right shoulder. It was probably caused by years of firing weapons and .303 rifles' strong recoil action. Steve had suffered slightly from firing the .303 himself and had sympathy for the corporal. But his nervous affliction could also have been caused by years of trying to train very reluctant National Servicemen! When it was Steve's turn to receive his money he marched smartly to the table, saluted, and picked up the princely sum of three pounds and ten shillings. The money did not go far, especially when boot polish, Blanco, Brasso and toiletries had to be purchased.

Early boot 'hurling' and morning parade had become the normal start to the day, and the recruits made sure that their 'best' boots were not available for Corporal Entwhistle to start the day with; working boots were sufficient for his early morning athletics!

Corporal Entwhistle still referred to Mac as 'Megeary' much to Mac's disgust. The corporal was always meticulous in his punctuality and Steve was certain that Entwhistle waited around the corner of the building, looking at his watch and not moving until the minute hand had reached 08.00 exactly.

After roll call and inspection the corporal looked at his clip board and flicked through the pages. He looked up and ordered Steve to report to the regimental office at 14.00 hours for an orientation with the 'Commanding Officer'. When Steve asked him what it was about the corporal replied, "You'll see, just don't be late!" The corporal flexed his shoulders, coughed and tried, unsuccessfully to stop the twitch in his shoulder.

Steve began to wonder what the order was for; it must be something serious if the C.O. was involved.

Perhaps it is to do with McVeigh and the barrack room incident, he thought to himself. A sudden panic overtook him; something terrible has happened to Aunt Maude! He jerked himself out of the thought, trying not to be so pessimistic. Even so, the hours until 14.00 would hang heavy on his mind.

The morning was spent on the parade ground practising 'close order' drill, a discipline designed to promote the platoon working as a team under single order. On the field of battle it was a very necessary discipline! At lunchtime Steve went to the cookhouse early for his meal in order to prepare for his interview with the C.O. at 14.00. He polished his best boots, pressed his battledress, and reported to the regimental office at five minutes to two.

The orderly corporal, told Steve to wait, and the corporal, after flicking a cloth over his own boots, knocked on the commanding officer's door and cautiously entered. The corporal re-appeared and told Steve to "March in." Steve did so, halted in front of the C.O.'s desk and saluted.

The C.O. looked up briefly, and then started to read some papers he had in front of him on the desk. The C.O. a major was a thin faced man with a small military moustache. He reminded Steve of the actor Alec Guinness in the film 'Bridge over the River Kwai', and he momentarily had thoughts of columns of men singing 'Adolf sat on a rusty nail'!

The C.O. finished reading the sheets of paper, stuffed them into a neat pile and looked at Steve. "Private Galway," he said with a commanding voice, "I have decided to promote you to Lance Corporal with immediate effect. During your early training here you have shown potential leadership qualities, and you have obviously decided to treat the army as your career."

The C.O. looked briefly at the pages again then said, "That's all, Galway."

The C.O. was a man of few words! Steve saluted and said, "Thank you, sir."

As Steve was turning to march out of the office the C.O. added, "One more thing, Galway, if you have occasion to charge a man with any offence and bring him before me, make sure the charge sticks, is that clear?"

Steve said it was, and marched out of the office, thankful to get the interview over.

The orderly corporal instructed Steve to report to the stores and pick up his 'chevrons' then take his tunics to the regimental tailor to have them sewn on. He would also be issued with an N.C.O.'s 'stable belt', a six-inch-wide elasticated web belt used when 'short sleeve' order was in progress during the summer months. The belt carried the regiment's colours, in this case, yellow and black horizontal stripes.

News of Steve's promotion had preceded him to the barrack room, and in the evening they all went to the N.A.A.F.I. to celebrate, which they did in some style. As the evening wore on the 'Blonde Bombshell' for some strange reason wearing a new dress and sporting an expensive 'hair-do', entered into the festivities, swishing her 'polka dot' skirt provocatively in front of Steve, much to the disgust of the ladies behind the serving counter.

The next day Steve decided to phone Lorraine, the girl he had met briefly on the train. He had found a telephone box after much searching on the outskirts of the vast camp area. In the evening after duties, he armed himself with a handful of loose change and Lorraine's telephone number that he had carefully kept in his locker.

After a quick fortifying beer at the N.A.A.F.I. he made his way to the only telephone box on the camp. It was situated in an isolated area on a piece of waste ground, and stood like a 'red sentinel' on its bleak surroundings. It was the only means of direct contact with the outside world, and in the evenings in constant use.

When Steve arrived at the kiosk there were four other people queuing, patiently waiting to use the phone. He joined the queue and waited his turn. He couldn't understand why people took so long making telephone calls. When he had made the occasional call in Somerset five minutes had always been enough time; people seemed to talk for hours, especially women!

Eventually it was his turn and he entered the kiosk and closed the heavy door. The back wall of the telephone box was festooned with telephone numbers, messages and idle doodles. He placed the small coins on the shelf beside the phone, fished in his pocket for the number and dialled. The dial tone seemed to go on for an eternity before a girl's voice said, "Hello." Steve instantly recognised Lorraine's voice and he breathed a sigh of relief; he had made contact!

Lorraine was surprised and pleased to hear from him. They talked about the train journey they had shared and Steve explained the situation at the camp and the fact that he was unable to leave until training was completed in two weeks' time. Steve always felt awkward when making phone conversations; it was like talking to somebody on the moon, distant and unreal.

Lorraine said that she understood the situation and suggested that Steve should phone again when he was free to leave the camp. She added that she looked forward to seeing him again, and perhaps tasting some of Aunt Maude's Macintoshes Assortment and possibly a cheese and pickled onion sandwich! Steve felt a sudden loving warmth for her, the fact that she remembered such things spoke much for their short meeting.

They talked for a few more minutes about the weather and her studies. Then there was a long silence, neither of them knowing how to end the conversation. Eventually they both heard each other say "Goodbye," and Steve put the phone down. After collecting his thoughts, he picked up the unused coins and Lorraine's number, put them safely in his pocket and left the kiosk. The waiting queue had increased to six people.

He decided to go to the N.A.A.F.I. for a celebratory beer, and as he strode along the road his chest swelled, and he felt like a million dollars! She had not forgotten their 'Brief Encounter' on the train, and wanted to see him again.

CHAPTER 11

It was normal practice during basic training for random barrack room and personal locker inspections to take place. The inspections would be carried out at any time of the day, seven days a week. It ensured that the rooms and lockers were always in good order and was part of the teaching of discipline and hygiene. Failure to maintain the high standards required would result in extra drill and guard duties for the whole platoon.

It was early evening and Corporal Entwhistle was carrying out a locker inspection. The barrack room door burst open and the Liverpudlian Docherty ran into the room, shouting in a strong Merseyside accent, "Hey, they tell me that old 'Twitchy' Entwhistle is leaving the army in a few weeks!"

Corporal Entwhistle emerged from behind a locker he had been inspecting. Docherty's jaw dropped. From that moment on, until the end of basic training, Docherty's life wasn't worth living!

The next day the platoon returned to the firing ranges, this time for instructions and firing of the B.R.E.N. machine gun. It was a bulky, cumbersome weapon but extremely reliable, and like the .303 rifle had served the army well over many years. Heavy rain had fallen during the night and groundsheets were placed on the sodden grass in order to fire the guns in the normal 'prone' position. But denims soon became damp under the conditions, and when it started to rain heavily again a premature end to the day was called.

It was to be the platoon's final visit to the ranges and they would miss the outings. It had been the only times they were allowed to leave the camp area, albeit for military purposes. They all longed for some 'leave' and freedom from the harsh restrictions of the camp. But there were a few days to go yet, plus the small matter of the official 'Passing Out' parade and inspection carried out by the area Garrison Commander.

The N.A.A.F.I. continued to be lively in the evenings with the odd fight breaking out to relieve the tensions. In general, the atmosphere was pleasant, and even the 'Blonde Bombshell' had a smile on her face after her financially lucrative 'liaison' with Mac! The cash had financed a new 'polka dot' dress, a complete hair-do at a prestigious salon in town and a manicure carried out by a specialist hired by the salon.

B.B. toyed with the idea of asking Mac to think up another 'scheme' to relieve the platoon of more of their money, but had second thoughts about it. She was content with her hairstyle and manicure; the 'Blonde Bombshell' was firing on all cylinders again. She was a great believer in the saying 'Life goes on', and a new intake of raw recruits had just arrived! When Steve went to the serving counter to order a beer and pie, B.B. gave him a half smile, but his thoughts were of another girl!

When Steve returned to the platoon's table they were discussing Judo and the other 'martial arts'. One of the more enthusiastic P.T.I.'s had started an after duties Judo class, and was looking for members, but the platoon would soon be finishing their training at the camp and moving on.

Docherty peered over his half empty jar of beer and said soberly, "I don't like martial arts or the ruddy Japanese; they locked Alec Guinness into a small hut in the Burmese jungle!" Although he was half joking it was unusual to see Docherty in a quite sombre mood. But his traumatic encounter with 'Twitchy' was only a temporary obstacle, and like all true Liverpudlians he would soon bounce back. He was also probably reflecting on his days in Liverpool and the fact that Cilla Black did not fall madly in love with him when he had frequented 'The Cavern' as a young teenager!

The final day of basic training would be the official 'Passing Out' parade. The inspection and 'salute' was to be carried out by the Garrison Commander, a lieutenant colonel. Before the parade, the whole area of the camp would be inspected by the colonel and his staff. The long serving officer was a strict disciplinarian and demanded high standards. He had a habit of wanting to inspect unusual parts of the vast camp, therefore the whole area and buildings had to be 'spic and span' on the day. Everybody was involved in some way to this end, and much 'elbow grease' was employed. Fresh paint was applied to the fire buckets and the surrounding white lines. Corner road kerbstones and bollards received the same treatment. One of the recruits asked what they should or shouldn't paint.

Corporal Entwhistle flippantly replied, "If it moves salute it, if it doesn't, paint it!"

The cookhouse floor received a new covering of 'Red Cardinal' polish. Dustbins were washed and scrubbed, inside and out, and any weeds at the side of the roads were meticulously removed using jackknives. Even the N.A.A.F.I. was given a spring clean.

The platoon was ordered to go to the regimental barber for a trim. When Docherty heard the order a shudder went through him. He had not yet recovered from his first encounter with 'Sweeney Todd' and was far from eager to enter the emporium again. He felt the top of his head and concluded that he had more hair on his chest!

The day of the big parade and inspection arrived, and the men were woken at 5.00am by the orderly sergeant with a final boot 'hurling' episode. The cast iron stove was showing the scars, just as the men were. As with all big occasions there would be last minute things to do, and the extra hour in the morning was much needed.

The platoon initially paraded as usual in front of their barrack room for pre-inspection. But today the check was more rigorous; everything had to be correct. Corporal Entwhistle was resplendent in his best uniform, the iron pressed creases, razor sharp. His medals were polished and proudly worn.

A large saluting dais had been hauled out of one of the store rooms, placed on the parade ground and suitably draped with the regimental colours and Union Jacks. A military band had been temporarily 'posted' in for the occasion, and they were the first to 'march on' to the parade ground, and prepared themselves in one corner of the square. The regimental sergeant major, as tradition required, was in charge of the parade and took control of each platoon as they, in turn, marched onto the massive square. The band played suitable marching music, under the baton of the band master in his spectacular dress uniform. The 'march on' procedure took some time, and was the start of a two-hour long parade.

Eventually the whole regiment was on parade, in line and facing the saluting dais, some eight hundred men strong.

Steve glanced around and thought to himself, *Prendergast would have had a field day!* It was a colourful moving sight, witnessed by invited family members and friends of those on parade, seated at the edge of the parade ground on chairs provided.

The garrison commander's staff car arrived, his personal flag fluttering in the breeze on the front of the shining bonnet. His driver, batman opened the rear door and the colonel, in full dress uniform, made his way to the saluting platform, accompanied by the regiment's Commanding Officer. The colonel, now in his fifties and suffering slight 'gout' blamed on imbibing in too many glasses of 'port' wine, gingerly climbed the three steps to the dais, faced the parade and stood to attention.

The R.S.M. called the parade to attention. On such a massive square this was no easy task and a healthy pair of lungs was called for. The parade came to attention as one man, their boots thudding into the tarmac ground. The timing of the movement was perfect and simultaneous. The ground shuddered and rippled under the men's feet and Steve could feel himself lifted momentarily into the air, as if experiencing a small earthquake.

When the shuddering sensation had stopped under the R.S.M.'s feet he lost control of his rigid discipline for a second and shouted, "Good!" He quickly regained his composure, and mentally slapped himself on the wrist for showing emotion. But it had been a rare moment, a phenomenon created by perfect timing, and one that most of the men on parade would never experience again.

The R.S.M. marched to the saluting dais, saluted and announced to the Garrison Commander, "All present and correct, ready for your inspection, sir!"

The colonel returned the salute and carefully stepped down from the dais. Escorted by the regiment's C.O. once again in full dress uniform, the colonel made his way along the ranks of men, all stoically at 'attention'. From time to time the colonel stopped to have a brief word with individuals. Noticing Corporal Entwhistle's medals he talked for several minutes with the long serving soldier, which certainly made the corporal's day.

The band played suitable music to accompany the inspection, and when each platoon had been inspected they were ordered by the R.S.M., who was loving every minute of the parade, to stand 'at ease'. When the colonel had finished his inspection he thanked the regiment's C.O., as was customary, and returned to the dais.

Steve's feet were aching and he could feel the sweat building between his toes in the completely non-ventilated army boots. He suspected the other men were experiencing the same discomfort, but that was little consolation, and more talcum powder would be required after the parade.

When everybody had been returned to their rightful position, the official 'March Past' began. As each platoon passed the dais the order 'eyes right' was given, and the colonel, standing to attention, returned the salute, while at the same time thinking how well a glass of port would taste now!

The march past and salute completed, the parade returned to its original position, and the R.S.M., pleased that all had gone well, marched to the dais, saluted for the last time and requested in military tradition to, "March off,sir!"

The Garrison Commander in turn replied, "Carry on please, R.S.M."

Military protocol had been satisfied and the R.S.M. took charge of the marching off routine, accompanied by brisk music from the band.

The parade, and with it, basic training, was now officially over and the men returned to their respective barrack rooms. The platoon gratefully removed their boots and sweaty socks, loosened their belts and collapsed onto their beds.

One of the National Servicemen uttered the immortal words, "Roll on death, demobs too far away!"

The men gradually wound down after the long day and looked forward to a beer and a pie in the N.A.A.F.I. Steve looked back over the six weeks. In retrospect, the time had passed quickly because of its intensity; there had been little opportunity for thought. He looked at the other men. They were all fitter and healthier than when they had first arrived at the camp, and even Charlie Strong's pallid complexion was looking more rugged, but the pills and potions still held sway. Steve thought about the 'Blonde Bombshell', and the platoon's vain attempts to 'woo' her. The new intake of recruits was in for a rude awakening from B.B. and 'boot hurling' alike! He wondered where Prendergast was after the parade ground fiasco, and couldn't help but admire him for his endeavour and single-mindedness. He spared half a thought for the Scotsman McVeigh, now languishing in jail, clearly a troubled man who needed help, not incarceration.

The next day, Sunday, was 'Church Parade', the traditional end to the six weeks training. It was a voluntary parade, but the entire platoon decided to attend. Mac said he wanted to go, if only to thank the 'Almighty' that the six weeks was over!

Military uniform was required for the church parade, but there was no inspection beforehand, all part of Sunday's general relaxation of discipline. The camp church was small and quite plain in appearance, almost as if military discipline required it. But the padre, a captain, had made the interior pleasant and inviting. A small upright piano had been donated to the church by a local dignitary, and was played every Sunday by one of the officers' wives.

Steve was not an overly religious man, but he enjoyed the service and said a silent prayer for Aunt Maude and hoped that she was well, and still happily 'pickling'. After church the men were allowed to make their way back to the barrack room, all reflecting in some way on the padre's well-chosen words.

Back in the barrack room they all felt an anti-climax, and decided to organise a football match to fill in the afternoon. They had no football boots, so black gym shoes would have to suffice. A fairly old full size football was available though and had been kept in working order by one of the P.T.I.'s. It being Sunday afternoon and not having anything to do he offered the football and himself as referee.

The men were all very fit after the six weeks training and enjoyed the light-hearted competition. Steve played at 'centre-half', and Mac decided to play in 'goal' a not too strenuous position! Charlie Strong was happy to play on the 'wing', pottering about and trying to stay out of trouble. In the evening the platoon enjoyed beer and pies in the N.A.A.F.I.; all in all, it was a pleasant end to basic training.

They all had two week's leave now. Mac decided to return to Dewsbury and see if his favourite barmaid was still working at his local pub. Taff went to Cardiff to see friends and watch rugby at Cardiff Arms Park. Steve toyed with the idea of taking the train back to Somerset, but decided instead to stay in the area and hopefully see as much of Lorraine as possible. He would write to Aunt Maude and tell her all the news.

When the platoon returned from the two week's leave it was planned that they would travel to Scotland for advanced training.

CHAPTER 12

Steve, with his new found freedom for two weeks, decided to venture into the nearby town the next morning and see what the shops had to offer. He would have a midday meal at a cafe and phone Lorraine in the late afternoon from a public telephone box. She would probably be finished with her day's study classes by that time.

In the morning he took breakfast in the cookhouse and then prepared himself for the bus journey into town. Most of the platoon had already left the camp, and room B2 seemed strangely quiet and hollow. He wore civilian clothes for the first time in six weeks. They felt very light in contrast to the heavy battle dress and army boots.

He left the confines of the camp showing his 'leave pass' at the guardroom; the pass was valid for the next fourteen days. He walked briskly to the bus stop, then realised that he was no longer in the military restrictions of the camp, and relaxed. Several people were waiting at the bus stop and Steve assumed that a bus was due shortly. As he joined the queue he idly wondered how many hours he would spend waiting for buses in his lifetime.

It was a dry, fairly sunny July day, and he was looking forward to seeing what the small town had to offer. He needed to buy a white cotton shirt and several pairs of civilian socks, hopefully of good quality and not requiring much darning. Needlework was not his strong point!

He wondered if the town was large enough to boast a 'Marks and Spencer' store. Aunt Maude always praised the quality of their goods, and would travel miles to give them her custom. Steve smiled to himself and thought, *If it's good enough for Aunt Maude it's good enough for me.*

The bus arrived and Steve boarded with the other passengers. The driver was a young, slim man, unlike the driver with the massive girth that Steve had encountered before. He wondered if his gearbox had finally collapsed! Steve recalled his first journey to Morval camp and the 'suffering' the bus had to endure at the hands of the driver. The sound of the crunching noise in the gearbox was still fresh in Steve's ears, and he could visualise the pieces of metal flying off the gear wheels and seeking sanctuary in the oil at the bottom of the gearbox. Steve was certain that sometime in the future gearboxes would be fully automatic and free from the molestation of ham-fisted drivers. But that time was to come.

He paid his fare and sat at a window seat. The bus was basically the same design as the previous one he had taken from the railway station to the camp. It had mahogany window frames, held in place by large brass screws. There was a hint of varnish aroma denoting that the frames had recently been painted. The seats were fairly comfortable, but the backs were very upright and certainly not designed for long journeys.

The bus made several stops before arriving at the station in town. It was the terminal and all the passengers slowly left the bus. The driver was busy sorting his 'takings' and placing the coins into a small cotton bag for handing into the cashier's office later. It reminded Steve of Mac and the 'Frugal Horn' episode.

Steve walked leisurely out of the terminal. It was difficult being a soldier and a civilian, but with practice he would succeed, it was a matter of wearing different hats. He reached the main street and decided to walk the length of it to see what shops it offered. He passed a 'Woolworths' store and a fairly large 'Boots' and assumed a 'Marks and Spencer' would be soon in sight. The three major companies usually plied their business in the same customer 'catchment' area. He came to the end of the street, but there was no M&S in sight.

Steve turned the corner and walked past a small public park. The shops seemed to have ended abruptly; the town wasn't as big as he had hoped. A sudden feeling of disappointment entered him; his new white shirt was not to be! As he was about to retrace his steps a young smartly dressed woman came towards him. She was carrying a large brown paper carrier bag, and on it was the logo 'M&S'. Steve politely enquired about the store, and the woman, who was about the same age as Steve gave him directions to the store. It was through a small arcade on a parallel street. Steve thanked her and wished her a 'good day'. The girl seemed in no hurry to go, but Steve had inner desires for Lorraine on his mind, and moved on. The M&S store was much the same basic layout as the stores he had visited with Aunt Maude as a young boy, and in a strange way gave him a sense of belonging. As he entered the store he held the swing door open to allow a woman to pass. She too carried a full carrier bag marked M&S. Steve thought to himself, *Another satisfied customer!*

He went to the shirt department, remembering his collar size was 14½". He selected a quality white shirt, ensuring that it had long sleeves and cuff-link holes before moving on to the sock department. Like most men he knew exactly what he wanted and completed his shopping in five minutes flat. He took his purchases to the cash desk and made his payment. The shop assistant put his shirt and socks into an M&S brown carrier bag and handed it to Steve. He had become a member of the social elite!

Pleased with his shopping, he decided to find a cafe for lunch. Time had gone by quickly and he suddenly felt hungry. He found a cafe just off the High Street and peered through the plate glass window. The interior looked clean and there were plenty of customers, always a good sign that the food and cooking was good.

Before going in Steve decided to buy a national newspaper from a nearby shop, something to read as he ate. He needed to catch up with the news, especially the sport. England had just completed a cricket 'test' series against the 'Aussies' and he had yet to find out the important result. The matches were always keenly contested, but having been 'locked away' for six weeks he had lost track of all sporting events.

The cafe was clean and pleasant inside. The white tablecloths were crisply starched and ironed. The upright chairs had cushions for customer comfort, something that the camp cookhouse needed, Steve thought, but such eloquence was not good for discipline or the toughening of bodies.

Steve sat at a table designed for two and put his shopping and newspaper on the spare seat. A waitress appeared holding a small order pad, a pencil ready in her hand. Steve looked up, surprised by the efficient service. The waitress was a small pleasant faced, cheerful girl. She was perhaps a little too plump for her own well-being, thought Steve, but pleasant nonetheless. She chatted to him whilst taking his order and Steve was grateful for the conversation. Having spent the last six weeks in the company of twenty men he was happy to have female company, if only for a few minutes. He silently rebuked himself for thinking that she was slightly overweight, and concluded that was a guarantee that the quality of the food in the cafe was good.

He ordered sausages, mashed potatoes and 'petit pois'. When the food was served it was enhanced with a small 'boat' of brown gravy, and the condiments were in an ornamental stainless steel holder which gave the table a touch of refinement.

Steve enjoyed the meal; it was his first 'civilian' food for six weeks. Army food was nutritious, but it left something to be desired as far as the taste was concerned! He followed the main meal with apple tart and fresh cream with white coffee to finish. He read his newspaper for a while to allow his food to digest before continuing his exploration of the town. Apart from the sport pages there was little to interest him. There were articles on the daily politics, but he was not a politically minded man and left that to others. As long as democracy prevailed and the rule of law was properly applied there was little to worry about.

Having read all the sports pages and completing half of the crossword he paid his bill, thanked the cheerful waitress and left the cafe. He made a mental note of the name of the cafe and its location, deciding to eat there again whenever it was possible. It certainly had the edge on the cookhouse corporal's meat balls!

Steve decided to retrace his steps and find the park he had passed previously. He needed some fresh air and to think about his oncoming telephone call to Lorraine. How should he approach it? What should he talk about? What should be the tone of his voice? He had so many questions, but he knew the call would be important for the future!

The park, although small, was well kept and new plants had been arranged in the verges surrounding the grass that had just been mown and was giving off its newly sweet perfume. Thoughts of the meadows and corn fields back in Somerset came to mind; he would always be a country boy at heart. A small duck pond was at the edge of the green, and several ducks, mostly Mallards with their colourful down, waddled around the area, completely happy and content in their environment. They stopped from time to time to preen their feathers before taking a refreshing dip in the water. Steve wished he had bought some bread from the cafe to feed them, but several people were throwing lumps of bread to them, and they were far from starving. He smiled to himself and wondered if they were partial to meat balls, or perhaps the extravagance of cheese and pickled onion sandwiches!

When evening approached it was time to phone Lorraine, and Steve slowly made his way back to the High Street and a telephone kiosk he had seen on his earlier exploration of the town. The kiosk was available, unlike the phone box at the camp which had a constant queue. He fished in his trouser pocket and took out sufficient small change for the call. As soon as he started to put his hand into his jacket pocket for Lorraine's number he knew exactly where it was, in his locker back at the camp! He cursed himself for forgetting it, he could remember the first four numbers, but the rest he was unsure of. There was only one thing to do, go back to camp and phone from the 'red sentinel'. He hurried back to the bus terminal, still soundly cursing himself.

He arrived back at the camp at six-thirty, still angry with himself. Before calling Lorraine he decided to go to the N.A.A.F.I., have a beer and try to calm himself. The medicinal treatment worked, and he put the mistake behind him. He picked up the phone number from barrack room 2B and walked fairly briskly to the 'red sentinel' on the piece of waste ground, time was marching on!

The 'red sentinel' was surrounded by a queue of people, and Steve joined them waiting patiently.

"The Post Office would do well to add another kiosk on this piece of waste ground," he said to another waiting client.

The recruit, who had obviously not visited Sweeney Todd's emporium yet laughingly replied, "One day we will all have phones we can carry in our pockets."

"Stranger things have happened," said Steve, and they resumed their vigil.

When it came to Steve's turn he quickly went through the routine of dialling and having his money ready. As soon as the dial tone started a female voice hurriedly said, "Hello!" It was unmistakeably Lorraine.

After they had exchanged greetings, she said that she had just arrived home from extra study at college, and heard the phone ring as she was opening her door. He had picked a good time, she said.

"Any earlier and I would have been out."

Steve immediately thought of his mistake with the phone number earlier. *Maybe it's fate,* he thought to himself.

They talked about the weather for a while, and she said he must be relieved to be able to leave the training camp after six weeks of 'captivity'. They joked about prisons and sentences. He thought about telling her of the McVeigh episode, but that would be for another day, when he knew her better. Steve suddenly became anxious about asking Lorraine 'out', for fear she may have changed her mind; that was a woman's prerogative after all! He wondered why he felt so strangely 'off balance'; the 'Blonde Bombshell' didn't affect him in this way. He took a deep breath and 'popped' the question, very aware that his voice was heightened with nervousness.

Eventually, after what seemed like a lifetime, she said, "This weekend I have been invited to a jazz festival, would you like to go with me and meet my friends at the same time, it would be a good way to 'break the ice' and get to know each other?"

Steve breathed a sigh of relief and said he would be delighted to go, it sounded great. They both sounded less anxious and decided to meet on Saturday afternoon near Lorraine's college that would be the nearest stop for him. She gave him instructions on the journey and the correct bus stop; it would be about an hour's ride from the camp she told him.

They talked some more, mostly about jazz and other music. The conversation flowed more freely now, the ice had been broken by music, the universal common denomination. Steve peered out through the kiosk glass. There were eight people now, all anxiously waiting to use the phone. He explained the situation to Lorraine and she agreed that they should say goodbye for now. They both said that they looked forward to Saturday and the music festival. After another tentative goodbye, Steve put the phone down. Telephones were such abrupt machines, one minute there was connection to another person, the next, you were alone!

As he left the 'red sentinel' the queue of people looked at him with irritation and 'black looks'!

Steve looked at his watch; he had been in the kiosk for three quarters of an hour! As he strode off down the road he thought to himself, *So that's what people talk about so long on the phone!*

He went to the N.A.A.F.I. for a celebratory beer, with the sound of Lorraine's beautiful voice in his ears. It had turned out to be a good day after all. He said to himself, "All's well that ends well!" as a writer of some repute once said.

CHAPTER 13

The July weather became sunnier and the temperature a pleasant 70°F so the regiment was ordered into 'short sleeve order' and battle dress tunics were stored away in lockers until the autumn. The summer ambience made the whole camp a different more acceptable place to be in, even the cookhouse corporal seemed to have added something extra to his famous, or infamous, meat balls! Steve was officially on 'Leave of Absence', and allowed to wear civilian clothes, but in the confines of the camp, beach shirts and sandals were frowned upon by the R.S.M. and recruits were required to look smart and 'carry themselves in a military manner'.

The next day was his meeting with Lorraine and the jazz festival. After a filling breakfast in the cookhouse he showered, shaved carefully wanting to look his best, pressed his civilian slacks, and polished his shoes to a standard that even the R.S.M. would have approved of. He decided to take a bus into the town fairly early, buy a small bouquet of flowers for Lorraine and have a light lunch before taking a bus to the college. It would be a longer journey but he wanted to buy the flowers for her, and lunch at the cafe he had visited previously, sounded inviting.

He wore his new white M&S shirt, which fitted perfectly, and together with his freshly ironed slacks and polished shoes he looked very presentable. His naturally wavy brown hair was recovering from the attentions of 'Sweeney Todd' the 'demon' barber, and he reminded himself the next time that the platoon visited the barber's 'emporium' he should warn Docherty to 'look out for the trap door'!

He had written a long letter to Aunt Maude telling her all about his six weeks training and his recent meeting with Lorraine. He put his letter securely in his back pocket for posting in the town, thinking that the service would be quicker than the well-meaning but somewhat ponderous N.A.A.F.I. shop mailing service. He told Aunt Maude he would write again when he returned from Scotland and the advanced training. By that time, he would know what his permanent posting was to be, and therefore what the future held for him. The decision was totally in the army's 'court'.

The bus journey was a welcome break from the camp and was becoming familiar. When the bus arrived at the terminal he went straight to the Post Office, bought a stamp and put the letter into the box provided. With luck Aunt Maude would receive the letter in two or three days, providing the postman had not been molested by an unfriendly dog!

His next stop was the florist's shop and a bouquet of flowers for Lorraine. Flowers were plentiful this time of year, and not expensive. He picked a nice mixed bunch, but romance, or no romance he still had to look to his budget of three pounds and ten shillings!

He took a stroll through the park in order to work up an appetite for lunch. He carried the flowers as matter-of-factly as he could, but still received some strange glances from passers-by, female, and male!

He found the cafe again without any problem. There was no need for a pre-inspection look through the window this time; he knew the place was all right. The same cheerful waitress greeted him, and he chose the same table as before. The waitress remarked to him about the flowers, and jokingly asked if they were for her. Steve almost felt that he should have bought her a bouquet, and he carefully removed one of the blooms and handed it to her with a solemn bow and smile. She seemed to appreciate the single flower as much as if he had presented her with the whole bouquet, and took his order with a 'flush' on her face.

Steve had a light salad lunch, not knowing what was planned for food later in the day, either with Lorraine or at the festival in the evening. He thought about the festival, it would be nice to hear some 'live' jazz, rather than second-hand on records. He finished his meal with a white coffee, leaving out the temptation of apple tart and cream. After he had paid the bill he waved to the waitress and she held up her flower and laughed; he had made somebody's day! As he left the cafe he thought what a cheerful soul she was!

He glanced at his watch, time had passed quickly and he quickened his pace towards the bus station. The temptation to march and swing his arms was undeniable; the training had left its mark! He remembered Lorraine's instructions on how to find the college and which bus to take. He was becoming used to bus travel now, and as he boarded the bus he asked the driver to let him know when the college stop was near. He clutched his bouquet of flowers and sat near the front in order to hear the driver's voice.

The bus made regular stops, and passengers came and went. Steve was interested in people and their mannerisms. He liked to assess their character by studying their faces and body language. The clothes they wore also gave an indication as to what profession they were following, or job they were engaged in.

A tall slim man boarded the bus. He wore a brown, pin stripe suit and had three fountain pens in his top pocket. Accountant, Steve decided, or possibly solicitor's clerk.

I should be studying human social behaviour, not training to be a soldier, he thought to himself. He smiled and wondered how the other people on the bus might be assessing him. Perhaps his close cropped hair and the proximity of the army training camp was a certain give-away! He continued with his assessments as the bus journey progressed, it helped to pass the time.

The driver shouted, "College," and Steve gathered his belongings together and left the bus, thanking the driver for his help as he did so.

The bus pulled away and Steve was left staring across the road at the college, a large grey stone building, surrounded by a high wall, also made of stone. He looked around for Lorraine, but there was no sign of her. He looked at his watch and realised he was early anyway, and crossed the street to take a closer look at the college. He stared through the massive black wrought iron gates. It was a very austere Victorian building, solid and quite formidable. In Victorian times it probably served as a hospital, or even a 'poor house', before being reformed into a place of learning.

Several students were walking along the gravel pathways, clutching their books and talking animatedly, but he could not see the student he was looking for. With an inner sixth sense he turned around and found her standing directly behind him, smiling!

"Hello," she said in a warm welcoming voice. He opened his mouth to reply, but no sound emerged. He vaguely remembered the flowers in his hand and offered them to her. "Thank you, they're beautiful!" she said.

He managed to say, "Hello," but couldn't understand his feelings. As soon as she looked at him he became a tongue-tied idiot!

Lorraine suggested they walk to her flat and await her student friends who were providing the transport to the jazz festival. Steve immediately visualised some 'fairly scruffy' Bohemian types with a broken down Ford saloon, held together with sticky tape, on a meagre student's budget.

Steve overcame his temporary vocal affliction, and they talked as they made their way to the flat. The conversation was naturally guarded. Although they talked on the train and telephone this meeting was somehow more personal and intimate, they could both sense each other's presence, and there would be some awkward silent moments.

Steve remarked that the college was very Victorian in design. She said that after the war it was used as a Catholic convent, and had been bought by the college some fifteen years ago with financial help from the government. The classrooms, she said, were small, and in the winter the cast iron heating radiators rattled, disturbing the students' concentration. But the general austerity was good for a student's self-discipline she said with a half-smile on her face.

Steve agreed, and told her about the National Serviceman Prendergast and his efforts to avoid it! She laughed when he described the parade ground incident and said that he was probably a born rebel.

He suggested that he should carry the bouquet of flowers, and she handed them to him, remarking that it wasn't every day that she received flowers from a handsome man. He had a sudden desire to hold her hand and kiss her, but this was not the time, or place, but it held well for the future and he thanked the 'Almighty' for presenting him with this wonderful woman.

They arrived at Lorraine's flat, a small block of flats owned by the college and designed specifically for student use. Lorraine invited Steve into the small lounge and suggested he should relax after his journey. She went into the small kitchen, put the flowers into a vase, and made a pot of tea. At the same time, she realised that she also needed to relax and assess the situation. She was very aware that her feelings were being emotionally disturbed, in a pleasant way, by Steve's presence. She had known boys before, but somehow this was a different relationship, and for the moment, inexplicable!

Steve looked around the room. It was a fairly average sized lounge, in keeping with the general design of the building, but nicely furnished and decorated. On one wall there were several paintings, all in water colour. They were mostly of woodland scenes or flowers. Steve stood up to study them more closely. They were colourful, pleasant to look at, and all were signed, 'Lorraine'!

Lorraine returned with a tray of cups, saucers, pot of tea and a small plate of biscuits. Steve remarked on how good her paintings were. She smiled and looked across at them with a self-questioning eye.

Steve thought to himself, *No artist worth his, or her salt is ever content with their work, it could always be better, such is the mark of a perfectionist!*

Lorraine said, "Painting is a hobby of mine, but my studies are becoming so intense and demanding there is no longer time for painting."

Steve smiled and said, "All work and no play?"

"I know," she replied, "but that's how it is at the moment."

Steve couldn't envisage studying for six to seven years simply to qualify for one profession. *The human body must be very complicated*, he thought to himself looking down at his own structure.

They drank their tea and nibbled on the biscuits and discussed Lorraine's paintings for a while until the doorbell rang, heralding the arrival of Lorraine's student friends. Steve mentally braced himself for a long, bumpy ride in a second-hand Ford. Lorraine quickly took the tray to the kitchen and they left the flat and walked out onto the street pavement. Steve stopped abruptly and stared at the car in front of him. It was a gleaming black, vintage 'Bentley' saloon!

CHAPTER 14

The front passenger window was open and Lorraine greeted the two occupants of the car. The driver was a man in his early thirties, the passenger a woman, slightly younger in age. They were both immaculately dressed.

Steve recovered his senses and opened the rear door for Lorraine. She slid into the beautifully upholstered seat and Steve followed. She quickly introduced Steve and they all said their hellos. The Bentley pulled effortlessly away from the kerb, and Steve could hardly hear the powerful engine and the amber trafficator, operated by its solenoid, signalled as if in salute!

Lorraine smiled at him. She knew what he had been thinking and cheekily said, "Not a bad little car is it?"

He laughed, took her hand and sank back into the luxury of the rear seat. She too had a 'sixth' sense. *Touché,* he thought to himself.

Lorraine leant forward and made conversation with the girl in the front seat. Steve took the opportunity to study the interior of the car. The polished walnut dashboard carried a variety of expensive looking dials and gauges. The seats were covered in high quality leather, probably the original upholstery, and the insides of the doors were covered in a plush, deep blue material. The whole car oozed quality and wealth! Steve suddenly felt strangely out of place, and wished he was back in the N.A.A.F.I. at 'Morval' with the rest of the platoon.

Lorraine finished her conversation with the girl and relaxed with Steve, soaking up the opulence of their luxurious transport. It was an experience that even she, with her fairly upper class background, felt stimulating. She quietly explained to Steve that the driver, whose name was Geoffrey, spelt with two F's, was in the final year of study, and hoped to qualify as a doctor shortly. The girl whose name was Audrey, was also a student doctor, but some three years younger than Geoffrey, and was at the same stage in her studies as Lorraine.

Steve toyed with the idea of engaging the driver in conversation, but Geoffrey was fully engrossed in his driving. Steve decided to leave any thoughts of interaction until they were at the music festival. The Bentley was obviously Geoffrey's 'pride and joy', and quite rightly so. Steve felt a pang of jealousy rip through him, and wondered why Geoffrey should be the owner of that beautiful machine, and he the custodian of a second-hand bicycle in Somerset?

He thought to himself, *Perhaps Karl Marx had the answer,* but he was languishing in a cemetery in London leaving the rest of the world to debate communism at its leisure. Steve envisaged himself as a prominent politician, grasping his lapel firmly and uttering the immortal words, 'We will fight them on the beaches'!

Steve jerked himself back to reality. Lorraine was admiring the countryside scenery and Geoffrey drove the Bentley smoothly, as if he was savouring the taste of an expensive vintage wine.

There will be no ham-fisted gearbox crunching today! Steve thought to himself.

The three passengers discussed the forthcoming jazz festival and Geoffrey interacted with the odd remark here and there. He spoke in a very refined way, and Steve could certainly picture him in a doctor's surgery, ministering to his patients.

The festival was to be an 'open air' event, held in the grounds of a private mansion on the outskirts of the New Forest in Hampshire. The landowner, a slightly eccentric, but enthusiastic jazz follower was allowing the festival organisers to hold the annual event free of charge. In return he would see a free concert, and meet all of his favourite musicians and bands. He would be the applauded host, and everybody was happy with the arrangement.

Steve looked out of the car window. The Hampshire weather was perfect for an 'open air' event: warm, sunny, and a clear blue sky. He started to feel as if he was on another planet. No early morning 'boot hurling', and no cookhouse corporal's meat balls!

When they arrived at the country mansion it was early evening, and already a steady streak of cars was entering the grounds and parking in the ample open spaces. They paid a small entrance fee to cover the car parking attendant's wages, and Geoffrey carefully drove the Bentley to an isolated parking space, well away from the other cars. Many a vehicle was damaged in the false mental security of a public car park and parking attendants bore no responsibility.

"More than my job's worth, mate!"

The girls wandered off to find a suitable spot to watch the concert from. A makeshift stage had been erected in the grounds and they found a pleasant lawn area near the stage front. Steve and Geoffrey climbed out of the car and stretched their legs. It had been quite a long journey, and comfortable as the Bentley was, their limbs were stiff. The girls seemed to have no such problems as they happily wandered off, and Steve admired their physical flexibility. Perhaps it was their ability for child bearing, he wondered as he rubbed his sore legs.

Steve knew a little about vintage cars and the rudiments of the petrol engine. As a young boy the theory of the 'Otto' cycle had interested him, and he remembered spending many hours at the local library in Somerset learning about 'four stroke' and 'two stroke' engines. The inventive endeavours of the German engineer Dr. Diesel also interested him, with his highly successful engine for commercial use in heavy transport, on sea, or land. Dr. Diesel had developed a method of utilising relatively unrefined fuel oil, the engine known technically as the C.I. (compression ignition) engine, as opposed to the I.C. engine (internal combustion). The fuel oil, universally called diesel, being unrefined was of course cheaper and made the rugged engine more financially viable. The diesel engine operated without the use of 'spark plugs' and their relative electrical apparatus making a further cost saving. Dr. Diesel accomplished this saving by increasing the compression ratio in the engine cylinders. The ratio in a normal petrol engine was 7-1, whereas the diesel engine operated at 20-1, therefore making the fuel / air mixture self-combustible in the cylinder. Steve admired German engineering, but as a race of people he found them arrogant and overbearing, and regrettably, responsible for two world wars. Not to mention the sturdy midfielder Franz Beckenbauer.

Nonetheless, Dr. Diesel's discovery, and other engines alike was responsible for the modern transport world, and to a great extent the luxury of easy living, rightly or wrongly.

Steve had a genuine interest in the vintage Bentley, and asked Geoffrey about its history and its mechanical technicalities. As soon as the driver realised that Steve had a 'learning' towards cars and engines in general, his attitude became more friendly. They chatted about cars and the merits of the Bentley. The car had been owned by Geoffrey's father, and handed down to him as a family heirloom. It was more than just a car to him, it was part of his family, and Steve began to understand the situation, and why Geoffrey had a special relationship with the Bentley.

The Bentley became the catalyst for conversation, and Steve no longer felt out of place, and relaxed. Geoffrey proudly lifted the car bonnet, and they studied the engine. It was a massive six cylinder, twin carburettor engine, quite capable of powering four ordinary cars. The engine compartment was as immaculate as the exterior of the car, and a neatly folded yellow cleaning duster was securely held by a bracket provided by the manufacturer of the special machine.

The girls returned from their survey, chatting happily as women do, probably about nothing in particular, but happily engaged nonetheless. Men seemed to talk about more serious matters, such as cars, cricket, beer and sex, not to mention cheese and pickled onion sandwiches!

Lorraine and Audrey found a suitable 'plot', and had staked their 'claim' by laying a car rug on the grass. Geoffrey went to the rear of the car and opened the boot with a theatrical flourish; he too had started to relax! In the very ample boot was a large picnic basket made of wicker and four collapsible chairs. He carefully closed and locked the Bentley, stroked his hand lovingly along its bonnet, and the four music lovers made their way to the concert area. The girls still chatted happily and carried the lightweight chairs. Steve and Geoffrey manhandled the large wicker hamper between them. The sun was starting to set now, and it was time for jazz.

The girls had picked a good 'plot' on a gentle slope, overlooking the stage. The mansion grounds were filling rapidly, and the slightly eccentric owner was making himself known, obviously enjoying the situation and playing the host. In reality he was probably a very lonely man, and revelled in the sudden party atmosphere.

Steve looked around him at the pleasant site. People were preparing picnics and putting up chairs, some had gone to the extent of bringing tables and were busy laying colourful tablecloths and arranging plates of food and drinks on them. Steve noticed that one table sported an ornate candelabra, complete with candles, to be lit when darkness came. It seemed to Steve that a certain amount of 'one-upmanship' was being invoked.

Geoffrey ceremoniously opened the picnic basket and handed the food, all neatly wrapped and packed, to the girls who arranged the fayre neatly on the tartan travel rug. The food looked delicious and had been prepared by Geoffrey's girlfriend. Steve and Lorraine congratulated Audrey; it must have taken much time and effort to prepare.

Steve glanced at Audrey and thought to himself, *If the couple do eventually marry, Audrey will make a perfect hostess for a successful doctor and his cocktail parties.*

Lastly, Geoffrey reached into the hamper and withdrew two large bottles of vintage champagne, four glasses, an ice bucket and some deep frozen ice in a special 'cold' bag. They had thought of everything!

A young girl was weaving her way around the tables and rugs selling programmes. When she reached their plot Steve bought a copy and studied the list of performers. He was surprised to see how many famous names were due to perform at such a relatively minor concert. But after discussing it with Lorraine and her friends he realised that unfortunately traditional jazz was losing its popularity, and the famous stars and bands could no longer fill large venues and command large payments. The younger generation was listening to 'The Beatles', Cliff Richard and the advent of 'Pop' music. Most young teenagers had never heard of Louis Armstrong, or Ella Fitzgerald.

Geoffrey expertly opened a bottle of champagne filled the glasses and handed them around. Steve sipped the 'nectar' which was giving off tiny bubbles. It was a new experience for him, he had never tasted the expensive drink before, but he was disappointed with its taste and secretly would have enjoyed a glass of beer instead. He glanced up from the bubbling glass to see Lorraine looking at him, a warm smile on her face. He smiled back and continued sipping his champagne. There had been a quite romantic moment between them; there was no need for words!

The concert started and Steve noted that top of the 'bill' was Humphrey Lyttelton and his band of 'All Stars'. Humphrey or 'Humph', as he was affectionately known as, started his adult life as an officer in one of the Guards regiments, but decided to give up the luxury of the Officers' Mess for the musical bandstand. Lorraine had seen him and his band on several occasions, but in the past Steve had had to content himself with records and magazines. Today was a magical 'first' for him.

Also on the programme was 'Acker Bilk' and his band. Acker was a Somerset man, and therefore Steve felt a certain kinship with him which added to the enjoyment of the evening. Acker, who played the clarinet, had learnt how to play his instrument whilst serving his two years National Service in the army, which strengthened the bond that Steve felt.

The audience enjoyed their picnics, and the music rang out across the mansion grounds. Very soon an atmosphere of warmth and goodwill was built. The musicians too were enjoying the open air scenario, and it showed in the music they produced. Steve nibbled at his sandwiches and sipped his 'bubbly', there was little time for conversation, but that didn't matter.

The concert was a great success, and as dusk fell the candelabras were lit, the last of the sandwiches and wine were consumed and the evening ended with all the bands packed onto the stage playing, 'When the Saints go marching in'. It was an evening that Steve would remember for a long time.

After packing up all of the picnic utensils and odd pieces of litter that had gathered they strolled back to the waiting Bentley. The journey home was a pleasant one; all four were happy and relaxed. Geoffrey whistled the 'Saints' quietly to himself, and even the Bentley seemed to be enjoying itself, the engine 'purring' under the driver's guiding hands.

It was totally dark when they arrived at Lorraine's flat and Geoffrey and Audrey said a quick goodnight, needing to get home and to sleep before a long home study day in the morning. As Steve said goodbye to them he felt that he had initially misjudged them when they first met. They were not aloof and snobbish, they were simply two fairly conservative, good people, and he hoped to see them again.

After the Bentley had disappeared into the night Lorraine asked Steve if he would like a coffee to finish the evening before he left for the camp. He gladly agreed and they went into the flat. Lorraine went to the kitchen and Steve sat on the small sofa and reflected on the evening. It had been a memorable day. Music was a catalyst for all people. His thoughts of Lorraine were warm and endearing, and although he hated to admit it to himself, tinged with more than just a hint of raw sexual lust!

Lorraine returned with the coffee and they talked about the concert. She had also enjoyed the evening and it had helped to break the ice as far as their friendship was concerned. Lorraine had a way of making people feel at ease, and Steve was sure that she would have a good 'bedside' manner when she did qualify as a doctor.

They finished the coffee and Steve looked at his watch, his bus was due in ten minutes, and it was the last one back to camp. They stood up and he put his hands on her shoulders and lightly kissed her on the cheek. She looked at him for a second and then kissed him firmly on the lips. It was her 'signal' that all was well, he had been given the green light to go ahead. They kissed again, moving closer together and holding each other tightly. Neither of them wanted to let go, but the bus would not wait! He gave her one last kiss and hug and they agreed that he should phone the next evening. They walked to the door holding hands, two people very aware that they were on the verge of an unstoppable romance.

As Steve made his way to the bus stop it was as if he was walking on a cushion of air, and as he boarded the bus he thought to himself, *Can this be love, or is it just the champagne?*

He arrived back at camp just before midnight, and feeling a bit like Cinderella showed his pass at the guardroom.

He went to his bed and imagined he was kissing Lorraine again. He could feel her soft lips, and her skin felt like silk. The aroma of her perfume was still with him. Today he had embraced the most wonderful woman in the world.

He flexed his limbs and felt strong; he smiled to himself, a contented man. Before many minutes had passed he was fast asleep, the smile still on his face!

CHAPTER 15

In the morning Steve woke later than usual, but was still in time for breakfast at the cookhouse. He allowed himself a full breakfast of sausage, egg, chips and baked beans in tomato sauce. Not a totally healthy meal, he said to himself, but he was on 'holiday' after all.

When he returned to the barrack room he was unsure of what to do for the next few hours. Later he would phone Lorraine, but there was time to pass before that. The rest of the platoon had dispersed in some way or another for the leave period. The quietness was welcome, but it was lonely. He needed more contact with Lorraine, and subconsciously thought about it, there must be a way of spending more compatible time with her!

Steve was still officially a member of the regiment's boxing team, even though he had not been called upon to fight in competition. He therefore had direct access to the camp gymnasium whenever he wanted to train, and decided to spend the morning working out. After exercising in the gym he would go for a run around the camp perimeter fence, a distance of some three miles.

The gym was well equipped, as all military establishments were for physical fitness. Steve started to 'warm-up' using exercises he had been taught over the past six weeks. He also tried to remember the basic calisthenics he had learnt at school in Somerset, and put them into practice.

After half an hour, two other members of the boxing team showed up and the three decided to don boxing gloves and spend some time sparring, but without the use of a boxing ring which was only erected for special occasions. Later, on Steve's suggestion, they agreed to run the three miles around the camp fence, and when they had completed the run agreed to meet again in two days' time for more boxercise. All three were very fit. Steve had enjoyed the workout and looked forward to the next meeting.

He returned to the barrack room, showered and relaxed for a while on his bed. One of the other recruits had left a paperback book on the trestle table and Steve picked it up and flicked through the pages. It was a 'whodunit' type of book, not his cup of tea, but he decided to read a few chapters to see how it evolved.

He relaxed on his bed and started to read the first chapter. He felt good after the exercise and warm shower. Halfway through the chapter his mind wandered back to the previous day and his first 'date' with Lorraine. He felt that it had gone well and was looking forward to seeing her again. She wore very little make-up he had noticed; she had a natural beauty, and simply didn't need cosmetic enhancement. He glanced at his watch, but there were hours to go before he could speak to her. When he did phone he reminded himself not to spend too much time talking. There would inevitably be the usual queue at the 'red sentinel' and he did not want to be the recipient of more 'black looks'. After finishing the second chapter of the book he closed his eyes and drifted off to sleep.

When Steve woke it was early afternoon and he was too late for lunch at the cookhouse. It was probably only meat balls and chips anyway, he said to himself. He dressed and went to the N.A.A.F.I. for a beer and a steak pie. The N.A.A.F.I. could always be relied upon to be open for business.

The 'Blonde Bombshell' was on duty and fussed with her hair as Steve approached the serving counter. She half smiled at him and asked why he hadn't gone home for his two weeks' leave like the other men. Steve replied that he was fully occupied in the surrounding area. B.B. looked at him quizzically, not completely understanding what he was talking about, but she assumed another woman was involved. The smile left her face. She placed his beer and pie on the counter purposely spilling some of the beer, and turned sharply to serve another customer. Steve left his money on the till, smiled to himself and carried his part filled glass of beer and steak pie to the platoon's adopted table.

He was the sole occupier of the table and sipped his beer and chewed thoughtfully on his pie. He reflected on the book he had just been reading. Normally he read adventure stories but somehow his mind centred on the 'whodunit'. The book had opened a new avenue of thought for him and he became totally convinced as to who the villain was. The murderer, or murderess, was positively the Irish born, frustrated, village postmistress! The clues were quite clear, he said to himself.

He finished his beer and pie and returned to the barrack room to read more of the book and prove his theory correct. As he walked to the barrack room he said to himself, "Who is this fella, Hercule Poirot anyway?" After reading three more chapters his theory proved to be drastically wrong. The book was returned to the trestle table in disgust, to await the attentions of the next amateur detective.

It was time to phone Lorraine. Hopefully she would have finished studying for the day. He armed himself with small coins and Lorraine's number. He had memorised the number but took it with him in case of temporary amnesia in the phone box. Telephones and 'red sentinels' can do strange things to the mind especially when six other people are waiting to use the line.

On the way to the 'red sentinel' he passed B.B. who had finished work for the day. Steve smiled as she approached, but she walked straight past, nose in the air. The 'Blonde Bombshell' had conceded defeat. But B.B. was a great believer in the saying 'life goes on'. A new intake of raw recruits had just arrived, and she moistened her red lips in anticipation.

The 'red sentinel' was fully occupied as usual, and he joined the queue of expectant callers. Steve looked at his watch and hoped that Lorraine would be in the flat. Two of the waiting queue lost patience and stamped off mumbling to themselves about the sorry state of England's phone system, or words to that effect! Steve gladly advanced in the queue and when his turn came he arranged his coins on the small shelf by the phone and dialled Lorraine's number. She answered the call almost immediately, and they exchanged hellos and 'how are you?' She had just finished studying for the day and was enjoying a cup of coffee, relaxing on the settee.

They talked for a while about the music festival and both agreed it had been a wonderful day. Steve looked out of the kiosk window, a queue was already starting to form, all looking at their watches. Steve explained the situation to Lorraine and the problems of long telephone conversations. She suggested that he catch the next bus to her flat, there were still hours in the day they could enjoy together. She added, slightly emotionally that she wanted to see him soon!

The tone of her voice prompted a surge of emotion in his mind and body, and after a quick, 'see you later' Steve put the phone down and left the 'red sentinel', much to the surprise of the waiting queue! He quickly walked back to the barrack room, the tone of her parting voice still ringing in his ears. She was potentially as expectant and passionate as he!

Steve washed and changed clothes, but after a second look in the mirror decided to have a shave. The 'five o'clock' shadow had started to appear, not a good basis for a possible romantic evening! Eventually he was satisfied with his appearance, and after applying a liberal amount of aftershave made his way to the bus stop. The journey was uneventful, and his mind was preoccupied with thoughts of Lorraine anyway.

He found the flat quite easily, taking his bearings from the college. Lorraine was waiting for him and in the privacy of the flat kissed him warmly. He wished he had bought flowers for her, but there had been no time, and the shop would probably have been closed, it being Sunday.

The sky was becoming overcast and threatening, but Lorraine suggested they walk to a nearby public park. She had spent the day studying in her flat and needed to clear her head with some fresh air.

Steve looked at her. She was clearly tired after a long day's study. He put his arm around her shoulder as they walked to the park, and Lorraine rested her head on his shoulder. The park was only ten minutes away, and although the sky was overcast and grey the temperature was pleasantly warm. They talked in general and Steve told her of his time exercising in the gym. As a doctor, or student doctor, she applauded him for keeping fit. She said that she wished there was more time for her to exercise, but her studies were intense now, and there were only twenty-four hours in the day.

They strolled through the park, enjoying each other's company and holding hands like the two young lovers they were becoming. On an impulse they turned to each other and shared a kiss. Neither of them understood exactly why, it was simply an act of romantic friendship, for the entire world to see.

They walked a little further, but the skies darkened dramatically and it began to rain quite heavily. Neither of them had brought raincoats and they had to make a quick decision on what to do. Lorraine said the local cinema was only two minutes fast walk away, and they headed for it, at least they would be in the dry.

The rain became heavier and they ran the last fifty yards to the cinema steps, still holding hands and laughing at the rain as lovers do. Steve bought two tickets and they went into the dark auditorium. They were greeted by an usherette who took their tickets and guided them to their seats using a small electric torch.

Their eyes soon became accustomed to the darkness and they made themselves comfortable in their seats. They were out of the rain and together, that was all that mattered. Steve looked at Lorraine. Small droplets of rain were resting on her cheeks, making her more beautiful and enchanting. He took the handkerchief from his pocket and gently wiped the droplets from her cheeks.

He kissed her lightly on the cheek and said, "The rain in Spain stays mainly on Lorraine!" She looked at him blankly for a second, and then the 'penny' dropped. They both smiled, and talked about George Bernard Shaw, Pygmalion, Audrey Hepburn and Eliza Doolittle.

The film show started and they settled back into their seats. The British Pathe newsreel was showing recent world events, and the latest ocean going liner to be built on the Clyde in Scotland. Steve marvelled at the engineering, and Lorraine couldn't understand how a ship of such a size could stay upright in a dry dock.

They sat as closely together as possible and held hands, awaiting the main film. He seemed to be building an obsession holding her hand. When he did so he felt secure, and not lonely. He thought to himself, *Hardly the emotions of a trained soldier, but we are all flesh and blood.* There was something beautiful in the softness of her fingers, almost massaging life into his manly, but empty being!

When the main film started it was ironically an Agatha Christie 'whodunit', featuring the Belgium detective, Hercule Poirot. They relaxed and forgot the slight dampness in their clothes and sat as closely as the conservative seats would allow. Their cheeks touched and Lorraine 'flicked' Steve's cheek with her long eyelashes. He gently squeezed her hand in loving recognition. It was a wonderful world, and Agatha Christie was playing her important part in the plot.

Steve had bought a bag of sweets in the foyer of the cinema before the show, and in the romantic confusion the bag slipped from his lap onto the floor. He leant down, picked up the bag, and as he retrieved the situation his hand touched Lorraine's knee. He smiled at her in apology and replaced the sweets on his lap. Lorraine took his hand, stroked his fingers, and put his hand back on her knee. She smiled at him in the darkness and 'flicked' her eyelashes on his cheek. Steve slowly slid his hand up to her thigh, and she opened her legs slightly. She was warm and inviting. Suddenly the film show became more enjoyable!

Hercule gradually unravelled the mystery and the film ended with all the suspects in the main lounge. The villain was pinpointed by Poirot and despatched to jail without delay.

Steve and Lorraine left the relative comfort of their cinema seats and went out onto the street. It had thankfully stopped raining, and Steve suggested that they buy fish and chips and eat them in the flat. Although it was Sunday he distinctly remembered the unforgettable aroma of a 'chippy' before they entered the cinema. Lorraine agreed, feeling quite hungry herself after a long day studying sustained mainly by cups of coffee and biscuits. She suggested that they buy a fairly cheap bottle of white wine at the off-licence to wash down the cod and chips. The food was wrapped in plenty of newspaper to retain the heat as they hurried back to the flat. Neither of them had forgotten the romantic closeness in the cinema and glanced at each other from time to time in an intimate sexual way. They were no longer platonic friends.

Their clothes were dry now and the evening air pleasant. As they hurried contentedly back to the flat Steve thought to himself, *Jazz, champagne, and now cod and chips with a 'cheeky' white wine, such decadence, whatever next?*

When they arrived at the flat Lorraine transferred the cod and chips to plates and Steve opened the bottle of Spanish wine which was quite cool and ready to drink. They sat on the settee and thoroughly enjoyed the fish and chips; there was something special about eating under such circumstances, far more enjoyable than a 'posh' restaurant, not to mention the 'cheeky' white wine and the occasional passionate kiss.

When they had finished the meal Lorraine made coffee and they sat, relaxing on the settee, listening to a long playing record of 'Nat King Cole' singing a selection of his well-known hits. Lorraine snuggled up to Steve and they kissed from time to time, Nat King Cole had that effect on people! They sipped the last of the white wine, the taste of the delicious cod and chips still on their palates. It had been another wonderful day, but once again time had been the winner. It was the hour to say goodnight. Without consciously thinking about it Steve said to Lorraine, "Would you like to go to London and see a live theatre show?"

Lorraine was taken by surprise at his sudden suggestion, but after a few moments thought said she would love to go, but it would have to be at a weekend, so as not to disrupt her study classes.

Steve understood and agreed it made sense. He said he would go into town the next day, find a theatre agent and see what shows were on offer. They sat back on the settee and looked at each other, strangely shocked by the plans they had just made. But both were inwardly excited about the prospect, and the thought of spending a whole weekend together was a magical fantasy, far removed from colleges of learning, and army training camps.

It was time for Steve to catch his bus. They kissed once more on the settee and then reluctantly stood up, Lorraine smoothing her crumpled skirt. They stopped at the door and held each other, coming closer now, a bond beginning to form between them. They kissed passionately, the emotion becoming almost too much to bear for both of them. The lust grew in him, and he knew that she would not say 'no'. But at this stage of their relationship he was aware that it was right for him to go. As soon as he returned to camp a cold shower would be in order! He was certain that Lorraine would appreciate his decision, and their relationship would be stronger for it.

The bus journey to camp was quiet; most people were already in their beds. He thought only of himself and Lorraine, the rest of the world could look after itself for a while. He went to his bed with memories of 'whodunits', Hercule Poirot, and raindrops on silk cheeks!

CHAPTER 16

Steve dreamt of Hercule Poirot running amok in the Westminster Houses of Parliament, searching for villains, and Agatha Christie waving to the crowds as she was driven down the Mall in the State coach.

When he awoke Steve blamed the richness of the fish and chips the night before! After washing and shaving he went to the cookhouse for breakfast, he needed some of the cookhouse corporal's meat balls to restore his gastric equilibrium! After two helpings of the bland meat balls and several mugs of coffee his sanity was partly restored and he prepared himself for the journey into town to find a theatre booking agent.

As he polished his shoes he reminded himself to take his bank book with him. During his working days in Somerset he had managed to save some money, and now was a good time to spend it. Aunt Maude had almost insisted that he put away part of his weekly wage, for a 'rainy' day, she always said. Aunt Maude led from the front, and was a regular monthly contributor to the Pearl Assurance company. Steve hoped that it didn't rain in London. As a young boy of five or six he remembered thinking that if you took out 'Life' insurance you would not die! It had sounded logical to him at the time.

The bus was almost on time, and as it rattled along the potholed roads he realised that it was possible to 'read' the general weather conditions by the amount of rattle on any given day. In dry conditions the wooden window frames, seats and other fittings dried out and shrank, allowing the parts freedom to move at will. In wet weather the reverse took place, everything swelled and tightened up, and the bus sped over the potholed roads as if it was new. After listening to the rattle for several minutes Steve concluded that the barometric pressure was high, and London should be dry for the weekend that was fast approaching.

The bus arrived at the terminal and he made his way to the main street where he was more likely to find travel and theatre agents. Steve had never ventured into the heady world of travel or theatre before; it was all new territory for him.

He found a smart looking travel agents shop next to 'Boots' the chemist, and after reading some of the adverts in the window decided to take the bull by the horns and go in. A smartly dressed young woman was sat behind a desk, busily tapping the keys of a typewriter in a very efficient manner. As Steve entered she took off her horn rimmed glasses, stood up and greeted him with a friendly but business like, "Can I help you?" He explained briefly what he required and the assistant nodded in understanding and opened a drawer at the side of her desk. She withdrew several shiny colourful brochures and handed them to Steve.

Steve glanced through the books, and she suggested in a helpful manner that he should take a 'package' deal that the agency was promoting. The deal included theatre tickets, rail travel and hotel accommodation. After enquiring about the price he gladly accepted the offer, it certainly simplified things and the price seemed reasonable to him for such a venture. Steve explained that he needed to go to the bank and withdraw the cash, and the assistant replied that she would have the tickets and other papers ready for him. She was the epitome of efficiency, and removed her horn rimmed spectacles as Steve rose to leave.

As he left the shop he thought to himself, *The world is full of beautiful women, what would we do without them?*

At the bank he decided to withdraw all of his money and close the account. In three weeks' time, after training in Scotland, he could be posted anywhere in the world. It was better to close the account, and move on.

When he returned to the agents the assistant was still busily tapping away at the typewriter, and Steve could almost see steam rising from it! Her slim fingers darted over the keys as if she was playing a musical instrument. She removed her horn rimmed spectacles with a flourish as Steve entered. She had partly let down her hair, and smoothed it down as he sat opposite her. It reminded Steve of the 'Blonde Bombshell', but this girl had a distinct sophistication about her and was playing in a higher league than B.B.!

She handed him a smart looking folder containing the tickets and other papers. After Steve had paid the bill she wished him a good weekend in London, perhaps with a certain amount of envy in her smile, and returned to her trusty typewriter. As Steve took the folder he remarked with a smile that her hair looked better the way she had altered it. She removed her spectacles again quickly and smoothed her hair. Steve had the thought that if she were to 'let her hair down' completely she would be a very sexual woman. There was a great deal of female frustration in her pent-up, conservative hairstyle!

He left the shop with the folder securely under his arm. He was pleased with his plans for the weekend; the money had been well spent.

He decided to do some more shopping whilst in town and then go to his favourite cafe for lunch. It would probably be for the last time, and he wanted to say goodbye to the cheerful waitress who had made his meals more enjoyable, simply by being there and having a friendly chat.

He was passing a florist's shop, and on an impulse went in and bought the waitress a small posy of flowers. It would be a nice way of showing his appreciation, make her day, and help the world go around. Steve was becoming a flirt and was aware that for some obscure reason the opposite sex was attracted to him.

"Must be the meat balls," he said to himself.

Before going to the cafe for lunch he looked around the shops for an inexpensive 'weekend' case. His khaki army kitbag, stuffed with clothes would not be socially acceptable in a London hotel. Nor would his dilapidated old holdall that he had hauled all the way from Somerset.

After some searching he found what he was looking for, something presentable but not expensive, he would probably only use it once anyway. It was basically made from compressed cardboard, covered with a light brown vinyl material, but it looked quite smart and boasted a decorative chrome plated badge between the two case securing clasps. He felt quite proud of his purchase, and toyed with the idea of buying Lorraine a small present. His love for her was starting to blossom, and he would gladly buy the world for her, and all its treasures, but there would be more shops in London, and 'pay parade' was a step away!

He walked to the cafe, weekend case in one hand, travel folder and posy in the other. Life was starting to become slightly complicated for a young unsuspecting lad from Somerset and he needed the guiding hand of Aunt Maude, but she was not there. His emotional thoughts were strangely torn between the 'Blonde Bombshell', the cheerful waitress, and Lorraine. Surely the 'Blonde Bombshell' didn't attract him? But there was no doubt that she had a basic sexual magnetism which could not be ignored! The cheerful waitress also had a strange allure, but Lorraine was a new scintillating planet, yet to be discovered. His young body was awakening in a turmoil of emotion, but the cold shower was a million miles away. He calmed himself, but at the same time realised he was a young virile man, placed on Earth to propagate the human race.

As he entered the cafe the welcome was as warm and inviting as ever. The cheerful waitress was on duty and with a smile said, "Hello, nice to see you again!"

Steve smiled back and produced the posy of flowers from behind his back. He presented them to her with a slight theatrical bow and flourish. He thanked her for the friendly service, and at the same time he became aware of a sexual desire for her. His male hormones were beginning to run riot, and once again he blamed the cookhouse corporal. He stifled the sexual emotion.

She probably doesn't feel the same way as me anyway, he said to himself, remembering that his new allegiance was to Lorraine. Life was becoming more complicated by the minute, and he wished he was back in the placid world of pre-puberty in Somerset.

The waitress was startled by his sudden show of emotion, but soon recovered, and like most women, regained control of the situation. Men were the instigators of passion, but women are the controllers, and quite rightly so. Men wander about, propagating the human race that is their purpose in life. But it is women who bear the responsibility of childbirth. A woman gestates a seed for nine months, and after that endures the responsibility of rearing a human being into a fragile, uncertain world.

Having discussed the human race with himself for a few seconds, he picked up the menu and turned his attention to the more important matter of eating and drinking.

Taking into consideration that it would probably be his last meal at the cafe, he ordered the same food he had enjoyed on his first visit, sausages, mashed potatoes and petit pois, followed by home-made apple pie and real cream. The waitress took his order, and in an unprecedented lax in waitress protocol, kissed Steve on the cheek! The meal was very enjoyable, and after paying the bill and giving the waitress a well-earned tip he returned her welcome kiss on the cheek, picked up his weekend case and went out into the street. Sausage and mash could be very satisfying under certain conditions!

After buying a bottle of aftershave from Boots, Steve made his way to the bus station, bought his ticket and awaited the arrival of the bus. The bus 'barometer' was still signalling dry as it rolled along the potholed roads. Steve was really looking forward to Saturday, and the journey to London with Lorraine. All the preparation was completed and the 'Big City' awaited them. He would phone Lorraine from the 'red sentinel' later, and they could make final arrangements.

After securing his new weekend case and papers in the barrack room he went to the N.A.A.F.I. for some liquid refreshment. He wasn't hungry after the sausage and mash at the cafe, but the bus journey had given him a thirst, and a pint of beer would go down well. 'Smoky' Funnell, the unfortunate punch-drunk corporal was in the N.A.A.F.I. with his latest boxing protégé, a young flyweight that Steve had met in the gym. After buying his beer from a very aloof B.B. he joined them at their table. The subject of conversation of course was boxing, and although 'Smoky' had his chronic affliction he was very well informed about the boxing world, and the champions and challengers. His memory had not been greatly affected, which was some consolation.

There was some time to spare before Steve was due to phone Lorraine and he suggested that all three go for an early evening run around the camp perimeter fence. Just a light jog would be enough, as the sausage and mash had not yet fully digested. They agreed to meet at the camp main entrance, and Steve went back to the barrack room and changed into 'gym' gear. The walk back to the room gave his pint of beer time to settle nicely. He would probably have one more later, as a nightcap!

The three met as arranged and began the jog around the perimeter fence. They concentrated on their exercise, it was difficult to talk whilst running, and Steve continued with his own private thoughts about boxing. 'Smoky' was a likeable man, and it was a tragedy that he had suffered from his sport by becoming punch-drunk. Steve thought that there was probably a technical medical term for the condition, but the result was the same. Steve was far from convinced about the 'noble art', and considered that the new protégé would do well to look at 'Smoky's' condition, and reflect on it. The new recruit was only a flyweight and would not be subject to any heavyweight pounding as 'Smoky' had been. But Steve would still have a quiet word in the boy's ear.

As far as Steve was personally concerned he decided that he had been far too enthusiastic during training when entering the boxing ring. When posted to another unit and the same routine applied he would show himself to be more inept than he actually was. He couldn't understand how the people in authority still allowed 'Smoky' to box. Perhaps they considered that it was one of the natural hazards of the sport!

After the run he returned to the barrack room, showered and dressed to go to the 'red sentinel'. He had spoken to the new boxing recruit, but the lad was too full of enthusiasm to listen, and Steve's words of warning fell on deaf ears. But he had tried, and sometimes that is all you can do.

The queue at the kiosk was long as usual, and Steve looked at his watch anxiously. Each time he looked at the dial it was as if time was standing still, and when it eventually came to his turn he went through the routine of dialling hurriedly. The dial tone sounded, and after what seemed an eternity Lorraine answered. She had just returned from extra study lessons at the college, and was still slightly out of breath from carrying her books, coat and all of the other accessories required for a day at college.

Steve explained the details of the trip to London on Saturday. She asked him what kind of show he had booked, and he replied that it was to be the American musical 'South Pacific'. Lorraine was pleased about it, saying she found straight plays so boring, a musical would be wonderful. They were both excited at the prospect of spending a weekend together in London. She had secretly decided not to tell her romantic plans for the weekend to her parents, as sometimes mothers, and conservative fathers could be less than understanding about such matters, and her father would probably ask to have a word with Steve enquiring if his intentions were strictly honourable!

They expressed their love for each other, and before saying goodnight, blew a kiss to each other into the phone, such was the frivolity of young love! His body ached for her and when he returned to the barrack room a cold shower would be in order.

Later, having dampened his ardour in the shower Steve went to the N.A.A.F.I. for his 'beer before bedtime'. He had 'wetted' the outside of his body, now it was time to moisten the inside. As he walked along the road he wondered about love. What was love anyway, was it something triggered off in the mind by physical attraction, was it a biological, chemical force, or was it, as a learned person once said, merely a temporary madness?

He decided to consult Lorraine on the subject; she was after all, a medical person, studying the effects of chemical electrolysis on the brain, and matters concerning the human heart!

CHAPTER 17

Finally, Saturday morning arrived and Steve went to the cookhouse early for a substantial breakfast. He steered well clear of the meat balls out of fear of them causing his young hormones to erupt completely. Thoughts of the fairly long train journey with Lorraine came to mind. To be arrested on a charge of sexual misconduct in a 3rd class compartment would not be a good way to start the weekend, pleasurable as the 'misconduct' might be!

They were booked into the West End of London hotel from four o'clock onwards, so there was plenty of time to enjoy their journey, and Lorraine's company. Steve prepared himself carefully, shaving with a new blade, and using more than the usual amount of aftershave he had bought in town from the ever reliable 'Boots'. After using the 'Old Spice' he screwed the top down tightly and packed it with his clothes in the vinyl case, hopefully for use in London under pleasant romantic circumstances.

Satisfied that he was ready for the weekend, he glanced around the barrack room and made sure his locker was secure. It had been a quiet time after the six weeks basic training. The platoon would be gradually filtering back from the leave period, and the room would not be as tranquil when he returned from London. He had missed the platoon and its interesting characters, especially Taff with his anecdotes of rugby football, and Mac dispensing his dry Yorkshire humour, and somewhat caustic blunt remarks, usually at the expense of the 'Lawyer' whose academic education seemed to irritate Mac.

When the weekend was over it would be time for them to prepare for advanced training in Scotland. The journey would take them to an infantry training camp near Fort William and Loch Ness. Steve was looking forward to the two weeks' training; he had never ventured over the border before, as the days of modern affordable travel were yet to come! The two weeks in Scotland would also complete the platoon's training, and on their return to 'Morval' they would learn what the permanent posting for the platoon was to be. It was an exciting time for them, National Servicemen and professional soldiers alike.

Steve smilingly said to himself, "Prendergast doesn't know what he is missing," and wondered if he was still wearing his beret back to front. Steve had met more colourful characters in his short army career than he had in his entire life back in Somerset.

The bus was on time and Steve stowed his vinyl weekend case under the seat. The bus 'rattle' barometer was still signalling fair weather and he made himself comfortable and thought about the weekend. He had bought a raincoat just in case; the English climate was after all, unpredictable. He said to himself, "There's nothing worse than a wet weekend," and for some reason thought of Corporal Entwhistle.

Lorraine was waiting for him outside the flat, and they kissed unashamedly in front of the passers-by. She had her weekend case the one Steve had helped her with when they first met on the train. She wore a light pink 'flared' skirt and a nicely fitting crisp white blouse. Her neatly brushed shoulder length brown hair contrasted beautifully with the white crispness of her blouse. She looked exquisite, obviously having had a good night's sleep.

Steve felt that he was being drawn toward her, as if by a strong magnetic force, and wanted to more than fully embrace her, but contented himself by holding her soft, inviting hand. A certain amount of self-discipline was required for the moment, but that could be relaxed when they reached the 'privacy' of the capital. There they would become lost in a multitude of people. They walked to the bus stop, glancing at each other, a mutual love and understanding holding them together. Her hand melted into his, and all was well with their young world.

The plan for the journey was to take the bus to the railway station, the train to Waterloo station and then get a taxi to the hotel. All the details were in the folder supplied by the travel agent. The girl with the horn rimmed spectacles had proved to be efficiency personified.

Lorraine had visited the capital many times as a young girl with her parents. She had brought some of her previous sightseeing maps and information brochures for them to study during the journey. Steve was very much the 'new boy' as far as London was concerned, and he left the general planning of the weekend to Lorraine. His main interest, apart from enjoying Lorraine's company, was to see a live musical show; the sightseeing would be an added interest.

Steve wasn't normally happy in cities. He preferred country villages, small quaint old pubs with low ceilings and solid oak beams, open hearth log fires and the aroma of the local brew. But London was such an interesting place, very historic, albeit a little noisy. There was so much to see: Buckingham Palace, the Tower of London, interesting museums, St Paul's Cathedral, the list went on and on.

On the train they were lucky to have a 3rd class compartment to themselves, and after stowing the cases on the rack above settled themselves on the bench seats opposite each other. Lorraine remarked that it was like an anniversary of their first meeting, and Steve seized the romantic moment by reaching across and kissing her warmly. They studied the maps and brochures and loosely planned the weekend. Lorraine was a mine of information, and obviously enjoyed playing the 'tour guide'. Steve wondered what he would have done if he had decided to venture into the capital alone, there was something daunting about big cities. Lorraine had the forethought to prepare and bring sandwiches from the flat, and after reading the colourful brochures enjoyed them like two young teenagers on a school outing.

The conversation turned to the musical show they were due to enjoy the coming evening. They had both seen the film of 'South Pacific', but the live stage show would be a very different experience for both of them. Lorraine had watched the film once, but Steve had seen and enjoyed it many times and for some reason it had made a strong impression on him. He had a fascination about the musical and had memorised many of the scenes. The film's leading female role, 'Nellie Forbush', was played by an American actress called Mitzi Gaynor, a curly haired petite girl who fitted in well as the nurse lieutenant. The male lead was played by the Italian actor Rossano Brazzi who gave a good performance as 'Emile' the French tea planter. Steve, after reading a film magazine was surprised to read that Brazzi didn't perform the songs in the film. They were actually sung for him by an Italian baritone named Giorgio Tozzi, and then dubbed onto the film soundtrack. But songs like 'Some Enchanted Evening' and 'This nearly was mine', were beautiful, no matter who sang them. After they had discussed the film for some time Lorraine said she was surprised at his extensive knowledge of South Pacific, and Steve somehow felt self-conscious about admitting to having watched the film so many times.

To the eyes of a 'country boy', Waterloo station was massive, with over twenty platforms. People rushed about, seemingly in complete chaos. The noise echoed from the high ornate glass roof. Lorraine knew where taxis could be found, and Steve bowed to her superior knowledge and busied himself by carrying the cases, saying 'no thanks' to a porter who wanted to take them.

The hotel was well situated, and most places of interest were easily accessible, including the West End theatres. They paid for the fairly short taxi ride. The traditional black London taxi had weaved its way through the dense traffic, almost as if the driver was not required, but perhaps that was testimony of the driver's knowledge and skill!

The entrance to the hotel was not overly luxurious, but they were not expecting Claridge's anyway. The package deal had been quite reasonable in price, and the hotel was just a base to work from, after all. They went to the reception desk and Steve handed the relevant pieces of paper to the receptionist. They 'cheekily' signed the register as 'Mr. & Mrs. Smith', giggling as they did so. The receptionist, a tall, thin faced woman with a long nose and greying black hair tied in a 'bun', read the register and sternly looked down her nose at them. They picked up the room key and their cases and laughed as they made their way up the carpeted stairway, the receptionist 'tut tutting' as they left. The two young lovers were like two unruly school children who had secretly just called the headmistress a 'sissy'. It was all part of the weekend, and they were determined to enjoy it to the full.

Steve thought about the receptionist and said to himself, "Surely there's not a branch of the W.I. in London?"

The hotel room was pleasant, but again not luxurious. It did have a large king-size bed though to compensate! The adjoining bathroom was more modern and well appointed. A small ornate wicker basket of potpourri was on the bathroom cabinet, which Steve thought was a nice touch, and made the air fresh.

After unpacking and continuing to giggle and joke about the Mr.& Mrs. episode, they decided to take in a little sightseeing before having a light meal and going to the theatre in the evening. Once again Steve left the decision making to Lorraine, and after studying the maps and brochures she suggested a visit to Hyde Park which was not too far away.

Steve handed the room key into the reception desk, and as they walked out of the hotel the receptionist gave them an icy look. They could feel the daggers going into their backs, and they started to laugh and giggle again.

The weather was warm and sunny; the bus 'barometer' had not let them down. After checking the small map again, they decided to walk to Hyde Park. They both needed to stretch their legs after the journey. After a while they asked directions from a passer-by as the park was further than they thought, sometimes maps can be confusing. On the 'Londoner's' suggestion they took a traditional red bus to Hyde Park corner.

London was full of hustle and bustle and it was difficult not to get caught up in the atmosphere. Everybody seemed to be running rather than walking normally and Steve had to consciously slow himself down.

They walked through Hyde Park and the atmosphere changed. Outside on the busy streets people were caught up in the crazy merry-go-round, but as soon as they entered the park they slowed down, as if in a different world. Steve wondered if perhaps it was the calming influence of the grass. The colour green was known to be a 'calmer'.

They bought ice creams and generally took in the atmosphere of the park as they walked, holding hands as usual. It had quickly become a pleasing habit, both holding out an inviting hand whenever they came together. They strolled to 'Speakers' Corner', still licking on their ice creams, and listened to the interesting characters expounding their favourite oratory, as they did most days, weather permitting. One of the speakers was demanding home rule for Lambeth, another, dressed in rags, denounced the capitalistic world for its selfishness and decadence, his up-market Mercedes Benz saloon car parked around a nearby corner with a full tank of petrol. Other speakers were obviously more serious, venting their anger at the present government's high taxes. Steve could easily imagine Mac stood on one of the soapboxes, extolling the virtues and superiority of Yorkshire Best Bitter against the more inspired inferior southern 'brews'. But then, Steve had sampled cider in Somerset that could knock the cotton socks off a person at fifty yards!

There was a good humour between the speakers on their boxes and the spectators, who interacted with shouts of, "What about the workers, mate?" It was a unique place, it was only a tiny part of England, but Steve realised that he was fortunate to live in such a democratic country. There were not many places in the world where such freedom of speech would be allowed.

Steve and Lorraine moved on, finished their ice creams, and on Steve's suggestion decided to hire a rowing boat on the Serpentine for half an hour. Lorraine wasn't too sure about the idea, but Steve assured her it would be all right and she agreed, with reservation.

The boatman held the stern of the boat as they climbed gingerly aboard. The elderly boatman, probably a retired sailor sported a battered sea captain's peak hat, and reminded Steve of a famous film actor. The only things missing were a short clay pipe and a jar of spinach!

Lorraine sat in the stern seat, it would be her job to steer the boat as Steve rowed. The steering was controlled by two lengths of rope attached to the rudder, one length on either side of the boat. Steve assured her that it was easy to steer and that she would soon get the 'hang' of it; what could possibly go wrong? There were several boats around them, none manned by apparent seafarers.

Steve struggled with the oars and Lorraine tugged at the steering ropes. They gradually made their way from the jetty, but the boat was far from under complete control. The boatman removed his captain's hat and scratched his head.

Steve partly mastered the art of rowing, but Lorraine was slightly unsure of the steering ropes and the boat went around in wide circles, colliding with other boats from time to time. No real harm was done and the other part time sailors entered into the increasing fun of it all.

Steve explained the nautical terms of 'port and starboard' to Lorraine, essential when steering a boat, whatever the size. She tried to put her new found knowledge into practice, but the boat insisted in travelling in ever decreasing circles.

They both laughed and Lorraine said, "I hope I make a better doctor than I do a sailor!"

Steve dipped his hand into the Serpentine and playfully flicked her with water. Lorraine let go of one of the ropes and returned the compliment with a full palm of water, resulting in a no holds barred water fight. Suddenly the boat ran aground, and both seafarers finished up in the bottom of the boat, hysterical with laughter.

The boatman looked at them from the jetty, shaking his head in disbelief. Landlubbers," he said to himself, and went to fetch the rescue boat.

CHAPTER 18

When they returned to the hotel room a small vase of freshly cut flowers had been placed on the small coffee table. There was a card beside the vase which read: - to Mr. & Mrs. Smith???, enjoy your stay. It was signed, Hotel Receptionist! They laughed at the woman's gesture, and Steve remarked, "At least she has a sense of humour, even if it is an icy, sardonic one!"

Their clothes were damp from the boating escapade, and Lorraine decided to take a bath before they went for a light meal and then on to the show in the West End. Steve busied himself by preparing his clothes and himself. He had pressed his trousers before leaving 'Morval', and had carefully packed them in his weekend case. His jacket had a few small creases, but they would soon fall out. The bottle of aftershave was still intact, and ready for use. He splashed a few drops on his face, as a refresher, and the scented 'tang' felt good.

As he started to polish his shoes Lorraine called to him from the bathroom. She had something in her eye, and could not reach the towel from the bath. He went into the bathroom, picked up a white towel from the rack and gently wiped her eyes and face. She thanked him, flicking her eyelash to make certain the problem was cleared.

"It must have been something from the boat," she said.

Steve, suddenly realising that he was seeing her naked body for the first time, leant forward and kissed her. She responded by touching his face with her slender fingers, and she made no move to hide her nakedness. He gently caressed her breasts, seeing them unclothed, firm and beautiful. Droplets of water clung to them, like rare diamonds enhancing a precious jewel. A warm glow entered his body and he kissed her again. She was exquisite, even if she couldn't steer a boat!

Lorraine remarked laughingly how big the bath was. The two redeeming factors of the apartment were the king-size bed and large bath. She laughed and suggested it was big enough for both of them! He looked at her; she smiled and nodded her head in approval. Steve had just been invited to the bath!

He didn't wait to be asked again and quickly removed his clothes, almost tearing off one of the buttons from his new white M&S shirt in his excitement. He said to himself humorously, in army 'Regulations' parlance, *Almost a 'self-inflicted injury'!*

The six weeks intensive training had tightened and toned his muscles, and he was pleased with his body. His arms were strong, his chest full and stomach flat. His thighs had strengthened with the many hours of assault course training, and he felt strong.

Lorraine looked at him as he stepped into the bath, and smiled in admiration. In her doctor's eyes he was the perfect human specimen, and she held out a welcoming hand to him. They both knelt down in the spacious enamelled bath, and he kissed her, gently at first, then with a growing passion. He wetted his hands and ran his fingers over her smooth wet body. She in turn caressed him, her hands and fingers already soft from the bath water.

Lorraine had bought a new bathroom product from 'Boots' called 'bubble bath', and had used it liberally preparing the bath. The lightly oily liquid tended to soften the water, and also produced a thick blanket of foamy bubbles on the water's surface.

They continued to kiss and discover each other's bodies. The oily 'bubble bath' made their skin sensuous to the touch, and Lorraine slipped her hand under the blanket of foam and touched and caressed him. Before long his young body was fully aroused, and he put his legs either side of Lorraine's body. He laid back, the foamy bubbles almost covering his body. She moved on top of him in a sliding movement, aided by the oily water. She became the aggressor, and demanding of him. He felt her tight breasts on his chest, and he stroked and gripped her silken buttocks. She lifted herself slightly, and he entered her.

They made love with a natural passionate rhythm, the foamy bubbles dancing around their bodies as the physical and spiritual enjoyment increased. Steve felt an ever increasing strength in his thighs. He became the aggressor now, and was in total control. She writhed with pleasure on his strong body, and began to gently sob and moan as their lovemaking came to a climax. Their bodies shuddered and erupted simultaneously, and the bubbles lay still around them.

It had been the first time for both of them, and perhaps ended too quickly. It was a raw, passionate young love, but in time they would gain experience and finesse in their loving. The crashing waves had ceased to pound on the beach, and they kissed lightly, as if to produce gentle ripples on the water and calm the wet sandy shore.

They continued to lie together. Steve was still fully aroused, and his 'manhood' remained with her. She in turn made no effort to move. He had fulfilled her, and was content with him.

The dish of potpourri had somehow found its way into the bath water from the nearby cabinet top, possibly from their flailing legs during the height of their lovemaking. The scent of lavender and aromatic herbs filled the bathroom, it was a fitting climax, but the chambermaid would not be pleased to see her sodden potpourri when she cleaned the room in the morning! Mr. & Mrs. Smith would also receive a further rebuke from the long nosed receptionist, over flagrant misuse of hotel property.

When the bath water became too cool they reluctantly stepped out, took white towels and gently dried each other in a display of mutual love and admiration. Later, Steve felt almost guilty about his raw passion. He would certainly not be discussing it with Aunt Maude, and once again the cookhouse corporal's cooking methods were brought in to serious question. Lorraine had been equally passionate, in a female way, and she in turn would not be trying to explain her feelings to fairly conservative parents. In the future the situation might change, and daughters would be able to discuss sexual matters with their mothers, but at the moment such talk was swept firmly under the carpet!

Preparation was naturally hurried after the prolonged 'bath', and Steve scooped up the potpourri from the water and spread it on to the cabinet in the hope that it would be dry by the morning. They both glanced at each other from time to time as they dressed. There was a happiness and contentment in their faces, and a deeper understanding between them. The theatre show would have to be very special to overtake the events of the afternoon.

Steve took the travel folder from his weekend case and removed the all-important theatre tickets. They had 'circle' seats, and the view of the stage would be good. He put the tickets carefully into the inside pocket of his jacket.

Lorraine had bought a black, full length elegant dress to wear to the theatre, and prepared herself in the spacious bathroom that sported a good size mirror. When she appeared in the doorway her beauty took Steve's breath away. She was no longer the young girl in the boat, acting as coxswain and playfully splashing water. With seemingly a few deft touches she had changed into a beautiful sophisticated woman. They looked at each other, decided they were ready to 'do the town', and left the room.

As they passed the reception desk the receptionist said, "Good evening," and touched the back of her 'bun' style hair-do.

As they walked to the door Steve looked back at the receptionist. She had the hint of a smile on her face, and Steve wondered if perhaps the members of the W.I. didn't have hearts of stone after all. They glanced at the large mirror in the foyer. They made a handsome couple quite capable of enhancing any West End theatre.

After a little searching they discovered a reasonably priced restaurant. Steve was surprised at the low prices; he had expected to pay much more. There was no need to dig deep into his pocket yet. A light salad based meal was ordered, not wanting to possibly feel uncomfortable during the show.

Steve was beginning to feel a 'buzz' of excitement about the show, and Lorraine could tell it from his animated conversation. She was not quite so enthusiastic, but was totally pleased for him. He had told her about the musical before, but she listened to him intently with love and understanding in her eyes, a quality that only a woman in love is capable of.

The musical 'South Pacific', written by Richard Rogers and Oscar Hammerstein, had been a great success when produced on Broadway in America. It had thrilled thousands of people, and was now pleasing audiences on the other side of the Atlantic. The leading lady on Broadway was the American actress Mary Martin, who played the nursing lieutenant Nellie Forbush. Mary made the role her own for a long time and always joked that she had the cleanest head of hair in the States, having to wash her locks during every performance of the musical when singing 'I'm Gonna Wash That Man Right Out of My Hair!' Mary Martin's son was the actor Larry Hagman, who in later years was to play the part of J.R. in the television series called 'Dallas', a role that he too was to make his own for many years. The episode, 'Who Killed J.R.?' was on everybody's lips for weeks, and made front page news in the daily papers. Quite a talented mother and son!

Steve and Lorraine took a taxi cab to the theatre. Earlier they had toyed with the idea of walking to the theatre, but time was moving on and the streets of London were strange to them and crowded with people. It would be stupid to risk possibly missing some of the show after coming all that way.

They arrived at the theatre in good time, thanks to the skill of the taxi driver who had weaved his way in and out of the evening traffic jams like Stirling Moss in his prime. As they entered the foyer of the ancient theatre they soon became aware of its long tradition. It had hosted many a 'hit' show and as they looked around at photos of the stars that had played there, they became aware that they were in the 'hallowed' quarters. The atmosphere was warm and exciting, and after buying a souvenir programme made their way up the palatial staircase to the circle seats.

They made themselves comfortable in the well upholstered seats. They were well situated, and once again Steve silently thanked the girl with the horn rimmed spectacles at the travel agents. He looked around him, the theatre was already half full, and there was a general hushed 'air' of expectancy in the audience.

He wondered what the audience reaction would be when seeing a live show and not on celluloid. In Somerset when he had watched the film version, he had glanced around him in the semi-darkness, and at the end of the film when 'Nellie' offered a full tureen of soup to her hero Emile, there had been many a tear being wiped from emotional eyes. Steve had to admit, even at his young age, that he was one of them. He was already an incurable romantic.

The show was all that Steve and Lorraine hoped it would be. Full of colour, vigour, romance and beautiful songs and music; Rogers and Hammerstein had created a masterpiece. The rest of the audience also loved it, spellbound by the sheer warmth and vitality of the players on the stage. After an emotional rendition of 'Some Enchanted Evening', Lorraine glanced at Steve to see him self-consciously wipe a tear from his eye. She said nothing, but squeezed his hand tightly. Steve felt her tighten her grip and slowly turned his head towards her stupidly overcome with emotion, and unable to speak.

The show came to an end, as all good things do, and they gathered their belongings together and filed out of the auditorium with the rest of the audience. They moved into the foyer and accustomed themselves to the brighter light. The foyer was full of happy contented faces, all talking about the show. 'South Pacific' had done its job, and the audience would return home and sleep well.

Steve and Lorraine walked, hand in hand for a few streets to take some air and to absorb the memory of the show, which would live in their minds for a long time to come. They took a 'hackney' back to the hotel. It was late but the streets of London were still bursting with life, London never slept! The atmosphere in the hotel was more quiet, the waiters and other staff going about their business in an orderly trained fashion.

Steve and Lorraine went to their room. There was a sense of anti-climax in the air. They had left a world of theatrical fantasy, and now had to readjust to reality. As late as it was, they decided to order a bottle of wine, and have it delivered to the room, it would be a good way to relax and finish the day. The night desk said that it was rather late for room service, but after Steve had told a 'white lie' saying they were on honeymoon, a bottle of white dry wine was delivered to the room, with the management's best wishes! Steve wasn't in the habit of telling lies, he had strong feelings on the matter, but the odd white lie did sometimes bear fruit, and add a certain amount of 'devilish' spice to life.

Steve took off his black shoes that were beginning to pinch his toes, and Lorraine went to the bathroom to freshen up. Steve opened the wine that had been nicely chilled and poured two glasses. Lorraine reappeared looking fresh and beautiful, still wearing her full length dress. They sipped the wine and gradually relaxed. They talked about the show, but subconsciously their minds were on their afternoon of love in the king-size bath. After two glasses full of inexpensive but pleasant Spanish wine, Lorraine said she was going to change into something more comfortable. The long elegant dress was tight fitting, and although perfect for the theatre was a little restricting for unwinding.

She disappeared into the bathroom, and Steve took off his clothes except for underpants and relaxed on the bed. He sipped on the last of the wine, his body feeling relaxed and strong. He looked up from the glass of wine. Lorraine was stood in the bathroom doorway wearing a pink chiffon nightdress. She walked slowly to the bed, smiling at Steve. She untied a tiny ribbon at the front of the nightdress and it slid gracefully to the floor, revealing her beautiful naked body. It was like unveiling a beautiful statue. She was the 'Venus di Milo', with arms.

He took a large sip of his wine and looked at her. She said nothing, but the words were in her eyes.

He put down his wine glass and thought , *Best follow Doctor's orders!*

They slid between the cool crisp sheets, and her body melted onto his. They both felt relaxed, partly by the wine, and partly by the experience and knowledge they had gained earlier.

Afterwards they relaxed in each other's arms, like two newborn babies, completely oblivious to the world around them.

As he held her Steve thought to himself, *All this, and South Pacific, what more do you want from life, Galway?*

He kissed her, and they both slept. It had been the perfect day!

CHAPTER 19

In the morning they both woke at the same time, and he kissed the beautiful woman beside him.

Steve stretched his body, relaxed and felt strong after a contented night's sleep. The white bed sheets were warm and still inviting, but this was their last day in the Metropolis, and there was much to see and do. He looked at his watch and started to leave the bed, but Lorraine grabbed his arm, and pulled him towards her. The race was won, but there was a lap of honour to be carried out!

They were still in bed when the chambermaid tapped on the door wanting to clean the room, and they guiltily jumped out of the bed and asked her to return in half an hour. They giggled and laughed about it, once again acting like two precocious school children. They held each other for a while, remembering the magical night they had just spent together. They were not children then!

After they had showered and dressed, the maid returned with fresh towels and sheets. She gave them a cheeky knowing smile and they thanked her for the kind, understanding service. As she left, Steve reminded himself to give her a substantial tip before they left the hotel. Smiles and thanks were very welcome, but they didn't pay the bills of a struggling young chambermaid.

Steve and Lorraine finished their preparations and made their way downstairs. They headed for the nearest cafe for breakfast; for some obscure reason a ravenous appetite gripped them!

After a satisfying traditional breakfast, they returned to the hotel room. The maid had finished her job efficiently and the room was back to normal. The potpourri had been renewed with a fresh dish and the aroma in the bathroom was pleasant. They looked at the newly made bed, and then at each other. They smiled, and shook their heads simultaneously; they needed fresh air not fresh relations! They were like two young school children who had discovered a new toy to play with.

They had to decide what to do before packing and leaving for Waterloo station and the train home. The hours had gone by so quickly and they both wanted to stop the march of time, but it was relentless, and disregarded their wishes. They had four hours left to enjoy London, and once again Steve left the decision to Lorraine. After studying the street map, she suggested a visit to 'Madame Tussauds Waxworks'. It would not take long, and then they could prepare for the journey home, though neither was looking forward to it.

The weather was still dry and warm, and they decided to walk to the waxworks. They walked along the busy streets hand in hand, two young people without a care in the world. Steve began to softly sing one of the songs from the musical show. He had memorised most of the songs from his many visits to the film show in Somerset.

After a while Lorraine turned to him and said, "You have a good voice."

He increased the volume of his singing, knowing he had an appreciative audience!

The words and music had been cleverly written by Rogers and Hammerstein, but some individual writers were able to produce both words and music. One notable composer was Cole Porter, an American born into a rich family who didn't need to work for a living, but produced some of the most entertaining and lyrical songs ever written. Another such individual was Irving Berlin, the creator of the perennial 'White Christmas', made famous by the much loved crooner Bing Crosby. Even the German Army in the Second World War had a soft spot for 'White Christmas' and Crosby whom they nicknamed 'Der Bingle'! The British Army 'squaddies' also had their enemy vocal 'pin-up' in the shape of Marlene Dietrich, and her song 'Lily Marlene'. War was a very strange thing, and seemed to bring out the worst and yet the very best in people.

When Steve had finished his open air recital and handed back 'Some Enchanted Evening' into the safe hands of Rogers and Hammerstein, he decided he would write a song himself, but where did one start? Was it the music first and then the words, or vice versa? Perhaps it was similar to writing poetry, and then adding music. The 'Lawyer' was a poetic man; he would seek his advice when the platoon re-grouped. Steve's mind was racing now, stimulated by the fresh morning air. If they did form a writing partnership they could call themselves Galway and Lawyer. Or should it be Lawyer and Galway? He wondered why it was that there appeared to be no famous women song writers. The same could be said about painters.

He asked Lorraine her opinion on the matter, and she laughingly replied, "Perhaps women are too busy working!"

His musical wanderings were curtailed by a sudden shower, and they ran to a nearby 'Lyons Corner' House to take refuge. The bus 'rattle' barometer had not proved completely correct, but 'Morval' barracks and the local bus was a long way away.

After a pot of tea and two 'fairy' cakes the rain subsided and they continued their walk to the waxworks. It had not been heavy rain; the Irish would have called it a 'soft morning'! The waxworks were a strangely haunting place. The characters were cleverly made, and lifelike. Much of England's history was portrayed: monarchs from bygone days, peers of the realm, and noblemen in their finery. Notorious characters were also there, and Dr. Crippen looked at them with a calculating eye, as if to be sizing them up to be his next victims! They both shuddered at the thought, and decided it was time to leave. They took a red bus back to the hotel, as sadly it was time to prepare for the journey home.

They packed their weekend cases and made themselves ready for the journey. Steve checked all the cupboards and drawers to make sure nothing was forgotten, as there would be no returning! Before locking the room, they said a fond farewell to the king-size bed and bath; they had happy memories of both! The long nosed receptionist was on duty and as Steve handed her the key she asked, in a straight faced non-committal way if the potpourri had been to their personal satisfaction. The two lovers blushed slightly, and answered in the affirmative. They picked up their weekend cases, said goodbye to the receptionist and walked to the exit door. Steve looked back momentarily. The receptionist was smiling, and Steve detected a hint of a 'twinkle' in her eye. Perhaps Mr. & Mrs. Smith had brought a little light relief into her humdrum life. Or maybe she was simply glad to see the back of them! Steve chose to believe the former!

The cases seemed heavier now that they were on the return journey, and a 'hackney' cab was hailed for the short ride to Waterloo station. The station was as busy as when Steve and Lorraine had arrived. All nationalities were represented, and people milled about in a partly controlled chaos. Steve heard many different tongues as he and Lorraine made their way to the waiting train. The cases were becoming heavy, and they settled for a carriage near the end of the long train, and Steve considered that a sizable locomotive would be at the head of it.

The compartment was not empty; two people were already settled into their seats. They paid no attention to the newcomers, totally engrossed in their

'Financial Times' and 'Daily Telegraph'. The cases were carefully stowed on the racks above them, and they gratefully sank onto the seats. There was something familiar about the atmosphere in the carriage, almost like a welcoming friend after a long, but happy journey. They sat opposite each other, smiled and held hands across the gap. They were aware of the other two passengers but that didn't matter, they were two young lovers totally lost in themselves and their own thoughts.

The train pulled away on time. Steve could not hear the sound of the steam engine, but he imagined the activity on the locomotive footplate. The driver would be totally concerned with his engine, ensuring that the driving wheels did not 'slip' on the rails and therefore lose adhesion. The fireman would be preparing for the long journey ahead; there was much coal to be fed into the fire-box, and water into the boiler with its insatiable appetite. The fireman would be sweating off a pound of weight, and Steve realised that he had never seen an overweight railway fireman!

After the logistics of packing the cases, paying the hotel bill and travelling to the station Steve felt hungry, as did Lorraine. But there was no possibility of buying food. It was at times like this that Aunt Maude's cheese and pickled onion sandwiches were worth their weight in gold. The thoughts of them increased his hunger, and he pushed desires for food into the back of his mind. His thoughts strayed back to Somerset and Aunt Maude. He decided that wherever he was posted in his army career he would write more often. She had, after all, become more of a mother figure to him than an aunt. Somehow she had been able to combine the roles of mother and aunt together, a fine and rare accomplishment.

Steve and Lorraine talked about the weekend in general, and then more specifically about the boating saga and having to be rescued from the Serpentine. They laughed about it, unaware of the other two people in the compartment. The person reading the 'Telegraph', it turned out to be a man, shook his paper and stared at them, a look of upper class annoyance on his face. Steve and Lorraine held their hands to their mouths, trying to stifle further laughter.

The reader haughtily returned to his paper clearly thinking to himself, *Young upstarts!*

The ticket inspector opened the sliding door, took a cursory look at his passengers, and moved on, closing the compartment door behind him. He was either satisfied there were no villains in the compartment, or simply too lazy to ask for the tickets.

The train was quickly leaving the 'Metropolis' now, moving into the suburbs, and the occasional green field came into view. The scene would fast change into the forest and farmland. It had been a long but totally enjoyable weekend, but they were both exhausted. In a way it was proof that they had both found it a satisfying experience.

Helped by the rhythmic swaying of the carriage their eyelids slowly began to close. Steve tried to stay awake, not wanting to miss a moment, but sleep overtook him, and he left the world to take care of itself for a little while. Lorraine looked across at him in his sleep and smiled. Within a minute her eyelids also submitted to the gentle swaying of the carriage, and she joined Steve in sleep.

When Steve awoke he looked at his wristwatch through bleary eyes. He had been asleep for over half an hour. He glanced across at Lorraine; she was still sleeping, her head resting against the seat's green cushioning. He looked out of the carriage window. They had completely left smoky London and were in the lush green of the English countryside. Cattle and sheep grazed in the enclosed fields, and corn was starting to ripen into a golden colour. Soon the combine harvesters would be at work, here and in Somerset. A pang of homesickness suddenly touched him at the thought. He wondered if they grew corn in Scotland.

They must make porridge out of something, he thought to himself, as he contemplated the fast approaching two weeks' training north of the border.

The train came to a halt at a station with a sudden jolt as the brake blocks gripped the wheel rims. Lorraine awoke from her sleep, also with slightly 'misty' eyes. Steve leant across and kissed her gently on the cheek. The man reading the 'Daily Telegraph' stared at them, shook his paper again, withdrew a fountain pen from an inside pocket, and proceeded to do the crossword.

When they were five minutes from their destination Steve took the cases from the rack, and they both shook off the last of the sleepiness from their cat-naps. They felt better for the sleep, but both needed a full night's rest to be fully recovered. The weekend had been wonderful, almost a fantasy, but now they were returning to the harsh realities of life, and a clear head was essential for tomorrow.

As the train approached the station they left the compartment and moved into the narrow corridor, joining the other passengers waiting to leave the train. As they left the compartment Steve looked at the person who was reading the 'Financial Times'. The reader had not moved a muscle during the whole journey! Steve smiled to himself and thought, *Perhaps it's one of the waxworks from 'Tussauds'!*

They left the train and made their way to the platform exit. Steve looked for the ticket collector, but there was no one in officialdom to be seen. They walked on and out of the station. Steve put the tickets into his pocket and said to Lorraine, "One more memento of the weekend."

After a short bus ride, they reached the flat and Lorraine quickly made coffee and sandwiches. They were both hungry and thirsty after the journey, and when they looked back, realised they had eaten very little over the whole weekend. There had been so much to do, and little time for incidental things like eating and drinking. Steve assisted in the sandwich making by buttering the bread, and giving Lorraine an affectionate 'peck' on the cheek as she sliced the cheese and cucumber.

They sat in the lounge and devoured the sandwiches and coffee in quick time. They talked about the weekend, and then of the oncoming two weeks. Lorraine had seven days of classes and then three days of important mid-term exams. In a way it was good that Steve was going to Scotland for two weeks, it would allow her to concentrate fully on preparing for the exams. She asked him where in Scotland he was going, and when Steve said it would be Fort William and Loch Ness she jokingly told him to be aware of the monster.

There was a pause, and then she said, "What comes after Scotland?"

Steve replied, "Well after Scotland I could be posted anywhere in the world, the decision is up to the army."

His sudden statement startled her, and she was quiet and thoughtful for some time.

After finishing the sandwiches and two more cups of coffee they held each other, and memories of their lovemaking in London returned. They kissed passionately, with the taste of their sandwiches still on their lips. Cheese and cucumber had never tasted so good. Steve reluctantly looked at his watch, it was time to go. Time waited for no man, or woman, and Monday morning was fast approaching, knocking on the front door, demanding to be let in! Lorraine asked him to phone from Scotland and he promised he would, providing he could master the 'foreign' telephones!

After one last kiss he made his way to the bus stop and back to 'Morval' camp. He checked his watch and decided there was time for a quick night-cap beer before the N.A.A.F.I. closed its doors at 10.00pm as required by camp regulations. The orderly sergeant would be stood at the door ensuring the strict rule was adhered to. He bought his beer and went to the platoon's table. The majority of the recruits had returned from the two weeks leave, including Taff and Mac. The rest of the stragglers would be arriving during the night, probably switching the barrack room lights on at 3.00am so a good night's sleep was probably not on the cards.

Taff had been to the rugby, and visiting relatives who were dotted around south Wales. It could be some time before he would see them again. Mac had returned to his local pub in Dewsbury, only to find that his favourite barmaid had moved to a pub around the corner. He therefore felt it his duty to patronise both establishments during his two weeks leave. It was very apparent by the bags under his eyes, but the training P.T.I.'s would soon 'knock him' back into shape again, Steve was certain of that.

They returned to the barrack room, and after stowing his weekend case under his bed, Steve made himself ready for sleep. After everybody was settled he switched off the lights and tried to relax before sleeping. But thoughts of Lorraine in her pink chiffon nighty, and memories of their torrid lovemaking in the king-sized bed and bath overtook him, and sleep was impossible. Scotland was a long way from Hampshire and for the first time Steve regretted his decision to join the army.

CHAPTER 20

The next morning came around far too quickly. Several of the stragglers had arrived in the early hours, switching the lights on and causing a general disturbance as they talked about their leave experiences. A selection of heavy army boots flew through the air signalling the owner's dissent at the sudden glare of light and unwelcome sound!

Steve rubbed his weary eyes. It had been far from the good night's sleep he hoped for; there was no privacy in an army barrack room. But the day was here, and it would soon be time for morning parade. He dragged himself out of bed, washed, shaved, and donned his army clothing for the first time in two weeks. The holiday was over and reality had appeared; it was a rude awakening. The words of the melancholic song came to his mind: - 'The party's over, it's time to call it a day, they've burst your pretty balloon, and taken the moon away'.

After breakfast the platoon paraded in front of the barrack room. Corporal Entwhistle arrived precisely on time, looking at his watch as he marched around the corner of the barrack room. He looked fresh after his two-week respite, and his boots had an extra polish and shine.

The platoon was all present and correct except for one National Serviceman who failed to report back from leave and was listed on Corporal Entwhistle's board as A.W.O.L. (Absent without Leave). The Military Police would be hot on his heels and no doubt before long he would be serving three or four days in Colchester Military Prison, regretting the error of his ways and his temporary bout of self-imposed amnesia! He may even meet the intrepid Prendergast in prison, and they would reminisce on happier days gone by. Steve thought it strange that some National Servicemen could 'buckle down' and serve their two years without rebelling, whilst others found it impossible to cope with, and spent their two years in total torment.

The time of departure for the journey to Scotland was fourteen hundred hours, 2.00pm and the platoon had until then to pack their kit and clean the barrack room, which would be inspected by Corporal Entwhistle at exactly 13.45. At 13.00 they would take lunch in the cookhouse, a last chance to savour the cookhouse corporal's meat balls! Charlie Strong still had plenty of his vile pink medicine, and placed it at the front of his locker for immediate use when the meal was finished.

After packing their kit and making a start on cleaning the room the platoon went to the N.A.A.F.I. for a coffee and a snack. Corporal Entwhistle, they learnt, would not be travelling to Scotland with the platoon. After twenty years' service it was time for him to return to 'civvy street' and a totally different way of life. They wondered how he would adapt to civilian life. It may not be an easy transition. They had grown used to the corporal and his very precise military ways, and had a sneaking admiration for him.

On Steve's suggestion they agreed to 'club' together and buy him a farewell gift. Steve had seen some cigarette lighters for sale at the N.A.A.F.I. shop, and as the corporal was a smoker it was the obvious choice of present. After they had gathered the money together, having to slightly 'twist' Mac's arm in the process, Steve went to the shop and purchased a 'Ronson' Varyflame lighter for the corporal's farewell.

At precisely 13.45 Corporal Entwhistle marched into the barrack room. The platoon stood to attention by their beds and a quick inspection was carried out. By now the platoon knew what was required of them, and the inspection was simply a military ritual that had to be carried out. A three ton 'Bedford' truck was parked near the barrack room, waiting to take the platoon on the first leg of its journey to the railway station and 'foreign' parts of Scotland.

Corporal Entwhistle, satisfied that the cleanliness of the room was up to standard turned to leave. Steve, being the N.C.O. in charge of the room, stepped forward and presented the 'Ronson' to the corporal, with the platoon's best wishes for his future. The corporal, clearly taken by surprise was moved by the show of sentiment, and the men saw him smile for the first time in six weeks of training. It was a simple, but fitting end to the platoon's association with him. He had taught them much and hopefully they had reciprocated, perhaps their interaction would serve him well to understand the complexities of 'civvy street', without two stripes on his shoulder.

The platoon's kit was loaded onto the 'Bedford' truck, and the men sat on the wooden bench seats at either side. The seats were solid, with no cushioning and the harshness of army life was apparent. The driver, satisfied all was well, closed the tail gate, and the 'Bedford' made its way out of 'Morval' camp.

At the camp exit barrier, the usual humorous calls and vulgar signs were made to the sentry on duty. He in turn completely ignored them, and moved his loaded rifle to his other shoulder, as if to let them know who was really in charge!

They made the short journey to the railway station with mixed feelings. They were relieved to have finished the severe basic training of 'Morval', but what of Scotland? Would that be more demanding, or less arduous?

When the train arrived the kitbags were loaded into the rear guard's van, and placed under lock and key. There was no catering service on the train. The platoon had been issued with army 'dry rations' before leaving 'Morval', and any drinks would have to be hurriedly purchased during train stops and changes.

They settled themselves into the 3rd class compartments and prepared for the long journey ahead. Some of the men played 'pontoon' or cribbage to pass the time. The 'Lawyer' scribbled in his notebook, recording his thoughts as the journey progressed. He lived in a different world to cribbage and pontoon players!

Mac looked at him over his hand of playing cards and after the 'Lawyer' had finished his third page said to him, "Why do you keep writing in that stupid book?"

The 'Lawyer' looked at him in a disdainful way and said, "One day I am going to write the story of my life, and you might feature in it. The story will have a bit of everything in it, some adventure, romance, drama, and of course a little pathos."

"What's pathos?" asked Taff who had been listening intently to the conversation.

The 'Lawyer' replied, "You know, as in Athos and Pathos."

Mac turned to Steve and said, "What's he on about?"

Steve laughed and replied, "I think it's something to do with the 'Three Musketeers', d'Artagnan, Athos and Porthos!"

Mac looked at him, none the wiser!

Steve was aware of the 'Lawyer's' quick mind and sophisticated sense of humour. But to explain to Mac would have taken hours. Mac was more into the world of Rugby League, Yorkshire Best Bitter and steak pies! The writings of Alexander Dumas were beyond him. They settled down into their games of pontoon and cribbage, and the 'Lawyer' continued with his literary deliberations!

The train journey continued, and after a stop at a station and a hectic dash to the refreshment room for plastic cups of coffee, Steve sat back in his seat and started to read a book he had purchased earlier. It was called, 'Ice Station Zebra', a story about international spies and the frozen north. Steve shuddered as he read about the sub-zero conditions; the temperature in the barrack room had been low enough!

From time to time he put the book down and stared idly out of the window. His thoughts strayed to Lorraine and their first meeting on the train, a very different journey to this one. The weekend in London was still very much on his mind, and thoughts of chiffon nighties and king-size beds and potpourri laden baths were never far away. He pondered his statement saying he could be 'posted anywhere in the world', and Lorraine's quietness afterwards. He began to think of the future, and it troubled him!

The compartment sliding door opened, and Docherty stood in the doorway. He had a 'captive audience', and proceeded to tell them the lengthy joke about the 'Actress, the Bishop, and the 'One-legged Jockey', who at the end of the joke stated, 'Don't worry about me, 'luv, I ride side saddle!' Docherty seemed to have an endless repertoire of jokes, and could reel them off, one after another without the blink of an eye. He had a unique Liverpudlian talent, and in the future would be priceless when the platoon was to encounter dramatic circumstances in pursuance of their duties abroad, and required a 'Morval boost'.

After a long and tedious journey involving three train changes and several dashes to buy drinks during the stops they arrived at a station near Fort William. They were in a foreign country for a first time, but a familiar 'Bedford' three tonner was available to take them on the final leg of the journey to the training camp. The kitbags were transferred to the truck and the platoon made themselves as comfortable as possible on the wooden bench seats. They were all feeling 'saddle' sore after the long train travel, and the truck's solid, un-cushioned seats did little to improve the matter. Steve looked at the surrounding countryside as the 'Bedford' made its way along the winding country roads. It was very green, hilly country, and they passed many small lakes, or lochs, as the local residents informed them. Over the next two weeks they were to learn much about Scotland and its ancient traditions.

They arrived at the training camp in the late evening, all hungry, and thirsty for a pint of beer. Mac wondered what type of ale would be on sale, certainly not Yorkshire Best Bitter; it would be sacrilege to sell the brew other than in Yorkshire!

The camp buildings were constructed of red brick, not at all like the wooden structures at 'Morval'. The barrack rooms were smaller, and more compact. Steve was surprised to see heating radiators attached to the walls. It was an unexpected luxury; maybe Scotland would not be so bad after all. The barrack rooms each housed ten men, and the platoon was divided into two sections for the purpose of training. Team competition would be a factor in training, and tended to bring out leadership qualities in people.

After organising themselves they 'fished' out their knives, forks, spoons, and enamel drinking mugs and made their way to the cookhouse. The food was plentiful, and after the long journey and meagre 'dry' rations they ate well. But the food certainly tasted different to the 'cuisine' at 'Morval', and Steve equated it to the fact that they were in a 'foreign' country with people who enjoyed a different palate.

Charlie Strong, the intrepid hypochondriac had already concocted a cocktail of medicines to combat any ill side-effects from the foreign food, and had placed the bottle within easy reach in his locker. The 'Lawyer' who had visited Scotland before as a teenager, requested of Charlie, that if he ate haggis over the next two weeks, he refrained from passing wind in the confines of the barrack room!

Docherty said to the 'Lawyer', "What's haggis made of anyway?"

The 'Lawyer' looked at him dramatically and replied, "I would rather not talk about it!"

The theatrical statement sounded ominous to the platoon, and the discussion ended abruptly. Perhaps the cookhouse corporal's meat balls were not so lethal after all! Charlie went to his locker and reinforced his cocktail of gastric remedies.

After a tentative meal the next stop was the nearby N.A.A.F.I. for a welcome pint of beer. The brew tasted different to the southern pint. The Highland water was probably purer here, being filtered as it cascaded down the mountains and hills. They sipped at their beers and looked around them; all N.A.A.F.I.'s seemed to be alike, no matter which country they were in, but there appeared to be no 'Blonde Bombshell' there!

Mac finished his beer, and signalled his approval by ordering another pint. After finishing their beers, the platoon returned to the barrack rooms and slept. It had been a long, tiring day, and there would be much to do tomorrow.

The next morning, they awoke to the sound of bagpipes! Steve looked at his watch through bleary eyes. Taff couldn't believe his ears and looked out of the window onto the small parade ground. A lone piper, dressed in tartan kilt and full ceremonial uniform, was vaguely visible in the morning mist, his haunting notes heralding the day. Another soldier also in full ceremonial dress unfurled and hoisted the regimental flag to the top of a nearby flagpole. This was to be the morning routine throughout the platoon's two weeks' training in Scotland.

After washing and shaving, Steve went to the cookhouse for breakfast. The menu was very Scottish, instead of cornflakes it was porridge, and plenty of it. There was eggs and bacon to follow, and together they made a very substantial meal. Mugs of strong coffee rounded off breakfast, and he was ready for the day ahead. Mac and Docherty returned for second helpings, and the corporal in charge did not refuse them. The army was strict on discipline, but if you could eat, you ate!

At 8.00am a sergeant arrived at the barrack room and ordered the platoon to parade on the road outside the barrack room. The sergeant had been seconded from the 'Black Watch' regiment, but wore normal khaki battle dress, not the traditional kilt. His name was McNiff, and he stood a good six feet tall. His back was as straight as a ramrod, and curly ginger hair tried to escape from his tightly fitting black beret. A neatly clipped military moustache completed the picture. His complexion was healthy and his skin tough from much outdoor living. He was very, very fit!

Sgt. McNiff explained that the first week of training would involve a certain amount of rock climbing and abseiling, but mostly trekking. The Scottish terrain was ideal for the latter; the ground was rocky and undulating and would build stamina in their legs. Steve was not aware of it at the time, but the training was to be put to good use in the future. The second week would be spent on waterborne activities, using light motorised beach assault crafts. McNiff added that a certain amount of first aid would also be taught. Steve could see the sense in that. Rock climbing and abseiling could be somewhat hazardous!

CHAPTER 21

After morning parade and meeting the other instructors, the platoon spent the day orienting themselves into their new surroundings and going to the camp kit store to be issued with suitable clothing for climbing, abseiling and assault craft training. The next two weeks would complete their training; six weeks at 'Morval' in Hampshire, and two weeks in Scotland, making a total of eight weeks hard endeavour.

The new kit was lightweight green denim shirts and long trousers of the same material. Their normal issue black boots, gaiters and web belt made up the uniform, plus of course the beret and coveted cap badge. Khaki battle dress used at 'Morval' was stowed away in lockers, and the new lightweight uniform was welcome. They were all looking forward to the freedom of the outdoor training, it was good to get away from 'square bashing' and the overly strict discipline of 'Morval' barracks.

The platoon's reservations about 'foreign' food were soon dispelled, and they enjoyed a meal in the cookhouse consisting of 'Scotch broth' and beef stew with so much goodness in it a fork could be stood upright unaided in the pot.

Having completed the six weeks basic training, the men were now allowed out of camp in uniform to mix with the local civilian population. The unit's C.O. was satisfied the platoon was a credit to the uniform and in a suitable state to be seen in public. After making themselves suitably presentable the men decided to continue their orienting and explore the nearby village.

Steve, Mac and Taff, whom the rest of the platoon had nicknamed the 'Three Musketeers', wandered off on their own, and Mac's delicate sense of smell soon detected the nearest pub. The small village hostelry was situated on a hillside, and overlooked a loch, a picturesque pleasant view to enjoy the local brew. The weather was warm and sunny. So far it had been a good summer in England, and Scotland was enjoying the same very agreeable climate. A small beer garden, equipped with tables and chairs overlooked the loch, and the trio picked a suitable table. A ginger 'Tom' cat was sprawled out on one of the tables. It was obviously his property and they didn't disturb him. The cat opened one eye, sized them up as 'foreigners', and went back to sleep. The view of the loch with its shimmering water was thirst making, and Steve went into the bar to order three beers.

The landlady behind the bar counter was a stern looking woman in her fifties, and wore a conservative tweed jacket and skirt. She was very much the 'I'm in charge' type of person, and it was clear that she allowed no frivolity in her establishment. Any person who dared to raise their voice in enjoyment would be quickly ushered to the exit door. There were several clients sat at the tables quietly sipping a glass of beer or a small glass of Scotch whisky. A group of elderly men sat at a lone table, deeply engrossed in a game of dominoes. A short, skinny, weasel eyed man, possibly the landlady's long suffering husband, darted nervously around the tables picking up empty glasses and polishing tables with a beer stained yellow duster.

Steve bought the three beers and asked the landlady for a tray. She reluctantly handed him one as if he had just asked for the keys to Edinburgh Castle! He went out and into the beer garden, past the 'Tom' cat that was deep in slumber, and placed the beers on the table. Mac, enthusiastic to try the Scottish brew grabbed his jar and drank half in one swift movement. Taff was a little more refined and sipped his beer thoughtfully. Steve explained about the stern landlady behind the bar and they immediately nicknamed her the 'Loch Ness Monster'!

The local beer was a dark brew and much stronger than the pints they had been used to in Hampshire. Mac reluctantly admitted it but added that Yorkshire Best Bitter was on a par. They decided to order a second pint just to confirm their evaluation of the dark brew! Mac took the tray and went into the bar. He was curious about the 'Loch Ness Monster', and wanted to see for himself. When he returned with the beers he looked at Steve and nodded his head. No words were required to describe the 'Monster'!

Mac said the old men playing dominoes in the bar reminded him of his grandfather back in Dewsbury. Grandad Joe had worked down the local pits for fifty years. He retired in reasonable health, and lived happily for a further twenty-five years. When asked to explain his longevity he always replied, "Regular sex, and plenty of tinned baked beans in a rich tomato sauce." He finally passed away with a smile on his face in a mistress' bed after indulging in the reason for his longevity. Eating tinned baked beans at 3.00am can be extremely exhausting!

They laughed about Mac's obviously colourful grandfather, and Steve remarked that 'Mr. Heinz' would be pleased to hear about Joe's theory for a long life, and the obvious advertising possibilities it produced.

They sipped their beers, the first one having quenched the thirst. They talked about Scotland and the oncoming two weeks of training. It was certainly a change from 'Morval', and Sergeant McNiff was a different 'kettle of fish' to Corporal Entwhistle. Taff and Mac were not too happy about rock climbing and abseiling. Mac made it clear that if God had meant him to fly he would have given him wings, or at least a twin-engine aeroplane!

After they had finished the beer 'The Three Musketeers' returned to camp and the N.A.A.F.I. The strong beer had made them 'heady', and confirmed their evaluation of the 'foreign' brew. Steve walked a little unsteadily past the ginger Tom's table and nudged it with his lack of balance. The cat looked up, shook its head, changed position on the table, and went back to sleep! They returned the tray and the empty jars to the landlady. She nodded in reply to Steve's word of "Thanks," but that was all he was going to get!

They strolled back to camp in the pleasant evening air and went straight to the N.A.A.F.I. All three had seen enough beer for the day, but the drink and evening air had given them an appetite, and a steak and kidney pie was in order. The rest of the platoon had commandeered a table, and after buying pies the trio joined them. The N.A.A.F.I. was much smaller than 'Morval's', and didn't have the same atmosphere. The aroma was more of whisky than beer, and perhaps the window curtains were slightly too clean to be comfortable. To some extent they even missed the 'Blonde Bombshell' with her overly made up face and provocative swishing skirt. Taff was the only exception; he didn't miss her at all!

When the N.A.A.F.I. closed at 10.00pm they made the short walk, still unsteadily, back to the barrack room. A notice had been pinned to the room notice board and was signed by Sgt. McNiff. The platoon was to parade outside the barrack room at 07.00 hrs for their first trek. Dress would be denims and full backpack. They all took a good night's sleep, greatly aided by the strength of the brew at the pub. At six o'clock sharp they were woken by the haunting skirl of the bagpipes, there was no sleep after that! Mac put his boots on and silently wished he was back in Dewsbury.

Steve washed and shaved, the sound of the pipes still ringing in his ears. It was only a short walk to the cookhouse, and the journey was made through the early morning mist. They were no longer regarded as basic trainees, and the strict regulation of carrying knife, fork, spoon and drinking mug behind the back no longer applied, but the eating 'irons', as they were called, would remain part of their issued kit and used throughout the years of service. In the cookhouse the sudden transition from 'Kellogg's' cornflakes to porridge oats was too much for some of the platoon to cope with. As with all things it would take time to change. Steve chopped a banana and carefully mixed it with his porridge, much to the disgust of the corporal cook as he made his routine inspection of the tables.

At 7.00am the platoon assembled in front of the barrack room. Sgt. McNiff had already arrived, dressed in green denims and wearing a full backpack strapped to his muscular shoulders. He flexed his limbs, eager to get started. The men had filled their backpacks to the required standard, and included a groundsheet that also served as a cape in wet weather. Spare pairs of socks, a change of underwear, 'mess' tins, eating 'irons' mug and filled water bottle completed the regulation pack.

Steve assembled the platoon into three ranks and reported to Sgt. McNiff stating the platoon was 'all present and correct', as required by routine military drill. Steve was learning his trade as N.C.O. (non-commissioned officer). McNiff addressed the platoon, and informed them that because it was their first trek it would be a short one of only ten miles!

Mac, who was stood next to the 'Lawyer' in the back row, turned his head slightly and whispered out of the corner of his mouth, "There's something of the sadist in that man."

McNiff overheard the remark, grinned at Mac, and flexed his muscles!

They marched out of the camp, and Sgt. McNiff set a fast pace, there was no time to 'warm-up'. The platoon marched through the village and past the pub, bringing back memories of the dark brew the night before. The water in the small loch was perfectly still, and the trees at the edge were mirrored on the blue water's surface. If one had to trek, this was the place to do it.

After two miles they reached the start of the open country, and McNiff ordered them to 'break step'. This was to enable them to master the rocky uneven terrain individually. The Scottish countryside was ideal for building stamina in the legs, and the backpacks added strength to their shoulders, backs and hips. As the week progressed they were to learn the use of a compass and some basic survival skills. Steve was not aware of it but he would be putting into use all of these skills and stamina training before long, and his life would probably depend on how well he learnt them.

After five miles McNiff called a halt, and the platoon gratefully took off their backpacks. They sank down onto the nearest available rock and loosened their boots. They were told not to take them off completely; the feet could swell and make it impossible to put them on again. Steve and Taff looked across at Sgt. McNiff. He was exercising as if he was just warming up for the day.

"The man's not normal," said Taff, and Steve was inclined to agree with him.

McNiff stopped exercising and took a sip from his water bottle, but it was not water he was drinking. Steve was certain that he could detect the aroma of Scotch whisky wafting across to them in the breeze.

After ten minutes had passed, they re-tied their boots that had cooled slightly, and generally made themselves ready for the second five-mile leg of the trek back to camp. The second leg didn't seem as long as the first one and Steve put it down to the fact that they were heading home, to a welcome shower and hot meal. When they arrived back at camp they all felt a natural tiredness but not exhausted. The six weeks of basic training at 'Morval' had served them well.

After a quick shower they grabbed their eating 'irons' and drinking mugs and made the short walk to the cookhouse, all with ravenous appetites. On the menu was 'cockaleekie' soup, followed by something called 'Mince Tatties and Skirlie'. Steve had heard of 'cockaleekie'; the other dish was new to him, but he was willing to put his doubts aside and give it a try. After the long trek he could have eaten a horse! Mac looked at the menu. The only thing missing he said was a 'dram' of Scotch whisky for afters.

The weather in the evening was warm and pleasant. Steve's legs and feet were still tired from the exercise, but he needed to talk to Lorraine, and he had promised to phone as soon as possible. She was always in his thoughts, and it was proving to be true that, 'absence makes the heart grow fonder'!

He changed into civilian clothes and put some soothing talcum powder on his feet before donning clean white socks and his lightweight shoes. They felt like dancing shoes after the ten miles in army boots. After arming himself with a certain amount of loose change he strolled into the village, enjoying the evening air.

The phone box was near the pub, and unlike the 'red sentinel' at 'Morval' there was nobody waiting to use it. He had become quite accustomed to public telephones, and went through the routine almost without thinking, and

Lorraine's telephone number was now imprinted on his mind. Steve glanced at his watch as the dialling tone sounded; it was just after seven o'clock. Lorraine answered his call. It was good to hear her voice again and he no longer felt lonely and in 'foreign' parts. It seemed like a hundred years since they had last spoken.

Lorraine was preparing for the mid-term exams. She said it was going well, but missed his company. Steve replied in the same manner, he wished fervently that they were in each other's arms, but they had to be content with talk, and the occasional kiss blown into the phone! He told her about the journey to Scotland and the first two days of training. She was surprised that he had trekked for ten miles, and said jokingly, "Rather you than me!"

They talked about the London weekend. It had been a wonderful two days, and they laughed about the 'Serpentine Saga' and their amateurish boat handling. Steve explained that during the training in Scotland he would be learning more about the technicalities of seamanship using small assault crafts.

Lorraine laughed and said, "That will be helpful if we ever have to 'storm' an enemy beach together!"

The conversation drifted on to the hotel, the king-size bed and foam bath. They both still felt slightly embarrassed by their raw passion and emotional lovemaking and it was difficult to talk of the wonderful sensations they had both experienced. Sometimes it was best not to talk, but simply look forward to the next time.

They talked until Steve's small change ran out. They blew a kiss to each other as young lovers do, and he promised to phone again. Lorraine said that when she went to bed she would wear the pink chiffon nightdress he liked so much; it would bring them closer together for the night. After a last 'kiss', Steve put the phone down, breathed a long sigh and left the kiosk.

A pint of the dark brew was required to soften the blow of having to say goodnight to Lorraine. He walked across the deserted street and into the lounge bar of the pub. The bar had its usual quota of locals, and the landlady's husband was still busy cleaning tables. Steve noticed nobody took time to speak with the man, and decided to put the matter right when the opportunity arose.

He went to the counter and ordered a pint of beer. The landlady looked at him and carefully inspected his money before handing him the beer. He sat down at a corner table and the ginger 'Tom' appeared as if from nowhere, jumped onto the table, glanced at Steve and went to sleep near his arm resting on the table.

The landlady's husband arrived carrying out his table cleaning duties. Steve said hello to the man and remarked how good the Scottish weather was. The man looked at him suspiciously, said "Aye," and hurriedly walked away flicking his yellow duster as he went.

The cat lifted its head and looked at Steve as if to say, "I told you so, don't bother." Steve picked up his dark brew and drank. The cat moved closer to him, nudged his arm, and went back to sleep. Steve had just found his first 'foreign' friend!

CHAPTER 22

In order to give their tired legs a rest the next day was devoted to lectures on first aid and survival skills. The first aid lessons were given by a senior N.C.O. in the R.A.M.C. (Royal Army Medical Corp). The lectures covered the basic methods of resuscitation, treatment of deep wounds and gashes in the field, head wounds and broken limbs. Mac asked the N.C.O. if he had a cure for alcohol hangovers, a question the N.C.O. chose to ignore.

Charlie Strong, the platoon hypochondriac, was in his element at the lectures and theoretically knew more about the subject than the instructor. As the lessons progressed the N.C.O. became visibly annoyed by Charlie's obvious superior theoretical knowledge and searching questions. If Charlie had not been such a raving hypochondriac, he would possibly have made a very good doctor. After the theory they put the learning into practice, and Charlie Strong succeeded in completely engulfing the 'Lawyer's' head in bandages, much to the disgust of the N.C.O. instructor.

Survival skills were more difficult to teach without going into the 'field', but the instructor, a sergeant from the 'Gordon Highlanders', made it as interesting as possible, and Steve was surprised at the variety of plants and shrubs that could be eaten for nourishment. Other methods of survival, especially in a jungle environment were not so palatable. The 'Lawyer' remarked that they were 'downright disgusting', and that he would 'rather die'!

The last lecture of the day was presided over by Sgt. McNiff, and covered the theory of rock climbing. Climbing was scheduled to start in about thirty hours' time. The platoon had time to study and absorb the theory before actual practice. Each man was supplied with a two-foot length of strong cord, and a sheet of paper showing how to make the basic knots required for rock climbing. It was essential that they learnt this basic skill well; it was a strict regulation that every man should be responsible for tying his own knots when climbing.

After explaining the theory of climbing, McNiff informed them that having rested their legs the platoon would be going on a 'forced' trek of fifteen miles the next day. 'Forced' being the operative word! The trek would be non-stop and would simulate a unit being called into emergency action. The only nourishment allowed would be water, or in Sgt. McNiff's case an illicit drop of Scotch whisky! The ten-mile trek had been bad enough, but the thought of a 'forced' march required a certain amount of extra sustenance, and the platoon retreated to the N.A.A.F.I.

Over a pint of the brew they discussed the trek planned for the next day. Steve remarked that it would be quite an undertaking, even for men as fit as they after the six weeks at 'Morval'. The 'Lawyer' pointed out that Steve's use of the word undertaking was unfortunate, and could quite easily be changed to 'undertaker'!

In order to change the subject, Docherty remarked that the previous day's meal in the cookhouse was spoilt due to the fact that the baked beans were only partially heated. He had made the fact quickly known to the corporal cook. For a man who had been brought up on 'jam butties' in Liverpool, he was very exacting regarding the standard of the cooking and quality of his food. Perhaps he thought the world owed him a good meal!

The mention of baked beans triggered off a conversation about Mac's colourful grandfather, and his fetish for consuming tinned baked beans in bed at 3.00am apart from other activities! Steve suggested they should open a camp wide competition to find the best advertising slogan to promote tinned baked beans and Joe's theory for longevity. First prize would be a tin of 'Heinz' baked beans. Second prize, two tins of baked beans, but not necessarily Heinz. The 'Lawyer' immediately licked the tip of his pencil and opened a new page in his notebook. Five minutes later he presented his entry to the competition, it read: -

Let Heinz be your true selection. You'll be certain to gain a good erection!

Mac said to him, "You're a bloody fool!"

The 'Lawyer' looked sternly at Mac, and put his name in the book!

Two days later the platoon received many slogans, unfortunately the majority were of a very lewd nature and unprintable, referring to the sexual abuse of baked beans in a rich tomato sauce!

After a final beer and further discussion regarding the merits of baked beans the men went to the cookhouse. It was essential that they ate a good filling meal before the trek in the morning. A fairly light, nutritious breakfast would be in order, and plenty of water on the march. Nobody wanted to be the first to 'drop out'; there was a certain amount of personal pride involved.

Charlie Strong stocked plenty of pills into his backpack. Steve still couldn't decide whether his little brown pills were 'yeast' or not. After the evening meal Steve practised making knots with the help of the instruction sheet provided. They might only be basic knots, but they had to be right. His safety and perhaps his life may depend on it. The other men, fairly reluctantly followed suit, Mac remarking he felt like a 'ruddy boy scout'! Everyone slept well after the mentally demanding lectures, and several pints of the dark brew. In the morning they were woken as usual by the sound of the bagpipes at 6.00am.

Breakfast was the proverbial porridge, and Steve fortified it with sliced fruit. He chopped two bananas and mixed them into the porridge with plenty of hot milk, which once again was looked upon disapprovingly by the corporal cook. Steve remembered Aunt Maude's words that bananas were a good source of almost instant energy, a resource he would need much of soon. Steve explained the banana theory to the cook, but the corporal was adamant that his oats had been tampered with!

When he returned from breakfast Steve made certain that his water bottle was full of fresh water. He put plenty of talcum powder into his socks, and securely tied his boots. Hopefully they would stay that way until the march was over. Being the non-commissioned officer in charge of the platoon it was essential that he set a good example and finish the course.

The platoon paraded outside the barrack room at five minutes to seven, in green denim and full backpack. Sgt. McNiff was already on parade, 'chomping at the bit', and eager to get started. After a quick inspection and reminder of what they were about to undertake, they made their way out of camp.

Another platoon was also on a forced march. They had left a few minutes earlier, and could just be seen in the distance. McNiff set a blistering pace, and Steve couldn't imagine any of them finishing the trek, with the exception of McNiff. After they left the camp area Charlie Strong complained to Steve that the rapid pace could quite possibly damage his follicles!

After two miles Steve's legs started to ache. None of the men had experienced such a pace. Even the stringent six weeks basic training at 'Morval' barracks had not prepared them for this. Sgt. McNiff on the other hand seemed to revel in the situation, but of course he had great experience of trekking, whether it be 'forced' or not. Not to mention the odd drop of 'Highland' stimulant!

A small W.D. (War Department) pick-up truck followed the platoon at a respectable distance and carried a junior N.C.O. from the Medical Corps, complete with first aid kit in case of anybody 'dropping out' from exhaustion.

After five, very quick miles McNiff ordered the platoon to drink water, on 'the march'. This was achieved by the man marching behind delving into the backpack of the man in front and handing him the full water bottle. The last man reversed their position at the right time to carry out the manoeuvre. In this way all drinks were taken without slowing down the march.

The aching in Steve's legs gradually wore off. He wasn't enjoying the trek, but was managing to cope well. Sweat was running from his forehead and trickling into his eyes, and the salt from his perspiration made his eyes sting. He wiped them with his sleeve, but that simply made them feel worse. He looked around at the others; Mac was obviously struggling, and sweating profusely. The 'Lawyer' seemed to have distanced himself mentally from the physical stress. He was probably mentally writing something of importance in his book!

So far nobody had dropped out, but there was a long way to go. Steve looked back down the road. The pick-up truck was menacingly close, and he could imagine the medical orderly busily preparing his first aid kit. There was something strangely sadistic about the way a person in the medical profession prepared their instruments. Almost like a dentist preparing his tools of torture!

Steve wiped the sweat from his eyes and looked across at Taff who was also struggling to keep up with the rapid pace. There was nothing Steve could do to help. Although they were a close knit platoon, at times like this they were very much on their own. The only thing Steve could do was to loudly offer words of encouragement, which in a strange way also helped him to cope.

McNiff continued to lead the march from the front, and Steve felt that he was gradually increasing the pace as the miles went by. With some two miles to go they had all switched over to 'automatic', and their body adrenaline was keeping them going. As they eventually marched into the camp their heads were held high. Nobody had 'dropped out', and a tighter bond had formed between them. The R.A.M.C. orderly had taken his journey in vain, and was probably sulkily repacking his first aid kit. Much to Steve's surprise, Charlie Strong had completed the course with flying colours. The 'yeast' tablets had worked yet again!

When they reached the barrack room and had been dismissed by Sgt. McNiff, they all collapsed onto their beds for half an hour, grateful for somewhere to simply lie down. Later, as each one gradually recovered, they went for showers and changed into fresh clothes.

Later Sgt. McNiff arrived, still looking disgustingly fit and fresh when the platoon was struggling to recover completely. He inspected the men's feet, and ordered two of the platoon to report to the M.O.'s clinic with some blisters that required medical attention. As McNiff started to leave they took the unusual step of inviting him for a drink at the village pub in the evening. It was far from normal for recruits to drink with senior training N.C.O.'s, but McNiff was a far from ordinary man. He relied on his leadership characteristics to gain respect of other men, not the stripes on his arm! But McNiff declined the invitation, saying he had an important meeting at the Sergeants' Mess. Later Steve learnt from another source that McNiff had been barred from the pub by the landlady some twelve months earlier. It followed an unfortunate incident involving the ceremonial 'Hogmanay' haggis, when McNiff and one of the locals were practising the intricacies of passing a rugby ball! Sgt. McNiff's opinion of the 'Loch Ness Monster' was interestingly colourful, but unprintable.

The second phase of the two weeks training was to be rock climbing and abseiling. In order to learn the discipline, the platoon had to travel to the coast each day. The surrounding area of the camp was ideal for trekking, but no steep rock faces were available. The training required leaving camp at an early hour and undergoing a three-hour drive in an uncomfortable 'Bedford'. This was then followed by four hours of climbing training on the coast before returning to camp by the same route. The usual 'dry rations' were supplied by the cookhouse, and the truck carried a small portable stove for coffee and tea making.

The training was hard on the body, and the granite rock faces unforgiving, but the feeling of freedom far outweighed the aches and pains.

The weather was unusually dry for Scotland, and after hours of training Mac sat back on the 'Bedford's' wooden seat, licked his parched lips, and exclaimed loudly, "I could murder a cold pint in the N.A.A.F.I.!"

The 'Lawyer' looked at him from the opposite bench seat and retorted, "Abstinence makes the heart grow fonder."

Mac looked at Steve his interpreter, and said, "What's the silly bugger talking about?"

Steve replied with tongue in cheek, "I've no idea, but I could handle a jar myself, army coffee and stewed tea leave a lot to be desired!"

Mac agreed, and they looked forward to a pint of the brew to sooth sore rock climbing bodies. Others seconded the motion and the 'Lawyer' was left in the minority. He removed his notebook, and wrote about absence, abstinence, and N.A.A.F.I. aromatic aperitifs!

After a relaxing evening and a good night's sleep they woke to the usual haunting strains of the pipes. It was always the same tune, and Steve assumed that it was the Scottish equivalent to reveille in England, signalling the start of the day, and time to put your socks and boots on. After going through the early morning routine of washing, shaving and breakfast they paraded outside the barrack room at 7.00am. The 'Bedford' had been loaded with the necessary equipment the night before, and Sgt. McNiff sitting in the cab passenger seat signalled them to board the lorry, time was of the essence, and there was still much to learn and practice. The morning routine was waived and the 'Bedford' made its way to the coast.

On the journey they talked of the previous 'forced trek'. They had all recovered well from the harsh experience, much to their relief. Possibly the six weeks at 'Morval' had paid off after all. Steve wondered why McNiff had measurably increased the pace towards the end of the trek. Mac enlightened him. Mac had met a fellow 'Yorkshire Best Bitter' man in the N.A.A.F.I., and over a pint of the 'foreign' brew Mac had learnt the trek secret. All of the trek instructors were in a six monthly pontoon. The instructor with the best average time over the six months 'scooped' the jackpot. Sgt. McNiff's habit of imbibing in 'Johnny Walker' was a costly hobby, and had to be financed from somewhere!

It was to be the final day of rock climbing and as usual time was marching on. They had trained for several days on the lower cliff faces, learning the techniques of climbing and safety, regarding the tying of knots, the proper use of ropes, and crampons, (steel spikes driven into rock to secure ropes). Charlie Strong, much to Steve's surprise, was enjoying the climbing training. He appeared to have no fear of heights, and scaled the rock faces like a mountain goat. Charlie's attitude to life was slowly changing and Steve had noticed that the pills and potions were no longer stored at the front of Charlie's locker.

They arrived at the coast after a bumpy ride. The 'Bedford' had to park some three hundred yards from the shoreline cliff face where they were to operate, and the equipment had to be transferred by hand. Steve looked at the coastline; the North Sea was quite rough, and sizable waves broke against the rocky shoreline. It was midsummer, and the sea, although rough, looked inviting. He cast his eye over the cliff face, it was almost vertical, and some eighty feet in height! They all looked at each other, the training slopes had been demanding, but this was real 'crunch' time and would sort the men from the boys.

After explaining again about the importance of safety harnesses and the proper use of ropes, Sgt. McNiff slung four sturdy ropes over his athletic shoulders and picked up a canvas holdall containing long steel spikes and a large mallet. He made his way by an alternative route to the top of the cliff. The platoon sorted out the harnesses and put them on as instructed.

One of the platoon members was a National Serviceman named Pearce. He came from a small village on the edge of Dartmoor, and was subsequently nicknamed 'Tom' by the rest of the platoon. Steve had grown to like the sincere, slow talking Devon man and his dry sense of humour. But Pearce was having obvious trouble learning the basic rope knots, and Steve took him to one side and spent the time before McNiff returned teaching him as much as possible in the time allowed. Pearce seemed to have a problem deciding which was his right or left hand. Therefore, the basic 'reef' became difficult with 'left over right' and 'right over left'.

Sgt. McNiff secured the ropes at the cliff top using two-foot-long steel spikes and threw the rope 'tails' over the cliff face. He gave each rope a good tug to ensure it was secured and then returned to the platoon. It was time for climbing to begin.

Steve and three other men secured their safety ropes to their respective harnesses, tying the knots themselves as required by the regulations, each man responsible for his own safety. Steve looked across at Mac who was the next to climb. He didn't look happy and definitely would have preferred to be back in the sanctity of the N.A.A.F.I.

The safety ropes were a last resort, and not to be used for actual climbing, it was hands and feet to the fore. Steve and the other three recruits gradually made it to the cliff top, all exhausted by the effort. In climbing terms, it was an easy ascent. Any self-respecting climber would have walked up the cliff face, but for the newcomers it was a great achievement, and they were all relieved and proud to have reached the cliff top. When they had completed the climb and recovered sufficiently they untied the ropes and dropped the 'tails' back down the cliff for the next Edmund Hillary's! They congratulated themselves before returning to the shoreline by the alternative route. Gradually all of the platoon made the climb and after two hours of tense climbing Sgt. McNiff called a half hour's break. For the newcomers it was exhausting work.

They took the harnesses off, loosened their boots, and gratefully tucked into the dry rations and coffee. The fresh air made the rations palatable, and the coffee acceptable. After eating and drinking their fill they still had fifteen minutes before resuming training. With McNiff's approval they decided to take a quick swim, the climbing had been hot work, and a dip in the surf would be cooling. They had no swimming trunks with them, but the beach was completely isolated and empty of people. They all stripped off, left their clothes on the rocks and dived into the foaming waves. After a few minutes, Docherty shouted to Charlie Strong over the noise of the breaking waves, asking him if his follicles were being stimulated by the cold water. Charlie grinned, but said nothing. His teeth were chattering so much he was unable to speak! Sgt. McNiff looked up and down the beach, and once he was satisfied they were completely alone, stripped off his uniform, took a deep swig from his water bottle, flexed his muscles and joined the platoon in the North Sea.

After an overly refreshing dip the platoon returned to the serious business of climbing. They were to scale the face again, but this time, after a brief rest at the top, they would then abseil back down the cliff face. This was once again a first time for all of them, and required a totally different technique to climbing.

Steve and his original other three men climbed to the top, released the rope 'tails' and took their rest break. Other members of the platoon slowly made the climb to the top, and after ten minutes rest it was time for Steve to abseil down the cliff face. He tied his rope following the instructions he had received to the letter. The abseiling method was to push yourself away from the cliff face and at the same time release some of the securing rope through the harness rings. It was a skill that required practice to make perfect. He reached the ground, but realised he had much to learn.

'Tom Pearce' had made it safely to the cliff top and prepared himself for the abseiling descent. He tied his rope and started down the face, pushing himself away from the face of the rock as instructed. The solid granite glistened in the afternoon sun.

Halfway down the sheer face, his rope slipped and Pearce crashed to the ground below. It happened so quickly and was over in seconds, as most accidents are. Steve ran to where Pearce was laying. His right leg was not in a natural position. He was still conscious, but obviously in a great deal of pain. Pearce's knot making had let him down, and had literally been his undoing.

Sgt. McNiff was quickly on the scene and took charge. He ordered two men to run and fetch a collapsible stretcher, splints and first aid kit from the

'Bedford'. McNiff looked at Pearce who was still conscious, and told him not to try to move. Steve doubted that he was able to move anyway, but it was all part of the first aid procedure.

The men arrived with the equipment and McNiff expertly strapped the wooden splints to Pearce's right leg, and then strapped the two legs together. He gave Pearce a pain killing injection which quickly took effect and then they gingerly lifted Pearce onto the stretcher. It was good to see a competent first aider at work, but Steve wished it had been under different circumstances. Seeing the likeable 'Tom Pearce' in such distress was not a good sight.

Four men each took a corner of the stretcher and they started to make the short journey to the 'Bedford. They were all still wearing their web harnesses, so there was little equipment to gather up before leaving. Sgt Mc Niff was annoyed with himself. As an instructor he felt responsible for the accident. He had failed to protect a student and felt bad about it. It was as if he had broken his own leg!

They drove straight to the nearest hospital which was in a nearby small town. It was a 'cottage' type hospital with little facilities for such an emergency, but a doctor and two trained nurses were on duty and a bed was quickly prepared in the single ward available. The unfortunate 'Tom Pearce' was in good hands.

The irony of the situation was that Pearce, although a National Serviceman, was actually enjoying his military service and had spoken to Steve on more than one occasion about 'signing on' as a professional soldier. It was quite possible now that he would be prematurely returned to civilian life, his two years military service finished. Steve smiled wryly to himself and thought, 'That's one ploy' that Prendergast didn't think of!

CHAPTER 23

The Sunday 'rest' day came around. It had been a tough week for all of them. The trekking and climbing had taken its toll, especially the long climbing days at the coast with the uncomfortable 'bumpy' rides, in the heavy springed 'Bedford'.

Steve relaxed on his bed and thought about the weeks training they had all experienced. In the main he had enjoyed it, and the hazardous climbing and abseiling, although testing, had been memorable and certainly not something he would have done as a civilian. A certain amount of danger in one's life somehow made it all worthwhile. Enlisting in the army had opened a whole new world for him, and he looked forward to more adventures in the future!

He thought about 'Tom Pearce' and his unfortunate accident. The corporal in the medical room had informed Steve that 'Private Pearce' had broken his 'tib and fib', and also had internal injuries. Steve didn't understand the technicalities, but a broken leg was a broken leg, and the bit about internal injuries did not sound good at all.

Charlie Strong walked past Steve's bed looking sorry for himself. Steve asked him what was wrong? I'm suffering from Cereal / Porridge Syndrome, said Charlie, and he hurried off to take some of his pink medicine. Charlie could always be relied upon for a little light relief in times of stress!

The small training camp had a very military style austere church, but there was a standing invitation for any soldier to attend services in the local village. Steve, along with other platoon members decided to accept the local vicar's invitation, if only to give thanks for surviving the cliff climbing and abseiling.

The village pub was closed for the Sabbath, and the landlady and her husband attended the service. The 'Monster' was dressed in her usual conservative tweed, and her husband looked quite 'dapper' in a pin stripe suit and red cravat, his grey hair smoothed down with plenty of 'Brylcream'.

The village church was small but 'homely' and like the chapel at 'Morval' barracks had been enhanced by the ingenuity of the vicar and his church helpers. Before the main sermon, given by the vicar, the pub landlady, who was a lay preacher, gave a short talk praising the virtues of sobriety in an ever increasingly self-indulgent society! Her husband almost applauded when she had finished, but contented himself by turning to the congregation and smiling slyly!

After the service the recruits returned to camp for lunch at the cookhouse and enjoyed more Scottish 'cuisine'. On the menu was 'Haggis', turnips and roast potatoes. Haggis was a new dish for all of them, and more aware of its contents. But together with the well-cooked turnips and potatoes made a good satisfying meal. It being Sunday the corporal cook had been inspired to produce a very commendable 'meringue' for dessert. Scotland was proving to be a very acceptable place indeed!

The rest of the day was spent preparing uniforms and other 'kit' for the start of the second week's training in Scotland. This would be S.A.B. (Small assault Boat) training. After the rigours of trekking, climbing, and abseiling, the thought of 'messing' about in boats was a welcome change.

The next day, parade time was a respectable 08.00 hrs and the platoon had plenty of time to enjoy breakfast, unlike the previous week that was had been a hectic time from start to finish. The cook corporal had come to accept Steve mixing fresh fruit with his porridge, and simply walked straight past the table on his rounds. Some of the other 'foreigners' had noticed Steve's fruity enhancement of the porridge and followed his lead. Some of the younger Scots also looked upon the dish with some interest. Steve had possibly started a new military trend!

The boat training was to be held on an isolated part of Loch Ness. A small secluded boathouse provided sanctuary for four S.A.B.'s. The powerful 'Evinrude' outboard motors however, were kept at the camp, and had to be transported each day to the loch. The highly powered 'Evinrudes' were expensive items and had to be guarded from some of the more unscrupulous 'Clansmen'! The boats themselves were made of lightweight aluminium, covered with multi-skin, thick canvas. They were very strong, and carried up to eight fully armed assault troops, plus a coxswain.

The platoon paraded at 08.00, and after a brief inspection by Sgt. McNiff they marched to a nearby warehouse and loaded four 'Evinrudes' onto the waiting 'Bedford'. There was a generally more relaxed atmosphere in the platoon as there was something inviting about playing about in boats, regardless of the seriousness of the training. Four 'jerry' cans of petrol, life jackets, and a dozen wooden paddles in case of engine failure made up the load. They clambered aboard the lorry, already feeling like seasoned mariners!

It was a short half hour journey to the loch, and they drove straight to the boathouse where four junior N.C.O.'s acting as coxswains were waiting for them. The coxswains would be in charge of the boats, and responsible for the safety of the men in their respective assault craft. Two of the coxswains had been seconded from the Argyle's the other two from the Cameron Highlanders. Sgt. McNiff would control operations from the shore, fortified by his ever present 'water bottle'! McNiff was 'at home' with trekking and cliffs, but not totally enamoured with water in any great depth! Steve began to understand the man and his show of 'super fitness'; he was only flesh and blood after all!

The S.A.B.'s, although fairly large were easily carried by two men, and the four boats were quickly taken from the boathouse and launched onto the still waters of the loch. The powerful outboard motors were off-loaded, and under the scrutiny of the coxswains clamped to the sterns of the boats. Safety chains were also attached from boat frame to engine in case of any mishap.

The Scottish weather continued to be pleasant, the sun quite warm and the sky clear. Getting wet feet launching the S.A.B.'s was acceptable, but it would be a different story in mid-winter with snow and ice cold water. The platoon was divided into four sections, each section being assigned to a particular boat. A competitive spirit would be nurtured by the corporal coxswains as the week progressed, making the training more enjoyable and productive.

The first day was spent trying to board the boats without capsizing them, learning the basics of craft handling, and control of the massive 'Evinrudes'. Being afloat reminded Steve of the Serpentine and Lorraine, an 'Evinrude' would have been exciting, but 'Popeye' would not have been pleased!

The training was fairly light-hearted; it was difficult to take 'messing' about in the boats seriously. Even McNiff seemed to be enjoying the proceedings from the shore, together with his 'water bottle' to quench his thirst!

In the late afternoon, after a long but enjoyable day, the motors were un-clamped from the S.A.B.'s and loaded onto the truck. The boats were returned to the boathouse and placed under lock and key for the night. The coxswains, pleased with the day's work, returned to camp with the platoon, and after an evening meal would be carrying out maintenance on the 'Evinrudes', ready for the next day's training.

The 'sea air' gave them all good appetites, and they enjoyed a meal in the cookhouse before strolling to the N.A.A.F.I. for a pint of the dark brew. They all felt relaxed after the day's training, but Charlie Strong did complain of slight sea-sickness! Steve thought to himself smilingly that Charlie would have been no good on the 'choppy' Serpentine! After a second pint of the brew and a steak pie to round off the day they enjoyed a good mariner's sleep!

The second day was spent learning more seamanship and craft husbandry. The boat hulls were inspected for any damage, and engine maintenance was studied. Spark plugs were removed from the 'Evinrudes', cleaned, and the electrode gaps meticulously checked and reset using the set of 'feelers' supplied. Propellers and shafts, and the all-important engine safety chains were checked for security. Sgt. McNiff took a 'back-seat' in the instruction proceedings, but at the same time kept a watchful eye on the junior N.C.O.'s and their words of instruction.

After another satisfying day and returning the S.A.B.'s to the safety of the boathouse, they left Loch Ness to its mysterious long neck monster and returned to camp. The platoon enjoyed a meal of 'Tattie soup' and 'Stovies' (potato soup and beef leftovers with onions). Later, Steve decided to shower, change into 'civvies' and walk into the village and phone Lorraine. There was plenty to talk about, and he missed the comforting sound of her understanding, bedside manner, doctor's voice. He had not talked to her for almost a week, and although he was engrossed in the training, his thoughts were still of her and their London weekend inspired relationship. He armed himself with the usual small change for the telephone and made his way to the village.

It was a pleasant walk, with little traffic on the roads, and any cars that did pass were travelling in a tranquil manner, in unison with the quiet surrounding countryside. Steve felt at peace with the world; he would shortly be talking to the special angel in his life. The thought of the king-size bath, and her silken body sliding onto his, made his heart flutter with joy.

Steve checked his watch. It was probably early for Lorraine to be at home after finishing college. He checked the amount of money in his pocket and decided to go to the village pub opposite the phone box for a quick pint of beer. A certain amount of 'Dutch' courage was welcome to assist the proceedings; telephone conversations could be very demanding!

Steve's feline friend, the 'Tom cat' was holding court in the lounge bar, accepting the attentions of the clients' fur stroking in an aloof 'monarchical way', as cats do.

Many of the locals Steve had seen in church were in the bar enjoying their favourite beverage. He ordered a pint of the dark brew from the landlady, and after paying, picked up his glass and said a polite, "Thanks."

To his surprise she replied, "You're welcome," and almost smiled.

Steve found a vacant table and sat down, grateful to rest his legs, but mystified by the 'Monster's' sudden friendliness. He concluded that it must be due to his attendance at the church, proving that he was not a complete foreign heathen after all! The cat appeared at the table, jumped up and nudged Steve's arm before settling down and going to sleep. Suddenly Steve felt more at home.

He quietly sipped his beer, not wanting to disturb his feline friend who had fallen into a relaxed slumber. Steve stayed as long as was possible, but the hour was racing by, and it was soon time to phone Lorraine. The ginger 'Tom' slept on, unaware of the increasing urgency. He carefully removed his arm from the cat, returned his empty glass to the bar and walked across the street to the phone box. It was a luxury not to have to queue for the use of a telephone box, and he silently wished the people queueing at the 'red sentinel', well. He glanced at his watch, took the small change from his pocket and dialled the number. Lorraine answered almost at once, and they talked endlessly for twenty minutes, there was so much to say!

Lorraine was taking her exams which were going quite well, but unfortunately her mother, who lived some distance away had been taken ill, which had put some extra pressure on Lorraine. Steve felt guilty that he was not in Hampshire, and able to help her in a time of crisis. But Lorraine was coping with the circumstances; she was ideal 'doctor' material. They talked for a further ten minutes, but towards the end of the conversation Steve detected a change in the tone of her voice. It was as if she was mentally trying to distance herself from him. They said goodnight in the usual way, but as Steve put the phone down he sensed something was wrong.

He walked back to the pub and ordered another beer. The landlady smiled at him as he paid his money, and he was grateful for that. The cat was still asleep on the table and awoke as Steve sat down, unaware that he had left. Steve stroked the ginger Tom, more in self-comfort than anything else. He continued to mull over the conversation with Lorraine, and suddenly remembered a talk he had with her previously about the future, and saying that after training he could be posted anywhere in the world. Perhaps Lorraine had taken more time to think about that statement. He finished his beer, said goodnight to the cat, and returned to camp. He went to his bed a troubled man, a seed of doubt had been planted in his mind.

The next day training resumed, and Steve put the problem at the back of his mind. Concerned as he was, he needed to concentrate on the current training.

Having completed the basis of seamanship, the platoon started to train for actual rapid assault beach landings. Rapid assault landings were designed to gain as great a surprise element as possible against an enemy force. Properly executed, the landings could be very effective, but needed much practice and teamwork.

Over the next two days the platoon practised the manoeuvre many times, and gradually became proficient, albeit with wet feet. For the final day of training a competition was planned. All four boats would compete against each other, the winning team being treated to an evening of free beer at the N.A.A.F.I., paid for by the losing crews!

CHAPTER 24

The final day of training arrived with the assault boat competition.

Charlie Strong expected 'severe turbulence' on the loch during the race, and had visited a chemist in the nearby town to purchase sea-sickness pills. In the platoon's twelve days in Scotland it had been the only time Charlie had left the camp and ventured alone onto 'foreign' parts. Steve gave him instructions on how to find the shop, and Charlie used the opportunity to re-stock his 'larder' with more pills and potions. He was a good customer to the chemists, no matter which town, or country he was in. But where he bought his vile pink anti-meatball medicine remained a mystery. Perhaps it was one of his own concoctions; the bottle suspiciously never carried a label!

Interest in the competition had increased dramatically, and Steve drew his boat team together in the N.A.A.F.I. to discuss strategy over a pint or two of the dark brew. The thought of an evening's free beer was incentive indeed, although Mac insisted that steak and kidney pies should also have been included in the prize.

As interest grew, little 'side' bets were placed. The 'Lawyer' promoted himself to 'Bookmaker' and made good use of his notebook and mathematical knowledge. He was no fool where money was concerned, and made sure of his ten percent profit in the dealings.

Steve, although not a gambling man, ventured two shillings each way on the race. In the N.A.A.F.I., during the evening's relaxation, the competitive spirit unfortunately over-spilled after several pints of the brew had been consumed, and a certain amount of robust fisticuffs ensued. After intervention by the camp police, Mac and another member of the platoon spent the night sleeping off their 'competitive spirit' in the guardroom cells.

The next morning in the barrack room there was talk that somebody was planning to 'spike' one of the 'Evinrudes' in order to reduce the gambling odds for the race. Docherty, with his vast experience in Liverpool of tampering with vehicles as a slightly renegade teenager, suggested that an efficient way to 'nobble' a petrol engine was to put some 'Tate and Lyle' in the fuel tank. Steve dismissed the 'spiking' theory as gossip; the engines were under lock and key in the warehouse after all!

The skirl of the bagpipes heralded the morning, and the boat competition. The pipes had become emotionally acceptable first thing in the morning, and after washing and shaving, breakfast of porridge and fruit was taken in the cookhouse. Somehow the boat teams had distanced themselves from each other. The competitive spirit had taken hold, and money talked! During breakfast Steve's team adopted his theory of eating bananas for energy.

The only exception was Mac who said, "You look like a load of 'ruddy' monkeys in the jungle!"

The 'Lawyer' in between bananas, continued to take bets. He was coming to the conclusion that he had wasted his talent studying law for two years when other professions could be more lucrative!

The following day, Sunday, would be Sgt. McNiff's birthday, and he had taken the unprecedented step of inviting the whole platoon to a celebration at a pub in a nearby town. The senior instructors normally stayed aloof of the trainees for discipline reasons, but training was almost over; the party in the evening would be a time for the men to let 'their hair down' before returning to 'Morval' on Monday. McNiff had grown to like the platoon and its unusual characters, and he recognised that when the individuals were put together as a unit, they were a 'bit special'! They were all looking forward to the party, but there was the little matter of settling the boat race first!

Charlie armed himself with plenty of his sea-sickness pills from the chemist. The shop assistant had asked him if he was going on an Atlantic cruise, but Charlie was reticent to answer. The other men in Steve's boat had eaten a good energising breakfast, and were ready for the competition. Some had wagered relatively large amounts of money on the race, and were in no mood to come second and have to subsidise free drinks in the N.A.A.F.I. for whoever won.

As the platoon was preparing for the 8.00am parade, Docherty strode into the barrack room and announced, quite proudly, that two pounds of sugar was missing from the cookhouse food store!

The weather was starting to break up, and dark clouds were beginning to form in the distant hills. They had enjoyed a good two weeks, but the forecast for the next two days was not optimistic. The loch surface could turn out to be very choppy for the race. Perhaps Charlie was wise to buy his pills after all!

After the routine parade and inspection, the platoon marched to the warehouse and loaded the four 'Evinrudes' onto the 'Bedford'. The petrol 'jerry' cans were filled and sealed against tampering. Steve kept in mind the fact that sugar had gone missing from the cookhouse, and it possibly wasn't simply to satisfy somebody's sweet tooth. During the short journey to the loch there was much light-hearted banter about the race, but from time to time Steve had fleeting thoughts about his last telephone conversation with Lorraine, and it still troubled him. The engines were unloaded and the S.A.B.'s carefully carried from the boathouse. Then the engines had been secured onto the boat sterns by the corporal coxswains, Steve posting one of his team to stand by his boat's engine, just in case of any type of skulduggery. After final instructions by Sgt. McNiff the teams boarded their boats and spent twenty minutes circling the loch to 'warm-up' the 'Evinrudes'.

Steve 'sorted' his crew out to provide the best trim for the boat. It was preferable that the stern was fairly low in the water in order to allow the propeller blades to 'bite' into the water. The bow of the S.A.B. needed to be high and out of the water. Mac and his like, being fairly weighty, were placed in the stern, and Charlie Strong, the 'Lawyer' and Docherty took up the bow positions. Steve and two other middleweights filled mid-ships.

When the 'enemy' beach was reached it was essential that the men disembarked in a speedy, but controlled way, and not in a mad scramble. Precious seconds could be won or lost. The winning team would be the first that safely landed its crew onto the shore. The time would be taken when the last man in the boat set foot on dry land. Sgt. McNiff would be the judge of that, and carried a stop watch for that purpose.

After the coxswains were satisfied that all was well in their respective boats, they signalled to McNiff that they were ready to race. Sgt. McNiff stood on the shoreline red flag in one hand, 'water bottle' in the other! McNiff brought the flag down sharply and the sudden roar of the four 'Evinrudes' could be heard across the wide loch. Charlie and Docherty were thrown backwards by the sudden surge of the S.A.B., and landed on top of Steve and the other men in mid-ships. The coxswain swore and Charlie and Docherty scrambled back to the bow.

The coxswain, annoyed at the disturbance in the boat, opened the engine throttle fully and the S.A.B. lifted out of the water and began to aquaplane. Steve glanced across at the other boats. Two of them were at least half a length ahead. Speed was increasing rapidly on slightly choppy waters that had been whipped up by the action of the boats and an increasing worsening of the weather. Charlie thought about reaching in his pocket for more pills, but his white knuckled hands would not let go of the bow! The shore seemed to be racing towards them at an alarming rate! Steve looked again at the other boats, they were all 'neck and neck' now, and the noise from the 'Evinrudes' was deafening.

The boat's speed increased even further and Steve was certain that they would end up in the bushes and trees that surrounded the loch's shoreline. When the S.A.B. was thirty feet from the shore the coxswain slammed the engine controls into reverse to decelerate the boat before striking the 'enemy' beach. The tortured engine's gearbox screamed in protest, and the engine tore itself from the stern securing clamps. It leapt a clear two feet into the air, and disappeared into the waters of the loch! There was a deathly silence and anti-climax as the other coxswains realised what had happened and shut their engines down. The corporal coxswain looked at the empty stern in disbelief. In his excitement for the race he had forgotten to secure the 'Evinrudes' safety chains!

In a moment of panic the coxswain stripped off his boots and dived into the loch in a vain attempt to retrieve the engine. But it was a forlorn gesture; the loch was deep and the water cloudy where it had been churned up by the racing propellers.

Sgt. McNiff, after the initial shock, had regained his senses, and after a quick reviving drink from his 'water bottle' started pacing up and down the shoreline shouting expletives at the offending coxswain, who appeared to be in a state of 'sodden' shock!

There was not a lot that Steve and the rest of the crew could do, but Steve noticed that there were two wooden paddles strapped to the inside of the boat. After unbuckling the leather straps, he and Mac paddled the S.A.B. to shore. The race was quickly forgotten, and Sgt. McNiff ordered a marker buoy to be dropped into the area where the 'Evinrude' had disappeared. The coxswain avoided McNiff's eyes as much as possible and inspected the safety chains for broken links. But the fault was totally his, and there would be much explaining to do!

The remaining three 'Evinrudes' were loaded onto the 'Bedford', and with it they had a sense of loss and defeat. The fourth engine had been part of the team, and it was lost in the deep waters of the loch. As they were about to leave, a dark green 'Land Rover' appeared carrying the loch sheriff. He was dressed in traditional kilt and tunic, and sported a well-worn deerstalker hat. A clay pipe protruded from his mouth, and Steve could detect the distinct aroma of moist 'Erinmore' tobacco.

The sheriff had been watching the scene from the opposite shore, and had witnessed the drama. Sgt. McNiff had to explain to him that they had just dropped an expensive piece of equipment into his loch. The water 'bailiff' looked at McNiff and nodded, took the clay pipe from his mouth and drove off, noting where the marker buoy was!

The journey back to the camp was subdued; the day had not been a great success, to say the least. All of the bets were off, and the 'Lawyer' reluctantly agreed to return the stake money. Maybe becoming a solicitor would have been a better profession; they seldom gave money back, whatever the circumstances!

McNiff sat in the rear of the lorry, and continued to 'bend' the offending coxswain's ear. The corporal, being a 'captive' audience, silently wished he was back with the Camerons! Sgt. McNiff decided to contact a nearby naval base as soon as they reached camp. The base was a training camp for Royal Navy divers, and they would probably welcome the chance of engaging in some practical work. In the back of his mind he remembered the loch sheriff's knowing look, and wished he had not divulged the engine's whereabouts. It may be a case of 'who dives first'!

Sgt. McNiff reported to the C.O. as soon as they arrived at the camp, and received the 'dressing down' he had fully expected. The corporal coxswain also felt the lash of the C.O.'s tongue, and was informed that his 'misdemeanour' would be put onto his official record. An official 'black mark' was not good if he expected to rise to the rank of sergeant one day.

The remaining three engines were cleaned and inspected before being returned to the safety of the warehouse. Charlie Strong had injured his wrist in the 'melee' on the boat, and reported sick. This time it was a legitimate ailment, and the M.O. welcomed him as if he was a breath of fresh air! Charlie returned, his wrist tightly bandaged and his arm in a sling. He received some sympathy from the platoon, but there was always a question mark about his visits to the surgery. The 'Lawyer' likened it to the Dutch boy sticking his finger in the dyke. When Mac asked Steve what he was talking about, Steve held up his hands and smiled!

After a shower and welcome meal of 'mince tatties' and skirlie in the cookhouse, the platoon retired to the N.A.A.F.I. for some much needed dark brew. The talk was naturally about the day's main event, losing the expensive 'Evinrude'. Steve felt sorry for the coxswain, he was obviously a responsible person, and he would not have been promoted to corporal otherwise. But the one 'slip' could cost him dearly in his efforts for promotion in the future, once it was in 'black and white' there was no going back.

Through the camp 'grapevine' they learnt that two navy divers had made a search of the loch, but there was no sign of the engine. The C.O. reluctantly reported the 'Evinrude' missing to the Garrison Commander, and contemplated the thought of much less 'Beaujolais' in the Officers' Mess for some time to come until the deficit was cleared.

As the beer flowed in the N.A.A.F.I. the men came to the very logical conclusion that the engine had been devoured by the 'Loch Ness Monster' in order to maintain its levels of iron! Either that or the 'twinkle' in the loch keeper's eye was not just a 'twinkle'!

The next morning the platoon was woken by the piper at 6.00am. His pipes sounded more lamentable than usual. He was possibly in mourning over the loss of the 'Evinrude'! Steve and the platoon were equally thoughtful, and it was sad that the two weeks' training should end on a low note.

After breakfast they attended a talk given by the C.O. which marked the official end of advanced training. No mention was made of the lost engine, but the corporal coxswain was very conspicuous by his absence. The men decided to forget the last twenty-four hours and move onto McNiff's birthday celebration in the forthcoming evening.

CHAPTER 25

Sgt. McNiff was a single man who had devoted his life to the army. He had joined the service as a boy soldier at the age of sixteen, and when he was eighteen years was transferred to the 'Black Watch'. Providing that he attained the rank of Warrant Officer, which was quite foreseeable, he could look forward to retiring into civilian life with a considerable military pension. It would ensure a good standard of living for him at a mature age, providing that 'Johnny Walker' did not look too closely over his shoulder!

By inviting the platoon to his birthday celebration he considered that it would give the evening a certain amount of substance, and with the help of a few 'drams' make it a party to remember. He had bribed the transport corporal into allowing him the use of the camp 'Bedford' to transfer all concerned to a hostelry in the nearby town. But the corporal, having had previous experience of Sgt. McNiff's parties, insisted that they find their own way back to camp when the celebration concluded. He vividly remembered one occasion when several ladies of 'ill repute' were found to be 'cavorting' with the overly 'merry' male party goers in the rear of the 'Bedford' as it entered the camp at 3.00am. The orderly officer had not been amused, and to date McNiff's ceremonial kilt and sporran had not been found!

Since being barred from the village pub by the 'Loch Ness Monster', McNiff had become friendly with the landlord of a sizeable hostelry in the nearby town. McNiff was an ardent Glasgow Rangers fan. The landlord, also a keen supporter of the football club was happy to host the sergeant's birthday celebration in his spacious lounge bar, which was fully adorned with blue and white Rangers' memorabilia. The prize possession was a football used in a Scottish Cup final when Rangers beat Glasgow Celtic 2-1.

In the afternoon the platoon had packed their kit in readiness for the long journey back to 'Morval' barracks in Hampshire on Monday morning. As they carefully placed their belongings in the kitbags to avoid more ironing at 'Morval' they were reminded of the cookhouse corporal's meat balls, the grubby N.A.A.F.I. curtains and the 'Blonde Bombshell', with her provocative swirling skirt, and heavy make-up.

The three-ton lorry was due to leave the camp gates for the party at 7.00pm sharp. The platoon made themselves ready before going for a last dinner in the cookhouse. The cooks, knowing the 'foreigners' were leaving the next day had excelled themselves and produced a very tasty meal of 'cockaleekie' soup and 'mince tatties' with skirlie, followed by the cookhouse corporal's lemon meringue speciality. After the meal a 'dram' of Scotch whisky was offered to each of the platoon as a parting gesture. The cooks, including the corporal, also took a 'dram' and the two 'Old Enemies' drank a toast together for 'Auld Lang Syne'!

After a preparatory pint of the dark brew in the N.A.A.F.I. the men boarded the waiting 'Bedford' at the main gates. The usual ribald remarks were aimed at the sentry on duty as the lorry left the camp, and he replied with a vigorous two fingered gesture, making sure that the orderly officer was not watching at the time.

They settled themselves into the lorry for the short journey to town. Charlie Strong was his usual disorganised self in his appearance, but in the main the men looked smart for the party. It was only when they were dressed in 'civvies' that their individuality came to the fore. Army uniform was very restricting in that way and one soldier looked very much like another.

Steve wore his new M&S white shirt with beige slacks and polished black shoes. Docherty, whose hair had almost recovered from the attentions of 'Sweeney Todd', had fashioned his locks into a 'Rock 'n' Roll' style, assisted by plenty of 'Brylcream'. He wore a high necked shirt, and his trousers were slim fitting 'drain pipes'! His thick soled shoes looked gigantic against the slim fitting trousers, and were known to people in the fashion trade as 'Brothel Creepers'! From somewhere he had found a gold coloured neck chain with a piece of jewellery in the shape of a guitar attached. With his cheeky 'Scouse' manner he had Liverpool written all over him!

Taff was more conservative, with a light yellow shirt, dark slacks and green necktie. Mac was content with plain shirt and slacks plus easy fitting suede shoes; beer and food was important to him, not dress! For once, the 'Lawyer' decided to leave his notebook and pencil in the barrack room, but his thoughts of the evening would be transferred to paper at a later date.

The men had 'clubbed' together and bought McNiff a small birthday gift. It was difficult to know what to buy; they knew so little about him. The sergeant was not a cigarette smoker, but Steve had seen him enjoying a small cigar from time to time, and they bought him a presentation box of 'Manikins'. Charlie Strong had donated one of his large brown paper bags from the chemists, and the box was carefully wrapped and everybody signed their name on the package. In a strange way the brown paper bag reminded Steve of McVeigh back at 'Morval' barracks and the sight of him being escorted out of the camp by two military policemen. He was a pathetic creature, but Steve silently wished that McVeigh was a better man, and had been there to enjoy the party in his own native land.

It was not a long journey to town, but uncomfortable when sat on the truck's solid wooden bench seats and they were all glad to reach the pub. The hostelry was a fairly large granite building, with dark oak beams set into the white walls. It looked almost English Tudor in style which was unusual considering Scotland's relationship in the past with the English kings!

At the rear of the pub was a cobblestone courtyard, and the 'Bedford' drove through the open steel gates. The men, sensing the aroma of beer, quickly climbed down from the truck and made strides towards the lounge bar, Mac to the fore! The truck driver made a three-point turn in the courtyard and the 'Bedford' returned to camp. They would not see it again that day, and as agreed, every man would make his own way back to camp when the celebration ended. Steve had heard about McNiff's previous parties, and could see a very late night ahead!

As Steve walked across the very ancient courtyard he could imagine its history. In the distant past many a 'coach and four' had used the inn and its sleeping facilities. He could almost see the coach, and its four horses, sweating from a long tiring journey. The coach driver, sat aloft, horse whip in hand and his knees covered by a thick tartan blanket against the harsh Scottish winter. His 'post horn' assistant, also suitably clad, would be sat beside him, and for just a moment perhaps, Steve imagined that he caught a glimpse of 'Bonnie Prince Charlie', tentatively peering out of the coach window, protective pistol in hand against the king's men!

Steve went into the spacious lounge where Sgt. McNiff was greeting his guests for the evening. He already had a glass in hand, and as he sipped his whisky his little finger protruded outwards in a show of drinking etiquette. The lounge was a perfect setting for the party. Six of the varnished wooden tables were fitted together to form one long banqueting table, and were surrounded by leather cushioned chairs with arm rests. The banqueting table was covered with crispy, starched white tablecloths, and platters of potato crisps, freshly made sandwiches and nuts. Unusually, plates of sticks of celery, sliced beetroot and pickled onions completed the table's adornment. The landlord had done them proud.

Sgt. McNiff introduced the platoon to their landlord host. He was a fairly rotund man in his fifties, and went by the name of James (Jimmy) McBride. After a fairly long conversation it became obvious that there were two things in life that mattered to Jimmy, firstly football, and secondly, football! He had followed Rangers football club for as long as he could remember. His wife, a buxom blonde who worked behind the bar, was also a fanatical Rangers supporter, and as a young girl had attended all of the club's home matches with her father. Their life was the pub and football, little else mattered! On Saturdays during the football season, the day was set aside for supporting Rangers. With a long standing agreement, 'Jimmy's' brother and wife minded the pub in their absence. Each Saturday some of the Rangers memorabilia was taken from the lounge walls and served a good practical purpose for the day. The pub was run well, and had a good, regular clientele and money was not a problem, and Jimmy paid his brother well for the Saturday service.

The bar staff were already filling the long table with pint jars of beer, and the serious business of celebration began in earnest. Steve presented McNiff with the box of 'Manikins' and the sergeant offered the box around after thanking the platoon for the gift. He was obviously moved by the gesture, and the senior N.C.O./recruit relationship was beginning to soften for the evening! None of the young recruits had taken to cigars, but the generous offer was noted. Docherty did accept a cigar, but only to give the party his impression of the American film comedian Groucho Marx. He had perfected Groucho's stooping walk, and it was obviously one of his party 'pieces'! It was a good start to the party, and being the extrovert that he was, there was possibly more to come later in the evening.

The lounge began to fill with the locals who had taken tables in other parts of the large room. The party began to 'warm-up', and after Steve's third pint of the dark brew, followed by whisky 'chasers', he was certain he could hear the clatter of a coach and four horses entering the cobblestone courtyard! He would not have been surprised to see 'Bonnie Prince Charlie' walk through the closed lounge doors, his trusty pistol in one hand and a 'dram' in the other.

Docherty decided to follow up his 'Groucho' impression by presenting his lounge audience with the benefit of his vocal experience in Liverpool's 'dens of iniquity' (pubs). After introducing himself, quite professionally to the locals, he offered them his rendition of 'Blue Suede Shoes', followed in direct contrast with his impression of Al Jolson singing his great hit 'Sonny Boy'! Many of the lounge audience were of 'mature' age, and able to relate with the American artist's song. Docherty, like all good entertainers, 'knew' his audience, and 'played' to them accordingly. His performance brought many a tear of joy to the audience, but looking at them, Steve could not be certain whether they were tears of pleasure, or simply relief that Docherty's act was finished! Nonetheless, he was proving to be the 'life and soul' of the party, and in some ways Steve felt envious of his talent. Steve knew just two party jokes, and when he told them, more often than not, made a complete mess of the punch line. Docherty was a master of timing, and had a God given gift!

Steve looked across the room at Docherty who was down on one knee, 'milking' the applause from his audience. It was strange how Liverpudlians had a natural talent for entertainment and comedy. Perhaps it was the warmth and talkative Irish trait in their character. Many of their ancestors had crossed the Irish Sea in the past, settling in Liverpool to escape the potato famine.

Sgt. McNiff, not to be outdone at his own party, arose, fairly unsteadily from his seat and proceeded to entertain the celebration with his melodic version of 'I belong to Glasgow', followed by 'The road and miles to Dundee'. Most of the platoon knew the words to 'I belong to Glasgow', and joined in with enthusiasm, but the 'Dundee' song was new to most of them, and they listened to McNiff with a 'foreigner's' interest. McNiff was in fine voice after several 'Johnny Walkers', and when he returned to his seat they applauded him soundly, as did the other appreciative locals in the lounge, the party was going well!

The locals were starting to 'integrate' into the party and were enjoying the atmosphere as much as the platoon. Some, aware that free drinks were on offer, moved their chairs closer to the banqueting table, and eventually the whole lounge was one big party!

Charlie Strong had taken the precaution of bringing a small bottle of his 'yeast' tablets with him in case of emergencies! He placed them carefully on the table in front of him, next to his pint of dark brew and whisky 'chaser'. McNiff had insisted that Charlie followed each beer with a whisky 'chaser', saying it was good for his health. Charlie was never a man to go against good medical advice, and he found the 'Johnny Walker' 'therapeutic'.

One of the local 'elders', who was purported to be a poacher, had, like

McNiff, been banned from the village pub for selling pheasants of dubious background in the saloon bar. The local 'squire' had long complained that his shooting stock was being depleted, and the 'Loch Ness Monster' was intent on putting the matter right!

The poacher, aware that free drinks were on offer, moved his chair closer to the banqueting table, and Charlie's chair. The poacher nonchalantly picked up one of the glasses of beer on the table, and asked Charlie what the 'wee brown tablets' were. Charlie, sensing a mutually interested person, explained in great detail his medical requirements, and finished by saying he was going through a twenty-five year 'transitional' period. The 'poacher' stared deeply at Charlie and nodded to himself. He had just had his opinion of foreigners reaffirmed. The poacher continued asking Charlie for medical advice, whilst partaking of the free beer and whisky.

A young woman walked up to the table and spoke to McNiff. He stood up, hugged her, and introduced her as his niece Moira. A space at the table was quickly made for her and a chair brought from another table. Moira looked a cheerful girl, with jet black hair and a pleasant outdoor complexion. Steve guessed that she would be in her early twenties, perhaps twenty-two, or three. She had an extrovert, sensual air about her, and Steve found her interesting. They all returned to the business of celebration, and Steve looked across the table at McNiff who was busy imbibing in the 'Johnny Walker', his little finger engaging in the social etiquette as usual; certain standards had to be maintained!

The banqueting table was overflowing with food, beer and whisky. The celebration was costing McNiff much money, and Steve concluded the trek pontoon business must be doing very well.

Steve was sitting almost opposite Moira, but the table was wide and the noise in the lounge made it impossible to converse. He caught her eye, and smiled across at her. She in turn smiled back, nodded hello, and said something, but the noise in the lounge blotted her words out.

Steve was later to learn that her second name was Theodopolis and that Moira's father had been a Greek sailor who visited the port of Aberdeen on regular occasions. He had met, courted and married Moira's Scottish mother, and settled in Scotland to raise a family. Moira had one brother, Andrea, but he had returned to Greece to live in his native land. Moira was a more flexible, outgoing person, and was quite happy to live and work in Scotland. McNiff ordered more beer and whisky, plus a large shandy for his niece. The platoon had seen little female company in the past eight weeks, and they were pleased to have Moira with them. She in turn was happy to be the centre of attention, and the party was further enhanced.

Sgt. McNiff rose unsteadily to his feet and announced in a solemn manner that it was time to toast and consume the birthday haggis. He waved a beckoning hand to his landlord friend who was serving drinks at the bar with his buxom cheerful wife. He duly arrived carrying the huge haggis on a large silver platter. To the platoon it looked like a large Christmas pudding, but its contents would be far removed. The haggis was served on small blue and white plates, in keeping with the Rangers theme of the lounge. The platoon nibbled tentatively on the delicacy, and washed down with plenty of the dark brew it proved to be quite palatable.

As the evening wore on Moira dispensed with the shandies and took a liking to a liqueur called 'Drambuie'. After several glasses, she and McNiff, who was equally 'relaxed', decided to demonstrate a Scottish reel for the benefit of the 'foreign' visitors. McNiff was extremely nimble on his feet and had a natural talent for dance. Moira's interpretation of the reel was half Scottish and half traditional Greek, having been taught by her father when a young girl.

Mac, not to be outdone by the Scots, staggered to his feet and started a 'Conga' line dance around the lounge. The line quickly increased and gathered momentum, the lounge double doors were opened, and the 'Conga' went out into the street. The only people left in the lounge were McNiff and Moira, completely lost in their reel, and unaware they were dancing alone.

At bar closing time the landlord closed the outer doors and secured them. Inside the party continued unabated. Sometime later two policemen peered around the rear door. The landlord waved his arm at them, as if to say, 'no problem here'! The policemen waved back and left for the peace and quiet of the police station.

Sgt. McNiff looked at his watch; it was time for his birthday speech. He rose, very unsteadily to his feet and withdrew a piece of paper from his tunic pocket. McNiff was not a good speaker, he was happier when trekking or climbing, but a celebration speech was essential.

McNiff looked at his slightly crumpled sheet of paper and started to speak, but his words were slurred, and coupled with his strong accent, they were almost unrecognisable. He tried saying the word 'congratulatory' three times, but without success. After the fourth attempt he admitted defeat and slowly sank back down to his leather cushioned seat. The haggis had taken its toll!

Steve had stopped counting the number of beers and whisky 'chasers' he had consumed. He didn't feel drunk, but his mouth and the tips of his fingers felt numb, as if they had been immersed in a bucket of ice. He vaguely became aware of someone tapping on his shoulder. He turned to see Moira smiling down at him. Steve returned the warm smile. She looked radiant, and her cheeks were aflame from the heat in the lounge and possibly the effect of the liqueur. She nodded her head, and her eyes said, 'you're the one'! Moira grabbed his arm, and he allowed himself to be hauled from his comfortable seat. They held hands and walked out into the solitude of the cobblestone courtyard, she taking the lead, a sense of purpose in her stride. Steve shook off the effects of the alcohol, and as he walked out of the lounge there was a feeling of expectancy in the night air!

It was almost dark in the courtyard and Steve looked around him. They were alone, and they stood by one of the stone walls. The sound of the party was muffled by the high walls; they had only walked a few yards but they were in a totally different atmosphere.

They held each other and he kissed her gently. Moira responded in a positive manner, forcing her mouth and lips onto his. Steve had momentary thoughts of Lorraine, but the whisky and his own masculine desire took over. Tomorrow he would feel guilty, but tomorrow was another day, and he was only flesh and blood.

Moira ran her fingers over his white shirt, feeling his strong chest. He replied by fondling her warm breasts. She wore no 'bra', and her breasts although ample were firm to the touch. She grabbed at his shirt in her rising passion, and one of the buttons tore from the material as she fought to touch the skin of his chest. (Steve made a mental note to complain to M&S about the quality of their workmanship). But Grecians could be very strong when sexually aroused! She squeezed his chest, and they kissed passionately, becoming oblivious to their surroundings. Moira was 'all woman'. The 'Drambuie' and Steve's masculine presence had unlocked her sexual passion.

Steve lifted her skirt and slowly pulled down her scanty, frilly panties. He felt her pubic hair, the curly tufts moist from her emotion. She started to moan in pleasure as he caressed her womanhood, and he slid a finger into her and deftly touched her clitoris. Moira moved her body in rhythm with his caresses, and she was in a different world.

Steve's own passion grew, and he forced her against the stone wall. The granite was cold on her buttocks, and enhanced her pleasure. She kissed him, and dug her teeth into the flesh of his shoulder, almost like a vampire demanding blood! She unzipped the front of his beige trousers and forced her hand into his underpants. Her slender fingers stroked him, and he was massive now. She guided him into her, and they shared a totally joyful carnal love. Her buttocks ground against the granite wall, and the skin became raw from her passionate movements.

Moira's body suddenly erupted, shaking violently, as if by a gigantic earthquake. She clung tightly to his shoulders as her knees grew weak from the massive climax. When their passion had subsided he kissed her gently. It was a kiss of love, and understanding of a woman's needs. At this moment in time she would have given her life for his continued love and affection.

Steve regained control of himself and glanced around the still courtyard. If 'Bonnie Prince Charlie' was to peer out of his carriage window now, he would be fraught with envy at the romantic scene, and not concerned with the ever searching 'king's men'!

Steve and Moira stayed locked together in the quietness of the dark courtyard, neither wanting time to move on.

CHAPTER 26

In the early hours of the morning Steve made his way back to camp. He 'hitched' a ride for most of the way in a red G.P.O. parcel delivery van, and walked the last half a mile to try and clear his head and walk straight! The alcohol and events of the past hours were making his head spin. The last thing he wanted was to end up in the guardroom cells, and being charged with self-inflicted injury the following morning.

He found his bed with some difficulty, and slept for three hours before being woken by the piper. He struggled to his feet and looked out onto the parade ground. The piper and his 'flag' man, in full ceremonial dress as usual, were shrouded in the early morning mist, which seemed to be common in those parts. It was the last time that he would witness the traditional ceremony, and although he was bleary-eyed and only half awake he found it a very moving, emotional scene, and one that he would remember for a long time to come.

He looked across the barrack room. Taff was fully clothed and fast asleep on his bed. Steve walked over to Mac's bed. He was spread-eagled on his bed, snoring loudly, and clutching a black sporran to his chest with both hands, as if it was a comforting hot water bottle! The other men were slowly coming back to life, probably having slept longer than the 'Three Musketeers'.

Steve shook Taff and Mac. They returned, with some indignation to the land of the living. Taff somehow found his towel, soap and shaving gear, and wandered off in the general direction of the washroom. Mac rose unsteadily to his feet, still clutching the sporran to his chest. Steve looked at him and then the sporran, asking the obvious question with his eyes.

In reply Mac said, "Don't know," grabbed his washroom gear and staggered off after Taff, still clutching the black sporran to his chest. From their condition he concluded that all three of them had enjoyed a good evening! Steve shook his head, trying to think clearly, but he too, like McNiff was still suffering from the influence of the haggis!

It was time to leave the camp and start the long journey back to Hampshire and 'Morval' barracks. After a sobering breakfast of mugs of black coffee and a bowl of porridge, a cursory inspection of the barrack room was made by one of the training corporals. Kitbags were secured and loaded onto the faithful 'Bedford'. The wooden seats were just as hard and unforgiving, but the reliable truck would deliver them safely to the railway station.

The truck skirted the parade ground, and Steve looked across at the flagpole with its regimental flag fluttering proudly in the stiff breeze. At sunset the flag would be taken down, carefully folded and returned to the guardroom for safe keeping. In the morning the piper and his flag man, both in ceremonial dress, would collect the flag, sign for it, and the ancient ceremony performed once more, quite possibly shrouded in the morning mist. The world moved on, and a new day would begin. It was just one of the many things Steve would miss about Scotland.

When the lorry reached the camp gates there was no exchange of ribald remarks. The men had enjoyed the two weeks training, and as they left were in a quiet, reflective mood. The 'Lawyer' was busy scribbling in his notebook, licking the pencil in concentration from time to time as he recalled the past two weeks. He had a subtle way with words, and if he did write a book one day the pages would be certainly worth the reading. Occasionally Steve had fleeting thoughts of writing a book, but soon dismissed the idea. There was so much to do in life, and little time for writing. The thoughts did remind him to write to Aunt Maude, and he made a mental note to do so when they returned to 'Morval'. The platoon would soon learn where the permanent posting was to be, and it was only right that Aunt Maude should be the first to know.

He had meant to buy a book to read on the train, but in the hectic schedule of the training camp it had slipped his mind. If there was a kiosk at the station he would buy one there, but there might not be time to browse, as the train would be due. But when they arrived at the station the train was half an hour late, and he was able to adjust his browsing time.

After ensuring that the platoon's kitbags were all stacked in the correct position for loading onto the train, he strolled along the platform to a small newspaper and bookstall. There was a limited selection of books available, after all it was not a main branch of W.H. Smith. After looking for a few minutes he decided on a fairly large book describing the exploits of Edmund Hillary the mountaineer. The platoon could soon be travelling extensively to whichever part of the world they were posted to, and plenty of reading material would be required to pass the time.

The train eventually arrived forty-five minutes late. The kitbags were loaded onto the guard van and placed under lock and key. Steve learnt from the guard that the delay was due to a broken gauge glass on the locomotive, and the engineers had been called from a 'Motive Power Dept.' to carry out repairs on the engine's footplate. It brought back memories of the station in Somerset to Steve, and his conversations with the engine crews about the technicalities of running a steam locomotive. The talk would be of 'big ends', valve gear, bogies, and of course gauge glasses that had a habit of 'bursting' without any warning showering boiling water over the footplate.

The men settled into the drab 3rd class compartments. The dark green cushioned seats were not luxurious, but a welcome change from the bare wood of the truck. The usual card 'schools' were formed, the players using matchsticks in lieu of cash. At the end of each game the player with the most matchsticks was declared the winner.

Steve opened his book, but decided to spend a few minutes reflecting on the two weeks in Scotland. It had been an interesting, eventful stay. The training had tested them to the limit, but he was sure that the platoon, including himself, was better for the experience. He thought about Pearce and his unfortunate accident. His broken leg would heel naturally in plaster, but the internal injuries were a different matter. He silently wished Pearce a full recovery and hoped he would see him in the future, perhaps as a professional soldier.

The small assault boat training had been a fairly light-hearted time after the tense rock climbing, and if it had not been for the loss of the 'Evinrude', would have made a fitting end to the two weeks training. Sgt. McNiff's birthday celebration was still in the forefront of Steve's mind, and his romantic experience with Moira Theodopolis. She was a pleasant, robust girl, but perhaps a little too dominant when it came to cotton shirts and 'physical' romance. Moira had been emotionally overcome with the effects of the 'Drambuie', and had practically destroyed the front of his new shirt. He smiled to himself, recalling the scene in the courtyard.

All's fair in love and war, he thought to himself.

One day Moira would be married, and make her husband a happy man. He may not live long, but it would be a very happy fulfilling period. He will certainly run out of cotton shirts!

Steve turned his attentions to the book. He had a strange fascination to learn about adventurers and their exploits. It was possibly due to his fairly restricted complicated childhood. He was eternally grateful for Aunt Maude's love and care, but nothing could replace the natural relationship with a mother and father.

He read about Hillary and his faithful Nepalese Sherpa 'Tenzing'. The Sherpa epitomised the tough, stocky Nepalese, upon which the famous and much admired 'Ghurka' regiments in the British Army were formed. Steve was to 'rub shoulders' with such men in the future, and he would come to know them as reliable, unswerving friends.

In between games of cards the talk amongst the men was of the permanent posting, which was soon to be revealed at 'Morval'. The British Army was stretched far and wide, from 'home' postings in the U.K. to the far reaches of the Orient. Unfortunately, there was no choice of posting; they went where they were sent!

After the Second World War a large number of British soldiers found themselves in Germany. Tens of thousands were still forming a military 'presence' in the country, and most of the men in the platoon agreed that Germany would be their choice, if they had one! Germany was regarded as a 'home posting' it being fairly close to the U.K. and home leave was therefore allowed.

Mac said, "Germany will do me for a year or two." That way his taste buds would not forget 'Yorkshire Best Bitter', and he could pay regular visits to his favourite barmaid in Dewsbury. The National Servicemen mostly wanted to remain in the U.K., feeling they had been press-ganged into the army anyway!

Germany had been split into two parts after the main conflict had ended. The West was 'overseen' by Britain, America and France, the East by Russia. A 'Cold War' was in progress, and Berlin itself was split into four sectors. One commanded by Great Britain, one by America and the other two by France and Russia. Rudolf Hess, Hitler's key man was confined in Spandau prison, which was situated in the British sector. Many a serviceman had grown used to German beer, bratwurst and 'wiener schnitzel', but Steve wanted to be more adventurous and travel further afield. The 'Far East' sounded far more alluring to him.

Singapore and Malaya were both popular postings with the long-term professional men, but the latter was partly an 'active service' posting, and weapons were being fired in 'anger'. Malaya had regained its independence in 1957, and was in a state of instability. Because of the 'power void' that had been produced when the British left the Malay Peninsula, the communist element from the north had decided to infiltrate the country, and take control.

In order to negate that situation British troops were deployed, together with other Commonwealth forces. Many servicemen had already been lost in the conflict which entailed much jungle fighting. In later years a medal was to be awarded by the Malayan Government in recognition of their services, and called 'Pingat Jasa', (Service to Malaya).

Steve was caught in two minds over the subject of postings. He wanted to see the world, but also felt the need to continue his relationship with Lorraine. The problem would be resolved by the staff at the War Office in London. The decision was out of his hands.

After he had finished a quarter of the book, and many matchsticks had been won and lost, the train arrived at their destination. It was late evening and they were all stiff from the long journey. A camp 'Bedford' was awaiting their arrival, and after a short journey they drove through the familiar entrance of 'Morval' barracks, they were back 'home'. After quickly 'dumping' their kitbags on their respective beds they went to the cookhouse where a meal awaited them.

Surprisingly the cookhouse corporal's meat balls were not on the menu, and in a strangely masochistic way they missed them. Charlie Strong reluctantly returned his bottle of vile pink medicine to his locker; there was no need for the anti-meatball remedy today! He gave the bottle a vigorous shake before returning it to the locker to ensure the molecules were still well mixed. As he shook the bottle a gaseous, volatile foam built in the top of the bottle. No self-respecting meat ball in the world could withstand that!

When they returned to the barrack room a corporal from the regimental office was pinning a notice to the board. It was short and to the point. The platoon was to be posted to Hong Kong for a tour of duty lasting a minimum of three years. A list of the men involved was printed below the short precise notice, there was no escape! In effect the whole of the platoon was involved, but the National Servicemen would only serve the obligatory two years before returning to the U.K. There would be no 'home leave' whilst on the tour of duty, compassionate or otherwise.

Steve was quite happy about the posting and looked forward to the adventure. The decision had been made for him, and in a way took the weight from his shoulders. He still had thoughts of Lorraine, but the die had been cast. Mac was still concerned about his 'Best Bitter', but Taff was his usual amiable self and didn't seem to be concerned either way.

"It's all part of life's rich pattern, boyo," he said to Steve, and wandered off to listen to the rugby results on his portable radio.

After absorbing the information and coming to terms with their pre-determined future, they retreated to the sanctuary of the N.A.A.F.I. The window curtains had gathered more dust, the smell of beer and steak pies was as strong as ever and the 'Blonde Bombshell' had changed her hair colour and style. It was now a bright orange, with light green tints. Taff, remembering his encounter with B.B. sarcastically remarked that she looked a bit like a 'Swan Vesta' matchstick! Steve wasn't quite as derogatory, but in his opinion she had done little to enhance her appearance, even if she had become more 'inflammably striking'!

Earlier in the day Steve had inspected the teeth marks made by Moira's sudden passionate outburst in the Scottish courtyard. She had not pierced the skin, but the imprint and bruising was clear to see. Several of the men had remarked on it with knowing jibes. It was difficult to conceal such a thing in a barrack's communal washroom!

Later, in the N.A.A.F.I. during the ritual relaxation and pie time, the platoon, tongue in cheek asked how he had incurred the injury. Many of them had watched as Steve and Moira left the party. But Steve would not be drawn on the subject. What happens between Grecians and Marks and Spencer white cotton shirts is strictly confidential!

The conversation came around to postings, Greece, Athens, and the fact that the traditional marathon originated there, all twenty-six miles of it! It seemed to put the platoon's efforts in trekking into perspective. But then, marathon runners did not have the drawback of wearing army uniform, plus a backpack and rifle. Docherty, always keen to hone his comedy timing, gave the old music hall joke an airing (what's a Grecian Urn?). The only one who didn't know the punch line was the academic 'Lawyer'. When Mac enlightened him, in his usual blunt manner, the 'Lawyer' licked his pencil and made a note in the book.

They discussed the posting to Hong Kong in more detail. Mac, having seen the film, 'The World of Suzie Wong', regarded himself to be an expert on the Far East and oriental women, and proceeded to enlighten the platoon on matters of eastern romance. But Taff and the 'Lawyer', who had accepted his advice on romance regarding the 'Blonde Bombshell', were reticent to heed his advice!

When the N.A.A.F.I. closed its doors and the long day was done the men returned to the barrack room, and dreamt of Hong Kong, Suzie Wong, and the mysterious east, all awaiting them!

CHAPTER 27

In the morning Steve went to the cookhouse for breakfast. He looked for the porridge, then realised that he had returned to the 'heathen' country and there was no Scottish nutrition available. He filled a bowl with cornflakes. The idea of using fresh fruit stayed, and he added a sliced banana before pouring milk onto the flakes and adding plenty of sugar. Mac wandered into the cookhouse, still half asleep, and had his usual sausage, egg, and greasy bacon. Some habits were hard to change.

Steve's thoughts turned to the day ahead. The platoon had been released from duties for twenty-four hours in order to re-group. Steve remembered the mental note he had made to himself, and the first job of the day would be to write Aunt Maude a letter. He had much to tell her, and now that he knew he was going to Hong Kong for three years the future was clear.

Aunt Maude had no telephone in the house. Writing letters was his only possible means of communication with her. She was reluctant, as many mature people were, to accept new technology. Maude did use the telephone at the end of the road from time to time, but was very wary of it. She couldn't understand how a person hundreds of miles away could speak to her. When the person did reply to her call she would have a sudden panic attack and put the phone down. She was gradually becoming accustomed to the instrument, but still would not have one in the house!

When he returned to the barrack room a notice had been pinned to the board and was being studied by several of the platoon. They were to report at 08.00 the following morning to the M.O.'s surgery for vaccinations and inoculations, in preparation for the tour of duty in Hong Kong. The men had not given the matter of health precautions a thought. But Charlie Strong had studied the subject in great detail, and proceeded to explain the horrible effects of malaria, beri-beri and yellow fever in detail to the platoon. Charlie could be quite macabre at times, and hopefully over imaginative! The 'Lawyer' felt his own pulse, and retired to his bed!

After finishing his lengthy letter to Aunt Maude, Steve turned his thoughts to Lorraine and their relationship. Because of his posting to the Far East the situation had changed dramatically, and he needed to come to terms with it. There would be no 'home leave' from Hong Kong for three long years. Was it right to ask a woman to wait that long? More to the point, did she want to?

He made up his mind to go to the 'red sentinel' and telephone Lorraine. She would probably be at college classes, but there was little time before he would be leaving for Hong Kong, and the problem had to be resolved, one way or the other. He gathered some small coins, made sure he could remember Lorraine's telephone number and made his way to the phone.

His mind was racing with the rapid change in circumstances. The platoon had barely returned from Scotland, and now they were preparing to embark for Hong Kong, some eight thousand miles away. As he approached the kiosk Steve was surprised that there was nobody waiting to use the phone, but as it came in to view he realised why. A stark notice in black and white, taped to the kiosk door read, 'Out of Order'! He swore to himself, frustrated that his plans had been foiled. He felt like kicking the door in his anger, but restrained himself. The 'red sentinel' had suddenly turned from being a friend to a foe!

There was no alternative but to go in to town and use a street phone. He would have to take 'pot luck' that Lorraine would be in the flat, but it was likely that he might have another wasted journey. He returned to the barrack room and made himself ready for the bus journey into town. His new white shirt was not available and he reluctantly donned his 'off white' second shirt, with fleeting thoughts of Moira Theodopolis! After changing and using liberal amounts of the perfumed aftershave, he put Aunt Maude's letter in his pocket for posting in town and walked briskly to the bus stop.

The bus duly arrived. For a small rural service, it was very efficient and reliable. He boarded the bus and paid his fare. The driver was the overweight, gear crunching individual that he had encountered on his first bus journey to 'Morval' camp two months previously. The driver looked surprisingly well, despite his obvious weight problem, but as the bus pulled away he continued to punish the gearbox cogs.

Steve looked at his watch, it was already almost midday, and he thought to himself, *Why does time always race when you need it to stand still?* Surprisingly he reached town safely without the gearbox collapsing onto the tarmac, and he made his way to the post office. After purchasing the necessary stamp, he put the letter into the box provided.

He had explained to Aunt Maude most of what had happened over the past weeks, and of course the posting to Hong Kong. He left out his dilemma about Lorraine. He knew that Aunt Maude would only worry if she felt he had a problem on his mind. Steve checked his watch again, it was one o'clock. Thankfully the phone box at the corner of the street was empty, and he prepared to phone Lorraine. The number was still imprinted on his mind, and he placed his coins on the small shelf beside the telephone.

Lorraine, when she answered his call was surprised he was calling at such an unusual hour. Steve quickly explained the reason, and they talked about his posting to Hong Kong. Lorraine said that Hong Kong was a long way from England, especially for a period of three years. They had much to say, but not over the telephone. Phone conversations always seemed to be distant and robotic.

Lorraine had a study class in the afternoon, but said she would be in the flat by about five o'clock. They agreed to meet at five-thirty at the flat. She suggested that she might cook a meal for them, and he could buy a bottle of red wine to accompany the food. Steve quickly thought about how much money he had in his pocket, it was not much, but perhaps just enough for a not too expensive bottle of Spanish table 'plonk'. They both said they looked forward to the evening together, blew a kiss down the phone and said 'See you later'. But both their voices seemed to have a sense of indecision in their words.

He left the phone box and 'fished' in his pocket to check the money he had. He was starting to feel hungry. There was sufficient cash to buy a cheap bottle of wine, a small snack and a daily newspaper. There was time to kill, and the cornflakes at the camp had not been as sustaining as the traditional porridge in Scotland. He thought of the lone piper in his ceremonial uniform, and a pang of nostalgia overcame him. His young life was being filled with more emotions than he could ever have imagined.

He bought a newspaper and went to his favourite cafe, possibly for the last time. The cheerful waitress was on duty and recognised him immediately as he entered. She jokingly asked if he had brought her a flower as before. Her smile was so welcoming that he wished he had, but he barely had money for the snack, and later the wine. Pay day was a long way off, the next 'pay parade' could possibly be in Hong Kong, and that would be paid in dollars!

He ordered a small snack, and settled down to read the newspaper. The second test match against the 'Aussies' had just finished, and the Australian fast bowlers had decimated the English batting order. But it was a five match 'series', with points even, so there was much to play for, but the 'spectre' of

Don Bradman still loomed on the horizon! The next match was at the Oval in two weeks' time. Steve looked forward to it, but in two weeks' time he would be in Hong Kong, there was little communication from there!

Steve was beginning to realise that he would lose contact with events at home, there would be no English daily newspapers to read, no cricket, no English cinemas, and no English girls. It was a sobering thought, and he looked forward to regular letters from Aunt Maude and possibly Lorraine.

After finishing his snack and reading the newspaper from front to back he beckoned the waitress and paid his bill. He explained to her that this was probably his last visit. Surprisingly she hugged him, gave him a kiss on the cheek and quickly turned away, an emotional look on her face. He left the cafe and walked towards the bus station thinking about the waitress. He was surprised at the impact he had made on her, and somehow felt guilty about it.

He found an off-licence on one of the side streets and bought a bottle of fairly cheap Spanish red wine. He studied the label on the bottle of table wine. It was in two languages, Spanish and English. The English translation had probably been written in the 'Bodega' in Spain by the vineyard owner, after taking several glasses of his own 'special vintage' red wine. Steve found the translation amusing, it read: - 'It is a pale colour, very bright and with golden glitters. On the nose displays a harmonious combination of fruity notes. Green apple on a background of aniseed. On the mouth is wee balanced and vitality, with a large palate, oily, and velvety'. Steve was happy to pay the price of the wine, if only for the label!

He checked his cash again. There was enough for the bus ride to Lorraine's flat, and when the evening was finished, for the return journey to camp. He reminded himself not to miss the last bus. It was important that he was in the camp for the 08.00 morning parade, and the vaccinations. If he missed that, he would be quickly placed on a charge of 'Absent Without Leave'.

He arrived at the bus station, clutching his bottle of wine, and after a short wait boarded the bus to the college and Lorraine's nearby flat. The driver was a young, slim man, who looked as if he played football at the weekends, possibly for the bus company's club. He was in stark contrast to the obese gearbox cruncher. The bus rattled along the uneven road surface, confirming the warm temperature and low humidity of a pleasant summer.

Steve arrived at Lorraine's flat fifteen minutes early. The bus had rattled over the tarmac efficiently under the control of the young driver, and the passengers had been few and far between.

Lorraine opened the door at his call and greeted him with a tentative 'peck' on the cheek. She was wearing a plain white blouse and dark coloured slacks. Her feet were bare, and red polished toenails 'peeped' out from under her slacks. Without shoes she was much shorter than Steve, and had a 'little girl lost' look about her. He towered above her, almost looking at the top of her head. He realised why women possibly wore high heeled shoes, they simply wanted to be equal to men! Steve idly wondered if Emily Pankhurst was wearing high heels when she chained herself to the railings in London.

A white, workmanlike kitchen apron was wrapped around Lorraine's slim waist, and the aroma of steaks cooking, wafted from the kitchen. He embraced and kissed her, but Steve felt that she was cool towards him, and certainly not dressed 'to kill' romantically.

Lorraine suggested that he should open the bottle of wine while she finished cooking the meal. He followed her into the kitchen, and she found the corkscrew and handed it to him. After another, slightly longer kiss she ushered him out of the kitchen and closed the door. Like many cooks she probably preferred to work alone and believed in the old saying, 'Too many cooks spoil the broth'. Or was there some other reason for her distant attitude?

Steve opened the bottle of wine in the lounge, his mind in confusion. Had he said something wrong? Perhaps he should have brought her some flowers or chocolates! Perhaps he should have fallen for the more basically minded 'Blonde Bombshell' who simply wanted a good time and to go to bed with him!

He poured a glass of wine for Lorraine opened the kitchen door and handed her the glass. Once again she thanked him, took the glass, and ushered him out of the kitchen. She was obviously having a 'culinary' experience, and was not to be disturbed! Steve continued to feel that 'all was not well', but he put his thoughts aside. He sipped his wine, and agreed with the 'Bodega' owner that it produced a 'bright palate and gold glitters on the nose'! Steve studied Lorraine's paintings on the lounge wall. He had admired them before, but now he looked deeper into them. They reflected her character, soft and understanding, but with an underlying strength. Just the quality a good doctor should have.

The kitchen door opened, and Lorraine appeared carrying two plates of food. She had prepared steaks, petit pois, deep fried chips, button mushrooms and sliced carrots. The steaks were wonderful; her 'culinary' experience had been a success!

They talked briefly whilst they ate, but there was a quietness about her that disturbed Steve. But he had his own deep inner thoughts, and probably appeared to be as quiet as Lorraine. He had thoughts of Hong Kong, three long years away from England, and recently his guilty feelings about Scotland and his sexual 'liaison' with Moira Theodopolis!

He handed Lorraine the wine bottle, explaining the English translation. She also found it amusing, and it helped to smooth over an awkward moment in the conversation. They finished the meal and moved to the comfort of the settee. The red wine tasted even better after the satisfying meal, and they listened to the soft mellow tones of 'Nat King Cole' on his latest 'long playing' record.

The sudden news of Steve's posting to Hong Kong had come as a shock to both of them, perhaps more for Lorraine, and she had obviously given the situation much thought. It is strange that in times of domestic turmoil it is usually the woman who makes the ultimate decision.

Lorraine explained that shortly she too would be 'on the move'. She would be moving to a 'teaching' hospital in London to continue her studies and gain practical experience. Steve's posting to Hong Kong, with no 'home leave' for three years, had cast a deep shadow on their relationship.

As the evening progressed they both realised that their futures were poles apart, and the distance, both spiritually and physically, would increase. After an agonising discussion they came to the conclusion that it would be the right decision to end their relationship, tonight. They agreed to write, but both secretly knew that this would be their last meeting.

After they had made the decision they both felt relaxed, and listened to the mellow voice of 'Nat King Cole' whilst kissing and caressing each other, perhaps in mutual understanding and commiseration. After a while Lorraine said that she was going to change into something more 'cosy'! They kissed once more, and she went into the bedroom.

Steve loosened his tie and rolled up his shirt sleeves, the food and wine had made him feel warm! Lorraine appeared in the bedroom doorway. This time there was no pink chiffon nightdress, just a naked, slim, beautiful woman smiling invitingly at him! Steve switched off the lounge light. The soft bedroom light turned Lorraine's naked body into a picturesque silhouette. He walked towards the bedroom door, and she held out a welcoming hand.

Their lovemaking was overly passionate, almost brutal, as if they were psychologically blaming each other for the break-up. They had nothing to lose, and everything to gain! Lorraine was totally aggressive, even without her high heeled shoes! Steve had never known a woman to be so physically strong, and afterwards they both collapsed, completely exhausted by the emotional and physical stress.

When he was able to, Steve went to the bathroom and looked into the mirror. He saw deep gouges on his shoulders and on his back. He bathed them with cold water and put some of Lorraine's hand cream on them. He tried to remember how passionate he had become, and hoped that she had not received the same brutal attention, it was all a 'blur' in his mind.

When he returned to the bedroom Lorraine was asleep. He looked as closely as he could without disturbing her. She had some minor scratches on her arms, and her bottom lip was bleeding slightly from their passionate kissing. He pressed his handkerchief gently onto her lip without waking her.

Steve looked again at his shoulders. Lorraine's fairly long fingernails had been the main cause of his injuries. He went to the kitchen and made himself a strong cup of coffee. He needed something stronger but they had finished the red wine. Thoughts of a McNiff 'dram' came to mind.

Lorraine awoke and joined him in the kitchen. They both drank strong dark coffee. No words were spoken; they were both in a state of shock.

They both gradually became coherent again and Steve looked at his watch, it was time for him to leave. They looked at each other's bodies, still not believing the result of their passion. He kissed her quietly on the lips, the bleeding had stopped now, and Lorraine put more cream on his shoulders. He dressed quickly and Lorraine put her house dress on. They both felt awkward, not knowing what to say. Steve kissed her, and they held each other before Steve moved towards the door to leave. As he opened the door she told him to wait; she had forgotten something. She went to the kitchen refrigerator, and Steve anxiously looked at his watch, time was running out. Lorraine reappeared holding a neatly wrapped square package. Inside was six, fresh, cheese and pickled onion sandwiches!

Steve walked to the bus stop, his mind in turmoil. He loved Lorraine, and she him, and yet they had just said goodbye for the last time. He tried to make sense of the last few hours. If two people loved each other, why should it be an impossible situation? Shouldn't love conquer all? He had shared some wonderful moments with Lorraine, and he came to realise that a minute, or even a second of pure happiness should be treasured, and never forgotten!

Having thought about the dilemma he felt slightly calmer, but as he stepped aboard the bus, there was moisture in his blue eyes.

CHAPTER 28

Steve woke from a fitful night's sleep, still troubled by the previous evening. He was not a person to seek advice or sympathy; Aunt Maude had taught him to stand on his own two feet, but Mac sensed that something was wrong. Mac was a rough diamond, and had survived many a relationship with barmaids and provocative landladies. But he had a Yorkshireman's philosophy of life, and he knew when to put a comforting arm around a troubled shoulder.

After a talk with Mac, Steve went to the washroom, and returned feeling fresher and more able to cope with a possibly difficult day ahead. He had no appetite for food, but knowing that the rest of the day could be demanding, forced himself to go for breakfast in the cookhouse. He half-filled a bowl with cornflakes and added milk and sugar. After 'picking' at the flakes, gradually his appetite returned. The talk with Mac had helped to offload a weight from his shoulders, and he went to the serving counter and helped himself, in the cook's absence, to sausages, egg, bacon, and two slices of fried bread; he had made a remarkable recovery!

The platoon went on parade at the usual time of 08.00, and awaited the normal inspection. Corporal Entwhistle had left the army for civilian life, and a new training corporal had been posted in. He arrived, five minutes late, still adjusting his web belt. He was a short stocky man with a 'ruddy' complexion and a 'bull neck'. He had 'aggression' written on his face, and the word 'bully' crossed Steve's mind as he took his first look at him.

The corporal was aware that the platoon was shortly to embark for sunnier 'climes', and he was to remain in the dull training camp. He took his frustration out on them. They were not the smartest platoon in the world, but he 'picked' at every hair. After he had left, they were all grateful to be going to Hong Kong, and understood how lucky they had been to encounter Corporal Entwhistle in their six weeks of basic training and not 'The Bulldog', as Docherty had quickly named him. Six weeks of him would have made them all into Prendergasts!

Steve left the ranks, took charge of the platoon, and marched the men to the M.O.'s surgery for the vaccinations and inoculations. Over a period of time the platoon had come to accept Steve as the leader, and it sat well with them. He tried to lead by example, and the men appreciated that. He hadn't thought much about it; it came naturally to him.

He reported to the Medical Officer that the platoon was 'present and correct'. The M.O. was not a strict military man. He carried the rank of colonel, but army protocol was of no interest to him. He was a doctor, and surgeon when required under military circumstances! The M.O. was 'looked up to' by the men, and the rank was one of respect, just as 'padre' carried the rank of captain'.

Two orderlies were busy arranging a selection of small needles and small bottles on a table covered by a white cloth. An aroma of antiseptic and disinfectant liquid was very apparent. The M.O. instructed Steve to bring the platoon into the surgery in single file, and the men entered with some trepidation! Steve was no exception to the rule. The only vaccination he had experienced was as a young child at school, and he could not remember what it was for. No doubt Aunt Maude would have remembered.

Steve filtered into the middle of the line of men, and they were instructed to roll up both of their shirt sleeves in readiness for the needles. They were to receive four 'jabs' two into each arm. The first was for protection against yellow fever, the second for malaria, and another against beri-beri. The fourth vaccination was not disclosed to them; they were merely told that it was very necessary for the part of the world they were being posted to.

Mac, with his one track mind, turned to Steve and said, "I expect it's a precaution against foreign beer!"

The inoculations started, and the two medical orderlies stood by in anticipation. Docherty, his sleeves rolled up was first in line, and regarded the whole thing as a joke. After 'being seen to' he rolled his sleeves down and returned 'whistling' to the barrack room. The line gradually moved forward, and the M.O. 'flicked' his needles in an expert manner before plunging them into unsuspecting skin! Charlie Strong moved forward, the M.O. picked up a large needle and gave it a quick 'flick'. Charlie looked at the needle and promptly fainted! The M.O. stood back and stared at the ceiling in frustration. The two orderlies applied a cold, wet sponge to the back of Charlie's neck. Within a few seconds Charlie was back in the land of the living, and was supported by the orderlies while the officer continued to administer the medication into his arms.

When it was Steve's turn he decided not to look at the needles, for fear of following in Charlie's footsteps. A large oil painting was hanging on the far wall of the surgery, depicting the regiment's colours and cap badge. At the bottom of the painting, written in Latin were the words 'Honi soit qui mal y pense' (evil be to him who evil thinks). On the cap badge was the regiment's motto also in Latin that read 'Ubique', (everywhere).

Steve's concentration was broken by the M.O. saying, "All done, move on."

Steve thankfully rolled his sleeves down, and with a relieved look on his face returned to the barrack room. The Medical Officer had given them the rest of the day 'off duty'. The men thought it was a very generous offer, but they were soon to understand why!

After cleaning the barrack room, the platoon went to the cookhouse for lunch. Their arms were already starting to ache and feel tight. Halfway through the meal Steve found it difficult to lift his arms to eat and drink. The other men felt the same way, and they all left the cookhouse with meals unfinished. The cookhouse corporal had seen it all before. He laughed to himself, and turned to make some more meat balls.

The men returned to their barrack room and went to their beds. The only way to rest was on their backs, both arms were quickly becoming stiff and swollen. In the afternoon the room was very quiet, except for the odd individual making very explicit exclamations about how swollen his arms were, and casting doubts on the M.O.'s parent's marital status! Steve had grown used to swear words, and used a few himself from time to time, but the vaccinations had taken the platoon to a higher dimension in their vocabulary!

Eventually Steve slept, and when he awoke it was evening and the sky was dark. His upper arms were still swollen, but he was able to lift his arms to shoulder level. The other men gradually 'came to' and it was agreed that the best aftercare would be a steak pie and a beer in the N.A.A.F.I. Beers and pies were purchased and they began to exercise their arms in the traditional way.

Charlie Strong had fully recovered from his fainting bout, and explained it away by saying that his fragile skin was 'biologically susceptible to Micronics intrusion'!

"In other words," said Mac, "you can't stand bloody needles!"

Mac was always one to call a spade a spade. Charlie looked at him, took a large green pill from his pocket, and washed it down with a swig of beer.

The beers started to flow and the steak pies were consumed, but after three pints they all realised that they were all disturbingly still sober! Their bodies, and minds, had become accustomed to the strong dark brew in Scotland. Extraordinary measures had to be taken, and it was agreed to change the usual beer to steak pie ratio. Instead of three beers to each pie it was democratically passed to drink four and a half pints of beer to every one steak pie, making it a mathematical formula of 4.8 – 1. The new formula soon became a success, and normal service resumed!

The 'Blonde Bombshell' walked around the table collecting empty beer glasses. She swished her skirt against the backs of the chairs, and as she went past Mac's chair playfully patted him on the head. She remembered their little lucrative deal, and the back row of the cinema. Mac laughed knowingly as she swished her way back to the counter. He had a way with women; there was no doubt about that. The 'Lawyer' was watching the proceedings, and made the appropriate observations in his notebook! After more beers and sustaining pies, the men returned to the barrack room. Their arm problems had sunk into the hazy background, and they slept. In the morning they would begin the long journey to Hong Kong.

The new day duly arrived, and when Steve awoke he automatically felt his arms. They had returned to normal, and he thanked the 'liquid brew' in the N.A.A.F.I. for a good night's sleep. As he awoke he half expected to hear the sound of the bagpipes, but then realised where he was. In a way he missed the haunting notes and the morning mist on the parade ground.

The men went to the cookhouse, physically able to handle a full breakfast of cereal, followed by sausage, egg and bacon. The talk was of the journey to the Far East, Chinese cooking, the mysteries of the Orient and Suzie Wong, whose voluptuous character had been suitably enhanced by Mac's inventive mind. The 'Lawyer' made more notes, in between sausages, and looked forward to the future with optimism!

The platoon returned to the barrack room and went through the routine of cleaning lockers, bed spaces and the room in general. Shortly it would be somebody else's responsibility, the platoon was moving on!

When they were halfway through cleaning the room for inspection the 'Bulldog' strode in, immediately making his presence felt by shouting the order, "Stand by your beds!" He handed each man a sheet of paper and said curtly, "Fill these in; I'll be back in half an hour to pick them up." He ran a hand over the top of a locker, checking for dust, turned sharply and strode out of the room, slamming the door after him.

The 'Lawyer' remarked, "What a nice chap!"

Docherty seized on the opportunity to give the platoon his impression of the 'Bulldog'. He dabbed some 'Cherry Blossom' boot polish on his top lip, 'Hitler' style, making a presentable 'Adolf' moustache, and strutted up and down the barrack room. Using the few words of German he had learnt from watching war films he proceeded to entertain the platoon. After inspecting several lockers for dust, and using his 'guttural' German expletives such as 'Schweinhund', 'Shizenhousen', and throwing a few 'Donner unt Blitzens' in here and there for good measure, he 'goose' stepped up to Taff's bed space and demanded, "Do you know 'vot' happens to British spies?"

Taff tried to keep a straight face, but broke into a smile as he said, "No!"

"That is a pity," continued Docherty, using his best Gestapo voice, "I 'vos' hoping you could tell me!"

Docherty had changed an unpleasant scene into one of good natured humour, simply by using his talent to entertain.

Steve took a moment from Docherty's performance to compare the 'Bulldog' to Corporal Entwhistle. They were two very different characters. Entwhistle had been a professional, efficient soldier who had experienced many a campaign, and relied on his own ability to see him through. The 'Bulldog' was an arrogant man, who 'blustered' his way through life, blaming every adverse situation on other people rather than himself.

After the men had stopped laughing from the Liverpudlian, Gestapo interrogation, they looked at the sheets of paper the 'Bulldog' had handed them, and were quickly brought down to earth.

Steve looked at his paper. It was headed, 'War Office', and subtitled, 'Last Will and Testament of Soldier'. He looked at the other men; they were as mystified as he was. It was true that they were going on active service, but the official papers seemed to be an overreaction by the people in charge. Or were they simply more aware of the dangers than the men?

Steve read the sheet of paper carefully. As far as he was concerned it was a simple matter, the other men, some of whom were married, possibly had more complicated problems. He had little money and few belongings, so he would leave everything he did have to Aunt Maude. Steve quickly filled in the form, signed it, and put it with the other forms on the barrack room table. He decided to forget about it as soon as possible, he was too young to be thinking of dying!

At midday a 'Bedford' arrived to take the platoon on the first leg of the journey to Hong Kong. They were to travel to R.A.F. Lyneham in Wiltshire. The 'Bulldog' collected the 'Last Will and Testaments', and as he left the barrack room gave Docherty a stern look. Perhaps he had learnt of Docherty's 'Gestapo' performance!

Wiltshire and the Lyneham airbase was a fairly long journey. They left the gates of 'Morval' for the last time, with mixed feelings.

The armed sentry on duty was aware of their ultimate destination, the exotic east, and with an air of envy, told them to, "Go forth you lucky illegitimates," or words to that effect!

They were to fly to Hong Kong by R.A.F. Transport Command. The air force operated a fleet of Bristol 'Britannia' aircraft, and was responsible for conveying personnel and supplies to all parts of the world where British Forces were engaged. It was a huge task; the aftermath of the Second World War had left the United Kingdom with responsibilities that stretched far and wide.

During the journey to Wiltshire Steve's thoughts, apart from the harsh understanding the wooden bench seats were just as uncomfortable, concentrated on the previous eight weeks, and all that had happened to him. Compared to his relatively quiet time in Somerset the last two months had been a hectic, complete change in his life, and was destined to continue. He looked at the other men; they too had mystified looks on their faces. Although the future was exciting, it was uncertain, and most were thinking about 'Last Wills and Testaments'!

They arrived at R.A.F. Lyneham. There were no facilities such as customs or passports, and after unloading the kitbags they marched directly on to the runway apron where the 'Britannia' was awaiting them. The platoon assembled under the wing of the aircraft and waited to board. Steve looked up at the 'Britannia', it was huge, and he wondered how something so heavy could ever leave the ground.

An R.A.F. officer, the flight engineer, appeared from the opposite side of the fuselage, obviously carrying out a pre-flight inspection. He looked up at the aircraft's port wing, put a hand into his pocket, withdrew a halfpenny piece and proceeded to tighten a loose screw. He completed his task, turned around and grinned at the platoon. They looked at each other in amazement. They were about to embark on a journey of some eight thousand miles in the aircraft, and it had just been maintained by using a small coin of the realm! Mac said he needed a beer, and the others concurred! Steve had a vision of the 'Blonde Bombshell' walking across the tarmac, swishing her skirt and carrying a large tray of cold beers. But it was a fleeting, hopeful mirage.

They reluctantly boarded the 'Britannia'; the journey to Hong Kong had begun!

CHAPTER 29

The men were directed to their seats by a grim faced R.A.F. corporal. It was an obvious disappointment. There were no perfumed air hostesses with tight skirts on this airline!

The 'Bristol Britannia' was a massive aircraft, and was fitted out to be used as a passenger / cargo transporter. There were forty passenger seats at the rear of the aeroplane; the front section was used as cargo space.

Steve looked towards the front of the 'Britannia'. The cargo space was filled with wooden crates and packing cases, all stencilled in black paint denoting the contents and their destination. The largest crate had aero-engine, and 'R.A.F. Gan' stencilled on it. Steve had no idea where Gan was, but that was to be revealed in due course. Other crates and cases were marked Aden, Bombay and Karachi. Two of the cases were stencilled 'Urgent Medical Supplies', and the destination was Singapore. Steve didn't think that Singapore was on the normal R.A.F. route to Hong Kong, and was surprised to see the cases on board.

Perhaps we are to be transferred to another aircraft, he thought to himself.

After ten minutes had gone by and the men were settled in their seats, the 'Britannia's' powerful turbo propeller engines were started up by the flight deck crew. The engines 'warmed up' while the routine pre-flight checks were carried out by the pilot and crew. The engines were 'revved up' slightly, and the 'Britannia' left the apron and slowly made its way onto the main runway. Steve looked at the mass of crates and cases, and that increased his apprehension about how the plane was able to leave the ground. As he looked out of the window, the wings appeared to be very small compared to the bulky fuselage!

They reached the runway for take-off, and were instructed to fasten seat belts by the flight corporal. Once again there was a pause while the pilot asked for, and received permission to take-off. The lulls in the procedure heightened the tension and apprehension the men were feeling; for most of them it was a strange first time experience. Steve glanced across the centre aisle at Taff. He looked calm and collected, but Steve noticed that Taff had his fingers tightly crossed. Steve suddenly thought that going to Hong Kong by troop ship would have been a better idea, but troop ships no longer appeared to be in use and air transport had taken over. Steve remembered the flight engineer securing the loose screw with a small halfpenny piece, had he been serious when carrying out the repair, or was he just having a private joke with the platoon? Steve was not a religious man, but said a few silent words in prayer. He looked at the locked fuselage door, there was no escape now, this was it!

The engines were brought to full power, the aircraft vibrated, trying to break free of its air brakes. The pilot released the restraining brakes, and the 'Britannia' gathered speed along the runway. When the correct speed was reached, the pilot pointed the aeroplane's nose upwards, and within seconds they were airborne.

As the aircraft left the ground and quickly gathered height, Mac held on to the arms of his seat, looked across at Steve and exclaimed loudly, in his broad Yorkshire accent, "Bloody Ell as like!"

The 'Britannia' gradually gained its cruising height, struggling under its heavy load. Steve looked out of the small circular window and down at the green land below. He could clearly see the fields and hedges, clumps of trees and cattle grazing. A lone car was travelling along one of the country roads, looking like a child's 'Dinky' toy. Steve realised this would be his last sight of England for three long, but hopefully adventurous, happy years. He kept looking down, committing the sights to memory until the aircraft entered a cloud level, and suddenly all he could see was a mass of grey. The aircraft climbed and burst through the blanket of cloud to reveal clear, light blue sky. He looked down at the tufted, cotton wool, white carpet of cloud. Below it was England, Lorraine, meat balls, Aunt Maude and cheese and pickled onion sandwiches!

The first stop on the journey was to be the Aden 'Protectorate', to deliver supplies to the small garrison of British troops who were keeping a necessary 'presence' in the area. The end of the Second World War had left certain parts of the world in an unstable condition, and the Middle East was no exception.

A small section of seats at the rear of the aircraft were curtained off and reserved for 'Officers use only'. When they landed at Aden two fairly high ranking Military Police officers left the plane, both carrying very official briefcases, which were secured to their wrists by a chain and handcuffs. The 'Protectorate', and the Middle East in general was becoming a hotbed of intrigue, and the reason for it all was oil!

The stop at Aden was only a short one and the platoon was not allowed off the aircraft. Steve stared out of the window, and found himself looking at sandy desert; there was no greenery, no trees, just flat desert. He asked himself, *Could there be such a change in landscape in a short space of time?* The 'Britannia' had travelled faster than he thought; speed was difficult to judge once you lose sight of land.

They were soon airborne again, climbing through the clouds as before and reaching open blue space. The next leg of the journey was to be a long one, the destination, Bombay, India.

Steve tried to read his book, but his mind was completely on the new experience that he and the rest of the platoon were experiencing. He looked around him, and out of the window. There was no sensation of speed, or height. They could be going to the moon for all he knew! He had not realised it before, but he had placed his life in the pilot's hands!

Eventually his mind settled down and he read a few chapters of his book about Hillary and Tenzing. In a strange way he too was climbing a mountain, and found it hard to believe that he was on his way to India, and eventually Hong Kong. Aden, Bombay and Karachi were simply stepping stones to reach Hong Kong, but for a young man from Somerset they were a giant stride! He looked across at the 'Lawyer' who was busy with his pencil and paper. There was much to write about, and the academic man would be purchasing many notepads and pencils in the next three years.

After reading four chapters of his book Steve was able to close his eyes and sleep, helped by the steady 'droning' of the 'Britannia's' turbo prop engines. When he awoke they were in darkness and approaching a new day. The aircraft was starting to descend and make its approach to Bombay Airport.

They would be staying in Bombay Airport for two hours, for refuelling and flight crew rest. When they took off again the 'Britannia' would be heading for Karachi, Pakistan. The aircraft landed safely under the efficient hands of the pilot and crew, and Steve began to feel that his life was in good hands. They left the aircraft whilst refuelling was carried out, and the men were grateful for the opportunity to stretch their stiff legs.

As Steve walked through the aircraft's doorway and onto the aluminium stairway he looked at the engine exhaust, and remarked to Taff how much heat was coming from it. Taff agreed, and wiped his brow. But when they reached the tarmac ground level, the temperature was the same. They looked at each other, amazed at the stifling heat, and hoped that Hong Kong was not as hot and 'sticky'! They walked across the hot tarmac and into the airport building, found a 'Coca Cola' machine and quenched their thirsts. 'Coca Cola' had never tasted so good, but a pint of the N.A.A.F.I. brew would have been more acceptable! After exercising their legs by looking around the fairly modern airport, strangely named 'Santa Cruz', they tended to their 'domestic' needs, and were instructed to board the 'Britannia' for the flight to Karachi, where several of the packing cases were destined for.

The 'Britannia' took off from 'Santa Cruz' and left the searing heat behind. Steve was curious about the name of the airport, and wondered if perhaps there was a certain Spanish influence in India. He smiled to himself and mused that possibly Hong Kong's airport was called Ghandi International! He joked with the flight corporal about it, but the R.A.F. corporal enlightened him that the airport at Hong Kong was called Kai Tak. The R.A.F. had a very poor sense of humour! Perhaps it was the blue uniform they wore.

During the flight some dry rations were issued by the straight faced flight corporal, together with tepid coffee served in disposable plastic cups. The quality of the cookhouse corporal's meat balls at 'Morval' were gaining in stature minute by minute.

They were becoming used to the routine of taking off and landing, and were no longer in awe of their strange surroundings. Steve was able to concentrate fully on his book, and as he glanced around he could see that the others were more relaxed and enjoying the flight. They were travelling east, towards the sun, and when the 'Britannia' landed at Karachi Airport watches and clocks were altered accordingly. The off-loading of cargo was to take some time, and the men were once again allowed to leave the aircraft and take advantage of the ever present 'Coca Cola' machine. It was still very hot and Steve began to understand why many Indians and Pakistanis wore long, loose fitting clothes for coolness and protection against the sun. As he looked out of the airport lounge spacious windows he could see several European passengers 'stretching their legs, none with protective hats against the sun. The words of Noel Coward's famous song came to Steve's mind, 'Mad Dogs and Englishmen'.

They all felt revived after the dry rations and drinks, and as they left the airport building to board the plane the flight corporal informed them that after a short stop at Gan, the 'Britannia' was to be diverted to Singapore in order to deliver urgent medical supplies to the British Military Hospital on the island. Steve's curiosity had been answered. The platoon would be staying in

Singapore for twenty-four hours before travelling to their final destination of Hong Kong.

Steve had heard about Singapore from some of the longer serving training staff at 'Morval', and he looked forward to the visit with enthusiasm. The posting was apparently very popular, especially with single men, the military discipline was not as strict as in England, many of the routine duties were carried out by civilians, and the night life was very pleasurable, to say the least! After the off-loading of cargo was completed, the routine safety checks of the aircraft were carried out by the flight engineer. Steve hoped he had no need for his halfpenny piece! The 'Britannia' was much lighter now. The atmosphere had been claustrophobic before with the large crates and packing cases. Now there was only the aero-engine, destined for the island of Gan, and the remaining cases for Singapore and Hong Kong. Steve still didn't know where Gan was, but that was to be the next stop on the long journey.

After going through the take-off routine the 'Britannia' turned south and across the Indian Ocean. The flight corporal was busy adjusting the securing straps on the crate and cases. When he returned from the front of the aircraft Steve took the opportunity to ask him about Gan. The corporal, still straight faced after the 'Ghandi' conversation, explained that Gan was a small island in the Indian Ocean, and was used as a 'safety net' for any aircraft experiencing problems whilst crossing the vast ocean. It was manned by a small detachment of R.A.F. personnel, and because of its almost complete isolation, the maximum tour of duty was six months. There were no civilians on the island, and no female company. Steve felt that under such circumstances six months could feel like six years!

After some three hours the aircraft descended through the cloud level, and the pilot banked the 'Britannia' over in preparation for landing. Steve looked out of the window as the plane banked over and turned towards the runway. He saw a tiny yellow sand covered island. It hardly looked big enough for the huge aircraft to land on and there was no room for error! It was simply a very small island with a tarmac runway across its middle, a control tower and half a dozen pre-fabricated single storey buildings.

The pilot made the final approach to the island; it was probably like driving a bus to him. He had carried out the manoeuvre many times before. As the engines slowed down Steve heard an unusual 'slapping' noise coming from the front of the cargo space. Two of the straps holding the massive aero-engine crate had snapped under the stress and the heavy crate started to slide across the fuselage. The 'Britannia', now only a hundred feet from the ground lurched to one side, the starboard wing perilously close to the tarmac runway.

Two of the flight crew, who had been strapped in their seats for landing, quickly unbuckled their safety belts and staggered towards the unstable crate and tried to drag the aero-engine back into position. The engineering officer appeared from the flight deck, and all three wrestled with the untethered crate. During the chaos the aircraft engines had returned to the full throttle, and the 'Britannia' pulled away from the runway and back into the relative safety of space.

The flight engineer beckoned to Steve for extra pairs of hands, and he and three others who were in the forward seats, made their way unsteadily towards the offending crate. Gradually the crate was returned to its original position, and new straps were taken from the side of the fuselage and attached to the crate's wooden frame. Eventually calm was restored, and the pilot, having made certain the cargo was secure, returned to the task of landing the aircraft safely. Steve returned to his seat, thinking, so much for buses!

The aircraft landed safely, and as they left the plane everybody, including the flight crew, breathed a sigh of relief. Steve looked around him, glad to have his feet on the ground once more.

He thought to himself, *At last I will have something to tell Aunt Maude about!*

The island, now that they had landed, was actually quite large, but very flat, hardly more than two feet above the sea level. A few palm trees added some greenery, but there was no other vegetation, just sand and a few small rocks.

The aircraft control tower was quite a modern building, made of concrete construction, with large windows and radar scanner on the flat roof. There were half a dozen 'half-moon' shaped 'Nissen' huts constructed of corrugated iron held together with large nuts and bolts. A single door at one end of each hut allowed entry and exit. The huts were painted black, and the only natural light was from two small square windows either side of the door. It was a very workmanlike place, with no frills! The 'rogue' aero-engine was off-loaded, and after drinks of cold water and visits to the washroom, they returned to the 'Britannia', ready for the journey south to Singapore.

The flight to Singapore was uneventful, and the platoon was grateful for that. They needed time to relax and re-adjust after the drama and chaos of the previous landing. Steve read a few more pages of his book, and then stared absent-mindedly out of the window. His mind wandered back to England, and

Lorraine. He missed her already, and the feeling was growing as each mile went by. He thought of writing to her as soon as they reached Hong Kong, but then he realised that he didn't know her postal address; he had visited her flat many times but the thought of writing the address down had never entered his head. They had agreed to part anyway, it would be foolish to create more heartache, for both of them.

Steve, and the rest of the platoon were looking forward to the twenty-four hours' stay in Singapore, it was an unexpected, pleasant deviation. The 'Britannia' landed perfectly, as if it was apologising for the previous inconvenience! As the aircraft came to a halt, Steve peered out of the window; a green painted 'Bedford' army truck was slowly making its way across the tarmac towards them. It was good to see the familiar shape of the 'Bedford' and a welcome reminder of home after all the foreign sights and sounds of the previous twenty hours.

The platoon was instructed to wait in the aircraft until the kitbags were loaded onto the truck. They were surprised that the task was not theirs. They did not realise it but in the Far East they were about to be strangely pampered with the luxury of Boot Boys', Laundry Boys, Chinese seamstresses to tailor their clothes and darn socks, and purveyors of very cheap cold drinks.

They left the 'Britannia' with stiff limbs after so much inactivity. It would be several hours before they were back to normal, both physically and mentally, the time differences alone would alter their body 'clocks'. Once again there were no passport or customs checks, in a way they were treated like V.I.P.'s, and drove away through a private airport gate.

The 'Bedford', painted in jungle green instead of the 'khaki' colour used in the UK, drove along the busy streets which were filled with rickshaws, trishaws, seemingly thousands of Chinese people, and above all, noise! They all marvelled at the 'rickety', ramshackle lorries, held together by pieces of rope, string, and odd pieces of wood. The lorries were filled to the 'brim' with all kinds of commercial goods off-loaded from the busy seaport.

Malayans and Chinese, many of them barefoot, carried bamboo poles across their shoulders, laden down with heavy wares. There was an air of 'busyness' about them as they scurried along the streets. A colourful festive dragon appeared from a side street, and weaved its way along the main road, Chinese firecrackers adding to the cacophony of sound. Strung across the road, advertising signs made of cotton material added to the colourful scene, and long bamboo poles protruded from upper windows, laden with washed clothes.

One of the workers stopped, relieved himself into the storm drain at the side of the road, and then hurried on his way, the bamboo poles across his shoulders bending under the weight of its heavy load.

From further down the road somebody was rapidly banging on a tin tray, increasing the almost deafening sound. The chatter of Chinese conversation was everywhere. The scene was one of total chaos, but wonderful!

The platoon looked at each other; they had just entered the 'Gateway to the East'!

CHAPTER 30

During the platoon's short stay in Singapore they were to be 'housed' with a squadron of Royal Engineers in the southern part of the island.

The Engineers, who were also on a three-year tour of duty, were responsible for operating a military seaport in an area called Tanjong Berlayer. They also had the task of operating the British Army railway network on Singapore Island. The network, although relatively small was a vital link in connecting the many base workshops and underground munition stores with the Malayan State Railway.

Malaya had gained its independence from the British Empire in 1957. The Malayan Communist Party (M.C.P.) was trying to take over control of the country from its safe haven in the north by filling the power vacuum that had ensued when the British left the country. Singapore was the base for operations against communists, and British, Australians and other Commonwealth forces were fully engaged in the conflict. The small islands of the south coast of Singapore provided secure bases and respite areas for many of the regiments engaged in the jungle fighting in Malaya, including a regiment of Ghurkas. The men from Nepal adapted well to the jungle fighting, and were proving to be the downfall of many groups of M.C.P. infiltrators in northern Malaya.

The army and Malayan railways were therefore an invaluable source of transport. The military port also played its part by connecting the small islands with the main island of Singapore. A fleet of vehicle / personnel carrying craft were in constant use, plus a number of motor launches for officers and Foreign Office personnel use.

The platoon arrived at the camp and off-loaded the kitbags into the accommodation that had been provided. The Engineer squadron was not overly large, some eighty or ninety men, and there were several barrack rooms available. The camp's accommodation was vastly different from the barrack rooms in the U.K. The rooms were bungalow design, housing six men. They were made of wood, with corrugated tin roofs. Steve could imagine the noise of rain hitting the tin at night, not being conducive to peaceful sleep! There was no false ceiling, and two large electric fans were suspended from the wooden rafters. There was a doorway, but no door, square window spaces, but no glazing or shutters. It was all designed for the free movement of air in the tropical climate.

After drawing bedding from the stores and taking out basic requirements from their kitbags, the platoon went to the Engineer squadron cookhouse for their first 'square meal' in twenty-four hours. In the cookhouse salads were the order of the day. Meat balls, beef stew and 'cockaleekie' soup were for the U.K. Lighter food was required in hot climates, with plenty of liquids to prevent dehydration. The latter requirement pleased Mac, and he looked forward to sampling the local brew.

The cookhouse was a very permanent building of concrete and red brick. But the design was the same as the single storey barrack room bungalows, but on a grander scale. The cookhouse did have more ceiling fans, but they had little effect, and sweating was accepted as part of life, day and night.

The ambient temperature was in the low eighties 'Fahrenheit' which was acceptable, but the humidity was high and made clothes stick to the skin. The platoon was allowed to wear civilian clothes for the duration of the journey and stopover. They would be issued with jungle green uniforms when they arrived in Hong Kong. The Engineers looked fairly cool and smart in their tropical kit, and the platoon looked forward to receiving theirs. Regulation black army boots still had to be worn with the tropical kit, together with knee length woollen socks. 'Putties' made of a felt material were used as a 'wrap around' cover between boots and socks, partly for smartness, and partly for protection against snake bites.

After a welcome meal the men followed their normal routine and went to the camp N.A.A.F.I. to sample the local brew. N.A.A.F.I.'s seemed to be the same the world over. The only difference was the design of the building and the materials it was made of. But of course, the 'Blonde Bombshell' was unique to 'Morval', there was no other!

Once again there were no doors or windows, but the aroma of beer, cigarette smoke and pies was unmistakeable, and B.B. would have fitted into the scene like a duck taking to water! The men almost expected her to appear from behind the counter, touching her hair, and swishing her flared skirt.

The majority of the engineers were busy at the port or running the railway. A small number were off duty, and shared a beer or two with the platoon. They were a mix of National Servicemen and professional soldiers, just as the platoon was. The engineers, or sappers, as they were traditionally called, were a friendly bunch. Most of them had served more than two years in Singapore, and were suntanned and hardened physically and mentally by the climate and experience of serving in the Far East.

Steve with his knowledge of steam engines soon made friends with the railwaymen in the squadron. They offered to show him the railway locomotives and the network, but there was no time as it was only a short 'flying' visit. Several of the 'loco' crews had worked for the railways in the U.K. before joining the army, and knew their jobs back to front. The engines they operated in Singapore were built in England, which made their job even easier; it was like taking your own car on holiday! They described the locomotives to Steve. Some were built by the 'Hunslet' Company in the Midlands, and others by Avonside Engine Company in Bristol. One of the engines sported a three-inch shell hole through its steel cab, a souvenir of the Japanese occupation!

The conversation in the N.A.A.F.I. came around to the Singapore nightlife. The sappers made it sound very inviting, and although the platoon was due to continue its journey to Hong Kong at midday the next day they decided to use every minute and visit Singapore City in the evening. The engineers described a typical 'night out' as going to the late night cinema show, (the midnight movie), followed by a visit to the notorious, but interesting 'Bugis' Street at 2.00am to savour the Chinese atmosphere of local food, beer, and very friendly female company! They should return to camp at daybreak, hopefully having had a memorable time. They could always try to sleep on the 'Britannia' during the final leg of the journey.

After several pints of the local brew, which turned out to be a lager type beer called 'Tiger', the men decided to rest on their beds for a few hours until it was time to venture into the city of Singapore. It was strange not to have uniforms to wear or duties to perform; they intended to enjoy the freedom while it lasted. The sombre duties of Hong Kong would come soon enough!

They slept well, tired from the journey, but when they awoke all were sweating profusely. It was harsh evidence that they were in a very different environment, and it would take some time to adjust. Steve wiped the sweat from his face and looked up at the roof beams. Small grey lizards were scurrying along the beams. At first sight they looked repulsive, but they were performing a very useful purpose by devouring mosquitoes, the carriers of malaria, which was something the platoon could do without. The lizards were the men's 'friends', and not to be discouraged in any way! The odd one, according to the sappers, was apt to drop onto their beds during the night. But that was a natural hazard of the job, and a friendly lizard running across your face at three in the morning was a small price to pay for warding off malaria!

The 'Three Musketeers' decided they would go into Singapore City together. None of them had much money to spend, and with all the travelling it was not certain when the next 'pay parade' would be. They 'pooled' their resources to check how much they could amass. They understood from the Engineers that a night out in Singapore could be quite cheap, but they needed as much as possible, in case of anomalies such as extra beers!

Taff was the more thrifty of the trio, and said that as it was a special occasion he would pay the 'lion's' share. He fished around in the bottom of his kitbag, and pulled out a large bag of money. Mac looked at Taff and beamed at him; he was a friend for life! Their cash was all in pounds 'Sterling', but they were told that it could be changed for Singapore dollars at the camp's wages office.

After sprucing themselves up, the trio left the camp armed with the knowledge passed on by the sappers, and full pockets, thanks to Taff. As they left the camp they were surprised by the lack of security and military discipline. It was a very different atmosphere to the very strict training camps they had encountered in the U.K., and although there was an obvious conflict being played out in the north, it was purposefully made low-key in order not to panic the population, or the forces.

They had arrived at the bus stop, and after a wait of fifteen minutes a green and cream painted single deck bus screeched to a halt. Steve looked at the bus, it was strangely familiar! He later learnt from the Engineers that the Singapore Bus Company had purchased a fleet of second-hand 'Leyland' buses from a county council in England, all part of the colonial relationship. The English council had decided to modernise its fleet, and were delighted to sell the well-worn buses to the Singapore Company. Steve smiled to himself, he had a fair idea who the English county council might be, and half expected to see the rotund gearbox 'cruncher' any minute; was it possible that he had been sold with the bus?

The 'Musketeers' paid their fare of fifty cents each, and the bus set off down the bumpy road to the city. The 'Leyland' was certainly very second-hand, and the worn body springs, coupled with the effects of the poor road surfaces produced a rattle that Steve had become used to in Hampshire. It reminded him of his visits to Lorraine and their happy times together. It was heart wrenching, but it was time to move on, and he silently rebuked himself for allowing the thoughts to enter his mind.

The bus reached the city centre. It had been an uncomfortable ride, but interesting. Steve saw very few private cars on the roads, and those that he did see were quite old and dilapidated. The main form of transport was the bus, or for European tourists the taxi. Strangely the taxis were quite modern, mostly driven by Indians or Sikhs in their traditional turbans. Rickshaws and trishaws, (a bicycle with an open sidecar attached), were more popular for short journeys into the town.

Using the sappers' instructions, the trio found the 'Britannia Club', which was situated directly opposite the famous Raffles Hotel on the seafront. They had some time to spare before the late cinema show, and sampling the local 'Tiger' beer seemed to be a good idea. The 'Britannia Club' was strictly for the use of personnel from the armed forces. It was a modern building of concrete and brick with large windows which made the interior very light and airy, much needed in the tropical heat.

They entered the club, which was well patronised by all of the services. There were very few servicewomen in the spacious lounge, and the singing of lusty rugby and other lewd songs seemed to be popular. Steve looked around him; there was more 'Tiger' beer on the floor than in the bottles and glasses on the tables. It wasn't Steve's ideal setting, but he decided to adopt the saying, 'When in Rome'! Mac on the other hand was immediately at home, and Taff, after two pints of 'Tiger' joined in singing the rugby songs. Steve was surprised how well he knew the dubious unprintable words! The 'Brit Club' was in stark contrast to the sedate colonial Raffles Hotel opposite!

When it was time, they left the loud, beer swilled club. It was obviously a place where servicemen could 'let off steam', and it seemed to work very well. The trio made their way to the cinema for the midnight movie. It soon became apparent why the show was held at a late hour. The temperature had dropped markedly, and the cinema was fairly cool and pleasant for watching a film. The movie was in English, and most of the cinema goers were European. The Chinese and Indian populations had smaller, 'open air' cinemas, which seemed to be a good idea to Steve. But colonial Europeans could not give up their traditional habits, and they would suffer the consequences, come what may!

When the show ended it was almost 2.00am. The film had been a dour dramatic story of early settlers in the 'Wild West' of America, and the

'Musketeers' were glad to leave and find the celebrated 'Bugis Street' that the engineers had highly recommended. They still had plenty of money, mostly Taff's, and hailed a taxi to Bugis Street, otherwise they could be looking in vain for the rest of the night. The taxi driver, an Indian, laughed when they asked for Bugis Street. He said something in his native tongue, but the trio had no idea what.

It was only a short journey to the street. If they had known the roads they could have walked the distance. Steve grudgingly paid the driver, and the Indian pointed to a small narrow street about fifty yards away. For some reason he was anxious about going any closer. The night was dark, and Steve had second thoughts about going any further, but after a brief discussion with the other two they decided to take the plunge. They turned the corner and walked into Bugis Street.

It was like entering a different world. The dimly lit street was a completely ramshackle Heath Robinson construction. Cafes and bars lined the whole street on both sides. Although the street was narrow, in front of the bars and cafes were Chinese 'wok' stalls, all cooking different selections of Chinese food. The stalls were all built of odd pieces of wood and material, possibly rescued from the flotsam of the nearby Singapore River and seaport. The pungent smell of Chinese cooking was everywhere, mixed with the aroma of 'Tiger' beer, and the fact that there were few toilet facilities in the area.

The cafes and bars were full of servicemen, mostly British and Australian. Bottles of beer and spirits filled the tables, and several of the servicemen were stretched out on the stone floor, obviously 'tired' from lifting heavy glasses of beer and spirits! Women, 'of ill repute', scantily dressed, mingled with the servicemen. They were mainly Chinese, but others were darker skinned, possibly from Indonesia or Sumatra which was not far away.

The trio found a free table and began to 'drink in' the heady Oriental atmosphere. Mac was in his element, and it wasn't long before the 'Three Musketeers' attracted plenty of female company. Compared to the Saturday night dance in Somerset this was complete debauchery.

'Tiger' beer was fairly weak in strength, but coupled with the heat and humidity was just as potent as the dark brew in Scotland. After six or seven pints Steve lost count and the trio moved to one of the outside 'wok' stalls to savour some authentic Chinese cooking. The stall holder, a mature Chinaman, with sunken cheeks and closely cropped hair was busy tending to the contents of his 'wok'.

Steve peered into the sizzling mixture of food, and could recognise squid, octopus, bean sprouts and chopped vegetables. There were several other ingredients, mostly types of meat and fish, but they were naturally foreign to him. The cooking and food was certainly authentic, but the stall hygiene was questionable. After many pints of 'Tiger', thoughts of hygiene and food poisoning had faded into the background. They were hungry, and any caution was thrown to the wind! They managed to convey their order to the stall holder, and he put more oil and extra meat and fish into the sizzling wok.

The rickety wooden stools, made from old pieces of packing cases were provided for the stall's clients, but they looked uncomfortable and unsafe. Mac gave one a shake, and decided to stand. The wok was sizzling well, and the stall holder was pleased that he had some well-heeled customers.

Mac was naturally feeling slightly 'tired' after consuming many 'Tigers' and whisky 'chasers'. He leant on the edge of the stall for support. The ramshackle construction collapsed under his weight, and the full wok, together with the bottles of sauces on the stall, shot into the air, and landed in the centre of the narrow street.

Within a matter of seconds, the whole street changed into chaos. The Chinese stall holder convinced that Mac had destroyed his stall on purpose shouted for help, and the other stall holders bore down on the unfortunate trio. They quickly agreed it was time to leave Bugis Street. They ran to the end of the street, the Chinese stall holders in hot pursuit, two of them brandishing very aggressive looking knives.

Fortunately, the surrounding streets were in total darkness, and the trio were very fit from their eight weeks of hard training in the U.K. They quickly put distance between themselves and the irate stall holders. Steve saw an open air amusement park further down the road, and the three decided to try and lose themselves in the throng of pleasure seekers, there was safety in numbers! But the stall holders had not given up the chase and wanted their pound of flesh. The amusement park, called the 'Happy World' was still crowded with people even though it was four-thirty in the morning, and the trio was glad of the respite. They were fit, but the heat and the 'Tiger' beer had drained their energy. For the moment they had lost the knife brandishing stall holders, and they mingled gratefully with the crowd of fun seekers.

After half an hour they ventured back out into the dark streets. It was quiet; the stall holders had given up the chase and returned to Bugis Street. Steve saw bright lights in the distance, and they walked quickly towards them. Eventually they found themselves back at the 'Britannia Club' and the 'Raffles'. The club, which operated under strict military regulations, was closed, but several taxis were parked outside the 'Raffles', and the trio gladly hired one, gratefully sinking into the well upholstered seats. The taxi made good time on the almost deserted streets, and before long they found themselves back at the camp, none the worse for their adventure in Singapore City!

It was six o'clock in the morning and daybreak. Steve looked out of the window space and into the breaking dawn. It was still warm and the sound of the insects and birds in the trees, created a morning 'symphony of the East'. He felt as if he could spend the rest of his life there. If Hong Kong was a similar place, he would be happy. Singapore was his Gateway to Life!

At midday the platoon packed their kitbags and loaded them onto the truck. They left the sappers to continue with the important work of running the seaport and railway. Not forgetting the equally responsible job of keeping the employees of the 'Tiger' beer company fully occupied!

CHAPTER 31

When they arrived at Singapore Airport the 'Britannia' was waiting patiently for them on the tarmac apron. The aircraft had become a friendly servant, delivering them safely to a destination, and waiting responsibly for them to return for the next leg of the journey to Hong Kong.

They settled into their seats and the aircraft pre-flight checks were carried out by the crew. The majority of the cargo having been delivered to their destinations, left the 'Britannia' with a hollow sound to it, and the interior of the fuselage looked even more gigantic than before. The hollow sounds of the aircraft seemed to heighten the hangovers the 'Three Musketeers' were feeling from their escapade in Singapore City the night before. But it was a small price to pay for such an experience. The hangovers would go, but the memory of Singapore City and Bugis Street would stay an enjoyable, dramatic memory forever. The stopover in Singapore had been an 'eye-opener' for all of the men, but Chinese stall holders wielding long knives was a little too realistic, and could have ended in a very different way. Once again the words of William Shakespeare came to Steve's mind, 'All's well that Ends well', but despite the drama he hoped that he could return to the wonderful island one day and discover more of its magic.

As the 'Britannia' took off and headed for Hong Kong he looked out of the window and said 'au revoir', not goodbye!

The sappers were fortunate to be there, and he knew from their conversations that none wanted to leave, including the National Servicemen. They came to the Far East as boys, and went home men!

The men's hangovers receded as the aircraft gathered height, and they were grateful for that. Mac recommended the cure; all one needed was a private 'Britannia' instantly available! The aircraft made good time with its lighter load, and travelled north over the South China Sea. As the last leg of the journey progressed, Steve talked with the other men. They had all enjoyed the stopover in their own way. The 'Lawyer' had carried out a sightseeing expedition, and now had much to write about. In the limited time he had done well, visiting the 'Tiger Balm Gardens' and the beautiful Botanical Gardens with its families of monkeys roaming freely in the exotic greenery. He even had time to visit the notorious 'Changi' jail in his sightseeing expedition, the jail being in the north of the island and fairly isolated as many prisons are. From the 'Lawyer's' description of the jail Steve was glad he had not experienced the Japanese occupation of the island during the Second World War. It must have been a very, very different place to be in, but life was life, and history was important. He made a promise to himself that if he did return to Singapore one day he would make sure to visit 'Changi' and study it, hopefully just from the outside!

The 'Britannia' started to descend, signalling its approach to Kai Tak Airport, Hong Kong. The huge aircraft broke through the bank of cloud to reveal the skyline of Hong Kong Island and the airport runway jutting out into the sea. The tarmac runway was surrounded on three sides by water. It reminded Steve of the island of Gan in the Indian Ocean, and as he looked out of the window he prayed silently for a minute hoping they would not have a similar dramatic landing. Chinese stall holders were acceptable, but crash landings are not to be recommended!

The 'Britannia' made a perfect landing, assisted by the competent pilot and crew. The majestic aircraft was making its last friendly gesture to them, delivering them to the final destination of their long journey. It was only a huge structure of metal, plastic and material, but it had played a part in the previous twenty-four hours.

They were met at the airport building by a sergeant and driver from the regiment, and quickly ushered to a private exit gate. Once again there was no passport check or customs ritual to contend with, and they enjoyed another moment of being treated like V.I.P.'s. But the sensation was short-lived when they saw the transport provided for them.

The truck detailed to carry them to their permanent camp was ancient to say the least. The transport, although well maintained and usable was an old 'Bedford' Q.L., the predecessor to the modern R.L. The three tonner was built in the U.K., but had served many years in the Orient, and had the scars to prove it. Chinese drivers were not the most careful in the world, as Steve was to find out in the near future. It seemed to Steve that the further east they ventured, the transport in general became less and less modern. The very second-hand buses in Singapore came to mind. Nonetheless, as they clambered aboard the Q.L.

Docherty picked the moment to shout to the driver, "Home, James, and don't spare the horses!"

The Q.L. was to take the platoon north on the mainland through an area called the 'New Territories', to their camp near the border with China. The island of Hong Kong and the 'New Territories' on the mainland were 'leased' to the U.K. from China for a period of ninety-nine years. When that time had expired the land would be returned to China, unless a further agreement was reached. But Hong Kong had become a commercial success under the guidance of the British, and it was becoming clear that the Chinese wanted to take advantage of the situation.

After loading the kitbags and making themselves as comfortable as possible on the harsh wooden seats of the Q.L., the truck slowly made its way along the crowded streets, weaving its way around the array of rickshaws and other transport unique to Chinese roads. At one point Steve noticed a wooden single bed, wheels suitably attached to form a means of transporting goods! The Chinese were inventive if nothing else.

The journey continued and a second Q.L. picked them up in Kowloon for the final leg of its journey to the camp. The road surfaces became worse and the terrain less interesting. The harshness of the seats became more noticeable, and Steve decided to pass the time away by writing a letter to Aunt Maude. Much had happened in a short space of time, and there was enough news to fill a long letter. He borrowed the 'Lawyer's' notepad and pencil. The 'Lawyer' handed it to Steve as if he was losing an old friend. Steve smilingly assured him he would not use many pages, and offered to buy him a new pad as soon as possible.

He started to write, and as he did so his thoughts went back to his young teenage days in Somerset. His first teenage 'love', Joy, would possibly be starting a family with her solicitor husband now. No doubt her meddling mother was fussing and 'clucking' about like an old mother hen, and keeping her fellow ladies at the W.I. fully informed of each nappy change! Steve wasn't one to normally hold a grudge, but with Joy's mother he made an exception. He enjoyed having a little silent self-indulgent 'dig' at her now and again. It was good for the soul!

Steve was certain that Aunt Maude would be interested in Hong Kong; it would be like something in a fantasy story for her. As soon as he could afford it he intended to buy a reasonable good quality camera, and send photos from time to time with his letters to her. With the advent of 'mass production' methods, cameras, and even washing machines, refrigerators, and even small family cars were becoming available to the ordinary working man in the street. They were no longer the sole right of the so- called 'upper classes'. The High Street businesses were also introducing the system of paying on the 'never never'. It was no longer necessary for a shopper to save a large sum of money in order to buy an expensive article. It was becoming possible to pay in instalments over a period of six or even twelve months. People purchasing items didn't seem to mind paying the extra interest that was incurred. The business fraternity had made a shrewd, clever move, and it was here to stay. Television was becoming popular and more affordable to the working man, once again by mass production and the financial hire/purchase agreements. TV was within the grasp of most household budgets, and the 'box' took pride and place on the living room table, sat on a white starched linen cloth, and several of the families knick-knacks either side of it to make it a show piece. The routine Saturday night visit to the cinema was fast disappearing. Film producers, ice cream makers and sweet companies were suffering losses, due to Logie Baird's and other scientists' inventions. Such is progress!

Steve wondered what modern technology was heading to. Weapons of mass destruction, a scientific invention, had been used at Hiroshima. Science could be used for good, or possibly evil! It was possible that man would be devoured by his own adventurous inventions and destroy himself and the world he lived in. Steve shuddered at the thought, and decided to end the letter, and with it his worldly, perhaps overly intense meanderings. He ended the letter to Aunt Maude saying he hoped she was well and that he missed her smiling face and firm words of advice. But most of all he missed her cheese and pickled onion sandwiches! It would be three long years before his taste buds could react to the flavour again. He licked his lips in memory of them and smiled. The sandwiches Lorraine had made for him on the day of their parting were tasty, but not the same. But there was consolation in potpourri and king-size beds! It was the little things in life that mattered; modern technology would have to take care of itself!

Steve handed the notebook and pencil back to the 'Lawyer', who accepted them with a look of relief on his face. He had watched closely as the sheets of paper were devoured, saying goodbye as each completed page disappeared into Steve's pocket.

The tedious journey continued and Steve looked out of the truck at the surrounding countryside. It was rocky, barren land, and he wondered why the

Chinese would want it back at all. Possibly there were precious minerals in the ground, or maybe huge oil reserves. They were heading to an area called Nee Soon, and their permanent camp called 'Gillman'. Steve assumed that it was named after a previous 'Governor' of Hong Kong or a prominent military figure.

After three hours' steady driving over the pot holed roads, the terrain became greener and the flat, uninteresting land gave way to rolling hills. Trees and shrubbery began to appear, and the feeling of being in 'no man's land' disappeared. They reached the camp in the early evening, all ready for a hopefully hot meal. The kitbags were off-loaded, and the exhausted Q.L. truck limped off to the transport garage. Steve looked around him, the camp was certainly isolated, but the interesting seafront of Kowloon was not too far away. To the north, a distance of about five miles away, lay China.

'Gillman' camp was much the same as 'Churchill' in Singapore but spread over a greater area; Singapore was a relatively small place. The bungalow type 'bashas' were the same design, but with the luxury of closable doors and glazed windows. They had travelled many miles north from the hot climate of Singapore, and the temperatures had decreased. Steve noticed a small number of lizards looking down at him from the roof beams, but they were not as large or plentiful as the wildlife at 'Churchill' camp. The men were growing used to having animals in the 'basha', it was almost like keeping a cat or a dog as a pet!

Steve took control of one of the 'bashas', together with Mac, Taff, Docherty, the 'Lawyer' and Charlie Strong. After unpacking their much travelled kitbags and drawing bedding from the stores, the platoon went to the cookhouse with empty stomachs; the rumbling noises from Mac's increasing girth were noticeable!

The buildings in the sprawling camp were connected by narrow pathways with greenery on either side, the grass almost knee high. The six newcomers, looking forward to a good 'square meal', strode along the narrow pathway towards the cookhouse, knife, fork, spoon, and drinking mug in hand. Although tired from the journey, they were all in a jovial mood. As they rounded a bend in the pathway a six foot long snake slithered across the pathway in front of them, and disappeared into the long grass. The six stopped in their tracks, not believing what they had just seen.

The 'Lawyer' made a rapid about turn, and announced that he was returning to the 'basha' for his 'routine' bowel movement! The other five said nothing, and after some hesitation continued making their way to the cookhouse. They picked up plates and joined the queue of men waiting to be served. Steve told the serving cook about the snake. He wasn't surprised.

"There's a few around here," he said. "Just leave them alone and they'll leave you alone." He accentuated his remark by 'dumping' a large scoop of mashed potatoes onto Steve's plate.

The 'Lawyer' finally arrived, hunger overcoming his natural fears. Mac asked him, tongue in cheek, "Did you discover 'perpetual' motion in the 'basha'?"

The 'Lawyer' looked at him sternly and replied, "My bodily functions are a strictly private matter between myself and members of the local sanitation department!" The 'Lawyer' sat down and licked the tip of his pencil, feeling he had made his point.

Charlie Strong in one of his rare moments of humour added, in his medically biological way, "When you gotta go, you gotta go!"

They talked about the snake as they ate; the experience hadn't dampened their appetites.

"The snake," Steve said, "was a python anyway," a little piece of knowledge he had learnt from reading adventure and explorer books. He continued, "Pythons are not poisonous, they kill their prey by squeezing it to death, and usually drop onto it from a branch of a tree."

"The thing to do," Mac interjected, 'was not to walk under too many trees!"

The 'Lawyer' made a quick note in his book, and underlined it heavily.

The universal ritual of retiring to the camp N.A.A.F.I. after a meal was followed. They shared a beer or two with some of the regiment's longer serving men. Many of them were due to return to the regiment's base in the U.K. The National Servicemen among them were looking forward to it, but for the professionals the posting was almost ideal and they would gladly stay. The life in Hong Kong was pleasant and returning to the U.K. with all of its guard duties, ceremonial parades and 'spit and polish' was not something to look forward to after being pampered in the Far East.

For the price of twenty cents a week they could hire a 'Boot Boy' to clean and polish their army boots and civilian shoes. For a further fifty cents a week they could employ a 'Laundry Boy' or woman to wash and iron their clothes. Guard duties were kept to a minimum, and ceremonial parades were allotted to other units. The platoon smiled at the news, things were looking up!

There were one or two negatives in the equation however. The beer in the N.A.A.F.I. was all bottled imported 'brew', the most popular being 'San

Miguel'. The news that no 'draught' beer was available was a 'bitter' blow to the experienced drinkers in the platoon. But it was an imperfect world, and there had to be a certain amount of 'give and take'! As far as Mac was concerned, he said that having someone to polish his boots everyday was a fair trade for having no draught beer. Mac, if nothing else was big hearted!

After coming to terms with bottled 'San Miguel', and consuming as much of it as their sensitive systems could deal with, they returned to the 'basha' and prepared for their first night's sleep in Hong Kong. Singapore had been a pleasant stepping stone to Hong Kong, but it was a long way from the security of Hampshire, and the U.K. In the morning they were to be issued with 'jungle green' uniforms, and attend an induction lecture given by the camp C.O.

The night temperature was warm. There was no need for blankets on the beds. Steve covered himself with a cotton sheet, the ceiling fans were put on half speed and the motors gave off a soft 'whirring' sound, but not enough to keep the men from sleeping. In the darkness Steve could hear the lizards moving to their own places for sleep, the day was done! The platoon was all suffering from travel 'time difference', but the 'San Miguel' helped to neutralise that. There was something to be said for bottled beer after all!

Before closing his eyes to sleep, Steve thought of the previous thirty-six hours. So much had happened in a short space of time, and there was to be no respite for the time being. In the morning they would receive new uniforms and attend the all-important 'pay parade' issued in Hong Kong dollars.

As the lizards settled down to sleep, he idly thought about the oncoming morning, and breakfast. Would baked beans in tomato sauce be on the menu as at 'Morval'? Heinz beans had become popular with the platoon since hearing about Mac's 'Grandad Joe' and his formula for longevity and sexual activity in Dewsbury. Docherty, amongst others, was convinced that he felt more virile since taking regular platefuls of the beans in a rich sauce. But Mac issued a word of warning to the platoon about the dangers of consuming too many beans, and the possibility of 'overdosing'! Grandad Joe, he said, at one time in his erotic career had suffered certain 'peculiar' side effects! He had made a large placard, suspended it from his shoulders using pieces of string and marched around the centre of Dewsbury dressed in his 'Fifty Shilling Tailors' brown suit and a black top hat. He wanted to write 'Beware the end is nigh' on the placard, but Joe couldn't spell the word 'nigh' so instead he wrote, 'Beware the End is Bloody Nearly Here'!

CHAPTER 32

In the morning after a 'brew' assisted sleep the platoon awoke at 7.00am to the sound of birds calling in the nearby trees, and grasshoppers in the grass that surrounded the 'basha', furiously rubbing their legs together in the morning conversation. Other smaller insects tried to compete in the morning call ritual. Chinese and Indian civilians who worked in the camp chatted animatedly as they went to their jobs. They were 'Boot Boys' and 'Laundry Boys'. The word 'boys' was used very loosely, some of them being in their late fifties! It was a vastly different sound to the early morning skirl of the bagpipes in Scotland, or maybe not?

The corporal in charge of the cookhouse was a Scotsman from Edinburgh. He had introduced porridge onto the breakfast menu, and apparently haggis had played a prominent part in the previous Christmas festivities. As Steve chopped a banana into his porridge he thought to himself, *It's a small world!*

Most of the platoon turned to porridge or other cereals for breakfast, but Mac in particular obstinately refused to give up his daily sausage, egg and bacon. His girth was increasing noticeably, and there was no longer enthusiastic Physical Training Instructors (P.T.I.'s) at hand to 'knock' him back in to shape. Basic training was over, and a certain amount of self-discipline was required now.

After breakfast the men paraded in front of the 'basha', and Steve marched the platoon to the clothing store for the issue of their long awaited jungle green uniform. The sizes were very loosely marked 'Small, Medium and Large, but they were assured by the issuing staff that for a few Hong Kong dollars the local Chinese seamstresses would alter the material to produce a perfect individual fit. They were also advised that for a few extra dollars and cents perfectly fitting sharkskin shirts could be made by the expert seamstresses, ideal for social visits to Kowloon and Hong Kong. The men were indeed becoming pampered V.I.P.'s.

When they returned to the 'bashas' clutching their newly acquired uniforms the Chinese seamstresses were already milling around the doorways, chatting excitedly to each other. They knew the camps routines better than the men, and the women quickly picked out their clients. They spoke little English, but that didn't seem to matter! With tape measures in hand they went about their tasks expertly, and after a little haggling over prices, mostly in sign language, they left the men in a somewhat dazed condition, minus their new uniforms. In the morning the seamstresses would return with the work completed.

It was the platoon's first encounter with Chinese efficiency. Having selected their clients carefully, each seamstress regarded him as her personal 'property' for the duration of his stay in camp, and heaven help any other seamstress who tried to 'muscle' in! The same principle applied to the 'Boot Boys' and 'Laundry Boys'. It was a system that had been tried and tested over a long period of time; the platoon had little say in the matter.

Later, still dressed in their civilian clothes, the platoon attended the Commanding Officer's induction lecture. The C.O. was a major in his late forties. He spoke like many officers of his kind in a very correct 'Oxford' voice, and as with most graduates of the Sandhurst Military College it was impossible to tell which part of the U.K. he came from.

The lecture was planned to last an hour, starting with some personal advice and instructions for the new platoon. They were advised not to drink the local tap water, which pleased Mac and the other beer 'swillers'. They were also instructed to stay out of the brothels in Hong Kong, which didn't go down so well.

The lecture turned to the more important work patrolling the border. It was essential that they fully understood the rules and regulations of the job. The Chinese authorities were almost paranoid about the border, and any error of judgement, whether it was great or small was immediately reported to the Hong Kong governor and officials at the Foreign Office in London.

The platoon was to be issued with Sterling semi-automatic guns for use when on border patrol duty. The Sterling was ideal for such duties, designed for close skirmish encounters, not a long range weapon like the 7.62 SLR. The Sterling was a sophisticated update on the cheaply manufactured Sten gun used for street to street fighting in the Second World War.

The C.O. made it clear that the weapons were to be kept securely locked in the 'basha' personal lockers. All ammunition was to be kept in the camp armoury, and only issued directly before a patrol. On completion of a patrol duty all 'rounds' of ammunition had to be returned to the armoury and accounted for. If any rounds had been fired during a patrol an immediate inquiry was held by the C.O. to ascertain why the bullets had been used. The border situation was always uppermost in the C.O.'s mind. In the morning after parade and inspection they would march to the camp's 'short' firing range, and become accustomed to their new weapons.

The lecture overran its scheduled time, and they had missed the cookhouse meal. But the N.A.A.F.I. was always available under such emergencies, and after the platoon had been dismissed from the lecture they took refuge in the club and the comfort of beer and steak and kidney pies. In half an hour's time they would attend the all-important 'pay parade', their pockets were extremely empty!

'Pay parade' was held in the 'basha', using the central table as the 'pay desk'. The Paymaster was the regiment's R.S.M., resplendent in his starched jungle green uniform and highly polished badge of rank on his wrist.

The men were paid in Hong Kong dollars and cents. It was strange not to pick up pounds Sterling from the desk. 'Docherty' counted his pay, calling it 'Mickey Mouse' money, but as Steve received his pay and pushed it into his pocket he seemed to have more dollars than he would have had pounds, Mickey or no Mickey!

Now that the platoon was on 'active service' a full corporal was to be attached to them from the main regiment, and would take overall charge of border patrols. Steve, as a lance corporal would be his second-in-command. The corporal had been introduced to the platoon at the end of the lecture without any undue ceremony by the C.O.

The corporal went by the surname of Hanson. He was a 'Geordie', and hailed from Newcastle upon Tyne. His grandparents were Scots, but 'Geordie' was Newcastle through and through, and a keen 'Toon' football supporter. Steve was to learn a great deal from the man who had served more than ten years with the regiment, and they were to become equally trusting friends.

In the morning, they awoke to a fresh sunny day, with plenty of Hong Kong dollars in their pockets. It was difficult to understand the true value of the new money, but there was no doubt that the exchange rate was in their favour, and they felt like millionaires. The seamstresses were waiting outside the 'basha' doorway with the uniforms duly altered, washed, and pressed. They had probably worked most of the night, but were cheerful and grateful to receive the meagre financial return for their work.

The men tried the jungle green uniforms on for the first time. It was very different compared to the heavy khaki battledress used in colder climates. Their knees looked strangely anaemic in the short trousers. They were issued with other long trousers, but these were to be used for night duty when the temperature dropped quite dramatically in winter. The complete uniform comprised of a green tunic/shirt, with breast pockets and lapels, short trousers, a green web belt, knee length socks, puttees and normal black leather boots. The original black beret, carrying the regiment's badge completed the uniform.

Steve, being a junior N.C.O. was allowed to wear a regimental 'stable' belt, a six-inch-wide elasticated belt in the regiment's colours. This made him easily recognisable, just as Military Police wore red caps to make them stand out in a crowd of people.

The seamstresses had made a good job of altering the uniforms, and it would not be long before the platoon felt at ease in them, they were a vast improvement to the 'off the peg' khaki battledress at 'Morval' training camp. They went to the cookhouse for breakfast, and with their white knees were instantly recognisable as 'new boys'. They had to endure a few minutes of derisory humour and 'wolf whistles', but in a week or so their knees would be 'weathered' and the platoon fully integrated. Steve enjoyed his porridge and fruit, as did most of the others. But Mac and other stalwarts of the traditional English fry up continued with their habit, and as Mac left the cookhouse he was seen to loosen his web belt and mutter to himself, "By gum, lad!"

After breakfast and a first inspection of their uniforms by the R.S.M. the platoon marched to the armoury for the issue of Sterlings. The armourer, a sergeant from the R.E.M.E. (Royal Electrical & Mechanical Engineers), instructed them on the mechanics of the gun and how to maintain it on a daily basis. They signed for their weapons, and were once again reminded that the Sterlings had to be kept in personal lockers under lock and key. They drew ammunition, and spent half an hour on the 'short' firing range, under the watchful eye of the armourer, becoming accustomed to the new weapons.

When they returned to the 'basha' the 'Boot Boys' had assembled outside of the doorway, all seeking employment. After a certain amount of traditional haggling over prices and some light-hearted banter with the 'Boys' who spoke some English, satisfactory deals were struck. But once again the men weren't completely sure who was employing who! Steve had the feeling he had been slightly conned but in a very pleasant way.

Steve's 'Boot Boy' was a fresh faced, cheerful fifteen-year-old Chinese boy called So Lo.

Amazingly he spoke very good English, possibly better than some of the platoon. His main job was as a 'Boot Boy', but for a few extra cents he would act as an interpreter. He also carried a large wicker basket full of cold drinks and salad filled bread rolls, the food all neatly wrapped in rice paper. So Lo with his mastery of the English language, and obvious business acumen, was destined for far greater things in the commercial world.

The civilians camp 'grapevine' had signalled the platoon was in their 'bashas', and open for business. The seamstresses returned, and with So Lo's help Steve spoke with his seamstress of the day before. Her name was Nani, and Steve considered she was possibly in her late thirties, but it was difficult to tell the age of a Chinese woman. They led a very harsh life, and coupled with a poor diet it tended to age them prematurely, so she could be ten years younger.

Steve decided to order two sharkskin shirts from Nani. He wanted long sleeved shirts, with two breast pockets, and pleats in the back to ensure a good fit around the waist. He always bought long sleeved shirts but had a habit of folding them neatly up to just below the elbow. So Lo conveyed all of his instructions to Nani, and she took Steve's measurements as before, deftly running the tape measure smoothly over his body as if she was using a technical slide rule. They agreed a price for the two shirts, and So Lo assured Steve that Nani would return the next evening with the work completed.

Steve paid Nani in advance, she had to buy the material after all, and it would show good faith on his part. Before leaving, Nani put her slim hands together as if in prayer and bowed slightly in a gesture of thanks. Steve smiled at her, and somewhat awkwardly returned the compliment.

The next evening the seamstress returned to the 'basha' and waited in the doorway for Steve to come back from the N.A.A.F.I. She handed him the two shirts, and to his surprise, a small circular rice cake. It was a signal that Nani was slightly enamoured with her new 'employer'. He accepted the shirts and cake, smiled at her, and bowed slightly in thanks. She giggled excitedly, returned the gesture and left.

Steve watched her walk away. She was barefoot on the harsh concrete path that surrounded the 'basha'. Her pink, high collared dress fitted her perfectly, accentuating her slim but shapely body. Nani's jet black hair cascaded down her back, making a stark contrast on the pink dress. As she reached the corner of the 'basha' she turned, smiled at Steve and waved her hand before disappearing around the corner, still giggling to herself. Steve smiled and took a large bite from his rice cake.

He tried one of the sharkskin shirts on, it was a perfect fit, and the stitching was immaculate. He felt that he should have paid more for such work, and decided to give Nani more work in the future to compensate, even if he had to manufacture the work needlessly. Perhaps he too was slightly enamoured.

Steve remembered his white shirt from Marks & Spencer that Moira Theodopolis had wrecked in Scotland. He found it at the bottom of his kitbag, it looked even worse now! He had intended to tear it up completely and use the cloth for cleaning boots and his gun, but possibly it could be put to a better use now. He looked at the shirt again and smiled to himself as he remembered the cobblestone courtyard in Scotland; Grecians could be extremely strong when sexually aroused. He would ask Nani to try and repair the shirt, it would, if nothing else be work for her, and he would pay her well whatever the outcome.

The next day the platoon returned to the firing range for more practice with the Sterlings. Steve had immediately taken to the weapon. Although it was a devastating gun capable of killing in the blink of an eye, it was a pleasure to use. He had mixed feelings about weapons, but as Aunt Maude always said to him, "You have to be able to look after yourself." After finishing the practice shoot they returned to the 'basha', cleaned their weapons and put them under lock and key. The fresh air had given them good appetites. They sniffed the air as they neared the cookhouse, whatever the food was, it smelled good!

The food preparation in the cookhouse was overseen by corporals and privates of the A.C.C. (Army Catering Corp) but the actual cooking was carried out by Chinese civilians employed by the British Army. When ready for serving, the food always had a distinct Chinese flavour to it, no matter what the dish. There was always plenty of fried rice and chop suey. The cook's 'Peking Duck' was always delicious, and the cookhouse corporal back at 'Morval' would have been impressed by their tiny meat balls. Even the traditional English roast beef and Yorkshire pudding had an Oriental taste to it.

Mac was resentful at the abuse of his beloved 'Yorkshire Pud'. But after his taste buds had become accustomed to the food, and the bottled 'San Miguel' beer in the N.A.A.F.I. he felt quite at home. It would not be long before he had a favourite barmaid in Hong Kong to complete the picture.

Some of the other members of the platoon would do well to learn from his flexible adaptability. In the fullness of time even the timid Charlie Strong was to benefit from Mac's indirect teaching, and he would leave the Far East a better man for the experience.

CHAPTER 33

The first week in Nee Soon went by very quickly. It was all new to them, and interesting. The new uniforms, new money, and the fact that they had civilians to clean and polish their boots and wash and iron clothes was strange, to say the least. Eight weeks before, training N.C.O.'s had been hurling their boots the length of a barrack room, sending them crashing into the cast iron stoves and brick walls. Now Chinese civilians were caring for the army boots as if they belonged to an emperor. Strange indeed, and very confusing. The new camp was officially called 'Gillman', but because it was situated near the small village of Nee Soon, the camp was known to one and all as 'Nee Soon'. Many of the civilians who worked at the camp lived in the village. It therefore became a natural step to unofficially name the camp after the village.

The platoon continued to orientate themselves in the very different scene. Charlie Strong had ventured out of the camp on his own for the first time, and described his adventure to the platoon over a beer at the N.A.A.F.I. He had hired a rickshaw in the camp and went on a 'tour of discovery' around the nearby village. Charlie was beginning to 'find his feet'. Soon there would be no stopping his emerging 'cavalier' attitude! But he did complain about the condition of the rickshaw, the wheels, he said, had several spokes missing and the seat was held together by pieces of string.

On hearing the word 'string', the 'Lawyer' dropped his pencil onto the N.A.A.F.I. table, and exclaimed in his 'Thespian' voice, "The time has come, the walrus said, to think on many things!"

Mac looked at Steve for the normal 'translation', but Steve laughed and held up his hands, the 'Lawyer' had them both at a disadvantage. Mac turned back to the 'Lawyer' and said, "You're a daft bugger!" The 'Lawyer' looked at him sternly, and put his name in the book!

The next morning Steve went for his usual breakfast of cereal and fresh fruit, but now the normal banana, apple and pears had been enhanced with oriental fruits such as lychee and rambutan, making the breakfast even more enjoyable. He would indulge himself from time to time with a plateful of sausages, egg and bacon, simply as a change from routine. He finished his healthy breakfast with three mugs of very overly sugared coffee, nobody was perfect!

When he returned to the 'basha' he looked at the notice board as a matter of course. He was surprised to see that he was detailed to carry out an armoury guard in the oncoming evening. He had become a V.I.P., but duties still had to be done! The guard duty was to start at 8.00pm and end at 8.00am the next morning. Steve didn't look forward to a twelve-hour night duty, but it did mean that he had until 8.00 in the evening to himself. He decided to use the free time to start exploring Kowloon and its seafront.

A daily civilian supply truck plied between the camp and Kowloon. He would 'hitch' a ride on it and return with the same truck in the late afternoon, in good time to make himself ready for guard duty at 8.00pm. The truck was due to leave at 9.00am. He had enough time to try and borrow a camera from somebody in the platoon. He would take some 'snaps' and send them to Aunt Maude with his next letter, and he made a mental note to start saving money for his own camera.

He took one of his new sharkskin shirts from his locker; it was time to 'christen' it. So Lo had polished his civilian shoes to a high gloss, and after dressing and applying a small amount of 'Brylcream' to his dark wavy hair he was ready for his first venture into the Orient. The 'Lawyer' was good enough to lend him his fairly sophisticated camera, and after a quick lesson on how to achieve the best results, Steve armed himself with sufficient Hong Kong dollars and made his way to the truck's leaving point.

The Chinese driver was quite happy to give Steve a lift, but made it fairly clear by sign language that a certain amount of remuneration would not go amiss! Steve handed him a dollar, the driver grinned, and opened the passenger door for him; the deal was done. Steve glanced at the driver as he took his place behind the steering wheel. He was a thin, gaunt faced man, and had a wild-eyed look about him. A half-used packet of 'Lucky Strike' cigarettes protruded from a small breast pocket on his grubby white cotton shirt. The steering wheel had a long piece of string wound around the shaft. Steve hoped it wasn't carrying out an overly important function! He looked quickly through the cab rear window at the ramshackle state of the rear of the truck, and then decided to close his eyes to any further investigation, he needed to get to Kowloon, and that was that.

The driver started the engine, which sounded quite healthy, unlike the driver and the rest of the truck. The driver gave Steve a toothy grin released the handbrake, and took off down the road to Kowloon as if he was being pursued by the Chinese devil! Steve clung on to the dashboard and looked at the driver. He was obviously a frustrated racing car driver. The journey that had taken the army lorry three hours was completed in under an hour!

They reached the centre of Kowloon, and the driver managed to stop the truck by applying the handbrake with all the strength he could muster. The foot-brake had given up the 'ghost' several miles back. The driver turned to Steve and grinned. Steve tried to grin back, but his teeth would not unclench! After gaining control of his senses he made it clear that he would be in the same place for the return journey, and by pointing to each other's watches came to a mutual time of departure. Steve thanked him, but he didn't know why. Perhaps he was simply glad to arrive in Kowloon in one piece!

The centre of Kowloon was a chaotic scene of people, trishaws, rickshaws, loudly 'hooting' taxis and the smell of Chinese cooking and pungent aromas of joss-sticks. Chicken and ducks seemed to wander about the streets unattended, but no doubt somebody was watching over them.

Steve regained his composure after his meeting with 'Stirling Moss', as he decided to call him, and after a comforting 'San Miguel' to restore his shattered nerves, made his way through the crowded streets and eventually arrived at the seafront. The sun was becoming quite strong with no clouds to filter it. Steve bought a 'rafia' sun hat, and together with the 'Lawyer's' camera slung around his neck he looked the complete tourist.

The Kowloon seafront was a magical place, with a character all of its own. Within a few streets the atmosphere had changed completely. The smell of salt water and seaweed was everywhere. The people on the approach roads and jetties were seafarers, far removed from the business people he had seen in the centre of town. He wandered along the seafront road, drinking in the scene. He took the 'Lawyer's' camera from its leather case and 'snapped' some pictures as he walked. He enjoyed his moment of being on 'holiday', because in a few hours' time he would be on night guard duty, carrying a loaded Sterling.

There were several jetties along the seafront, but one of them was much larger than the rest. Suspended from long bamboo poles was a green and cream painted sign that announced 'Star Ferry'. The ferry to Hong Kong! Across the street from the jetty was a small cafe, aptly named, 'Star Cafe'. Steve took photos of the jetty and the 'Star Cafe'. The temperature was increasing as the sun rose higher in the sky, and a cool beer in the cafe was very inviting. He put the camera back into its case, checked the money in his pocket, and walked across the busy street to the cafe.

Two small tables and four chairs stood invitingly outside the cafe, and Steve gratefully sat at one of the tables. He had walked for almost an hour in the warm sun. He continued to 'drink' in the colourful scene whilst waiting to be served. The Chinese scurrying along the street reminded him of Singapore. They had the same single purpose in life, to get the job done, and earn a 'crust'.

Steve settled himself down. His limbs had taken a severe jolting at the hands of 'Stirling Moss' and he was glad to sit in a comfortable chair for a while. The table was covered with a clean, starched cotton cloth, and had a traditional willow pattern embroidered on it. The chairs were made of bamboo and wicker, and were surprisingly very comfortable.

A Chinese waitress suddenly appeared from inside the cafe, and his thoughts quickly returned to a cool beer. Steve ordered a 'San Miguel' by pointing to an advert on the cafe window. The waitress smiled in acknowledgement and went back into the cafe. She reappeared with a glass of cold beer and placed it on the table. Steve said thank you, as a matter of course, and although she probably didn't understand what he said, it was simply good manners that had been drilled into him by Aunt Maude.

To his surprise the waitress replied in good English, "You're very welcome, enjoy your beer." Steve laughed and held up his hand, as if to say 'Touché'. She smiled, and continued, "I speak very good English, yes?"

Steve lifted his glass in salute and said, "Yes you do." She smiled again and disappeared back into the cafe. Steve sat back on his wicker chair, sipped at his 'San Miguel' and smiled to himself. The mysterious east was full of surprises, and they were good looking ones too!

He looked across the large jetty opposite and its 'Star Ferry' sign suspended across its entrance. Chinese workers were milling around the jetty waiting for the next boat. It was probably the main source of transport to the island that Steve could see in the distance. He finished his beer, stood up and stretched his body. His arms and legs were still stiff from his joyride with 'Stirling Moss'. More lubrication was required! He opened the cafe door, went in and ordered another beer. The waitress smiled and took a fresh glass and bottle of 'San Miguel' from the fridge, and a handful of ice cubes from a freezer.

Having established that the waitress spoke English, Steve thanked her more freely and asked her how much he owed her for the beers. He paid the price and added a suitable tip, still feeling like a tourist. Strangely, the waitress was very well dressed, unlike the people in the street, or the seamstresses back at Nee Soon. He put the thought to one side, and returned to his wicker chair. The second 'San Miguel' had more effect than the first, and he could feel his body relaxing. He thought more about the waitress, perhaps she owned the cafe, or was a partner. Steve had a lot to learn about the Chinese, and his curiosity knew no bounds. He smiled to himself and thought, *It's a good job I'm not a cat!*

He sipped at his beer and continued to enjoy the interesting atmosphere of the seafront with its ever changing scenery. People came and went, all carrying on with their busy lives. The Chinese seemed to have a single purpose in life, to work! Steve wondered as he studied them whether they ever had time to relax. Maybe that's why most are so slim he concluded!

After finishing his beer, he looked at his watch. There was still time to explore more of the seafront before returning to Nee Soon with 'Stirling Moss', and preparing for the night guard duty. He wasn't looking forward to either. He put the thoughts to one side and concentrated on his Oriental explorations. As he left the 'Star Cafe' he promised himself that he would return as soon as possible.

He wandered along the quayside. Boats of all shapes and sizes plied across the bay to and from Hong Kong Island. They made perfect subjects for Steve's photographic studies. Aunt Maude would find them interesting, providing he had partly mastered the camera's technicalities! It was more upmarket than a 'Kodak' box 'Brownie'! His thoughts went back to the cafe and the Chinese waitress. She was obviously Chinese, but some of her facial features were European She had traditional jet black hair and high cheek bones, but her lips were fuller, almost as if she was pouting, and when she spoke in English it was with a Continental accent, perhaps slightly French or Italian. His curiosity grew as he walked. Why did she have expensive clothes, most waitresses wore very drab attire; was her mother European, or her father? He was totally intrigued, and looked forward to seeing her again.

After an hour of more sightseeing and putting the 'Lawyer's' camera to good use he decided that it was time to turn around and make his way back to the pre-arranged truck pick-up point. He must not miss the guard duty, no matter how distasteful it was. He found the place without too much difficulty and the ramshackle truck and the equally ramshackle 'Stirling Moss' were waiting for him. He climbed into the passenger seat and greeted the driver who grinned and said something in Chinese to him. Steve hadn't fully realised how difficult communication could be between people of different languages.

'Stirling' started the engine, and Steve braced himself for a hectic ride back to camp, but strangely the driver was very subdued, and drove as if he was on a Sunday afternoon outing. Steve decided not to question why in his mind. He relaxed and enjoyed the journey, thinking of Kowloon and the Chinese waitress.

When they reached the camp, Steve handed Stirling another dollar. He intended to visit Kowloon regularly in the future. The driver and his truck were far from perfect, but the transport was reasonably priced, and it was door to door!

After taking a shower and shaving again to make himself presentable for guard duty, he put his civilian clothes away and donned his uniform. As he was changing he made a mental note that it was time to employ a 'Laundry Boy'. He took his Sterling from the locker and glanced at his watch. He had twenty minutes before parade time, enough to go to the armoury and draw ammunition. The R.E.M.E. armourer issued him with ten live rounds of ammunition, and Steve signed for it in regulation manner.

Guard duties were usually boring, tedious duties, but part of a soldier's life. The only consolation was that at Nee Soon they were cut to a minimum because of patrol duties on the border which were more important. It would be at least two months before his next armoury duty. The armoury was situated directly opposite the main guardroom, making it easily protectable. The duty would last for twelve hours, the men working in pairs, two hours 'on', and two hours 'off'. The two hours 'off' were spent in the guardroom, resting or sleeping.

The theory of two men working together was that one, armed soldier stood in front of the armoury door, whilst the other guard secluded himself in the nearby bushes. If the door guard was attacked, it was a simple matter for the second man to raise the alarm. It was highly unlikely that the authorities in China would sanction any raid on the armoury. But there were rebel gangs in Hong Kong, mostly working for the drug syndicates and over a hundred Sterlings plus other weapons and ammunition would be a useful haul.

After a brief inspection by the guard commander, the men were allotted their duty times. Steve and his working partner, a National Service private who hailed from Cheltenham, were to take the 2.00am – 4.00am stint. They therefore had time to rest or sleep in the guardroom until then. The temporary 'camp' beds in the guardroom were not comfortable, and the men were not allowed to return to their 'bashas' to sleep. They were on duty for twelve hours, and that was that!

The extensive travelling and events of the previous week had caught up with Steve, and releases of adrenalin could not cope forever. The beds were far more compatible, but as soon as he closed his eyes he fell asleep. He remembered nothing until the guard commander shook his shoulder at 1.45am. He was still wearing full uniform, and they were not allowed to take their boots off in case of sudden emergencies. All he had to do was to wake himself up and concentrate on the job at hand.

Steve and his partner from Cheltenham took over the guard duty from the previous pair. It was pitch black outside and the National Serviceman elected to stand guard at the armoury door, Sterling loaded for use, but the safety catch 'on'.

Steve found a suitable place in the bushes where he could watch his opposite number. Their eyes had become accustomed to the darkness, and he could clearly make out the other guard's silhouette. The night was warm, but two hours was a long time to stay alert, especially when your mental 'time clock' was telling you to sleep. He felt like finding a soft spot in the greenery and sleeping, but the 'orderly officer' could turn up at any time, and to be caught asleep on duty was an automatic 'Serious Offence' charge. It was certainly, enough for him to lose his N.C.O. status and become a private again. Steve kept himself alert by planning the next day that he was completely off duty. He would 'grit' his teeth and travel to Kowloon with 'Stirling Moss'. He would pay a return visit to the 'Star Cafe' for a 'San Miguel' and hopefully see the waitress again. He would then take the 'Star Ferry' to Hong Kong. A full, but interesting day.

He looked at his watch, the luminous hands read 2.30. His legs and feet were stiff from inactivity, and he flexed them as much as possible without moving his position. Steve looked across at his partner; he was stood, completely still in front of the armoury door clutching his Sterling to his chest.

In the distance Steve heard the sound of two people singing. As they drew closer he recognised the tune and words of 'I belong to Glasgow'! His partner also became aware of the noise, and 'cocked' his Sterling ready for use. In the darkness two people's silhouettes appeared around the corner of the armoury, obviously the worse for alcohol.

The National Serviceman shouted the regulation command, "Who goes there, friend or foe?"

One of the singers answered in a loud Glaswegian voice, "We're foes, you Stupid B…..d'! The guard raised his Sterling and was about to pull the trigger when Steve leapt out of the bushes and restrained him.

The sudden noise had alerted the guard commander and he switched the floodlights on, lighting up the fronts of the armoury and guardroom. Steve recognised the men as two Scots from a different platoon. When the two 'revellers' had seen the guard pointing a loaded Sterling at them they became sober in seconds. Steve looked at them. They were both wearing Oriental dresses, and boots without socks, and orchid like flowers in their hair. Somewhere in a nearby village were two Chinese women dressed very smartly in jungle green uniforms!

Steve laughed at the Scotsmen. They had obviously enjoyed a good evening in the village, and the few minutes of drama had broken up the otherwise boring duty.

In the morning, the two Scots were 'hauled up' in front of the C.O., still nursing giant hangovers. They had been drinking the villagers' home brewed beer and distilled whisky, and not even a hardened Glaswegian could deal with that! They were both awarded three extra guard duties as punishment. The Scots had got off lightly; they could both have been very dead, under the hands of a 'nervy' trigger-fingered National Serviceman carrying out his first guard duty.

Steve returned to the 'basha' after the duty, thinking to himself, *That's another little episode that Aunt Maude will enjoy hearing about;* she always did like a 'sing song'!

In the evening after the usual beer and pies, Mac came up to Steve and asked if he had recovered from the relationship with Lorraine. Steve replied that he was gradually coming to terms with it. But time was the only possible healer. No medication can cure heartache! Mac put a hand on Steve's shoulder and said, 'There's plenty more fish in the sea lad'. It's just a matter of whether you feel the urge to get your fishing gear out!"

Mac's advice was seldom subtle, but it was always to the point!

CHAPTER 34

After a 'dummy' patrol with one of the experienced platoons to show the 'new boys' the ropes, the men were deemed to be capable of carrying out their first 'live' patrol of the border undivided.

The first patrol would be a daylight duty, starting at 8.00 in the morning and ending at 8.00 in the evening. Night patrols were a different matter, requiring extra knowledge of the land. Everything looked different at night, and moonlight could play strange tricks on the eyes. When the platoon had proved itself on day duty they would take a share of night patrols.

It was a normal routine for an officer of the Hong Kong Police Force to accompany the regular border patrols. Illegal immigrants and drug smugglers were always a problem in the 'New Territories' and the police played a constant role, in conjunction with the army, to control the border. The immigrants usually travelled in groups of six to ten people, taking extreme risks to evade the Chinese Army patrols on the other side of the border. The smugglers preferred to operate in twos, making them flexible and elusive. Every consignment of drugs safely delivered to the drug 'Barons' and Hong Kong, carried a big reward, and was well worth the risk.

On the day of the patrol Steve awoke early and went to the cookhouse for a good sustaining breakfast of sausages, egg, bacon and baked beans. The patrol duty would last for twelve hours, and the only sustenance would be from 'dry rations' and water. Dry rations were nutritious, but certainly not enjoyable on the palate!

After drawing ammunition from the armoury and checking their Sterlings, the platoon paraded in front of the 'basha' for inspection before leaving. The inspection was carried out by a young National Service 'second' lieutenant, serving his two years for 'Queen and Country'. He would have preferred to have been continuing his profession as a surveyor, but duty called! Due to his education he was fortunate to carry the rank of a junior officer. His two years would be pleasantly spent. No sleeping in a communal dormitory for him.

After inspection, the officer gave the platoon last minute advice and instructions on their job at hand.

He completed his advice by saying, "If you are suddenly confronted on the border by six members of the Chinese Republican Army, all carrying loaded weapons, what steps would you take?"

Mac immediately put up his hand and replied, "Ruddy great big ones, sir!"

The young officer looked at him and threatened him with a charge of 'insubordination', but Mac considered that it was worth the risk, and the others had to hide a smile. The lieutenant eventually saw the humorous side of it, and no harm was done.

The 'Bedford' Q.L. three tonner duly arrived and the men were taken to the border five miles to the north. 'Geordie' Hanson took control of the platoon, the young lieutenant having returned to the tranquillity of the Officers' Mess for breakfast! 'Geordie' knew the terrain well, and as leader carried the map, compass and binoculars, all army issue.

They arrived at the drop-off point where the night patrol was waiting to be picked up and taken back to camp. They looked tired and drawn, night patrols were not good. They had also encountered a batch of illegal immigrants trying to cross into Hong Kong. The Chinese were desperate, distressed people, but the patrol had no alternative but to turn them back over the border.

After exchanging information, the new patrol started on their trek of the twenty-mile section of the border. They all carried extra water bottles, and as Steve looked at the already warm morning sun he knew they would need every drop. The land was hilly, but not overly difficult to trek. Trees and bushes dotted the landscape, and large rocks made the terrain interesting. It was quite different to the 'no man's' land that Steve had seen between Kowloon and 'Gillman' camp. He looked around him, there were few landmarks to gain direction from, and he was glad that 'Geordie' was with them. His knowledge of the area was invaluable.

After two hours trekking they stopped for a welcome break. Dry rations were reluctantly 'nibbled' at and water bottles brought into use. The first stage had been very routine; they had seen nobody, and as far as they knew, nobody had seen them. The 'Lawyer' scribbled in his notebook. Charlie Strong took two of his brown pills with his water and Docherty made a joke about Chinese laundries and the possible use of rick-shaws for somewhat lewd romantic purposes. Steve glanced around him, all was well.

As the patrol continued, the sun became high in the sky, and water bottles were put to good use again. Steve thought about Sgt. McNiff in Scotland, and wished that his own bottle was filled with something stronger than water. He licked his lips and looked forward to a cold 'San Miguel' in the evening at the N.A.A.F.I. after the patrol duty finished at 8.00pm.

In the late afternoon, the patrol rested under a clump of trees to gain the shade from the hot sun. Their feet were beginning to feel sore, and they loosened their boot laces for relief. They had used three quarters of their water, and there was still a way to go. The platoon would have to gauge things better on future patrols, there were no 'Coca Cola' machines available here!

'Geordie' discussed the terrain with Steve. It was important that he should learn as quickly as possible, and 'Geordie' passed on his knowledge of compass and map reading. They continued with the patrol, and reached a high point on the route. They looked across the border and into mainland China. Steve could clearly see the 'paddy' fields with the workers knee-deep in water. With the aid of binoculars, he could make out the army guards patrolling the edges of the paddy fields, all fully armed and ever ready to discourage any worker from making a dash towards the border and freedom in Hong Kong.

Steve said to 'Geordie', "No wonder they wait until darkness to try and make their escape!"

The sun started to make its descent, and the men rested after a long leg of the border had been covered. They were all feeling tired, the novelty had started to wear off, and thoughts of 'San Miguels' and steak pies were entering their heads rather than possible encounters with the Chinese Republican Army, drug smugglers, or immigrants!

There was a sudden rustling noise above them, and Steve reached for his Sterling, but it was only the breeze becoming stronger in the tops of the trees. Nerves were starting to become frayed, and they all looked forward to seeing the 'Bedford', and the journey home.

They reached the pick-up point just before 20.00 hrs . The water bottles were empty, and most of the dry rations eaten. The truck arrived, carrying the new patrol that would protect the border during the night hours. In their turn they would be picked up at 08.00 hrs the next morning, and a new patrol would take over to continue the twenty-four-hour border cover.

The 'Bedford's' hard wooden seats were welcome for a change, and thoughts turned from duty to 'San Miguel' and pies. On the way back to camp 'Geordie' asked them what they thought of the first patrol.

"Piece of cake," said Docherty, and the others agreed.

Piece of cake, what's all the fuss about? Steve thought to himself. *It can't be this easy! There's a catch somewhere!*

Their feet were aching, but a night's rest in bed would probably put that right. After a pie and a 'San Miguel' in the N.A.A.F.I. they all thankfully put the theory to the test.

The next day the platoon was placed on 'release of duty' for forty-eight hours. They were relieved that the first border duty was over; they were no longer 'new boys' in the regiment. Their feet and bodies had stopped aching and most of the day would be spent relaxing barefoot in and around the 'basha'. Beach flip-flops were allowed in the cookhouse as footwear providing feet were washed and clean.

As the morning progressed, Nani appeared at the 'basha' doorway carrying a rice cake. Steve greeted her in the usual way, putting his hands together and bowing slightly. Nani returned the gesture and giggled! So Lo was not available to translate, but Steve thankfully received the cake, and in return handed her some woollen socks to repair. Nani left, and giggled her way around the corner of the 'basha'.

After that visit by Nani the rice cakes arrived thick and fast becoming larger and larger by the day. But there are only so many rice cakes that one man can eat, and Steve eventually started to distribute them around the 'bashas'! The men in turn handed their clothing repairs and orders for sharkskin shirts to Steve for passing on to Nani. The system worked well, and in the words of a prominent English Conservative Party politician, Nani had, 'Never had it so good!'

The men were in a pensive and reflective mood after the border patrol. Taff relaxed on his bed as much as possible, but he was missing Wales, Cardiff Arms Park and rugby. Most of the other men in the platoon were soccer fanatics, following Arsenal, Manchester United or Chelsea. Rugby and its finer points were lost on them, and discussing 'drop' goals and conversions was beyond their sporting knowledge!

Taff delved into his kitbag, and found his battered old rugby ball that he had rescued from a rubbish bin after Wales had been unexpectedly beaten by Scotland in a four nations international match. The ball had seen better days but was still usable. He took it outside the 'basha' and idly began to kick it about on the grassed area surrounding the 'basha'.

So Lo, on his daily round of selling cold drinks and bread rolls, stopped and watched Taff with interest. He was an intelligent lad and could see that the man from Wales was not happy. He parked his laden bicycle against a tree, and looking at the strange oval shaped ball asked Taff if he was sad because his football had become misshapen. Taff explained to him that it was not a football, but a rugby ball! The two games were very different.

So Lo was instantly interested, eager to learn anything that might help his chances of commercial success in the future. The European market could be very lucrative for an aspiring Chinese businessman! Taff kicked the ball to So Lo, who duly kicked it back. Taff picked up the rugby ball and threw it to So Lo, passing the ball as if in a rugby match. So Lo carefully placed the ball back on the ground and kicked it to Taff. As far as So Lo was concerned it was a football and had to be treated as such!

The young Chinaman was eager to learn, but when Taff tried to explain the game and its rules So Lo naturally became confused. There was only one thing to do in order to explain fully. He would organise a rugby match, the 'Boot Boys' versus the platoon. They shook hands, as gentlemen do on such occasions, and Taff bought a cold drink and salad roll in order to seal the contract.

News of the forthcoming match soon spread through the camp. The regimental sergeant major was notified as routine, and he decided to take it upon himself to be referee for the game. That way he could control matters and make sure that there were no breaches of discipline. He hurriedly placed an order with one of the seamstresses to make him a black referee's uniform, and found one of his spare regimental blazer badges to have sewn onto the left breast pocket. The R.S.M. quickly became enthusiastic about the match; it would fulfil one of his boyhood dreams. He decided to start an immediate fitness programme, and donned his P.T. kit that had not seen the light of day for some time.

The R.S.M. jogged across the road from his quarters to the football pitch opposite. He practised 'press ups' and 'knee bends' for five minutes. He then retired to the Sergeants' Mess for a celebratory double whisky. There was no sense in over doing it!

CHAPTER 35

Having rested completely on the previous day, Steve awoke feeling fresh and ready for another visit to Kowloon and more exploration. This time he would venture across the water on the 'Star Ferry' to the island of Hong Kong. When he returned, it would be time to prepare for the platoon's second daylight patrol, starting at 08.00 the next day. At a later date they would take on the responsibility of their first night patrol duty; but there was much to learn about the terrain before that.

In the cookhouse Steve took breakfast of cereal and fresh fruit. The following day he planned to indulge himself and have sausage, fried egg, bacon and baked beans, to compensate for the 'dry rations' that would be issued by the cookhouse for the patrol duty. He thought for a minute about the previous patrol. It all seemed very easy, and he hoped it would stay that way. But he had the uneasy feeling that the platoon was being 'lulled into a false sense of security.

In the 'basha' he prepared himself for the trip to Kowloon and Hong Kong. His shoes had been polished as usual to a high gloss by So Lo, and he reminded himself to pay his 'Boot Boy' the weekly salary of fifty cents. It was also time to appoint a 'Laundry Boy'. Some of his clothes were starting to look drab and in need of washing and ironing. He would select a 'Laundry Boy' as soon as possible, relying on So Lo's advice and recommendations. The new responsibilities of employee management were daunting!

Steve wore a second sharkskin shirt, it fitted perfectly just as the first one had. He would ask Nani to make him one more, just in case of over emotional Grecian women! He smiled to himself and wondered what Moira would have made of sharkskin. Understanding Moira's sexuality his money was on Moira, not the sharkskin!

He finished dressing and looked in the mirror. His dark wavy hair had fully recovered from its 'Sweeney Todd' treatment at 'Morval' and he applied a small amount of 'Brylcream' to keep it in place. He flexed his shoulders, feeling good about himself and made his way to Stirling Moss' race 'starting' place.

The truck was being loaded with empty boxes and wooden crates when Steve arrived. Stirling was supervising the work, 'puffing' on a 'Lucky Strike'. Steve handed him a dollar note before climbing into the passenger seat. Stirling grinned at him as he joined his passenger in the cab, and stuffed the dollar note into his breast pocket with his new packet of 'Lucky Strikes'; carrying passengers was a lucrative addition to his transport business.

Steve looked around the cab. The string wrapped around the steering column had been re-enforced with steel wire! He decided not to investigate further, and fixed his mind on the visit to Kowloon and Hong Kong Island. He would go to the 'Star cafe', hoping that the waitress was on duty. He was fascinated by her unusual accent and very pleasant manner, and it was wonderful that she spoke good English. He looked forward to hearing her voice again, and simply enjoying her company. Talking to the men in the platoon over a beer and steak pie was all very well, but the interaction between a man and a woman was a totally different experience.

'Stirling Moss' started the engine and grinned at Steve. He grinned back, and knew exactly what to expect! 'Stirling' made sure that the ashtray was empty, and revved the engine, he selected first gear with a positive movement, released the handbrake and they were off! 'Stirling' put his foot down on the accelerator and leant over the steering wheel as if he needed spectacles to see the road. He looked at Steve and grinned! Steve clung to the dashboard as the boxes and crates shot to the rear of the truck with the sudden inertia.

After half an hour, the black gear lever knob unscrewed itself with the aid of the extreme vibration in the cab and rattled around the cab floor. 'Stirling' kicked it to one side, grinned at Steve and carried on regardless! Steve made a mental note to re-think the transport situation.

They arrived in Kowloon and 'Stirling' lit his tenth 'Lucky Strike' of the journey. They made the usual arrangements by sign language regarding the time of leaving for the return trip to 'Gillman' camp. Steve massaged his hands, trying to encourage the blood to circulate after gripping the dashboard for nearly an hour. He needed a 'San Miguel', and headed straight for the 'Star Cafe'.

The streets were crowded, and rickshaws and trishaws weaved their way through the throng of people. The pedestrians seemed to disregard any pavements that were available; perhaps they felt the road was safer! Steve decided to take the same approach, as there was safety in numbers!

When he reached the cafe, the outside tables were occupied by foreign tourists. A modern cruise ship was in the port, bringing well-heeled holiday makers to swell the already prosperous Hong Kong banks. Steve went into the 'Star' and found an unoccupied table. He looked around the small room, there was more time to study it now, and for some reason that he couldn't explain to himself, the cafe was more important now. The walls were brightly coloured in red, with dark green carefully intermixed. Small traditional lanterns were suspended from the ceiling. It was totally Chinese, with the aroma of 'joss' sticks in the air. The only foreign influence was a very American 'Wurlitzer' jukebox that sat very dominantly in the corner of the room. It looked completely out of place, and somehow spoilt the ambience of the room. Steve was tempted to look at the records on selection, but was fairly certain that they would be 45 RPM's of Elvis Presley, Bill Haley and possibly Englebert Humperdinck, with a 'smattering' of Frank Sinatra for good measure. Perhaps he was a musical 'prude', but you could have too much of a good thing!

The waitress appeared through a beaded curtained doorway that divided the room from what was presumably the kitchen. She greeted him in her almost perfect English. The waitress had remembered him!

Steve smiled and said, "Hello!"

She looked completely serene in a well-fitting high collared red dress, beautifully embroidered in gold lace.

He ordered a cold beer and she disappeared into the back room, returning in a minute or so with a bottle of cold 'San Miguel' and a frosted glass.

As she put the beer on the table the waitress smiled in her refined Oriental way and said, "It's nice to see you again."

Steve smiled at her, and replied in the same manner. His throat was dry from the hair-raising ride with 'Stirling Moss' and he downed the beer in a matter of seconds and handed the empty glass to her for another 'San Miguel'. She went into the back room and duly returned with a second beer. Steve sipped the cool brew, having quenched his thirst with the first bottle.

The waitress left to attend the needs of the tourists. They were mostly American, in fairly 'loud' clothing, and voices to suit!

At least they should enjoy the jukebox, Steve thought to himself. He continued sipping on his beer, contemplating why it was that many Americans were of a flamboyant nature. Perhaps it was their 'cosmopolitan' background.

The waitress returned to Steve's table. She seemed eager to chat and he assumed that she wanted to practice her English. Her voice continued to fascinate him, and he longed to ask her about her parents, they were obviously not completely Chinese, but he 'shelved' the question in case it was embarrassing for her. He explained that he intended to take the 'Star Ferry' to Hong Kong and explore the island for the first time.

She said, "That should be nice, you will enjoy Hong Kong," and wished him a pleasant trip. The waitress turned away, stopped as if having an afterthought, looked back and said, "I finish work in one hour and if you like I can be your guide to Hong Kong!"

Steve was slightly taken aback, and her face saddened thinking he was going to say no. He recovered his senses and smiling said, "Yes I would like that."

She looked relieved and smiled back. They arranged to meet in front of the cafe in one hour. She walked away, her shimmering black hair cascading down her back, almost to her slim waist. Steve watched her depart. How very different she was to the 'Blonde Bombshell' back at 'Morval' barracks in Hampshire!

Steve left the cafe and wandered along the seafront. He had forgotten to bring the 'Lawyer's' camera, but hopefully there would be other visits to Hong Kong. He thought about the waitress and her strangely mystifying character. He was fortunate to meet her. Sometimes he felt that such events were fate, and preordained. A sudden surge of excitement swept through him. She was special; there was no doubt about that. He looked at his watch, there would be little time to explore the island, and it was important not to miss 'Stirling' for the return journey to camp, hectic as it might be. There was certainly no bus service to rely on. They would possibly have one and a half hours in Hong Kong, but that didn't matter. He knew that with the company of the friendly waitress it could be the start of something very beautiful, and unforgettable.

When he returned to the 'Star Cafe' the waitress was waiting for him sat at one of the outside tables. The American tourists had moved on, and she was alone. She had changed her clothes from the high collared traditional dress into a white blouse with a light green coloured skirt. She still wore the low-heeled shoes that Chinese women seemed to prefer. When she stood up to greet him she looked even more European than before, and increased Steve's curiosity about her. He knew before long he would have to ask about her parents, but the saying 'Curiosity killed the cat' came swiftly to mind!

He remarked on how beautiful she looked. She blushed slightly, and they crossed the street to the 'Star Ferry'. Steve bought two tickets from the small office on the jetty. Everything was cheap compared with European prices, and his money didn't seem to diminish in his pocket. It was another reason why the professional soldiers in the regiment enjoyed the posting so much, and wanted to stay beyond the term of the three-year posting. There were also no 'Boot Boys' or convivial Chinese maidens in Hampshire to make 'home' life more pleasant!

The 'Star' jetty was crowded with people, most of them Chinese and women carrying goods for sale in Hong Kong. One old Chinaman had a large square wicker basket with four black feathered chickens 'clucking' fairly contentedly in the confined space. Steve assumed they would be for sale in Hong Kong, possibly to a restaurant. The old man flicked the basket from time to time with a grubby white handkerchief, trying to deter the multitude of flies that hovered around the basket.

The ferry boat arrived from Hong Kong and the passengers from the island quickly made their way down the wide gangway. The new passengers started to board, and Steve and his 'guide' joined the throng, all holding their tickets in hand to be clipped at the gangway by a sailor. He appeared to be wearing an admiral's peaked cap 'perched' on his bald head, in contrast to a very dirty off white shirt and short trousers. Steve smiled and toyed with the idea of saluting him as he clipped their tickets.

There was little comfort on the boat; the passengers were packed in like sardines by the crew members. The trip across the bay was short and interesting enough, but Steve was glad to reach the other side. The gangplank was put in place, and he shuffled off the ferry, still packed 'sardine' style. He was closely followed by his 'guide' for the day. She knew the problems of the ferry, and kept a careful eye on her 'tourist' who stood head and shoulders above most of the other passengers. Steve was surprised how many people were on the ferry, the crew were expert 'sardine' packers!

They walked along the seafront and his guide began to explain a little of the history of Hong Kong. She was certainly well informed and educated, which further fuelled his bursting curiosity.

A waitress with all this knowledge? he wondered to himself. He listened intently to every word, but had to admit to himself that he was more interested in her dark shining hair, and high cheek bones and sensual lips. The fantastic sights and scenery came a poor second.

She suggested that they should go to the island's highest point, known as the 'Peak'. He would have a good view of Hong Kong and the surrounding islands from there. He readily agreed; she was the 'boss'. They strolled through the busy streets; the Chinese seemed to live at a hectic pace wherever they were. They reached the 'Peak's' cliff lift and more tickets were purchased. The view from the 'Peak' was stunning, and Steve could also see some of the smaller islands. They were beautifully green, the lush greenery stretching down to the water's edge. Loaded 'junks' slowly travelled along the narrow waterways that separated the tiny islands, and smaller boats, also laden with goods completed the picturesque scene.

Steve remarked to his 'guide' how beautiful the islands were, and she explained that Hong Kong, translated into English meant 'Seven Islands'. He was standing close to her as she continued to explain the history of Hong Kong. He felt a sudden urge to put his arm around her shoulder; it was such a romantic setting, but he realised that such a show of emotion would be taboo in Chinese culture. It was all very formal between them, and he decided it was time to introduce himself. He did so, and she spoke his name for the first time. It sounded like 'Steafe', but her accent was all part of her natural charm.

She held out a slender hand to him, smiled, and said in a petite way, "My name is Mai Lee."

As he took her hand a strange power ran through his body, almost like an immense electric shock. After a while he felt he should let it go, but her hand was like a magnet, and they simply stood hand in hand, neither fully realising what was happening to them.

As they left the 'Peak', still hand in hand, she turned to him and asked if he would like to visit Hong Kong again.

He gently squeezed her hand, smiled, and simply said, "Yes." She hardly needed to ask the question, he was already completely mesmerised by her. As they walked their hips 'nudged' together, it was almost like making love!

Steve looked at his watch, time was quickly running out, and they had walked quite a long way from the ferry point. He didn't want to leave, but 'Stirling Moss' waited for no man! Steve and Mai Lee continued to hold hands as they walked back to the ferry. They had arrived as 'tourist' and 'guide'. They were leaving as 'lovers'.

They reached the 'Star Ferry' and Steve bought more tickets. He would keep the ticket stubs and send them to Aunt Maude with his next letter and some photos; she liked that sort of thing. Steve and Mai Lee managed to squeeze on board the ferry, the 'sardines' were packed even tighter than before, but it did allow the new 'lovers' to be very close together. On a crowded Chinese ferry it was acceptable cultural behaviour.

As they left the ferry the light was fading. In the semi-darkness and shadows of the 'Star Cafe' Steve said goodnight to his new love, Mai Lee. He kissed her gently on the lips, and she held him to her. He promised to return as soon as he could. Mai Lee smiled, and promised to have a cold 'San Miguel' waiting for him. She was like a precious, delicate Oriental jewel in his arms, and he could tell by the warm look in her eyes that everything was perfect!

CHAPTER 36

Steve left Mai Lee at the 'Star Cafe' and walked back to 'Stirling's' pick-up point. There was a spring in his step, and love in his heart. He was looking at the world through rose coloured glasses again!

The driver was waiting for him; he was always punctual and dependable, if nothing else. Steve climbed into the cab and handed 'Stirling' a dollar note. He realised that he still didn't know 'Stirling's' real name, and knew no conversational words of Chinese to ask him. He would ask So Lo the next time he was having one of his many interesting talks with him. So Lo was a mine of information. 'Stirling Moss' would probably be pleased and even flattered with his English name, especially if he knew he had been likened to a famous racing driver.

The driver grinned at him on receipt of the all-important dollar. He folded it carefully and put it with the packet of 'Lucky Strikes' in his breast pocket. Steve looked carefully at him; 'Stirling' seemed to have changed in attitude since the outgoing journey! The black gear lever knob had been re-fixed, and the insect spattered windscreen meticulously cleaned. He drove off at a moderate pace, and the rest of the journey was pleasantly passed, just as the previous return trip had been. Steve thought about the driver's rapid change in demeanour. Could it be that when 'Stirling' was in Kowloon he was purchasing, and taking a certain illegal powdered substance, and didn't want to attract any undue attention?

When they reached the camp Steve thanked him in his usual English manner, and the Chinaman replied. Neither of them knew what the other was saying, but that didn't seem to matter. 'Stirling' drove off at his subdued speed, and Steve went to the cookhouse in the slender hope that the evening meal had not yet finished. A plate of fried chicken legs and chop suey would go down well. He was in luck; it had indeed been a fortunate day!

After a satisfying meal and preparing his kit for the next day's patrol duty he went to the N.A.A.F.I. The rest of the platoon were enjoying beer and pies, and discussing the forthcoming rugby match between the platoon and the 'Boot Boys'. Taff was presiding in the 'chair'. He had picked his team, which apparently included Steve, who had been 'selected' in his absence. Steve didn't know whether he should be pleased or not, it was possibly a double-edged blade!

Taff was busy coaching his team on the rules and tactics of the game. Most of the items on the table, bottles of beer, empty glasses, cigarettes and boxes of matches were used to represent players and where they should be on the field of play. The 'Lawyer' complained that he should at least be represented by a bottle of 'San Miguel', not a box of 'Swan Vestas'! There were limits after all! Taff grudgingly changed the position, which placated the class conscious 'Lawyer'. Part of a coach's job was to keep his players happy; a contented player was an efficient player, providing the 'Lawyer' left his pencil and notebook in the 'basha'.

Steve tried to enter into the spirit of things, but his mind kept wandering to thoughts of Mai Lee, and nudging hips on the 'Peak'. He wondered if he should have been bolder, regardless of Chinese protocol, and put his arm around her! He became aware that somebody was talking to him, and he jerked himself back to the present time and the all-important rugby. Taff was saying that with So Lo's help they had found four long bamboo poles, and that they had been tied to the existing goal posts to simulate rugby posts. They were nowhere near long enough, but apart from Taff it was doubtful that anybody could kick the strangely shaped ball that high anyway!

So Lo was apparently having problems getting a team together. The 'Boot Boys' were not exactly athletic, but with So Lo's natural selling ability and powers of persuasion Taff was certain he would eventually be successful. The game was planned for the following Saturday, 'kick off' at 3.00pm as was traditional at Cardiff Arms Park. Through the 'grapevine' they heard that the R.S.M. had started an intensive fitness training programme in order to carry out his referee's duties on the day. Taff hoped that the R.S.M. would not insist on them marching on the field before the game; anything was possible in the army!

Taff continued with his coaching session over more pints of 'San Miguel', the instructions becoming more blurred with every pint consumed. When Mac pointed out that they were only playing the 'Boot Boys', Taff fixed him with a look that would have turned a pint of Yorkshire Best Bitter stale.

As the evening wore on, the talk changed from rugby tactics to the more interesting subject of women, and its accompanying problems. Docherty had 'struck up' a relationship with a bar girl in Kowloon, but was having trouble with his love life. He blamed it on the heat and the fact that his girlfriend insisted on burning six 'joss' sticks in the bedroom before they made love. Docherty was experiencing premature ejaculation, and it was becoming very frustrating for him, and his overly sexual girlfriend.

Mac, who had knowledge of such matters, offered his advice over a pint of the brew, purchased by an anxious Docherty. Mac, after a satisfying swig of the free beer, (it always tasted better when you didn't have to pay for it), explained the biological and psychological aspects of the problem in his blunt Yorkshire miner's way. But that confused everybody, and put one or two of the more 'sensitive' men off their steak and kidney pies with his explicit exclamations.

He concluded his extensive lecture by saying, in slightly slurred words, "You need to drink more beer before you and your bar girl get into bed, and then you should practice what is known in the medical books as 'Coitus Interruptus'." He took another large swig from his glass and settled back in his chair, content with his diagnosis.

Docherty looked confused and said, "Does that mean I can't have sex at all?"

"No it doesn't mean that," replied Mac, feeling more like a family doctor by the minute. "Basically," he continued, "in strictly technical medical language, you need to take a 'tea break' in between it all! The 'joss' sticks shouldn't be a problem, but tell your girlfriend not to light them when you're both naked in bed, that could lead to serious inflammable consequences!"

Docherty looked even more confused, and left to buy a beer.

Taff listened to the lecture with interest. He too had started to date a girl, between his rugby interests which took paramount position in his life. He did concede that women had a certain part to play in the way of the world. Taff explained to Mac that when he and the girl were on the couch together, he never knew where to start!

Mac thought about the problem for a minute, took a mouthful of beer, wiped his mouth with the back of his hand and said, "Well, lad, you do as anybody else does in the world, start at the bottom and work your way up."

Taff nodded, and the 'Lawyer' made notes. He underlined his notes, 'For future reference'. The 'Lawyer' had not yet engaged in carnal desire! The more 'robust' of the seamstresses referred to him as 'The Cherry Boy'! But one day a woman would enter his life, and the notebook would take second place.

They all retired to their beds, Mac in particular satisfied with his evening's work. Others had thoughts of rugby, some about the girlfriends they had left in the U.K. But one romantically inclined individual had his mind totally fixed on a certain 'hip nudging' waitress at the 'Star Cafe'!

In the morning Steve had his pre-patrol breakfast of sausage, egg, bacon and beans. The thought of existing on 'dry rations' for twelve hours was not something to contemplate. The chef who had invented the recipe for 'dry rations' was either a complete sadist, or simply mad.

After drawing ammunition and going through the routine inspection, the platoon boarded the waiting 'Bedford'. It was a fresh morning with blankets of cloud hiding the early sun. The truck made good time and they looked forward to another uneventful patrol. Most of the men had taken the big fried breakfast in the cookhouse; the 'dry rations' were not popular with anybody. They settled down to let the breakfasts digest as well as possible, taking into account the bumpy roads and the 'Bedford's' wooden seats. Halfway to the drop-off point the 'Bedford' uncharacteristically broke down. The plastic distributor head had shattered, and the engine immediately died. There was complete silence for a few seconds. They had come to rely on the well-built trucks, and to be suddenly let down was an unwelcome surprise.

Mac broke the silence by stating sullenly, "The bloody elastic band's broke!"

The truck carried a certain amount of communication equipment, but field two-way radio was still in its relative infancy, and very much a case of 'hit and miss'. The driver set up the equipment and began trying to contact 'Gillman' camp. If time had not been an important factor the platoon would have trekked to the border area, some two and a half miles to the north, but time was of the essence, and the night patrol would be waiting to be picked up and returned to camp and their beds.

The patrol was accompanied by an officer of the Hong Kong Police Force, as was normal routine. Steve took the opportunity to talk to him about the problem with drugs in Hong Kong. He told the English speaking officer of his suspicions about 'Stirling Moss'. The officer wasn't surprised at 'Stirling's' possible activities, the problem was rife in Hong Kong, and Macao, the not too distant Portuguese owned island.

Apart from his very subdued driving on the return journeys, it was quite possible that 'Stirling' was selling drugs to civilians in and around the camp. There were also rumours that some military personnel were experimenting with illegal substances. The situation reminded Steve of the opium addicts he had seen on the Singapore stopover. They were sat at the side of the road, simply waiting to die. It was difficult to ascertain their age, they looked very old, but some were possibly no more than thirty to forty years of age.

The drug trafficking in Hong Kong was controlled by the 'Barons' and the police had little success in bringing them to justice. When a consignment of drugs was seized by the police, the smuggler accepted his fate and was confined to prison without disclosing the 'Baron's' name, as to do so would mean almost certain death. They also knew that when they had served the prison sentence a substantial wad of money would be waiting for them. In this way, the 'Barons' further protected their anonymity.

The officer said that one such 'Baron' was an Italian named Busetti. The police, although highly suspicious of him, had not been able to prove his guilt. He was a shrewd, clever man, but they knew that one day he would make a mistake. All they had to do was watch and wait.

The relief truck, an older 'Bedford' Q.L. eventually arrived, possibly having been quickly taken out of 'moth balls'. It had seen better days, but hopefully it would get them to the border. They transferred the kit and were on their way in five minutes. The driver of the broken truck had to wait for a mechanic to arrive with a new distributor head. He was well supplied with some of the platoon's 'dry rations' and a bottle of water. Strangely he seemed quite content to be left on his own.

They were only fifteen minutes late for the patrol change over; the old Q.L. had made good time over the rough roads. Its rest in 'moth balls' had done it some good! The weather was overcast, helpful for trekking. They set off at a good pace, trying to make up for lost time. They needed to reach the other pick-up point by 20.00 hrs where the night patrol would be waiting to take over.

Steve continued to practice his map reading and use of the compass. 'Geordie' pointed out some of the more not so obvious landmarks. Steve gradually felt more confident about possibly leading the platoon in the future without 'Geordie's' guidance. One day the friendly giant from Newcastle would return to the central regimental depot, and they would be on their own.

The patrol went smoothly, apart from the 'Lawyer' twisting his ankle on loose rocks. Taff looked at the ankle that was starting to swell and his thoughts turned to the rugby match the next day. He had just lost his star 'fly-half', and would have to find a substitute. The pendulum was starting to swing in favour of the 'Boot Boys'. Taff was a worried coach! The 'Lawyer' was helped by two other men to the pick-up point. His ankle was painful, but he wasn't exactly distraught at missing the rugby match.

In the evening the 'Lawyer' managed to hobble to the N.A.A.F.I. for his 'medicinal' 'San Miguel', and he took his pencil and pad to make the necessary entries for the day. The men's feet were aching, but several pints of the brew softened the blow. Taff had 'roped in' a substitute for the 'Lawyer', and all was well until Charlie Strong came into the N.A.A.F.I. and complained that his left leg had broken out in a nasty rash during the last mile of the patrol.

Since Mac's explicit medical advice to Docherty and Taff, Charlie had reluctantly handed over the mantle of 'Medical Adviser' to him. He decided to seek Mac's professional advice on the matter of his left leg. Mac studied the rash carefully and 'tut tutted' a lot.

Charlie said to him, "Will it be all right?" Mac finished his beer and studied the rash once more. Charlie was becoming agitated. "Well?" he said.

Mac finally said, "I think it will be okay, just don't start reading any serials!"

Charlie looked at him quizzically and then went to order another 'San Miguel'. Steve watched him saunter to the counter. Charlie was changing quickly now. In the past he would have raced off to his locker and taken half a dozen of his pills, followed by a good measure of Linctus.

CHAPTER 37

Saturday arrived, and with it Taff's big day. The morning weather was cool and sunny, with slight broken cloud, perfect for Taff's rugby match at his very own 'Cardiff Arms Park'.

The cookhouse corporal had entered into the spirit of things and was busy providing a selection of sliced oranges and melon for the half time break. One of the cookhouse stainless steel tea urns was commandeered to be used for cold orange drinks. There was a general 'buzz' of excitement around the camp, nobody had seen the 'Boot Boys' play rugby before, it should prove interesting! The enthusiasm had even reached the camp's married quarters, and soldiers' wives were busy preparing picnics for their families; it was to be a 'day out'. The R.S.M. awoke early and prepared his well- laundered and starched black referee's uniform with the regimental badge neatly sewn onto the blouse pocket. He filled his hip flask with 'five star' brandy; the 'intensive' training programme was complete!

When Steve awoke in the 'basha' Taff was already washed and shaved and sat at the central wooden table working on his pre-match team talk. Steve couldn't help feeling that he was getting a bit carried away with it all. He looked at Taff again, turned over, and went back to sleep.

The platoon eventually clambered out of their warm beds, the previous night's 'San Miguel' still fresh on their taste buds. Steve looked around the room and idly wondered how many pints they had collectively consumed and whether it was advisable fayre for aspiring young rugby players.

Steve had a late light breakfast of cereal and fruit. The thought of running about with a full fried meal did not appeal to him. But Mac was adamant, and said that Leeds and Widnes trained on fried sausage and eggs all the time!!Steve took his word for it, but stuck to his cereal and fresh fruit.

At 2.30pm Taff assembled his team and gave them a final lecture on tactics before jogging to the playing field. With the aid of So Lo's bicycle pump the ball had been fully inflated, and a small amount of 'Dubbin' was applied to protect it from any possible moisture. Nobody had seen the 'Boot Boys', and there was speculation that they had 'cried off'. But So Lo and his 'Boot Boys' were made of sterner stuff, and were busy preparing themselves for battle.

On the playing field Taff organised his team into small groups for warming-up. Some of them, it being a Saturday, would rather have been 'swanning' off to Kowloon or Hong Kong, and Docherty was one of them. But his bar girl, and practising 'Coitus Interruptus' would have to wait!

So Lo and his team of 'Boot Boys' arrived, So Lo on his bicycle, the team in single file behind him. He was a natural leader of men, riding his 'stallion' with great aplomb!

The R.S.M. trotted onto the field, looking resplendent in his new black referee's uniform. The regimental badge stood out from the well starched blouse, and his whistle dangled menacingly from the white ribbon around his neck. The referee called the team captains together for the coin toss. So Lo and Taff trotted to the centre of the pitch, followed by some of the 'Boot Boys'.

Taff had instructed So Lo on the routine to follow, and they shook hands with the referee as was traditional. But it was noticeable that the R.S.M. shook the Chinaman's hand with a certain amount of 'coolness'. An amount of class distinction had reared its ugly head! The referee took a fifty-cent piece from his pocket and flicked it into the air. The coin dropped to the grass, and immediately one of the 'Boot Boys' grabbed it and dashed off the field. He assumed that it was a strange little European game, and he had won! So Lo quickly called him back, explained the strange ritual, and the 'Boot Boy' reluctantly handed back the fifty cents. The ritual was carried out again, and Taff won the toss.

He studied the weather carefully, the sun was slightly to the west, and he decided that the 'Boot Boys' should have the disadvantage of looking into it. All's fair in love, war… and rugby!

Steve looked around at the 'Boot Boys' team. They were wearing the same clothes that they worked in; they probably had little else to wear. So Lo had presentable white tennis shoes on, but the others wore open toed sandals, or no footwear at all. Steve spoke to Taff about the situation, and it was agreed that both teams should play barefoot in order to make the game equally fair. Steve also considered that it wouldn't harm some of the platoon to toughen up their feet, making the border patrols easier.

A good 'sprinkling' of spectators had arrived, and Steve noticed that the Commanding Officer and his wife were sat under a nearby shady tree. The

C.O.'s 'batman' hovered in the background, preparing sandwiches and cocktails from a large wicker picnic basket. 'Batman's' jobs were cherished, and closely guarded. To have the post meant having no guard duties, or cookhouse and trekking patrols to carry out. The 'batman' had the C.O.'s ear, and if he pleased the C.O.'s wife, he had a job for life.

The families from the married quarters were also spreading blankets on the grass and carefully placing the contents of their picnic baskets on them. A carefree party atmosphere was quickly building.

The referee blew his whistle, signalling which half of the pitch each team should take up. Nobody, except Taff, knew where to stand, and they all spread apart, trying to look as professional as possible. The perplexed 'Boot Boys' followed suit, commanded by So Lo. The R.S.M. had forgotten to appoint linesmen, and two of the spectators were coerced into the role. The only qualification needed was a fairly clean white handkerchief!

The R.S.M. checked his watch, it was exactly 3.00pm. He looked around him, and satisfied that all was in order, blew his whistle to start the match. Taff kicked the ball as hard as he could into the 'Boot Boys'' half, and immediately started to limp. Rugby was a different 'kettle of fish' without boots!

The 'Boot Boys' had a distinct advantage with their toughened feet, and Taff realised he had made a mistake agreeing to the 'no boots' rule. The 'Boys' made good use of their superior kicking but couldn't understand why the ball had to go 'over' the goal, and not into it. It took So Lo some time to explain, but they learnt quickly, and started to score freely, enthusiastically encouraged by the spectators.

The pace of the game picked up momentum, the 'Boot Boys' were proving to be a handful, and Taff had to rally his troops. The R.S.M. was having trouble keeping up with the play. His 'strict' training programme had not paid off, and he stopped play to take a large swig of brandy from his hip flask, insisting to all around that it was purely for medicinal purposes!

But part of the referee's mobility problem was his knee length black shorts. His Laundry Boy, sensing the importance of the occasion had put three times the normal amount of starch in the laundry water, and the shorts, although smart, looked as if they were made of stiff cardboard. After a further ten minutes of hectic play the referee's knees turned a nasty shade of purple. He blew his whistle and announced that he was returning to his quarters to change into something 'more suitable'!

The Commanding Officer immediately stepped into the breach. He tested the whistle and hung the ribbon around his neck. The R.S.M. hurried off to his quarters, cursing his Laundry Boy, and using language the padre would certainly not have approved of.

The game restarted, to the applause of the spectators, they had never seen anything as funny, and the party spirit continued. The 'Boot Boys' enhanced their score, but the platoon also began to score freely. The game was very much 'end to end' and enjoyable to watch. The real Cardiff Arms Park in Wales would have been proud to host such a battle, and it wouldn't have damaged their sacred grass! The C.O. seemed to know quite a lot about the rules of the game, and awarded the 'Boot Boys' a penalty directly in front of the platoon's goal posts. Taff forgot himself and shouted words of unprintable dissent at the referee, but he had the presence of mind to salute first!

The R.S.M. reappeared ten minutes later, dressed in full ceremonial uniform. He marched onto the pitch to the applause of the crowd that was growing by the minute. News of the unusual spectacle was spreading quickly. The R.S.M. accepted the handover of the whistle as if he was being presented with a medal. He straightened his back, flexed his shoulders, and re-started the game. He managed a smile as he did so, but his Laundry Boy would be out of favour for some time to come.

The Commanding Officer returned to the shade under the tree, loudly applauded by his wife, and 'batman', who was holding a freshly made cocktail for him after his service in the 'breach'. The C.O.'s wife smiled at the 'batman', his job was safe!

After forty minutes play the R.S.M. blew his whistle to signal half time. The platoon was relieved; they were receiving a drubbing at the hands of the 'Boot Boys'. Taff would have his work cut out to revitalise his team, as to be beaten by a bunch of 'Boot Boys' simply wasn't on. He would never be able to show his face in Cardiff or the Arms Park again.

The slices of orange and melon were handed around. Four of the 'Boot Boys' assumed that the game had finished, and gratefully started to walk away. So Lo laughingly explained to them that there was a second half to play. The news wasn't received well by them; they had given their all in the name of boot cleaning, and wanted to go home, even if it was to a nagging wife and a bowl of rice! So Lo managed to persuade them to stay, mainly by threatening them with expulsion from the camp as 'Boot Boys'. So Lo was their spokesman and 'shop steward', and his voice carried weight.

After slices of fruit and drinks of juice they all felt revived, and applauded by the growing number of spectators the R.S.M. re-started the game. Both sides began to score more 'tries' and 'conversions', and the party spirit continued well into the second half. But gradually the hectic pace began to tell, and tiredness crept in. The R.S.M. was sweating profusely in his ceremonial uniform, and required regular 'top ups' from his flask.

The platoon began using their distinct weight advantage to 'secure' the ball, and many of the 'Boot Boys' found themselves flattened, whether they had the ball or not! After the platoon had scored three more 'tries', one of the 'Boot Boys' in his frustration, grabbed the ball, stuffed it up his shirt and made a dash for the trees and shrubs that surrounded the pitch. As he left the field he shouted something over his shoulder.

So Lo said that loosely translated it meant, "Sod you, you silly bastards, I'm going home!"

The spectators applauded loudly, amused by the 'Boot Boy's' action, and the C.O. raised his cocktail glass in salute. The referee and the other players waited patiently for him to return with the ball, but after ten minutes it became clear that he was not in the mood to return. The 'Boot Boy' had played enough rugby for one day, nagging wife or not!

The R.S.M. declared the game a draw, and made an official note in his referee's book stating: 'match abandoned after sixty minutes due to rugby ball being 'Absent without leave'. He also noted the weather conditions prevailing at the time, and the direction the ball had disappeared into. Lastly he wrote a note to himself, reminding him to refill his hip flask!

The crowd of spectators drifted away. They had enjoyed a good day, even if it had ended prematurely. In a way, the 'Boot Boy's' dramatic exit had been a fitting end. So Lo went to his bicycle, lifted the large wicker basket from its cradle and placed it on the grass. He had filled it with bottles of 'San Miguel' and salad rolls, all packed with blocks of ice. So Lo was never one to miss a selling opportunity! The platoon agreed to buy the whole contents, and pay him the next day. They and the 'Boot Boys' sat on the grass and enjoyed their picnic. All things considered it had been an enjoyable day, and through So Lo's interpretation all agreed to have another match. The R.S.M. was invited to return as referee, and he agreed to do so, as soon as he had re-trained his Laundry Boy!

Two days later the rugby ball re-appeared on Taff's bed. It had been liberally coated in boot blacking, and polished to a deep lustre!

CHAPTER 38

Sunday was the second day of the platoon's forty-eight hours 'release of duty' following the day patrol.

Most of the men were taking advantage of the Sunday relaxation of discipline and sleeping late. The rugby match against the 'Boot Boys' had been strenuous, especially on the feet. The 'Boys' were fitter and tougher than they looked. Steve thought about the game as he slowly awoke, a slight breeze wafting through the open window making the Sunday morning 'lie-in' pleasant.

The match with the 'Boot Boys' had been a public relations success for the army, and had drawn the camp closer together, military and civilians alike. The results would not go unnoticed at the regiment's headquarters, and the C.O. could look forward to having a star placed on his military record; further matches would be encouraged. Taff was to be in charge of rugby operations, all with the full backing of the R.S.M. who intended to put his new referee's uniform, and hip flask to good use in the future. Other platoons in the regiment were forming their own teams, and possibly a competitive league could be started. The league would include the 'Boot Boys', and possibly the 'Laundry Boys' who had shown an interest in the strange new foreign game.

Steve yawned and looked around the 'basha'. The other men were gradually coming back to life, and filtering off to breakfast in the cookhouse. Sunday could be quite a pleasing day, provided that you were not detailed for duty. He wondered what plans to make for the day, with no duties to perform. He had enjoyed the rugby match, and fulfilled his moral obligations to Taff and the platoon. Today would be for him, and he would venture into Kowloon with 'Stirling Moss' again and pay a visit to the 'Star Cafe' and Mai Lee. She had been very much in his thoughts and he had promised to return as soon as possible, but it being Sunday there was a chance that she was not working, and at home, wherever that was. There was only one way to find out.

He felt isolated in the camp; there wasn't even a 'red sentinel' to contact the outside world. 'Stirling Moss' was his only lifeline, albeit a very precarious one. He was grateful for the transport, but with 'Stirling's' rigid timetable there was little time in the day to enjoy Kowloon, and hopefully Mai Lee's company. He decided to try and extend the hours in Kowloon; it may be that 'Stirling' might be open to a little financial bribery.

After breakfast, he made himself ready for the day, and possibly Hong Kong with his attractive 'guide' Mai Lee. He longed to know more about her, there were so many unanswered questions. Did she have many friends, possibly other boyfriends? She was certainly beautiful enough to attract any man! And what of her mother and father, were they still alive, or dead? The lifespan of people in the Far East was not great. He rubbed his upper arms, remembering the disease protecting vaccinations and inoculations he had endured at 'Morval' barracks. Most Chinese were not able to avail themselves of such life protecting serums.

Steve had run out of aftershave and reminded himself to buy more from the camp N.A.A.F.I. shop. Mac allowed him to use some of his 'special' lotion he had bought in Dewsbury during his two weeks leave to impress his favourite barmaid. But after Steve had 'sprinkled' himself and his sharkskin shirt with it he decided he smelled like a 'Soho tart', the only thing it had done was to sting his face after shaving and leave red blotches on the skin. He hoped the blotches and obnoxious aroma of the aftershave would be negated by the fresh air on the journey to Kowloon. Mac's choice of aftershave left a lot to be desired. It was possibly acceptable to his favourite barmaid, and perhaps the 'Blonde Bombshell', but Mai Lee was a 'cut above'!

'Stirling Moss' was supervising the loading of his truck as usual, and after casually greeting him Steve climbed into the passenger seat and waited for the driver to finish his task. He looked around the cab, but decided not to inspect it too closely; they had always completed the journeys unscathed anyway, what could possibly go wrong?

When 'Stirling' joined him in the cab, Steve held a five dollar note in front of him, and through sign language and much pointing of fingers at watch faces 'Stirling' grinned, nodded, and stuffed the money into his top pocket. The deal was done, and it would give Steve a further four hours in Kowloon.

'Stirling' lit a 'Lucky Strike', casually spat out of the open window, and the journey commenced. 'Stirling' was his usual 'hectic' self for the outward journey. The accelerator was pressed to the floor, and his knuckles were white as they held tightly onto the steering wheel. Steve took his normal precaution of holding onto the dashboard with both hands. After ten minutes on the rough road the passenger door flew open and flapped wildly on its loose hinges. Steve grabbed the door and hauled it closed, one hand for the door, one for the dashboard. 'Stirling' laughed and handed him a piece of string for 'running repairs'. Steve tied it to the door handle and secured the other end to his seat frame. 'Stirling' carried on at the same speed as if nothing had happened, it was situation normal!

Steve regained his composure; he was becoming used to the odd unexpected drama where 'Stirling Moss' was concerned. Because of the language difference conversation was impossible, and tended to make the journeys more fraught. Steve had a few words in Chinese, which included 'good morning', happy birthday, and 'you look beautiful today'! The latter was to encourage Nani to make him more rice cakes for the platoon, but it wasn't much use in general conversation, especially when talking to a man!

'Stirling' knew four words of English. They were: 'Liverpool', football, and 'never happen' and he practised them regularly between 'puffs' on 'Lucky Strikes'. His previous passenger client had been a Liverpudlian. But it could have been worse. The passenger might have come from Scotland! Hearing the words 'haggis', 'och aye the noo', and 'cockaleekie' for the duration of the journey would be enough to drive anybody mad!

When they reached Kowloon Steve reminded 'Stirling', by the use of sign language, of the different pick-up time. He walked through the busy streets, dodging tri-shaws and horn blowing tactics when crossing the streets.

Life was never this hectic in Somerset! he thought to himself.

He reached the 'Star Cafe' massaging his fingers back into life after clinging on to 'Stirling's' dashboard. He fervently hoped that the passenger door would be repaired for the return journey. The thought of landing on the road halfway through the trip did not appeal to him.

As he approached the 'Star Cafe' he saw Mai Lee sitting at an outside table. She was smoothing the tablecloth against the breeze, a natural instinct for a 'tidy' waitress. She looked content with herself, and settled back in her wicker chair after putting the table 'to rights'.

Steve smiled as he saw her contented smile and thought to himself, *Maybe it's the fried rice, and plenty of 'joss' sticks at romantic times.* It reminded him of Docherty and his overly sexual girlfriend! The sudden thought gave him lustful feelings about Mai Lee, and he quickly pushed them into the background. There was a time and place for everything!

Mai Lee was dressed in European style clothes, and reading a glossy magazine. It was her day off work, he was in luck! She looked up from the fashion magazine and saw him waving to her as he weaved his way through the crowd of tourists. The foreigners were listening intently to a young female guide who was speaking in fluent French, the tourists with their black berets and dapper manner from Paris.

Steve had his own personal guide, and she picked up her magazine and walked towards him. The tourists moved on, cameras clicking as they went, leaving Steve and Mai Lee to greet each other. When they were ten yards apart she suddenly rushed towards him and threw her arms around him. Steve was surprised by her sudden show of emotion, and he held on to her trying not to lose his balance. They kissed gently in the shadows afforded by the overhanging roof of the cafe. Mai Lee sniffed slightly at his sharkskin shirt, and laughingly asked if he had been eating garlic, or 'chilli peppers'.

Steve smiled awkwardly and replied, "No," then he silently cursed Mac and his 'favourite' barmaid!

They kissed once more, the 'chilli peppers' forgotten. He held her to him. She was like a golden jewel in his arms. He felt guilty for touching her, in case of tarnishing her beauty. She in turn grasped onto him, feeling secure in his strong arms. East and West had come together!

They reluctantly drew apart and Steve recovered from her sudden show of emotion. The European side of her nature had certainly shown itself, in stark contrast to the reserved Chinese part of her being. Steve had never seen the Chinese show any kind of emotion, but what they did in the privacy of their own bedrooms was possibly another matter!

Mai Lee asked Steve if he would like some tea, in Chinese tradition.

"Yes, that would be nice," replied Steve. A 'San Miguel' would have been more acceptable, but if she wanted to drink tea, then tea it was!

He started to sit down at one of the cafe tables, but she said, "Would you like to take tea in my apartment?" Once again Steve was taken aback! Was this the European, or Chinese side of her nature? Mai Lee continued, "I live above the cafe." She said it as though he should have already known, but that was simply her female logic, albeit illogical.

They went into the cafe and through a back room where stairs led up to Mai Lee's apartment. As they walked into the apartment a grey coloured cat jumped down from a sofa and greeted Mai Lee by rubbing itself against her leg. She reached down and stroked its shining fur; it was obviously well cared for.

Mai Lee said to Steve, "This is my cat Chow-Chow." She looked at the cat lovingly and said, "Chow-Chow, this is Steafe." The cat stared at Steve, as if to be 'sizing' him up. Chow-Chow turned its back on him, and walked away, tail in the air! Mai Lee looked disappointed and said, "Don't worry, it will be all right, Chow-Chow is partly Siamese and a little highly strung."

Steve smiled, and thought to himself, *I prefer dogs anyway*. He didn't, it was just sour grapes.

Mai Lee went into her kitchen to prepare tea for them. Steve took the opportunity to look around the lounge. It was tastefully furnished, and seemed to be half in European style, and half Chinese. But the two went well together. Steve wasn't aware of furniture prices, but he knew the pieces of furniture in the lounge were not 'run of the mill'! Once again a question leapt into his mind, but he had no answer for it.

He sat on the comfortable sofa, and looked at the cat, fast asleep at the other end, its paw shielding its eyes from the light. Chow-Chow certainly knew how to relax, and Steve felt envious of it.

Mai Lee returned with a tray of cups, saucers, pot of tea and a plate of chocolate biscuits. Chow-Chow awoke from its siesta, sniffed the air, and went back to sleep. Mai Lee smiled lovingly at the cat, and put the tray onto a small coffee table in front of the sofa. She sat next to Steve and they enjoyed lemon tea, nibbling at chocolate biscuits. From time to time they 'nudged' hips, and the cat turned contentedly in its slumber.

Steve looked around the lounge again, and remarked how well it was furnished. Mai Lee said, "Most of it was bought by my father," and then almost as an afterthought added, "he owns the apartment, and the cafe downstairs. He is in the import/export business."

Steve felt it was time to ask about her parents, as he could restrain himself no longer. She replied to his curiosity by saying, "My mother was Chinese, from Peking, but she died ten years ago from consumption."

Steve said he was very sorry, and silently cursed himself for asking the question. She could see the concern on his face and said, "It's okay, but I miss her very much. She was a wonderful woman and taught me a lot, quite apart from being a loving mother." Mai Lee continued, "I went to school here, but the teaching was very basic, my mother taught me a great deal more, and we were very close."

Steve said that he wished he had known her and that she sounded like she was a special person, just as Aunt Maude was to him.

They had 'broken the ice' about her family and she continued by saying, "My father, who lives along the coast on a boat, is called Giorgio."

Steve in his inquisitiveness, blurted out, "That doesn't sound very Chinese."

"It's not," she said, "he is Italian. His name is Busetti, Giorgio Busetti." Mai Lee hurried into the kitchen to avoid any more searching questions.

Steve remembered his conversation with the Hong Kong policeman about drugs and the controlling 'Barons'. But Busetti was quite a common Italian name; there could be dozens of Busettis in Hong Kong. He decided to 'shelve' the matter until a later date, possibly over a pint of beer in the N.A.A.F.I. Alcohol always assisted clarity of thought At least to a certain degree!

Mai Lee returned from the kitchen, and Steve changed the subject of conversation by explaining to her about his financial 'deal' with 'Stirling' and the fact that he had more time before returning to camp. He suggested that they might take the ferry to the island again.

Mai Lee thought for a moment and then said, "Would you like to see more of the Kowloon coastline? It is beautiful." Then she added, "We could go to Hong Kong another day." Steve was pleased to hear the phrase 'another day', as it meant that she had accepted him, and there was more to look forward to.

He had planned his day for Hong Kong, but Mai Lee had other ideas, and that was okay by him. The way he felt about her he would gladly go to the moon!

He asked which bus they should take for the coast road.

She replied, "It's all right, I have a car."

Once again his mind was thrown into confusion. She owned a car? Most Chinese waitresses could hardly afford a second-hand bicycle. Cars in Hong Kong were for the well-heeled aristocrats and businessmen. Mai Lee was growing more mysterious by the minute. He asked her what make of car she had and she said that she couldn't remember, but it was a red one.

Steve thought to himself, *She's a typical woman.*

When they had finished the tea and biscuits Mai Lee suggested that they go for a sightseeing coast tour in her car. The weather was fine and sunny, but it was the time of year when rain could come in the evening, and sightseeing in wet weather was not good. She jokingly said she would be his official 'guide' again for the day. Steve smiled, and said he wasn't sure he could afford a full time guide, being a fairly low paid soldier. She was not totally surprised that he was in the army, his short haircut and military bearing had already given him away.

They prepared themselves to leave, and Mai Lee stroked Chow-Chow saying, "Goodbye, be a good cat."

The cat half awoke, looked harshly at Steve, and then went back to sleep! They left the apartment and walked down the stairs that connected with the cafe's back room. Mai Lee spoke briefly to a waitress who was on duty, and Steve held the exit door open for her as they walked out into a narrow quiet cul-de-sac. It was in complete contrast to the busy seafront road at the entrance to the cafe.

Mai Lee was wearing a white blouse, light green skirt made of thin material in keeping with the warm weather, and low heeled shoes. She seemed to prefer European style clothes when not working. The tourists though, demanded that Chinese waitresses wear traditional 'cheongsam' and 'sanfoo' in the cafe, all in keeping with their oriental vacation and photographs to show the folks back home.

Steve glanced at Mai Lee as they walked slowly along the quiet road to the car garage. She was about 2'' shorter than him. With a pair of high heeled shoes, they would both be the same height. He didn't feel that a woman should be taller than the man she was with; he didn't know why exactly, it just didn't look right. He remembered that Moira Theodopolis in Scotland was much taller than him, and had been very dominant in the courtyard! He smiled to himself, and automatically looked down and smoothed his shirt front.

They came to a recently built modern garage at the end of the cul-de-sac. It stood out amongst the old, fairly untidy Chinese buildings that needed more than a coat of paint. The dark green wooden doors were secured with a large padlock. Mai Lee took a key from a small leather shoulder bag, and opened the double doors to reveal a gleaming red sports car. The badge on the bonnet read 'Ferrari'!

Steve's jaw dropped open; Mai Lee smiled and said, "It's a nice little car, isn't it? It was a birthday present from my father."

Steve closed his mouth. Mai Lee opened the passenger door and Steve thankfully sank into the beautifully upholstered seat. For some reason his knees felt weak. He blamed it on the recent barefoot rugby match, but a certain very, very, expensive red car could also be a factor! He wondered how many more revelations were to be unfolded; it was all too much for a young lad from Somerset!

Mai Lee started the engine and gently pressed the accelerator. The exhaust sounded throaty, deep, and very powerful. Steve could visualise the engine under the bonnet. It would be at least six cylinders, and possibly supercharged. Mai Lee put a pink head scarf over her hair, and tied it neatly under her chin. She took off her shoes to drive barefooted. She explained that she had been taught to drive that way by her father. He said she would get a better 'feel' of the accelerator that way. Steve had read in a car magazine that many 'Rolls Royce' owners did the same in England. Her father scored a 'point' with him, whoever he was!

Mai Lee drove out of the garage, and Steve automatically gripped onto the dashboard, thinking that she might be of the same ilk as 'Stirling Moss', but she drove carefully, and seemed to recognise that she was driving a very expensive and special piece of engineering.

As they drove along the winding coast road Steve took a minute to try and absorb all of the recent information he had acquired. But his mind was confused; he was pleasantly confused, but confused nonetheless!

As the car picked up speed, the breeze in the car gradually blew Mai Lee's skirt up towards her thighs, revealing her slender beautiful legs and slightly tanned skin. A beautiful confusion indeed!

CHAPTER 39

As they drove along the coast Steve drank in the scenery, listened to the 'purr' of the 'Ferrari' engine, and sneaked the odd glimpse or two at Mai Lee's slender legs. He felt a sudden pang of envy and jealousy that she owned the car and not he, but he glanced down at her legs again and realised there were distinct compensations in non-ownership!

Mai Lee didn't appear to be self-conscious about showing her legs; it was possibly the extrovert Italian side of her nature coming to the fore again. He wondered what kind of man her father was, he certainly sounded very generous! If he could afford to give her expensive birthday presents the import/export business was doing very well!

They stopped at a small fishing village to stretch their legs. The picturesque place was strangely called 'Aberdeen'. Mai Lee explained about the 'Boat' people, who were born, lived, and died on their boats. They knew no other life, or home.

Steve and Mai Lee strolled along the shoreline, and after a while he took her hand, half expecting her to draw back. She looked at him in her quizzical Chinese way, and then gripped his hand, moving closer to him. Steve breathed a sigh of relief, and they smiled at each other, as if saying 'hello'!

Mai Lee was curious about him as he was of her. She knew nothing about him, except that he was called 'Steafe' and was a British soldier. As they walked he began to tell her about himself, he hadn't realised that she would be as inquisitive as he always was about other people. Perhaps that was one of his faults, selfishness?

He told her about Somerset and Aunt Maude. It was difficult to explain about his parents, he knew little about them, and he decided to try and explain on another day. Sometimes he needed somebody to explain to him! He talked more about Aunt Maude and her locally famous cheese and pickled onion sandwiches. Mai Lee said she would like to try them one day, perhaps with a little 'soy' sauce!

They continued holding hands as they walked. Steve picked up seashells, and Mai Lee put them in her shoulder bag. She said that she would take them back to the apartment and make a toy for Chow-Chow to play with. Steve thought about the Siamese cat, and why it obviously disliked him. Maybe it was jealousy over Mai Lee; animals could be very strange that way, as could humans. Or perhaps the cat simply didn't like foreigners! He saw it as a challenge and decided to try and win the cat over.

The conversation came around to Mai Lee's parents again. Her mother had been a school teacher in Peking before meeting Giorgio. He was already a successful businessman, and swept Mai Lee's mother off her feet with his flamboyant Italian ways. They moved to Hong Kong at his suggestion. Business opportunities were more available in the democratic Hong Kong. China itself was far too restricting for a 'cavalier' entrepreneur that had his eye on other markets.

Steve was still curious about her father, and to keep the conversation moving in that vein said, "Which part of Italy does your father come from?"

She replied, "He was born in a place called Napoli, but I have never been there." She added, "Giorgio comes from Napoli, but most of his brothers and sisters live in Sicily, I think his grandfather is from there." They were both quiet for a few minutes, and then she said, "Would you like to meet my father?"

Steve wasn't sure that he was ready for such a move, but replied, "Yes, I would like that."

Mai Lee said, "He lives on a boat in Wan Chai, we can drive there, it's not far."

Steve glanced at his watch; there was still plenty of time before his return journey with 'Stirling'. He idly wondered what state of mind the erratic Chinaman would be in.

They cleaned their shoes of sand and rocky grit before continuing the ride in the 'Ferrari'. Mai Lee drove without shoes again and re-tied the pink scarf to keep her hair in place. Her slender legs looked even more attractive without shoes, and Steve tried to restrain certain feelings he felt in his loins. Mai Lee looked the part behind the wheel of the expensive 'Ferrari'. Nobody would have taken her for a lowly cafe waitress. She and the car could easily have fitted into one of the modern spy secret agent adventure films.

They reached Wan Chai, a pleasant, fairly busy fishing village with a large picturesque bay. Trees reached down almost to the water's edge. The shoreline itself was quite rocky, unlike the sandy 'Aberdeen' shore. Mai Lee parked the car and they started to walk around the bay. Fishing nets were strewn across the rocks, drying out and being repaired by mature fishermen. They were probably repairing the nets for their sons and grandsons who fished the waters of the South China Sea. The old men had seen their days at sea, and were content now to sit and tend the family nets, puffing on their clay pipes.

Steve looked out across the bay at the mixed array of boats moored on the calm blue waters. There were a few sizeable commercial 'junks' mixed in with the smaller boats. Steve assumed that Mai Lee's father had bought one of the 'junks' and transformed it into a type of 'houseboat'. It was the kind of thing an extrovert entrepreneur would do.

Having convinced himself that his theory was correct, Steve asked which boat belonged to her father. She said his boat could not be seen from the shore, they would have to go further along where a small ferry boat operated. When they reached the ferry point the small boat had just returned from a 'junk' moored in the bay. Mai Lee explained that the ferryman made a meagre living taking owners to and from their boats.

Mai Lee and Steve sat in the bow of the tiny boat, having paid the fare of two cents each. Steve ran his fingers through the warm water as the boat weaved around the other moored vessels. It was a far cry from the Serpentine in London, and going around in circles with Lorraine at the helm.

The small ferry boat was propelled by using a single oar fixed through a 'rowlock' on the middle of the wooden stern. The boatman expertly used the oar to propel, and steer the boat. He made it look easy, but it was not a simple skill.

The number of boats around them increased. They encountered more 'junks' amongst the smaller vessels, their large sails flapping in the breeze. Steve wondered why they should have their sails set, when they were clearly not making ready for sea. The ferry boatman, although skilled, was finding it difficult to navigate through the tightly packed vessels.

Eventually the ferry boat rounded the high stern of a 'junk' to reveal a sleek, modern, white motor yacht.

Steve looked at Mai Lee in amazement.

She smiled and said, "This is my father's boat."

Steve looked back over the stern of the ferry. The tightly packed 'junks' and other boats were acting as a protective security barrier to hide the white yacht. He turned his attention to the luxury yacht. It was at least sixty feet long, very streamlined, and very expensive. A sloping aluminium ladder was fixed to the side of the boat, and as they approached it Mai Lee said they should take their shoes off.

She explained, "My father is the only one allowed to wear shoes on the boat."

Steve raised his eyebrows, but did as instructed.

The ferry boatman held onto the sloping ladder as Steve and Mai Lee climbed to the deck of the yacht. Steve looked up to see a swarthy crewman waiting at the top of the ladder. He was dressed in a white 'tee' shirt, black trousers and was barefoot. He also carried a small pistol in a holster belt around his waist! Mai Lee reached the deck and the crewman formally greeted her. When Steve reached the deck, shoes in hand, the crewman eyed him to board the yacht.

Steve followed Mai Lee who was walking towards the stern of the yacht. A large white canvas sheet was stretched across the rear of the boat, tied to uprights on either side of the boat. The rear of the yacht was designed as an open lounge, with small black leather armchairs and two glass topped coffee tables, with vases of freshly cut flowers adorning them. Almost hidden from view was a luxurious fully stocked cocktail bar. A Chinese steward was stood at the bar, waiting to serve. He was dressed in a white uniform, with well-polished brass buttons at the front of his tunic, and gold embroidered epaulettes on the shoulders. He too was barefoot!

Steve and Mai Lee sat at a coffee table and she asked him what he would like to drink. "I believe the steward's 'special' cocktails are very good! Giorgio drinks them all the time."

Steve agreed to try one. His mind was still reeling from the shock of seeing the hidden yacht. Mai Lee did not drink alcohol; a glass of orange juice with some ice was quite sufficient to quench the thirst, but she was happy for Steve to indulge himself.

She looked at him seriously and said, "A man should be a man, and a woman a woman."

Steve readily agreed with that philosophy on life. The bar steward made the drinks, and polished the buttons on his tunic with his sleeve before placing the glasses on the coffee table.

After finishing her orange juice Mai Lee said she was going to look for her father, he was probably working in his office, or 'day cabin', as he called it. She spoke to the bar steward in Chinese and he made another cocktail for

Steve. After Mai Lee had left, Steve sipped his cocktail and looked around him. Everything he saw was of the best quality, and the deck looked as if it had just been varnished and shone in the bright sunlight. The yacht was spotless, as if it had just left a showroom. He wondered what the rest of the boat was like, and more importantly, why was the Chinese crewman carrying a possibly loaded gun around his waist?

Mai Lee returned and said that her father was finishing some important paperwork, and would be with them shortly. Steve finished his drink and asked Mai Lee as nonchalantly as was possible, why the crewman was wearing a gun.

She shifted slightly in her chair and replied, "My father is overly concerned about security and there are some very expensive paintings on the boat!"

Steve accepted that, and moved on.

Fifteen minutes later Mai Lee's father appeared and the bar steward immediately made him a large special cocktail. Steve stood up, waiting to be introduced. Mai Lee made the formal introduction and the two men shook hands. Her father's handshake was positive, but quite businesslike; there was no warmth in it. Steve studied him quickly, trying to form an instant opinion of the man; sometimes 'gut' feelings can be very much relied upon.

Giorgio had a fairly gaunt face. He was a typical Italian, with black hair swept back from a high forehead. His eyebrows were dark and in a thin line, as if they had been 'plucked'. His nose was aquiline, almost aristocratic, but his mouth was tight, and quite cruel. Steve noticed a heavy gold chain around his neck, and he wore a large gold signet ring on one of his long artistic fingers. Steve glanced down at his feet. He was wearing expensive leather shoes, possibly Italian!

He said to Steve, "I understand you are a British military man?"

Steve replied that he was, and he was stationed near the border with China.

Giorgio turned and spoke to Mai Lee, but he spoke in Italian, not English. Steve didn't understand what he was saying, but he talked to Mai Lee as if she was an employee, not his daughter. Steve summed him up, and took an instant dislike to him!

Giorgio turned to Steve and said, "I have to go to Hong Kong for an important business meeting, but please stay and enjoy the special food that my chef is preparing."

He said it in an almost condescending manner, and Steve wondered whether he should bow in gratitude.

A crewman appeared carrying a black leather briefcase and a light coloured 'Fedora' hat. He handed them smartly to Giorgio, turned quickly and walked away. Steve watched him hurry away. Giorgio had his crew well trained, or was it that they were simply terrified of him?

Giorgio said something further to Mai Lee, then turned to Steve and said curtly, "Arrivederci!" He placed the 'Fedora' neatly on his head, made certain that the briefcase was locked and made his way to the aluminium ladder. A small launch drew alongside and took Giorgio to his meeting in Hong Kong.

As he left Steve thought to himself, *So much for prospective father-in-laws!*

Mai Lee turned to Steve and said, "My father is always very busy with his import/export business."

Steve replied, "Well, he is very successful, this is an expensive boat."

"Yes, it is," she replied. But when she spoke there was sadness in her voice, as if she disliked the yacht and all that it stood for.

A waiter arrived carrying two silver platters of food. He placed them on the coffee table and put serviettes and condiments with them. He spoke to Mai Lee, bowed slightly and left without even glancing at Steve. He began to feel that for some reason he was not welcome on the yacht. The delicately prepared food was hors d'oeuvres and thinly cut sandwiches, all high quality, but not filling. Steve would rather have had a steak and kidney pie from the N.A.A.F.I., followed by a 'San Miguel'. He looked at Mai Lee who seemed to be covering a thin wafer with a red lumpy jam. He asked her what kind of jam it was.

She laughed and replied, "It's not jam, Steafe, it's caviar!"

She handed him a small piece of the wafer for him to try. He took a bite, winced slightly and said, "Maybe it's an acquired taste."

She laughed again and replied, "It is probably not as good as cheese and pickled onion sandwiches!"

Steve drank a last cocktail while Mai Lee went to 'powder her nose'. He looked at his watch and was pleased to see that there was still a good two hours before he was due to return to camp with 'Stirling Moss'. He had struck a very good deal with the Chinaman.

They left the yacht, the crewman still guarding the ladder. Steve glanced at the pistol and saw that it was certainly not a toy. The small ferry boat took them to shore and the waiting 'Ferrari'. They were both quiet and reflective on the journey back to Mai Lee's apartment. The 'Ferrari' 'purred' like a contented lion under Mai Lee's barefoot control. The 'Ferrari' was the 'Rolls Royce' of all sports cars and the pang of envy returned.

When they had returned the car to its garage and settled themselves into the apartment, Mai Lee made coffee, and they sorted out the shells that had been collected on the shore. Steve studied them as Mai Lee carefully cleaned them. They were much like the shells he had collected as a young boy on holiday with Aunt Maude in Bournemouth.

It's a small world, he thought to himself.

They talked about the day in general; it had certainly been an 'eye opener' for Steve. He thought about Giorgio Busetti. The Italian was a cold, calculating businessman, but whether he was a drug 'Baron' was another matter. Nevertheless, Steve found Mai Lee's explanation of why the crewman carried a gun a bit hard to swallow. She was obviously telling the truth as she saw it, but was she being misled by her father?

As they sipped the coffee Steve told Mai Lee a little of England and the U.K. in general. She was keen to learn. Her thirst for knowledge was insatiable, and she bombarded him with questions ranging from Charlie Chaplin, The Houses of Parliament, Blackpool, Judy Garland, and the famous Yellow Brick Road, where did it lead to? His head started to spin with the non-stop questions.

He looked at his watch; time had raced on. They only had another twenty minutes before he had to leave. She asked if he could stay one more hour, but it was impossible; to miss 'Stirling Moss' would be a big problem. Mai Lee became agitated and to his surprise took the initiative and kissed him, running her slender fingers through his hair. After his initial surprise and thinking her Italian side was taking over again, he kissed her fully on the lips. Once more the electricity shot through his body. Mai Lee ran her fingers down the front of his shirt, searching for buttons. He kissed her again, pushing his tongue against her teeth. She opened her mouth, and their tongues caressed. Mai Lee grabbed his shirt front with both hands, and in a frenzy started to tear his buttons. Steve had visions of a repeat Moira Theodopolis performance, and he quickly removed the shirt before serious damage was done! Sharkskin shirts were not two-a-penny!

She took his hand and they walked towards the bedroom. Mai Lee was already loosening her blouse and skirt. Chow-Chow awoke and watched them disappear into the bedroom. The cat licked its front paws, glanced at the ceiling, and went back to sleep.

Mai Lee uncharacteristically threw her clothes on the floor, stretched out on the bed and eagerly awaited the attentions of her man.

Steve unzipped his trousers, and as he removed them thought to himself, *So this is what the Chinese do in the privacy of their own home!*

He gently placed himself over her, and she was grateful for his masculine presence.

CHAPTER 40

After saying goodbye to Mai Lee, Steve walked and half ran to 'Stirling's' pick-up point. He looked at his watch, hoping the hands would slow down, but time waited for no man, or even lovers!

He reached the rendezvous with five minutes to spare and congratulated himself on his effort. He looked down at his trouser front, his zip was undone, and his shirt unbuttoned. He quickly put the matter right, and combed his ruffled hair. They had cemented their relationship in no uncertain manner, and his shirt was still intact! Under her controlled Chinese facade Mai Lee was a passionate woman, and any reservations in her character had been swept away by their lovemaking.

Steve looked for 'Stirling's' truck but there was no sign of it. He checked his watch again; it was exactly on the agreed time. Corporal Entwhistle at 'Morval' barracks could not have planned it better with his paranoid meticulous timekeeping! Steve sat at the side of the road, exhausted by the combined efforts of making love and the dash to make the pick-up time. He waited for twenty minutes, but no truck appeared. Had there been a breakdown in their sign language communications or had 'Stirling' simply let him down? Once again thoughts of drugs entered his mind.

He had two options, one was to go back to Mai Lee's and ask her to drive him back to 'Gillman' camp, the second was to trek it on his own. It would be nice to arrive in an expensive red 'Ferrari', driven by a beautiful girl, but Mai Lee had work to do tomorrow, and needed a good night's sleep.

He decided on the trek. As long as he was in camp for the morning parade there was no problem. He was fit and there was only one road, so there was no danger of getting lost. He went to a nearby bar for a fortifying 'San Miguel' before starting his journey. He also needed a few minutes to re-live and think about the extraordinary day he had just enjoyed. It wasn't every day that one met a Siamese cat!

After two satisfying pints of beer Steve started his trek back to camp. The evening was growing cool and there was a slight breeze blowing through his sharkskin shirt. He was glad that he had 'rescued' the shirt before Mai Lee had a chance to vent her passion on it. Perhaps it would be a good idea for Nani to make one more, just in case of emotional accidents in the future.

The road to camp was fairly straight, but the terrain was very uninteresting, it was simply a matter of switching off the mind and letting the legs do the work. But his light shoes were not suited for long distance walking, and he was certain to have blisters to tend to tomorrow. He walked for an hour, and then stopped to rest for ten minutes. The routine of the border patrols was fresh in his mind, and after ten minutes relaxation he was ready to tackle a few more miles. He looked back down the road, hoping to see 'Stirling' approaching, but the road was deserted. Perhaps the truck had simply fallen apart; there wasn't too much holding it together!

He walked for another half an hour. It was dusk now, and would soon be dark. He heard the faint sound of a petrol engine, and turning around saw headlights in the distance. The lights were close together, so it wasn't 'Stirling's' big truck. He took off his shirt and waved it at the oncoming vehicle. As it approached it slowed down and stopped in front of him. He peered through the dusk and into the cab window; grinning at him from behind the wheel was So Lo. Steve gratefully joined So Lo in the cab.

It was a very small commercial van, with little leg room, but he was glad to rest his feet. They set off and Steve asked So Lo how long he had held a driving licence.

So Lo laughed, and said in his best 'Oxford' accent, "I do not have a licence, but I hope to have one in the future!" He then added, "I practice now!"

Steve looked at So Lo and laughed. He was a character to behold, an entrepreneur in the making.

So Lo said he had borrowed the van from his uncle to replenish his stock of cold drinks. He knew a trader in Kowloon who obtained low priced drinks from a source that was possibly not entirely legal! Steve decided not to ask about the source, that was So Lo's business. He looked around into the rear of the van and saw that it was filled to the brim with cans of drinks and bottles of the ever popular 'Coca Cola'!

They talked as the van bumped along the uneven road, the cans and bottles rattling in the rear. Steve enjoyed his conversations with the young Chinaman and had learnt much about the Chinese way of life from him. With a little coaxing, So Lo told him about himself. His father was a gambler, and had been addicted to it for years. He spent most of his time, and money, in the back street gambling dens. So Lo's voice was full of resentment as he explained his family circumstances. His father had little time for So Lo, or So Lo's mother. His uncle, a businessman had taken the young boy 'under his wing', taught him English, and steered him away from his wayward father and gambling dens. The nearest So Lo came to gambling was to play 'Mah Jong' with his uncle and aunt. His uncle taught him much about business during the games and the need to learn English if he was to have an international business career. There was no doubt in Steve's mind that the intelligent young Chinaman would be very successful.

When they reached the camp Steve offered So Lo a dollar for the lift, but So Lo smilingly refused it saying he was happy to help. He was also glad they had talked about his family's problem, and said in his Chinese way that the conversation had taken the problem 'from his head'! Steve smiled, understanding how difficult the talk must have been for him. He shook the Chinaman's hand and they said goodnight.

So Lo drove off to unload his new stock and prepare for tomorrow's trading, as every day was a working day for the Chinese. Steve looked at his watch; there was half an hour before the N.A.A.F.I. closed its doors. He entered the atmosphere of cigarette smoke, beer, pies and noise, bought a pint of 'San Miguel' and two steak and kidney pies and joined the platoon at their table. The thinly cut sandwiches on the yacht were very nice, but far from filling. He sat at the table and consumed one of the pies in seconds. The platoon was enjoying their final beers before retiring to the 'basha' for sleep. They greeted Steve, and when he told them he had just returned from a yacht they politely asked him what he had been drinking in Kowloon, methylated spirits?

The next day was pay and mail parades, both important, and eagerly awaited by all. The mail was the only link with home, and if a parcel arrived it was cause for jubilation. The recipient became a celebrity for the day, and if he had received something not quite to his liking much bartering and auctioning took place.

Steve received his first letter and parcel from Aunt Maude, and he placed them on his bed without opening them, it was a moment to savour, and ponder what was inside. Aunt Maude would have given it much thought, but to hope that the parcel would include a cheese and pickled onion sandwich was beyond the realms of expectancy!

Mac had received a short letter from his favourite barmaid in Dewsbury, covered in perfume from a doubtful source, possibly Woolworths!

Mac was more interested in the contents of Steve's parcel. "Do you know what's in it?" he said to Steve.

"No," replied Steve, smiling at Mac's curiosity, and sniffing at the barmaid's letter that Mac had handed to him for perusal. Nothing was sacred or private in a barrack room, or 'basha'! Mac picked up the parcel and shook it, but there were no clues to the contents, the sender knew what he, or she, was about.

Several more of the platoon joined in, having read their own letters. Steve decided to put them, and himself, out of their curiosity and carefully opened the parcel, all eyes centred on the gift from far off U.K.; the crown jewels could not have commanded more attention!

Aunt Maude had wrapped it well, not many packages reached their destinations intact after an eight-thousand-mile journey. The tension mounted around Steve's bed, and there was much speculation about the possible contents. Several of the men were already offering sums of money for part of the contents, even though they had no idea what was inside. Such was the importance of receiving something from the homeland to alleviate the feeling of homesickness. A stick of rock from Blackpool, or a whelk from Southend would have been treasured. Steve would settle for a cheese and pickled onion sandwich!

Steve built the tension for as long as he could, enjoying his moment of fame. Taff arrived and joined in the humorous banter. He had just finished a rugby training session with some of his 'star' men, making ready for the next big match with the 'Boot Boys'.

Steve finished unwrapping the parcel with a theatrical 'flourish' to reveal a large square biscuit tin. He slowly opened the lid and all heads peered into the tin. It was well packed, not a square fraction of space had been wasted. With due ceremony he lifted out a small tin of peaches, which drew a round of applause from the onlookers. Next a tin of 'Macintoshes Assortment' appeared, and offers of money were quickly made. Steve insisted that nothing was for sale, but everybody had their price, no matter what their moral values were, and the platoon had just been paid!

Next out of the tin were two pairs of woollen socks, in Steve's favourite shade of blue. Aunt Maude had done him proud, but there were no financial offers for the socks! Steve carefully put the socks in his locker; they were like Blackpool rock to him, regardless of what the others thought. Three tubes of 'Colgate' toothpaste followed, together with a new toothbrush, a reminder to

Steve about cleaning his teeth every day! Lastly Steve removed a tightly sealed tin, and opened it to reveal four beautiful moist cheese and pickled onion sandwiches, which provoked an immediate financial response. But they definitely were not for sale!

Steve opened the box of 'Macintoshes Assortment' and gave the onlookers one each, but that was as far as his generosity went, charity began at home, and that meant, him! He realised that there were people starving in Africa, but maybe it was time for Africa to look after Africans.

When he was on his own he read Maude's letter. She said that things in Somerset were fairly quiet as usual. The French onion seller still paid regular visits and Maude continued to make her locally famous sandwiches, much to the annoyance of the vicar's wife. Aunt Maude seemed to enjoy goading the vicar's wife for some reason. Perhaps Aunt Maude had secret desires about the fairly good looking man of the cloth? We are all human after all!

Maude said that Steve's first girlfriend Joy had separated from her husband and was living with her doting, suffocating mother. The solicitor had 'put up' with his mother-in-law as best he could, but after months of unrest had filed for divorce pleading 'parental intrusion' in the marriage. The divorce was granted, but the solicitor lost most of his money in the proceedings, which was unusual for a solicitor, and a timely reminder of the strength of the Women's Institute!

Steve wasn't sure about his feelings when he read the news, he would think more about it later, but there was no doubt that a parent's advice could be positive, or negative, regarding their off-spring's relations and could have far reaching effects; how many grandchildren blamed their demise on their forebears?

Aunt Maude finished her letter by saying she hoped he was well and enjoying army life. She promised to send him more sandwiches later, perhaps with lettuce leaves to keep them moister, it was a long way to send a cheese and pickled onion sandwich! Steve carefully put the letter away in his locker, and reminded himself to have the film he took of Kowloon developed, it would go well with his next letter to Maude. He had returned the camera to the 'Lawyer', but the film was still in his locker.

In the evening the rest of the platoon went to the N.A.A.F.I. as usual, but Steve was feeling tired and decided to rest on his bed. Apart from the tiredness he had a lot to think about, and that wasn't possible in the noise and hectic atmosphere of the N.A.A.F.I. The previous day had been a revelation from start to finish and required much thought to absorb it all.

Steve's relationship with Mai Lee had 'blossomed' very quickly; they seemed to have an almost telepathic understanding of each other. They had made love in a hurried frenzy of passion, and Steve was certain that in the future their lovemaking would become more sophisticated, tender, and loving.

Giorgio Busetti was not a likeable man, but he was Mai Lee's father, and Steve made the decision to be as friendly towards him as possible, assuming that he was invited to the yacht again! The yacht and its hidden location was another question; could even a very successful import/export businessman afford such luxury? And what of the armed Chinese crewman? Surely normal security did not warrant such drastic measures? The only complete negative of the day was his inability to win over Chow-Chow, and he resolved to increase his efforts in that direction.

Steve relaxed on his bed, and was about to close his eyes when a platoon private from another 'basha' walked in. Steve recognised him as a National Serviceman called Trevor Smith. He had only passed the time of day with him before, and knew little about him. Smith walked down the centre of the 'basha', and didn't appear to notice Steve on his bed. Steve looked at him more closely, he seemed to be in a trance, and unaware of things around him. Steve left his bed and walked over to Smith. He greeted him and asked if he was all right.

Smith said, "Hi," but that was all. His face was strangely different, as if all emotion had been removed from it.

Steve asked once again if he was all right. Smith smiled, still as if in a trance, and handed him a crumpled letter he was holding tightly in his hand. Steve unfolded the letter and glanced through it. It soon became clear that it was a 'Dear John' letter from home. He suggested to Smith that they sit down at the central table whilst Steve read the unwelcome news more carefully. Smith didn't say a word, but sat on a chair that Steve pulled out from the table. He looked at Smith closely; the man was in a state of shock!

Steve read the letter carefully. Smith's girlfriend of many years had met another man in Smith's military absence, and had recently married. He looked up from the crumpled letter and said to Smith, "I'm sorry!" What else could he say? Sometimes there were no words that might help.

Smith said, "We were to be married as soon as my army service was over." There were tears in his eyes when he spoke.

Steve looked at Smith, his eyes were filled with tears and he obviously required special attention for shock. It was a new situation for Steve, and he knew that he was 'out of his depth'. He suggested they go and have a chat with the regiment's padre. Smith was unsure at first, he was a very private person, and to seek advice from an officer was completely foreign to him, even if the officer was a vicar! After some reassurance from Steve he reluctantly agreed; he smoothed out the letter and placed it in his pocket. Steve felt the first hurdle had been cleared.

The padre, a captain, lived in the officers' married quarters on the perimeter of the camp. Steve knocked on the front door and the padre's wife answered. She was a jovial, helpful woman and invited them into the lounge. The padre put down a book that he was reading, and after greeting them, beckoned them to sit on the sofa. Steve briefly explained the purpose of the visit, and the padre listened understandingly. He had dealt with similar situations before, and he asked his wife to make a pot of tea, the English reaction to all dramatic problems!

They sat and talked, sipping their tea as they did. There was little that anybody could do. Smith's girlfriend had married in his absence and that was legally binding. The only thing that could be applied was a bit of tea and sympathy. The padre drew Steve to one side and said that he wanted to speak to Smith alone, and thanked him for what he had done, and Steve left for a relaxing beer at the N.A.A.F.I.

Most of the platoon was still enjoying beer and pies. The usual convivial conversation complemented the fayre, and ranged from totally unimportant matters to putting the world 'to rights'! After buying a 'San Miguel' Steve explained about Smith and his 'Dear John' letter, and the talk changed to thoughts of home and domestic matters.

National Servicemen went through a difficult period when serving their two years. The service sometimes completely disjointed their lives, and Smith was a typical case. If National Service had not come along, he probably would have married the girl and all would have been well.

Mac concluded the discussion by saying, in his blunt Yorkshire way, "She couldn't have loved him that much anyway if she wasn't prepared to wait'."

They all agreed, finished their beer, and went off to their beds, each man thinking of his own individual romantic circumstances.

CHAPTER 41

The next day, when normal duties were finished, Steve was called to the padre's residence. After the traditional cup of tea and biscuits provided by his wife, the padre explained that he was concerned, (quite rightly), about Smith's domestic problem and to some extent the man's state of mind. Even with the padre's position and rank of captain there was no possibility of Smith being returned to England, and the padre had to make the best of the situation. He asked Steve to keep an 'eye' on Smith over the next week or two, and provide the padre with regular reports on the state of the National Serviceman's mental health.

Steve didn't consider that he was qualified to carry out the instructions, but reluctantly agreed to keep a watch on Smith. The padre did not convey his wishes as a military order, but it amounted to the same thing. Over more tea they talked about Hong Kong and the difficulties that men faced when serving long terms of duty without any home leave. The professional soldiers, in general, coped with it well, and enjoyed the three-year overseas duty; it was their choice to be in the army. But for National Servicemen it was a very different matter, and Smith was no exception with his added domestic problem. A sense of resentment and bitterness was bound to creep in during their two year stay.

The padre advised Steve how to approach Smith when engaging him in conversation. It was essential not to dwell on the subject of 'Dear Johns' but to move on from the episode. But that was easier said than done!

Before going to see Smith, Steve thought more about the padre's words of advice on how to help Smith without being too intrusive. The padre, being a man of the cloth, had seen many similar situations in his military service. He was correct when he said that individuals reacted in very different ways to the same circumstances.

Steve wondered how he would react given the same situation. In retrospect he was glad that he and Lorraine had agreed to end their relationship before he left England for the Far East. If they had become engaged Steve could have eventually been involved in the same unhappy problem as Private Smith. It was easy to be blasé thinking theoretically, but perhaps it would not be so 'cut and dried' if it actually happened to him. He tried to assess how other men in his platoon might react given the same problem. Mac and Docherty would simply shrug it off, and the problem would be forgotten in a matter of hours. Steve could almost hear Mac saying 'There's plenty more fish in't sea, lad'!

The 'Lawyer' and Charlie Strong on the other would almost certainly react in the same manner that Smith had. They would take it very much to heart and become quite introvert. He wondered how carefully women considered their actions before sending a 'Dear John' letter to their loved one thousands of miles away. Perhaps the female sex was more selfish than he had previously thought, or were they simply impatient? Somebody once said, 'Patience is a virtue, seldom found in men, and never in a woman!'

Having armed himself with the proper physiological armoury, he went in search of Smith to have a friendly chat, as advised by the padre. He went to Smith's 'basha' but the room was empty except for three men playing 'Rummy' at the centre table. They were playing for matchsticks as usual, in lieu of cash, the debts to be paid after the next 'pay parade'. To Steve's question about Smith's whereabouts they said he was probably in the N.A.A.F.I. The card 'school' quickly returned to their game, annoyed at having to break away from their intense concentration and matchsticks, there were more important things in the world than Smith's woman problem! Steve could never understand the interest some people had for card games, and to play for matchsticks seemed to be even more uninteresting. He thanked them anyway, and made his way to the N.A.A.F.I.

The 'watering hole' was busy as always in the evening. Cigarette smoke filled the air, mixing with the aroma of beer and hot pies. There was an atmosphere of good humour in the room, but Smith was sat alone in a far corner. Steve studied him before approaching the table. He was staring into a half empty glass of beer, and there were several empty bottles on the table. Smith was oblivious to the noise and general hilarity around him.

Steve went to the serving counter and bought two beers, one for himself and one for Smith. As an afterthought, he purchased two steak pies; sometimes eating was a comfort, as well as alcohol! He fought his way through a crowded room and arrived at Smith's isolated table. He looked up as Steve placed the beers and pies on the table and sat down, but Smith's face was expressionless, and Steve knew that he had his work 'cut out' to get through to the lovelorn individual.

Steve said hello and Smith returned the greeting, but his voice was flat and subdued. It was a difficult moment, and Steve was unsure how to start the conversation, as Smith was clearly in no mood for talking! He tried to think how the padre might start 'breaking the ice', but no 'divine' inspirational thoughts came to him. In the end he relied on the fact that most people had some interest in sport and used that to start 'breaking the ice'.

Smith was not an overly athletic man, and had declined to take an interest in the recent rugby match. But he had mentioned his general interest in soccer, and Steve decided to use that as a starting point of conversation.

He poured the cold 'San Miguel' into the glasses, and offered one of the pies to Smith who said, "Thanks," but didn't touch the steak pie.

They talked about football in general, with Steve making most of the conversation. They sipped at their beers and gradually Smith began to relax and contributed more to the discussion. He had played some football at school, but preferred indoor sports rather than outdoor physical pursuits. He was a good chess player, and belonged to a club in his home town. As the conversation continued Steve began to understand more about the man, and a picture of his character was beginning to form. Steve knew nothing about chess, but showed an interest in the game, albeit slightly falsely, and Smith started to explain the rules and finer points of the ancient game. The 'ice' was broken, and Smith started to nibble on his steak pie.

Later Steve bought more beer, and as the evening wore on Smith became more jovial and relaxed. Steve encouraged him to talk as much as he could, merely offering the odd sentence here and there to keep the conversation flowing. He did not mention Smith's problem, it was better, the padre had said, to keep his mind off it completely. Steve was quietly pleased with the way the evening had gone, and when the N.A.A.F.I. closed at 10.00pm they walked back to Smith's 'basha', still discussing chess. Steve wished him a good night's sleep, and returned to his own bed.

Most of the men were already in bed, but Steve 'bent' their ears for five minutes telling them about his talk with Smith. Docherty said the situation reminded him of a girl he knew in Liverpool.

"It was one of those love/hate relationships," he said, "I loved her and she hated me!"

In Docherty's mind, there was humour in everything. But Steve detected a slight sadness when he said it. Perhaps it was a case of 'Many a true word spoken in jest'. Every comedian has his tragic side, lurking in the background!

Steve prepared himself for bed and a well-earned sleep. He went to the washroom, cleaned his teeth and rinsed his face. He looked into the mirror, pleased with his evening's work, and smilingly visualised himself in a padre's uniform, complete with three 'pips' on the shoulders! He wondered if he had possibly missed his vocation in life.

The 'basha' was quiet now, interrupted only by the sound of soft snoring emitting from Mac's bed. When Mac was ever questioned about his chronic snoring he blamed it on his many years working down the coal pits, so who could dispute that? Taff, also an ex-miner, suffered slightly from the problem.

Steve made himself comfortable on his bed, using a sheet and one blanket to cover himself. The night air was warm, and a light breeze wafted through the open windows. As his eyelids started to close, his thoughts returned to Smith and his problem. Relationships between men and women could be very complicated, and his mind turned to his new friendship with Mai Lee. His Hong Kong posting of three years was quite a long time, the army's maximum for any one tour of duty. Many things could happen during that time, but one day it would be over, what then?

In many ways his relationship with Mai Lee could be very similar to his friendship with Lorraine! Steve and Lorraine were incompatible because of her profession and upbringing; his life as a soldier would be very different. Mai Lee came from a totally foreign part of the world to Steve and because of that there would be obvious difficulties ahead. It reminded him of Puccini's opera 'Madame Butterfly', and the American officer 'Lieutenant Pinkerton'. Could Steve and Mai Lee one day face the same situation? Would Mai Lee be staring out to sea, waiting for the return of her 'Lieutenant'? He realised that nobody was immune from the complexities of life, and he felt a greater sympathy for Smith. Eventually his eyelids closed, and the last thing he remembered of the day was Mac's snoring.

The following morning arrived, far too quickly for most of the platoon who were sleeping off the previous evening's joviality in the N.A.A.F.I.! Taff was one of the first to awake, having taken to his bed earlier than most. In between border patrols and other duties, he had been busy organising the newly formed rugby league and platoon team training. A regimental team was also in its infancy, designed to play against other units in Hong Kong and possibly further afield. Everybody had thoughts of Singapore; there were many 'sports' to be enjoyed there! Taff was fully employed in all the projects, and was enjoying every minute of it; he had found his 'niche'. Soccer was still the main field sport, but rugby was fast becoming a popular alternative, and promoted friendly rivalry, unlike soccer that seemed to promote overly inflated aggressive emotions. Rugby of course was synonymous with pleasant beer drinking after the game, unlike football where many supporters chose to take alcohol before the game, usually leading to unpleasant circumstances. To Steve's surprise, Taff knew many raucous rugby beer drinking songs and when he had time was busy writing copies. But it was very laborious and there were few volunteers to help! Much as they were growing to like rugby they had better things to do with their free time. They were all getting to know and enjoy Kowloon and Hong Kong, and even Charlie Strong was venturing into the wild unknown, discovering the world and himself at the same time. Song sheets would have to wait!

The next rugby match between the platoon and the 'Boot Boys' was planned for the coming Saturday. The R.S.M. resumed his strict training programme, and he had fully re-trained his Laundry Boy regarding the overly enthusiastic starching of his referee's uniform. He was confident that he would have complete freedom of movement on the day. His knees had ceased to show signs of purple stress, and with a little extra 'fluid' training at the Sergeants' Mess all would be well! He had also written to the English R.F.U. (Rugby Football Union) to update himself on the latest rules of the game, essential when dealing with barefoot 'Boot Boys'! A new whistle and hip flask purchased from the N.A.A.F.I. shop completed his kit. He would be ready for anything come what may.

Some of the 'Boot Boys' team were losing their enthusiasm for rugby training, and several dropped out, much to Taff's disappointment, the Chinese were simply not compatible with the ways of Cardiff Arms Park! They complained to So Lo that the extra exertion was affecting their boot polishing abilities, not to mention their domestic sexual responsibilities! Certain wives were beginning to become irritable!

Under the watchful eye of So Lo, it was agreed to form a 'Consortium' team, which would include members of the 'Boot Boys', 'Laundry Boys', and a 'sprinkling' of the more robust seamstresses. This would add a slightly feminine touch to the proceedings, and was voted for by one and all. The women immediately entered into the spirit of things, and using pieces of old cloth made black and white hooped blouses and shirts for the 'Consortium' team. Under a So Lo negotiated financial agreement, they also made red and white squared shirts for the platoon's team, all good business for the seamstresses.

The day of the match arrived and the long bamboo poles were re-tied to the goal post uprights. It had rained heavily during the night, almost a monsoon downpour. The rugby pitch was soaked, and parts of the field were slippery and muddy. Some of the men were against playing in such conditions, but Taff said it was ideal for rugby, and a bit of mud was good for the complexion!

Taff wasn't happy about his team playing barefoot again, but after much discussion with Steve and the rest of the men he agreed to continue with the 'Barefoot Rule'. There was no doubt the rule would give the 'Consortium' a distinct advantage, their feet were like leather, women included! In comparison, the platoon's skin was comparable to a baby's bottom!

The teams assembled on the pitch. They made a colourful scene in their newly acquired shirts and blouses. The R.S.M. looked equally resplendent in his not too harshly starched uniform. The seamstresses had brought a brightly coloured garland of flowers for the referee and ceremoniously draped it over his head and shoulders. Steve wasn't sure if it was simply a local custom, or whether they were trying to bribe him! Regardless of their motives, the R.S.M. was very impressed with the gesture and wore it for the entire match. Taff was disgusted; it would never happen at Cardiff Arms Park!

The game started with the usual confusion of tossing the coin and Taff trying to organise the teams into a presentable formation on the field. But gradually the game began to flow. The 'Boot Boys' had practised well, and the seamstresses soon adapted to the slippery conditions and handling the oddly shaped ball.

The game attracted many spectators who remembered the previous game, but the soggy conditions did not allow picnics to be taken and there was not the same festive atmosphere as in the previous match. But the inclusion of the seamstresses into the 'Consortium' team did partly make up for the wet conditions, and the male spectators in the crowd were very vociferous in their encouragement of the seamstresses who were, after all, playing their first game of rugby. The men's encouragement spilt over into pure adoration when the women's rugby blouses became wet, and clung invitingly to their well-endowed upper bodies!

The inter-mixing of platoon, 'Boot', 'Laundry Boys' and seamstresses proved a great sporting and social success, and after refreshments of sliced oranges and pints of 'San Miguel' at half time, it was even more enjoyable! It became far more satisfying for the platoon to tackle a seamstress than a 'Boot Boy', particularly when the seamstress tried to hide the ball under the front of her blouse! The women's actions completely confused the referee, and he hurriedly flicked through his rule book trying to find a ruling on the matter, but the English R.F.U. had not catered for such a complicated feminine situation, that was all in the future for the male dominated game! The Chinese women had unknowingly entered a man's domain, and they were fully intent on making the most of it.

More spectators arrived, the word had spread that women were playing rugby, a new phenomenon in the sporting world, and conjured up all kinds of emotions for male, and female spectators alike. The seamstresses became aware that they were commanding attention and continued to enter into the spirit of the game. It was an 'elixir' to them, and they were all aware that their wet blouses and shorts were drawing attention from the men as the material clung to their bodies.

Four of the seamstresses, 'flush' with their new stardom, made a concentrated charge towards the 'Cherry Boy Lawyer' in an effort to release his suppressed sexuality even though he had released the ball tens of seconds before! But the Lawyer was not about to give up his virginity lightly, and raced off the pitch and into the nearby bushes. He had given enough for one day by consenting to play rugby! As he disappeared into the trees and bushes a cramp seized his stomach, but he smiled grimly and said to himself, "A stitch in time saves nine!"

He stopped to gather his breath. He had outrun the lustful seamstresses, but he had to admit, it was exciting to be pursued by a horde of sexually intent women! The day had produced plenty of material for his notebook. He rounded a large bush, thinking that when the excitement had died down he would return to the rugby match. A ten minute rest in the solitude of the bushes would be welcome, and he could return to the game a fresh man.

He found a pleasant spot, and stretched out on the grass. The ground was damp, but so were his clothes, and the weather was warm. He listened to the noise of the match in the background, somebody had just scored, and perhaps it was the seamstresses in their new found freedom. He relaxed on the grass and stretched his limbs, he felt strong. Rugby wasn't so bad after all! He closed his eyes thinking, *Discretion was the better part of valour, and I've lived to 'write' another day!*

A rustling sound in the bushes behind him disturbed his thoughts, and one of the more buxom seamstresses appeared. She had carried out a 'pincer' movement after the others had returned to the rugby. She was breathing heavily after the chase, and her ample breasts swelled under the wet cotton blouse that clung tightly to her. She looked down at him, as if eyeing a prey, she had just cornered. He was hers, regardless of what he desired!

The 'Lawyer' shifted uneasily on the grass, and instinctively reached for his reassuring pencil and book; he felt naked without them! The seamstress opened her blouse, and her unfettered breasts burst onto the scene. From that moment, the 'Lawyer' was a lost man! She lay down beside him and kissed his stunned lips. The instincts and forces of nature overtook him, and he stroked her wet, heaving breasts. The grass grew warmer under him. Twenty minutes later the 'Lawyer' was no longer a 'Cherry Boy' and the seamstress was complete.

Meanwhile the rugby match continued and was well into the second half. Aided by the very muddy conditions it had turned into a carefree for all! Many of the spectators, men and women alike, felt the need to express themselves in the extreme conditions and their bare feet and clothes were soon covered in mud as they joined in the game. The ball became coincidental as the players grappled with each other, acting more like children than children!

Steve, when he could stop laughing, tried to play a normal game. But halfway through the second half found himself being tackled by Nani. She had quietly found her way onto the pitch, even though she had not been picked to play for the 'Consortium'. She enthusiastically followed Steve around the field, throwing her arms around him at the slightest hint of the ball coming near him. After a few mutually agreeable 'tackles' Steve was fairly certain that more rice cakes would be in the offering the next day.

Even though the playing conditions were decidedly soggy the game was just as enjoyable as the previous encounter. The R.S.M., in his garland of flowers, relaxed the rules and had the odd playful kick of the ball himself after partaking of some refreshment from his trusty hip flask! As the game was drawing to its end one of the 'Boot Boys', having tackled a seamstress in error, kissed her in repentance, and they both disappeared into the bushes, never to be seen again!

Nani continued to throw her arms around Steve, and he made little effort to stop her advances. Nani was having the time of her life, so who was he, a mere man, to deny her that?

The 'Lawyer' and his 'Mistress Seamstress' appeared from the secrecy of the bushes and re-joined the game. Her wet blouse front was held together by only two lower buttons, and her deep cleavage was soon spattered with mud. The 'Lawyer' naturally saw it as his military duty to wipe it off, and he did so using his bare hands, for sensitivity. He was feeling slightly weak-kneed from his exertions on, and off the field of play, but he concluded that rugby matches could be, 'quite good fun'!

As the game drew to its close Taff looked around him at the laughing faces. It had hardly been Cardiff Arms Park, but still wonderfully heart-warming and enjoyable.

The R.S.M., with a final flourish of resignation, tossed his rule book in the air, took a large swig of his hip flask and entered the fray. Tomorrow his 'Laundry Boy' would be fully engaged in scraping mud from the referee's black uniform!

Later, as the sun started to set, the R.S.M. brought the game to an end. Everybody was covered in mud, but filled with a joy that was hard to express.

In the evening, after a shower and cooked meal the platoon retired to the N.A.A.F.I. and discussed the game. Although it was only a friendly match and not to be taken seriously, they wondered why the 'Boot Boys' always won.

The 'Lawyer', who had been listening intently to the discussion whilst writing in his notebook, offered this explanation, "Champions are made from people who hail from harsh backgrounds. They have a burning desire to succeed because of it. Those of us who are born into a soft life have no such desire or ambitions in the stomach. A silver spoon simply requires polishing, from time to time!"

They all agreed, and filled their glasses!

CHAPTER 42

The following morning in the 'basha' washroom Docherty asked the 'Lawyer' why he had green grass stains on his buttocks. The 'Lawyer' blushed slightly but said nothing. Later he made a short entry in his notebook.

It was time for the platoon to carry out another daylight border patrol duty. In recent weeks there had been several minor skirmishes on the border, mostly involving illegal immigrants, desperate to escape from the overly restrictive ways of the Chinese regime.

As a result of the disturbances, border patrols had been increased, much to the disappointment of the platoon which was quite pleasantly occupied playing rugby, enjoying evenings in the N.A.A.F.I. and, not forgetting the night life in Hong Kong, which 'upstaged' border patrols by a long way!

The problems on the border were tending to escalate into something more serious. The Hong Kong Government blamed the Chinese regime for the unrest, and diplomatic relations between Peking and London were becoming stretched. There was a growing speculation that the Chinese Government regretted signing the extensive ninety-nine-year lease on Hong Kong, and were seeking ways to prematurely regain the land of New Territories, and Hong Kong itself. Hong Kong had become extremely prosperous under U.K. rule and was a thorn in the Chinese side.

It was another early start for the platoon, and when they formed up for inspection at 07.00 a 'Bedford' was waiting for them to appear. N.A.A.F.I. hangovers were not totally cured, and Sterlings plus ammunition were signed for as a matter of 'blurred' routine. Steve watched Smith as he took control of his weapon and bullets. He seemed to be in better spirits, and joked with the men around him. Steve congratulated himself on the success of his counselling. It was satisfying to have helped somebody, and he understood the job satisfaction that charity workers felt.

They boarded the truck and the journey to the border was the usual bumpy, uncomfortable ride. Smith sat next to Steve and after discussing the previous evening in the N.A.A.F.I. Smith 'fished' in his back pack and withdrew a small booklet entitled, 'The Rules of Chess'. He suggested that after Steve had studied the rules they might have a game or two in the 'basha' at a quiet time, which unfortunately was very rare. Steve was not totally enthusiastic about chess, but it was one way to forget the bumpy ride, if nothing else!

Smith busied himself by cleaning his Sterling, and the other men slowly recovered from the previous night's drinking. The usual conversational banter started to fill the air, and Docherty updated Mac on the progress with his Chinese girlfriend and 'Coitus Interruptus'. He was quite explicit in his description of recent happenings in his love life, and the rest of the platoon listened intently! Smith continued with his weapon cleaning seemingly not interested in Docherty's bedroom antics, but Steve noticed that his face reddened at Docherty's blunt remarks.

Mac continued to give Docherty his 'fatherly' advice, and the general consensus of opinion was that Docherty appeared to be making good progress in his sexual readjustment. The 'Lawyer', since his sexual 'awakening' at the hands of the buxom seamstress in the bushes, felt he was now partly qualified to talk on the subject of sex, and submitted his own advice to Docherty, which was surprising to the Liverpudlian. But it did explain the grass stains on the 'Lawyer's' buttocks!

The discussion continued, it was a pleasant way to forget the journey and the fact that they were about to perform another twelve-hour duty. Mac was still concerned about the safety of 'joss' sticks in the bedroom. Many a Chinese bedroom had been razed to the ground by irresponsible use of the sticks and unguarded candles in the heat of passion!

The 'Bedford' lurched to a halt, and the driver let down the tail-gate. The men gathered up their backpacks and weapons, glad the ride was over as they needed to stretch their legs, even if it was for twelve hours! The night patrol had already reached the pick-up point, and was eager to get back to camp and their welcome beds.

The night patrol had arrested two male drug smugglers during the night. Steve looked at them as they were being placed aboard the 'Bedford'. They were both young, hardly out of their teens. They would serve a prison sentence in Hong Kong, which was not something to look forward to. But at the end of the sentence it was possible they would be allowed to stay in Hong Kong and not be sent back over the border. For some Chinese it was a way of gaining access to freedom, the drugs and prison sentence were simply a means to an end.

The patrol started its twelve hour trek and 'Geordie', as senior man took the lead and Steve as second-in-command was the last man in line. It was his job to ensure the patrol kept together and acted as a unit. Smith was in front of Steve, and as the patrol progressed they talked about sport in general, and Smith in particular about his love of chess, and its intricacies. Steve likened it to life itself, and wondered if Smith was trying to equate his life using the theory of the game.

The first leg of the patrol was completed without any complication, and most unusual circumstances occurred at night under cover of darkness, but Steve had a sense of foreboding, and was uneasy. After a rest period they continued along the border route, and reached a high point. Steve studied the Chinese side through the binoculars. The civilians were toiling in the paddy fields as usual, up to their knees in water. But there were many more soldiers on duty, and as Steve looked along the border, extra flag poles were being erected and the red flag of China was more prominent, and fluttered defiantly in the stiff breeze. The situation was far from normal, it was clear to see! It was the Chinese way of heightening tension, and they did that very well. 'Geordie' had served in the Korean War, and had many a spine chilling tale to tell of what happened before the 'thirty-eighth' parallel was reached.

The patrol continued and although it was without incident, Steve still had an uneasy feeling in his stomach. He put it down to his fairly wary and pessimistic attitude about life. It had probably started in his early formative years without having the care of a mother and father to guide him. Aunt Maude was a wonderful woman, but hers was not the womb he came from.

Steve's feet ached, and he began to doubt that he had been designed for trekking. Before the final leg of the patrol the platoon took a twenty minute rest. It was mid-afternoon and the hot sun bore down on them relentlessly. The cooling breeze had died down to a whisper, as if deciding it had completed its work for the day. Sweat ran down the men's faces and backs, the backpacks 'digging' into their wet skin. Tree cover was sparse, and Steve wondered why patrols didn't carry parasols against the heat. Perhaps they were not considered to be 'military' enough!

On reflection, he could imagine the Chinese patrols laughing at them from across the border, and he dismissed the idea, perhaps he had a 'touch of sun'!

The men spread out, trying to find shade behind the large rocks that were scattered around the area. Steve found a sizeable piece of granite with a slight overhang that gave some protection from the sun. He drank from one of his water bottles. He had purchased a third bottle from the N.A.A.F.I. shop, and the extra water was welcome. It was slightly tepid now, but quenched his dry throat, and the thought of a cold beer in the N.A.A.F.I. later, sustained him. He felt as if he'd be able to drink a gallon of 'San Miguel'!

The rest of the platoon had spread out all seeking the elusive shade, and Steve was on his own. He took off his backpack and settled himself on the ground with his back against the rock. The granite was solid and uncomfortable, but better than nothing. He placed his Sterling carefully beside him, making sure that the safety catch was 'on'. He drank more warm water, and thoughts of cold 'San Miguel' came to mind again.

He began to relax, and looked forward to resting his aching body on a soft bed at 'Gillman' camp. He glanced at his watch and saw that the platoon had fifteen minutes before starting on the final leg of the patrol. In his mind he pictured Somerset, and watching the cricket match on the village green. Resting his head against the rock reminded him of hours sitting on the lush grass with his back against one of the elm trees that surrounded the village green. It was there that he had first seen 'Joy', his first love. Their eyes had met across a wooden trestle table as she prepared cucumber sandwiches for the players, neatly slicing off the crusts to feed the birds later. She had smilingly presented him with a sandwich, and they shared a sudden recognition of each other. No words had been spoken, simply a mutually inviting glance and smile that said, 'see you again'! A few weeks later they were officially introduced at the village dance, and after joking about cucumber sandwiches had shared their first quick-step, accompanied by Victor Sylvester!

The cricket matches on the green were always light-hearted affairs, one village playing host to another. The result was not important; it was very much a case of 'the game's the thing'! Steve remembered a team's 'twelfth' man taking a pint of beer out to the umpire on a hot afternoon. Whether it was a gesture of sportsmanship or a ploy to 'blur' his decision making capacity was a matter of opinion!

Aunt Maude always enjoyed the village green cricket, even though she was not completely aware of the complex rules of the game. She was happy to enjoy the sunny afternoons and the company of other people, always willing to engage in conversation, whether she knew the person or not. Such was the convivial atmosphere of the place.

He had recently written to Aunt Maude, enclosing the photos he had taken in Kowloon. They had developed well, and he was certain that she would enjoy them. His next set of photos would include a 'snap' of Mai Lee. It was time that Maude was aware that he had a new girl in his life, and Steve was certain that Aunt Maude would not allow racial bigotry to cloud her mind. He looked forward to owning his own camera, and had placed several dollars at the back of his locker shelf for that purpose. The 'Lawyer' was a generous man to lend his expensive camera, but there was a limit to everybody's goodwill. With the thoughts of Somerset and the warmth of the shade relaxing him his eyelids began to close.

Suddenly he was jerked back to being fully awake by the sound of a single gunshot. His mind changed in an instant from being totally relaxed to a state of animal awareness and tension. The harsh sound of the gunshot was probably from a '9mm' Sterling; Steve had grown to recognise the 'staccato' noise from practice on the firing range. The gunshot had sounded deafening in the early evening air. His mind raced; was it problems with smugglers, immigrants, or even the Chinese Army? He quickly slung the backpack over his shoulder and warily made his way in the direction of where the shot came from.

Mac joined him, his own Sterling at the ready. He asked Steve what was going on. Steve shrugged his shoulders but said nothing. They rounded a large boulder, and saw Smith lying on the ground, his weapon two feet from him. Steve went closer, and was horrified to see part of the back of Smith's head was missing! Steve's stomach 'churned' at the sight, and he was violently sick. Smith had clearly pointed the muzzle of his Sterling to the underside of his chin, and pulled the trigger!

Mac took off his own uniform jacket and draped it over Smith's head and shoulders. He turned away and vomited, swearing as he did so to relieve the tension and emotion. The rest of the platoon arrived, and 'Geordie' took a quick look at Smith. Death had been instantaneous and there was nothing anybody could do.

They all sat down, stunned by what had happened. 'Geordie' knew nothing of Smith's previous circumstances, and Steve explained about the 'Dear John' letter and the visit to the padre. Steve couldn't understand Smith's action, when they had spoken earlier he appeared to have the situation under control, but obviously not.

When they had sufficiently recovered, 'Geordie' supervised the making of a makeshift stretcher using Smith's own groundsheet and two sturdy boughs wrenched from a nearby tree. They lifted Smith onto the stretcher, his head still covered by Mac's jacket. Smith had not been a 'weighty' man, but it took four men to carry the stretcher over the rough terrain. Thankfully they were not far from the pick-up point, and a steady trek would see them there in under an hour, and hopefully the 'Bedford' would be waiting.

The last leg of the trek took longer than expected. They had all taken their turn in carrying the makeshift rickety stretcher and their bodies ached from the exertion. They were all exhausted, physically and mentally. The night patrol was waiting for them to arrive. At first they were irritated by the platoon's lateness, but when they saw Smith they were shocked and quiet. They went about their business, and left the platoon to get Smith's body back to camp. Few words were spoken on the journey, shock and dismay had taken over!

When they arrived at 'Gillman' the R.S.M. was immediately informed, and he in turn went to the Commanding Officer's quarters and told him about the tragedy. The C.O., after seeing Smith and talking briefly to the platoon, ordered a 'Court of Inquiry' to take place in his office at 10.00am the next day.

The men had no appetite for eating, and went to the N.A.A.F.I. for a sustaining, calming 'San Miguel'. The sight of Smith's head, partly blown away by a 9mm bullet would live with them forever, so a certain amount of 'sedative' might help! For a while. There was no light-hearted banter in the N.A.A.F.I., or the camp. Everybody by now had heard the news. After a few quiet, thoughtful beers they all left, feeling more sober than when they came in.

Steve did not sleep well, waking every hour of the night, his mind racing. At 10.00 the next morning the 'Court of Inquiry' was convened in the C.O.'s office which was fairly spacious. The Commanding Officer sat behind his oak desk, his face ashen and concerned; he too had not slept well. Steve wondered whether his insomnia was out of sympathy for Smith, or how badly it would look on the C.O.'s record regarding promotion in the future. He was an ambitious man, and had already psychologically polished his colonel's insignia!

The padre and Medical Officer sat at his right hand side, the R.S.M. on his left. The platoon was stood at 'ease' taking up the remaining space. After hearing evidence from everybody the C.O. asked why it was Smith had been allowed to draw live ammunition from the armoury when he was in a suicidal state of mind. The padre in his own defence said that Smith had appeared to be dealing with his own problem satisfactorily, and nobody could have foreseen he would take his own life. Steve endorsed his remarks, and related his own conversations the previous evening with Smith, and again prior to the shooting.

The C.O., trying to build a clear picture of the scene before the fatal shooting, asked Docherty what he had been doing prior to the tragedy. Docherty replied that he had been having thoughts of a highly personal nature regarding a certain attractive bar girl in Hong Kong who had a fetish for 'joss' sticks! The C.O. looked at him strangely and decided not to pursue the matter further. He adjourned the inquiry until a later date, and after being dismissed the platoon returned to their 'bashas', via the N.A.A.F.I.

The padre left the office with the platoon, and took the unusual step of sharing a beer with the men in the 'Other Ranks' drinking sanctum. The padre was shaken to the core by the tragedy, and began to question his belief in the 'Almighty'. He needed fortification before returning to his teapot and biscuits.

Steve's mind, like the other men's, was still spinning and trying to come to terms with the shooting. Why had Smith been so keen to suggest chess games if he had decided to take his own life? Was it all a smoke screen to cover his eventual intentions? Perhaps Smith didn't kill himself. Was it possible that he had been murdered by somebody in the platoon? Smith wasn't the easiest of men to get on with. In the past he had 'fallen foul' of several men in the platoon over minor incidents, and even minor problems can escalate in a person's mind.

Steve jerked himself out of the way he was thinking. He was becoming irrational in his thoughts; the idea of Smith being killed by somebody in the platoon was logically unthinkable. He needed somebody to talk to, a person not involved in the shooting. Aunt Maude would have been the perfect listener, but she was thousands of miles away.

He changed his clothes, contacted 'Stirling Moss', and made his way to the 'Star Cafe', and the comforting, sympathetic arms of Mai Lee! As they drove along the stony road, 'Stirling' tried to explain by sign language, what had happened to make him miss the previous 'rendezvous' in Kowloon. Between laughing, gesticulating, and wildly letting go of the steering wheel, 'Stirling' made loud 'hissing' sounds through his uneven, tobacco stained teeth. Steve assumed the 'hissing' noise was escaping air, and that the truck had suffered a 'flat' tyre.

It was not uncommon on the rough roads, plus the fact the truck's tyres were thread bare and down to the fibre casing. 'Stirling' had no choice but to exchange them for new, 'second hand' replacements. Steve laughed, and signalled his understanding by using the international communication of OK, OK, OK. Stirling laughed, and replied, OK, OK. They drove on, and 'Stirling' put his foot hard down on the accelerator. Steve held on to the dashboard, it was white knuckle time again.

CHAPTER 43

The platoon was 'stood down' from duty for four days until the inquiry into Smith's death was completed. It was a sombre time for all, and minds tended to dwell with the enforced period of inactivity.

A captain from the R.M.P. (Royal Military Police) arrived from England, and carried out further interviews and investigations. The tensions of the border with China were becoming more acute by the day and a major problem for the Foreign Office in London. Any possible suspicious circumstance had to be fully investigated. After a lengthy final meeting in the C.O.'s office the Board of Inquiry came to the decision that Smith had taken his own life whilst the balance of his mind was disturbed. However, in order to relieve his relations in England of any unnecessary stress, it was agreed that the official record should show that Private Smith had died in the line of duty.

When Steve had spoken to Mai Lee about the shooting she was naturally shocked. But she was made of Oriental sterner stuff where drama was not uncommon. She soon recovered, as if she had read of the tragedy in a newspaper, and not experienced it first hand as Steve had the misfortune to do. They talked well into the night, and as they did so Steve felt the ton weight being taken from his shoulders. Later they went to her bed and held each other tightly, but not to make love. They paid homage to the tragic Smith, as if entering into a short period of mourning. There was a time and place for everything, and in a strange way it made Steve and Mai Lee's romantic bond stronger. Mai Lee had not known Smith, but if his death troubled her man, it also troubled her!

Gradually the platoon returned to normal life and routine, and the whole unpleasant matter drifted into the back of their minds, and life went on! Tomorrow was another day.

Over the following weeks and months Steve and Mai Lee formed a growing and beautiful relationship. He looked forward to his every visit to the 'Star Cafe'; it became a shining 'beacon' to him, far from the cares of army discipline and duties on the border. On their free days off from work and duty Mai Lee continued to show him Hong Kong.

She grew to worship him; he was like a god to her, as if from another planet. He was not like the Chinese men she had known, he had different ideals, a totally different way of thinking about the world, and of course there was the added mystery of the strange game called cricket! She longed to know more about him, and it became a fixation in her partly Oriental curious mind. She tended to his every need, and in return learnt of his European ways, such as eating toast and marmalade for breakfast, and even more strangely, tinned baked beans in a rich tomato sauce!

Steve in turn treasured every moment he spent with her, her every word, touch and kiss remained in his memory. Her quiet sophistication and natural elegance overwhelmed him, and he always felt he was in the presence of a goddess. She was a far sight from 'Joy' in Somerset, Lorraine in Hampshire, Moira Theodopolis in Scotland or the 'Blonde Bombshell' in the N.A.A.F.I. at 'Morval' barracks. Perhaps she was all of them put together in one wonderful package? B.B. did, after all, have at least two good points to present to the world!

Mai Lee taught him a great deal about Hong Kong, and Steve felt privileged to gain the knowledge first hand. It was similar to having one's private tutor, and a beautiful one at that. She was equally inquisitive about England, and wanted to know about Buckingham Palace, London Bridge and the Queen of England. Was it true that 'Elisabet', as she pronounced it, held garden parties at the palace and could you actually meet her and share a cup of tea? Such things were not possible in China!

To Mai Lee, England was a magical place, almost a fairy-tale land that one read about in books, but did not really exist. Steve did not make promises lightly, but said that if it was possible he would take her to England one day, to Buckingham Palace, Somerset, and to meet Aunt Maude. He told her about eating traditional cod and chips, usually bought from a High Street shop after an evening's visit to the local cinema. The food, piping hot and sprinkled with plenty of salt and vinegar, was wrapped up in sheets of paper and warmed the hands on a cold evening as they made their way home after a good night out. Mai Lee was enthralled, but couldn't understand when Steve remarked that the food tasted better when wrapped in last Sunday's copy of the 'News of the World' newspaper. She came to the conclusion that it was a deeply religious tradition, and Sunday was a special day in England after all! Apparently the

'News of the World' was a much revered newspaper, and featured exciting stories of local vicars, bishops, and famous actresses!

Mai Lee was also inquisitive, but mystified, by the strange English game of cricket. Steve had spent many a pleasant hour trying to explain the ancient game to her, using tightly packed paper tied with string as a ball and a piece of driftwood they had picked up at Aberdeen coast village as a makeshift cricket bat. She appreciated his explanation about 'googlies', the 'full toss' and the 'leg before' wicket rule, but she could never understand why it was that when the umpire regularly announced 'over' the game continued for several more hours, or even days! Steve regarded it as a teacher/student 'learning curve'; Rome wasn't built in a day!

The intensity of border patrols continued, and the platoon was preparing for its first night patrol. The trauma of losing Smith was still with them, but life and duty had to go on. They had prepared well for the night patrol. Steve knew the terrain from many long day duties, and the platoon had trained as a unit at night in the surrounding area of the camp.

Smith's replacement in the platoon was a professional soldier, named Kieron O'Driscoll, from Innisfree in Ireland. He had served in the regiment for over fifteen years and slotted in as if he had soldiered with the other men for years. He was an amiable man, not overly ambitious regarding promotion, quite content as he was, a private of long standing without a hint of trouble on his record sheet. He preferred to be called 'Paddy', not Kieron. The only person who did call him by his proper name was his mother back in Innisfree, and he suffered that from time to time for her sake! Sometimes a son had to make sacrifices for family unity! Steve liked the man. He was a totally different character to the unfortunate Smith.

It was time to put the platoon's night patrol training into practice. They had learnt much from the other platoons, but now it was time to go it alone. The daylight hours before the patrol in the evening were 'release of duty' time, in order to prepare kit and take some rest before the twelve hour trek.

Steve spent the morning preparing his kit and then went to the cookhouse with the rest of the men for lunch. The previous patrol and the memory of the tragic episode of Smith's death were still on their minds. Some had come to terms with it, but for others it remained a problem in their minds, and the 'Lawyer' for one, had written many pages in his notebook about the matter. As an academic person the tragedy had opened many questions to him, and he equated them by putting his thoughts on paper. They ate a good meal of fried chicken, chop suey and fried onions and then retired to the N.A.A.F.I. for a dessert of 'San Miguel', and one steak pie! In the convivial atmosphere of the N.A.A.F.I. the 'Lawyer' showed Steve his notebook and his profound thoughts on the subject of Smith. His final paragraph read: - 'If the role in life was changed, and the woman was sent off to war, would she have committed suicide under such conditions?'

Steve put the question to the other men at the table. After several pints of 'San Miguel', they came to the conclusion that self-preservation was important, and not to give your life because of others. Steve thought about Mai Lee, would he die because of her, or for her? It left many emotions darting about in his mind, but after another beer and steak pie he went to his bed a satisfied man. An afternoon 'siesta' was enjoyed, and he understood why the Spanish people were so relaxed!

It was late afternoon, and after final preparations for the night patrol the platoon went to the N.A.A.F.I. for sustenance before duty. It was the day before 'pay parade', and like many others, the 'Lawyer' was as he put it, somewhat financially embarrassed! He had been scribbling in his ever present notebook, and seeing that his glass was empty, stood up, and read aloud in his best 'Shakespearean' voice,

"To be benign, and lost in time, is something so mystere!
And if I had a 'San Miguel', I know I'd find it here!"

Steve laughed, picked up the 'Lawyer's' empty glass and bought him a beer. The 'Lawyer' could be quite lyrical in times of financial distress.

Steve, like most of the platoon, rested on his bed prior to the night duty parade at 19.00 hrs; the trek itself would start at 8.00pm. It was to be a long night,

and nobody was looking forward to it. As dusk fell, the men paraded in front of the 'basha'. They felt strange parading at such an abnormal time. Their 'body' clocks were telling them to slow down and prepare for sleep, but instead, they had to carry out a twelve-hour duty, in darkness!

The 'Bedford' delivered them to the border pick-up point, and the day patrol boarded the truck and returned to 'Gillman' camp, leaving the platoon to start their night vigil.

The trek started in semi-darkness, and as they walked the now familiar path, memories of the previous patrol flooded back into their minds. It was now almost nine weeks since the shooting tragedy, but the sight of Smith lying dead on the ground would be fresh in their minds for some time.

'Paddy' O'Driscoll, the new man and not having been involved in the drama was a source of light-hearted conversation, and took their minds off the past. Like most Irishmen, he could talk the 'hind leg off a donkey', and he was a welcome distraction.

After an hour complete darkness took hold of the night, but the sky was clear of cloud, and a half moon provided some light as their eyes grew accustomed to the night. Steve could see the stars quite clearly; it would have been an ideal romantic time to be with Mai Lee, perhaps on the 'Peak' in Hong Kong. He pictured them later, driving along the coast road in the 'Ferrari' to a seafood restaurant in Aberdeen. But tonight was for duty, and he tried to concentrate on that.

After two hours trekking without incident, the platoon stopped for the usual rest break. It was much quieter than Steve imagined it would be. There were no sounds from the birds or insects that helped to make the daylight hours more interesting, and less lonely. It seemed as though the whole world was asleep, except for the platoon. A light breeze rustled the greenery in the few trees that were dotted around the sparse terrain, and Steve could faintly hear the rock lizards as they scampered over the higher rocks, keeping watch on the platoon as it made progress through their territory!

Steve drank from his water bottle. He had only brought two bottles for the night duty; the third was kept in his locker for the next day patrol when the sun would be on his back, and sweat trickling down his face. From their high point on the terrain Steve looked through his binoculars over the border. There were no lights to be seen, no noise, just an eerie stillness. He wondered why night patrols were required, there was nothing happening at all. Steve thought to himself grimly that they could all be asleep in their comfortable beds, after a few beers in the N.A.A.F.I.!

Suddenly the quietness was shattered by a military flare bursting in the night sky above him. The flare hit the surrounding area as if somebody had switched on a massive bright light. Steve dropped the water bottle and grabbed his Sterling, automatically switching the safety catch to 'off'. He heard the sound of voices shouting, some in English, but others in Chinese! He couldn't understand the Chinese, but it sounded like words of military command. It certainly wasn't smugglers or illegal immigrants fleeing the scene.

Steve's mind started to race; had the platoon been caught up in a Chinese patrol immigrant/smuggling incident, or had they accidentally strayed into Chinese territory? He was certain in his own mind they had not, but the night played tricks on people's eyes, and it was easy to lose direction. He looked around him, straining his eyes against the darkness as the flare died down. He could see silhouettes of bodies darting from rock to rock, but whether they were his men or the Chinese was hard to tell. He almost wished another flare would hit the sky, but if it did he also would be exposed to the enemy he was now facing.

The situation was totally confusing. He had to assume that not all of the men in the area were 'friendly', and were possibly 'foe'. In daylight it would have been clearer, but the darkness cast a shadow over everything, whether it be on the terrain or the mind! For a second his mind leapt totally out of control and a panic struck him, but the word 'discipline' reasserted itself in his head, and he jerked himself back to the situation, and regained self-control. The basic training at 'Morval' barracks told him that clear thinking was the order of the day. The endless hours of 'square bashing' had been well devised after all, and not simply a reason to wear out boot leather!

A second flare did burst in the sky, illuminating the scene once more. Pieces of hot phosphorous spiralled to the ground, making an almost grotesquely 'festive' scene. In other circumstances people would be reaching out to dance with each other, and not possibly intent on aggressive hatred, using weapons of destruction. Steve's eyes became accustomed to the glare of the bright light, and he looked around for the platoon. There was no sign of them, he was on his own! Somehow the platoon had been split up, either by chance or perhaps by other people's planned action.

The sound of gunfire opened up, but it was not from a Sterling. The harsh sound was unfamiliar to Steve; it was a foreign weapon to his ears. He cautiously peered over the rock he was sheltering behind. In the light of the dying flare he could see the body of a man on the ground, some thirty yards away.

The gunfire started again, some Sterling fire, but mostly foreign weapons. They had a distinctly, unfriendly noise about them. Steve looked again at the man, prostrate on the ground. He was trying to move, but had been shot in the leg. Steve moved to another rock where he would have a closer view of the man; as the flare faded he recognised the unfortunate figure as Charlie Strong! As Steve looked over the rock at Charlie, a lizard scurried away, as if it was saying, this is your problem, not mine!

Steve took off his backpack and prepared to run and help Charlie, but as he did so he saw a figure in the semi-darkness dash up to Charlie and drag him to the safety of a nearby rock. Steve recognised the bulky form of Mac in the rescue, and realised that many a good man was made in the harsh coal pits of Yorkshire, Charlie was in safe hands. But Mac would need help, and Steve checked the bullet 'clip' on his Sterling. Everything was quiet now, the shooting had stopped as abruptly as it had started and there was an eerie 'stillness' in the air as if the episode had never happened. Could he have dreamed the last twenty minutes? He sniffed the cordite filled air, and realised it had been very real.

His mouth was dry, and he took a minute to quench his thirst and to recover his senses. He peered over the rock and could hear movement, but there was nobody in sight, no silhouettes, nothing. He noticed that the lizard had not returned; Steve thought to himself sardonically, *Fair weather friend!*

He heard a sound behind him, turned around and found himself looking at a Chinese soldier pointing a rifle at his head! The Chinaman signalled to Steve to drop his Sterling, and he reluctantly did so, there was no point in playing the dead hero! The Chinaman held the 'ace' card; all he had to do was pull the trigger.

The soldier nudged Steve with the barrel of his rifle, directing him to move. A second Chinese soldier arrived and picked up Steve's Sterling. They walked for ten minutes, one soldier in front of Steve, one to the rear. They said nothing to each other, which tended to heighten the tension and drama for Steve. He realised that his backpack was still under the rock, but it was too late now to retrieve it. Perhaps an illegal immigrant would find it helpful, fleeing the regime in China!

They came to a truck parked in a clearing. Unfortunately, it was not a friendly 'Bedford'. The small truck probably designed to carry six people, had a canvas awning over it and the red star of China was prominently painted on the side.

Steve was ordered into the rear of the truck, followed by one of his captors. The other soldier climbed into the cab and the truck rumbled along the track. Steve tried to grasp the situation and what was happening to him. One hour earlier all had been well and the trek had been going normally. Now the world had suddenly been turned on its head.

He looked at the Chinaman pointing his rifle in Steve's direction, and realised that he was a prisoner of the Chinese Republican Army. He looked out of the rear of the truck, but there were no other vehicles in sight, no other members of the platoon. Although it was not a cold night a shiver went down his spine, and he felt very isolated.

In desperation he said to the soldier, in English, "Where are the others?"

The Chinaman's face was expressionless, and he looked straight through Steve.

The truck rumbled on through the dark countryside and eventually came to properly made up 'tarmac' roads. Steve stretched his arm and glanced at the luminous dial on his watch, it was almost midnight. The Chinese soldier pointed to the watch and gestured for Steve to take it off. Reluctantly he unstrapped the watch, and the Chinaman grabbed it, grinned to himself, and greedily stuffed it into his jacket pocket. Steve thought to himself, *That's the last time I will see that watch!*

They came to a set of buildings, which in the darkness appeared to be an army camp, or a military prison. The truck drew up at a grey, daunting stone building. Steve was ordered off the truck by the rifle wielding guard, and ushered at gunpoint into the building. The entrance to the building was draped with the Chinese flag, and as the soldier passed under it he saluted with his rifle. Steve looked up and remarked to himself, "It would make a good tablecloth!"

The guard prodded Steve in the back with his rifle, forcing him into a small office. The room was bare except for a table, and a Chinese officer, sat very upright on a high backed wooden chair behind it. He wore a very austere, highly starched and pressed uniform. Steve stood in front of the table, and couldn't help thinking that the R.S.M.'s referee's uniform had carried more starch.

The Chinese officer looked at Steve, his eyes filled with hatred. He shuffled some papers on his desk top. His actions were robotic and prearranged, as if he had practised it many times.

He stared at Steve with cold steely eyes and said, "You are an enemy of the Republic of China, you will be tried before the people's court. Until then you will be held in solitary confinement." The officer said nothing more, and continued to shuffle his papers.

Steve was led away at gunpoint to a cell at the rear of the building. The steel door slammed behind him, the key turned in the lock and he heard the soldier march away, Steve's watch in his pocket.

For the first time in his life he felt totally alone.

CHAPTER 44

The prison cell was almost in complete darkness, except for a shaft of moonlight from a high barred window at the opposite end of the room.

Steve felt around the door frame, in the slender hope that there might be a light switch, but there was nothing. The wall felt damp and cold to the touch. He stood still waiting for his eyes to become adjusted to the darkness. After a while he could make out the opposite wall, and he carefully explored the cell. The floor was made of uneven granite slabs, and the walls of brick. He ran his fingers down the wall, and his hand became wet. The only ventilation was the small barred window at the top of the far wall.

Against one wall, at low level, were three long planks of wood, on sturdy square legs. Presumably that was to be his bed! He shuddered at the thought of trying to sleep on it, what would he give now for his comfortable bed in the 'basha'? On the other wall was a single brass water tap, no sink or drain, just a solitary tap. He opened it cautiously and cold water ran freely from it. He cupped his hands and drank. The water tasted sour, and he closed the tap quickly. The water that had fallen to the cell floor disappeared through the open joints in the slab floor, and he was grateful for that. There was enough moisture to contend with without more water in the cell!

He sat on the plank bed and tried to take stock of the situation. He had only the clothes he was wearing, his backpack was under a rock on the border, and his treasured wrist watch was now adorning a Chinese soldier's scrawny arm. He felt no real malice against the Chinese; he was in love with one of their kin after all. But there were limits; it just wasn't cricket to take another man's watch! He looked around him at his bleak surroundings, and decided that the person that said, 'iron bars do not a prison make', had obviously never been incarcerated in a damp Oriental cell.

He tried to remember what had happened on the border. Why had they been attacked? He was certain the platoon had not strayed from their normal route. What had happened to the rest of the platoon? Had they managed to escape?

And what of Charlie Strong, was he still alive? The questions kept pounding into his head, but there were no answers. He came to the conclusion that the Chinese had 'manufactured' the situation in order to increase border political tension. He relaxed as best he could on the solid planks and slept, simply from pure exhaustion.

The sound of Chinese voices awoke him, and he automatically looked at his wrist for the first time. It was daylight and he glanced around him. For a few seconds he was completely disorientated, then realised where he was, and why! The voices he had heard were probably the guards changing duty, it was silent again now. His body was stiff from lying on the wooden bed. He wryly thought about the wooden seats of the 'Bedford', he would gladly exchange the bed for the seats any day!

He struggled to his feet, went over to the water tap and splashed some of the unpleasant tasting water over his face. He took a few sips to wet his dry mouth, but that was all. It was a taste he would have to get used to for a while, he realised, but for how long? He sat down again on the planks, fully awake now. He began to think about Mai Lee in Hong Kong. She would possibly be thinking that he was deserting her, he had no idea how long it might be before he was with her again, if ever! The thought chilled his spine, and hatred built in his mind for his captors.

The sound of heavy boots approaching the cell distracted him from his thoughts. A small ceramic bowl was being pushed through a small flap at the bottom of the steel door; it was filled with rice and water. Steve reached down and picked it up; there was no spoon, just cold rice. He was hungry, and scooped the rice up with his fingers. The rice was tasteless, but he could have eaten a ton in his desperation. Thoughts of the cookhouse corporal's meat balls flashed through his mind. What price were they now?

He tried to gauge what time it was. It was full daylight now, and a weak sun was sending a shaft of light through the small barred window, so he assumed that it would be about 7.00am. After eating the cold rice, he sat down on the planks of wood he loosely called the 'bed'. He needed to use a toilet. Nature did not change; it was oblivious to a person's plight and surroundings. He hoped that a guard would appear before too long! About half an hour later the cell door was opened, and an armed guard ordered Steve out of the room. The guard was the same man who had taken Steve's watch. As he left the cell he looked at the Chinaman's wrists, but could not see the fairly expensive timepiece, the guard had probably sold it already, possibly to an officer.

Nobody in the regime was overly paid, and few luxuries were available. The watch had been a present for his sixteenth birthday from Aunt Maude, and therefore of great sentimental value to him and at times such as this, personal belongings took on great importance! The Chinaman had made an enemy of Steve. He wore a different uniform to Steve and carried other loyalties, which could be partly understood. But he was also a common thief, and therefore not to be admired. At the moment the guard held all the playing cards in the pack, but if the tide turned, the Chinaman would rue his greedy ways!

The guard ordered him at gunpoint along the corridor, and Steve steeled himself, not knowing where he was being ordered to go. Was it the so called 'trial' and if it was, what was to be the charge? He had merely been carrying out his duties as a soldier!

The guard walked behind him, prodding Steve's back with the barrel of his rifle. They went along the narrow corridor that had cell doors on either side. Steve looked for an office door where a 'trial' might be held, but there were only the steel cell doors, and in a way he was relieved.

They came to the end of the corridor, where a solitary door remained. The guard unlocked it, and motioned Steve to go through. He walked into a large open courtyard. The brightness of the daylight hurt his eyes, and he put his hand up to shade them. A tall tree stood at one end, which provided some shade. The yard itself was surrounded by a ten-foot-high wall, made of rough granite blocks.

Steve breathed a sigh of relief, at least it wasn't the 'trial', and the fresh air and open space was welcome. The guard said nothing, his face robotic and blank. He leant against the trunk of the tree, his rifle slung loosely over his shoulder. Steve assumed this was to be his exercise time, and he took the opportunity of flexing his muscles and generally loosening his stiff body. He didn't know what the future held, but there was no point in being too pessimistic and allowing himself to degenerate. A certain amount of British 'stiff upper lip' was called for!

After half an hour, he was returned to the cell by the guard. The steel door was locked, and the guard's footsteps diminished as he walked down the corridor. Steve was alone again. He looked around the cell and noticed that a large steel bucket had been placed in one corner!

Later he made a closer inspection of his pockets. He had a handkerchief and two Hong Kong dollars. They had left him that at least. The dollars would not be much use to them anyway. He looked at his black beret and noticed that the cap badge had been taken.

He tried to rest as much as possible, but the wooden planks were unforgiving and dug into his body, and he wondered how many other prisoners had occupied the same unfriendly planks and tasted the sour water from the brass tap. Perhaps Chinese political prisoners had been held there, and if so how many had returned to normal life? The thought troubled him and he moved his mind on to other things.

At about 4.00pm he heard the sound of heavy boots in the corridor, and the cell door was unlocked. Once again he was ordered out of the cell and prodded in the back by the guard's rifle then taken to the exercise yard. The prods in the back were beginning to infuriate Steve and self-restraint was difficult. He wondered if the Chinaman's gun was even loaded. But it would be foolish to try and find out!

Steve breathed in the fresh air, and this time the guard returned to the main building and left Steve to exercise alone. He immediately looked for ways to escape, but it was hopeless. The big tree was far from the stone wall, and the walls themselves were too high to be scaled. The guard knew that he had nothing to be concerned about, and was probably drinking tea or coffee, or perhaps something stronger.

Steve was glad to get out of the damp cell for a while, regardless of thoughts about escaping. He was becoming quite claustrophobic in the small cell, and did not look forward to going back and the door being slammed behind him. The turning of the key was like a knife stabbed into his back.

When he was eventually returned to the cell he tried to shut his mind down and not think of his predicament. At 7.00pm another small bowl of food was pushed through the 'cat flap', and Steve inspected its contents. It was cold rice again, but seemed to have small pieces of white meat in it. He decided not to look at it too closely; he was very hungry and would have eaten almost anything.

When darkness fell, he tried to sleep, but it was impossible. He thought about the day that he had just endured. It looked as if it was to be the routine whilst he was in captivity, two very meagre meals a day, two exercise periods, and all the sour water he could drink!

He tried to 'switch' his mind off, but the more he did the greater the thoughts became. His mind centred on the platoon and what had possibly happened to them. In a way, not knowing was worse than being aware of the facts! He thought about Mai Lee. When would he see her again? Puccini, 'Lieutenant Pinkerton' and Madame Butterfly staring out to sea, flooded his mind. He missed her more than he could ever have imagined, but he pushed the thoughts of her into the background. If he didn't, he would go mad.

He eventually slept fitfully, waking every hour, his body aching and stiff. During the night he relieved himself into the steel bucket, but the smell of his own urine only made the atmosphere in the damp cell worse, and he covered his nose with his handkerchief to lessen the smell.

In the morning, another bowl of rice was pushed through the 'cat flap'. He scooped the cold rice out of the bowl with his fingers, feeling almost grateful to his captors. He felt wretched, his uniform was dirty and he had not washed or shaved since parading for the night patrol two days before. He rinsed his face in the tap water, and he rubbed his teeth with his finger.

At mid-morning, the same exercise routine was carried out. The blank faced guard left Steve to his own devices, in the knowledge that escape from the courtyard was impossible. Steve looked at the high granite walls, if only he had a length of rope, or even some bedsheets to tie together, but he had neither. The films he had seen in the past where the hero had made his dramatic escape against all odds were a myth, and strictly for 'Metro Goldwyn Mayer' and cinema shows! The harsh reality of life was very different.

It had been raining during the night, and the soft ground of the courtyard was quite muddy. There were small pools of rainwater, and he scooped some up and drank. It tasted far better than the sour tap water in the cell. He looked at the tree and the branches hanging down laden with green leaf. He wondered what type of tree it was, and whether the leaves were edible. He was still very hungry; the small bowl of rice had not been a sustaining breakfast. Thoughts of sausages, bacon, eggs and baked beans in the cookhouse at 'Gillman' came to mind. He plucked three or four of the green leaves from the tree, broke them up, and chewed them well before swallowing. They tasted quite good, but whether they would poison him was another matter, but somehow it didn't seem to be overly important in the circumstances.

The guard returned and Steve was prodded back to the cell, and left to his own thoughts once more. He felt the stubble on his chin and wondered what the regimental sergeant major at 'Gillman' would say about that! Steve had often contemplated growing a beard before joining the army, and now was his chance to see how a 'full set' would feel and look, providing he could find a mirror somewhere. The sophistications of life were not abundant at the moment! Even a chair would be welcome to rest his back. He vowed in the future never to criticise the austere seats in the N.A.A.F.I., assuming he was to make their acquaintance again.

He needed to keep a record of the days otherwise he would become more confused and disorientated. He decided that he would pick up one of the small pebbles in the courtyard every day, and keep them in his pocket. He had no idea how long he might be held captive, but he had to have a plan for survival.

He rested on the bed as best he could, and at 4.00pm he heard the familiar sound of heavy army boots and the cell door opening for him to take more exercise. However, instead of turning towards the courtyard door the guard prodded him in the opposite direction.

Steve's mind switched to 'overdrive'. Was this to be the 'show trial' that had been threatened, or was it just more mind games? He straightened his shoulders, took a deep breath, and prepared himself for the possible ordeal.

The guard stopped at an office door and looked slyly at Steve as if to say this is 'it', your time has come! Steve looked at the door. It was not the same office he had been ushered into on the night of his capture. The wooden door was adorned with Chinese writing, and had a red star underneath the letters.

The guard, his face once again blank, opened the door and beckoned Steve to enter. Steve reluctantly walked in and the guard shut and locked the door behind him. Steve glanced around him. Compared to his cell the office was spacious, and a sizeable window allowed plenty of light into the room. A large desk was at the far end of the room, and a thin faced, bald headed Chinaman sat, very upright, on an uncomfortable small wooden chair.

Thinking about his own cell, he thought to himself, *The Chinese do not believe in creature comforts.* Perhaps it was Chairman Mao's directive!

The thin faced Chinaman wore a plain grey uniform; there was no insignia on the tunic apart from a small red star embroidered on one of the breast pockets. Steve assumed he was a civilian, possibly from a branch of the Chinese Secret Police.

The Chinaman completely ignored Steve, and read some sheets of typewritten paper on his desk. Steve looked beyond the Chinaman, and at the wall behind the desk. A large framed photo of the 'Chairman' stared menacingly down on the scene. Directly below the photograph, on a small wooden plain table was a little red book.

The Chinaman finished reading his papers and looked up at Steve. He had a singular look of hatred in his eyes. The whole room was designed to be cold and intimidating. Steve stared back at him, refusing to weaken. The Chinaman averted his eyes, and resumed shuffling his papers. Steve knew that he had won the first round. Chairman Mao would not be pleased!

The interrogator finally looked up from his papers and said in an almost robotic way, "What is your name?" Steve told him his full name, and added his army rank and number, the only three pieces of information he was obliged to divulge under the 'Geneva Convention'. The Chinaman wrote them down carefully on a new sheet of paper. He fixed his eyes on Steve's face and said loudly, "Why did you invade Chinese territory?" Steve replied quite calmly that he, and his platoon were not on foreign land, his platoon was following the recognised route on the Hong Kong side of the border.

The interrogator repeated his question in a more forceful, agitated manner. Steve replied with the same words he had used before, keeping his voice as calm as was possible under the circumstances. The Chinaman shifted uneasily in his seat and began to study his papers again.

He said to Steve, in a quieter tone of voice, "Do you realise that you are simply a pawn in the British imperial game of chess?" As soon as he said the word 'chess' Steve thought of Smith, but the Chinaman moved quickly on, saying, "You will be returned to your comfortable cell, I suggest that you reconsider your answers to my questions." He pressed a 'buzzer' on the side of his desk and the armed guard opened the door, signalling Steve to follow him. Steve felt that he had won the 'bout'. 'Smoky' Funnell back at 'Morval' barracks would have been proud of him!

Three days passed without any further visits to the interrogator's office. On the fourth day, when Steve returned to his cell from the morning exercise he found a small red book on his plank bed. He flicked through the book that had been translated into English. He started to read the first page, but then decided to ignore the rest of the book. He was being 'brainwashed'. In retaliation, he used the paper in connection with the steel bucket in the corner of the room!

The days passed by, and Steve's beard grew longer. He became aware that his trousers were becoming slack around his waist, and he tightened his belt. By the eighth day Steve was beginning to feel the mental stress of solitary confinement. Although his beard was quite full, his cheeks were starting to sink into his face, and because of continuously lying on the wooden bed he was finding walking difficult. He began to understand why people signed forced, untrue confessions.

On the tenth day, before any bowl of rice or exercise, the cell door was opened and Steve was ordered out of the room. The guard prodded him along the corridor towards the interrogator's office. But instead of stopping at the wooden door they walked further on down the corridor to more cells with steel doors.

They stopped at one of the cell doors, and the guard unlocked it. He pushed the barrel of his rifle into Steve's ribs, ordering him to go in. Steve looked into the darkness. He had just left one 'hell hole' and was in no mood to enter another. His instinct was to turn and run, but the guard prodded him fiercely in the back.

From inside the dark cell a broad 'Geordie' voice shouted, "Come in, lad and sit down, you're making the place look untidy!"

CHAPTER 45

The pure joy and relief of the next few minutes were indescribable! There was no British 'stiff upper lip' machoism! The comrades hugged each other, and everybody talked at once. But even in the semi-darkness Steve could see by the drawn faces of his friends that they had suffered just as much as he had over the past ten days.

The cell door slammed shut, and the key turned in the lock. But Steve had the feeling it was the guard who was now lonely and isolated not him!

In the darkness of the cell they talked about border patrol and what had happened during the last ten days as captives of the Chinese Republican Army. When the ambush occurred the platoon had scattered, trying to evade capture. But eventually all had been taken prisoner by the Chinese who had far outnumbered them. Four of the men had been taken to an army barracks, the others to a military prison. From their accounts, they had all undergone the same 'softening up' process that Steve had endured. The only physical casualty, apart from Charlie Strong, was Taff who had a severely bruised shoulder, his arm in a makeshift sling. He was more concerned about not being able to play rugby for a while, rather than the fact he was being held prisoner by a foreign power! Mac was his usual happy-go-lucky self; all he missed was a pint of 'brew' in the N.A.A.F.I. and the attentions of his favourite barmaid in Hong Kong.

They began to wonder why they had been brought together again. Had diplomatic relations been restored between London and Peking? Or was it in preparation for the threatened trial, or 'show trial' as Steve thought of it. There was no logical reason for it.

The cell door opened and a guard appeared with a large bucketful of rice. There were no bowls or utensils to eat with, and the bucket did not look overly clean. They had no option but to scoop handfuls of the tepid mixture into their hungry mouths, and drink sour water from the wall tap. The 'Lawyer', devoid of his notebook, made mental notes regarding the 'Geneva Convention' and prisoners' rights!

There was no exercise time, and any stretching of the arms and legs had to be carefully carried out in the cramped cell. The weather was warm and humid, making the overcrowded cell very depressing. The hours dragged by, but at least they were together, and strength and resolve was gained from that. In the evening a second steel bucket was placed into the cell by the armed guard. The first 'breakfast bucket' was still in the cell, and later in the evening a desperate platoon used it for other necessary purposes!

The cell, although bigger than the one Steve had come from, was certainly not designed to take a dozen men. There were no beds, not even the wooden planks that Steve had endured. They spent the night sitting on the granite floor, their backs supported by the cold brick wall. They literally had their backs against the wall, in more ways than one!

Steve wanted to know about Charlie Strong and where he was being held, but nobody was the wiser. 'Geordie' had spoken to a Chinese officer, but because of poor translation and secrecy, the information was very sketchy. Charlie was in a nearby hospital, under the 'care' of the Chinese People's Republic, and that was all the officer had chosen to say.

Mac said bluntly, "Well if he's getting the same 'care' that we are receiving then he is in bloody trouble!"

They all looked at each other, and felt for Charlie.

Steve ironically thought, *What good are Charlie's pills and potions now?*

The matter was out of their hands and they just had to hope for the best. They counted their blessings, there were not many, but they would have to do!

In the morning the 'soil' bucket was removed from the cell, and an hour later more rice was served for breakfast. They drew their own conclusions about the steel bucket!

By mid-morning they were hoping that the guard would appear, and some exercise could be taken in the courtyard, but no footsteps sounded in the corridor, and it was all menacingly quiet. The cramped conditions and lack of communication was beginning to tell on their nerves, and irritation turned to frustration and anger. By Steve's reckoning this was his twelfth day as a prisoner, it was long enough, and desperate plans for escape entered his mind.

The day dragged by, minutes seeming like hours. They tried to keep their spirits up by talking about Hong Kong, and Steve allowed himself to think about Mai Lee. A hair-raising ride in 'Stirling's' ramshackle wagon to Kowloon would be more than welcome at that moment! Docherty, a natural comedian, was a constant source of humour with his ribald 'Liverpudlian' jokes. Steve looked around him, and was grateful for their company. He wondered what state of mind he would be in if he was still on his own.

The evening 'meal bucket' was delivered by two armed guards. Perhaps they knew that the prisoners would be in a more desperate state of mind now, and possibly thinking of escape. The long night was spent trying to sleep, but they passed the time mainly by talking about methods of escape, which became more bizarre as the night went on. In the morning the men were all becoming more anxious and desperate about the situation. Their health would not last much longer; they were all beginning to suffer the effects of malnutrition, lack of exercise, and confinement.

After the 'breakfast bucket' had been delivered and dealt with, the talk of escape resumed. Even if it was not possible, the planning, albeit a little theatrical, would keep their minds alert. At about midday the cell door was unlocked and two guards ordered the platoon into the corridor. Once again Steve's mind began to race. Was a trial about to begin, or had diplomatic talks been successful? But the courtyard door was opened and the men tasted fresh air for the first time in three long days and nights. The two guards were joined by three more fully armed soldiers. Any thoughts of overpowering them would have been foolish. They looked at each other, and settled for the fresh air!

The platoon exercised for at least one hour. The Chinese were being far from consistent, and still playing 'mind' games. The guards finally ordered them back into the corridor, but instead of returning to the cell they walked along several long corridors to a different part of the prison. Steve looked at 'Geordie' with a question on his face, but the Newcastle man just shrugged his shoulders as if to say, 'don't ask me!'

They stopped at a wooden, office type door and were ordered in. The room they entered was certainly not a cell, or an office. It was more like a barrack room sleeping quarters. Steve looked around. The large room was probably designed to accommodate twenty men. A dozen 'camp beds' had been erected and placed around the room. A plain central wooden table, much the same as the one in the 'basha' at 'Gillman' completed the furnishing. There were no chairs, just the lone plain table. At the far end of the room a large window allowed ample light into the sleeping quarters. It looked out onto a spacious courtyard, but the glass and frame was well and truly barred, there was no escape!

Steve noticed an adjoining door at the other end of the room. He cautiously opened it to reveal a washroom and toilet facility. Perhaps the Chinese were not so bad after all!

After fully exploring their surroundings the platoon discussed the situation, and came to the general opinion that diplomatic talks had been successful and their return to Hong Kong was imminent. They relaxed, settled onto the wood and canvas camp beds, and slept for twenty hours!

They were woken by sunlight streaming in through the large window, and gradually took stock of their new surroundings. The Chinese were certainly presenting them with a roller coaster ride of emotions! The door was unlocked and four guards entered, each carrying a tray of food. The men looked at each other; where was the steel bucket of rice? The trays were placed carefully on the table, and one of the guards beckoned them to eat, almost in a friendly manner, which the men found strangely unnerving. They had almost become accustomed to their captors' callous nature and brutality.

The platoon enjoyed their first nutritious meal in two weeks. It was made up of white bread, fresh fruit and mixed nuts. Their stomachs 'reeled' at the sudden relatively rich food, but it was welcome nonetheless. Mac emitted the odd belch as he consumed the food, and the rest of the men hoped he would not suffer his usual bout of flatulence afterwards! Later the guards appeared with tea, together with a jug of milk and bowl of sugar. If the Chinese were feeling guilty about their previous behaviour they were certainly making up for it.

An hour's exercise followed and the men could feel the strength returning to their bodies. Later they took full advantage of the washroom facilities. The plumbing was basic, to say the least, but bars of soap and Chinese army issue towels were provided. The platoon was now fully convinced that the return to Hong Kong would be today.

Steve washed as well as he could in the cold water which was far from pure. It probably came from the same source as the supplies in the cells. The large blocks of yellow soap were welcome, but refused to lather, no matter how enthusiastically it was rubbed. 'Paddy', who had been rubbing his block for several minutes, remarked that properly sawn up it would make good brake blocks for his bicycle back in Ireland!

Steve looked into the wall mirror. They were all carrying well established 'full set' beards now. With their longer than usual hair and sunken cheeks they resembled out of work bank robbers, rather than fully trained British soldiers. But they were in a happier state of mind now, the ordeal was almost over.

As they returned to the main room the outer door was unlocked and two armed guards entered. They were closely followed by an officer, in full uniform. Around his waist was strapped a highly polished leather belt and gun holster. A modern automatic pistol protruded from the open holster strap.

The officer carried several sheets of paper, and without any explanation began to hand each of them a sheet. Steve looked at his piece of paper. It had an official heading, but that was in Chinese and had a prominent red star either side of the writing. The rest of the typewritten script was in English. Steve looked at the other men, all of whom were engrossed, reading their papers. It was the first written 'communique' they had received from the Chinese authorities, and their captors. He read his own sheet, anxious to ensure that he understood every word; it was not a friendly letter from Aunt Maude!

When he had carefully read his official sheet of paper he looked up at the other men. They were staring at each other in disbelief. The papers were 'Confessions of Guilt', and a fabrication from start to finish!

The officer broke his silence and said curtly, "You have invaded Chinese territory, which is an act of war. You have abused the terms of the lease on Hong Kong, and therefore political action will be taken to terminate that agreement." Before anybody could speak he withdrew a pen from his jacket pocket and said, "You will sign please." It was the first time Steve had heard a Chinaman say 'please', even if it was in a sly commanding voice.

They all turned to 'Geordie', the senior man and platoon leader. Without any hesitation he walked up to the officer, ripped the sheet of paper into minute pieces, and threw them over the officer as if it was confetti at a wedding!

The officer's face reddened dramatically and he withdrew his pistol. The two guards, flustered by the sudden drama, raised their rifles and released the safety catches. Within two minutes the platoon found themselves back in the damp, dark cell. As they heard the door slam shut and the key turn, they sank down onto the granite floor thinking to themselves, *Another roller coaster ride!* The Chinese officer had lost face in front of his men and the platoon would surely pay for that!

In the evening a steel bucket of rice was placed on the cell floor and the guard who had half smiled earlier, left with a blank look on his face. The men spent most of the night coming to terms with the situation and their recent actions. Should they have signed the confessions, even though the facts were not true? If they had, they would probably be on their way to Hong Kong and safety. But there were other thoughts to take into consideration. If they had signed the papers they would have betrayed their own standards of decency. The situation had brought into focus the question of what was right, and what was wrong. As they sat forlornly on the cold floor they all knew that they had made the right decision.

The long night continued, without any real sleep. Just before dawn the cell door was unlocked and the men were ordered out. They were tired and confused, the Chinese 'mind games' had taken their toll of them. They were taken, half asleep, into the courtyard, hardly aware of what they were doing.

In the courtyard six soldiers stood uneasily in one corner. The officer that the platoon had encountered before strode into the courtyard, brandishing his pistol, which was undoubtedly fully loaded. The platoon was ordered to stand in a line against the granite wall. The six Chinese soldiers lined up at the opposite end of the courtyard and raised their rifles, safety catches clicking to the 'fire' position.

Steve looked at the other men. Was this it? Was this to be the end of their lives? No more Mai Lee, no more enjoyment of life. It was not possible, or was it? Steve looked around him and glanced at the wall, there were bullet scars in the granite blocks!

The officer shouted a command holding his pistol menacingly in the air. The squad of soldiers brought their weapons to their shoulders, and took aim. The officer shouted another sharp command. The rifle triggers 'clicked' but there were no bullets in the magazines! The sound was deafening, but it had simply been another Chinese 'mind game'. Steve felt sick, and one or two of the other men became aware of dampness around the area of their groins!

The officer returned his pistol to its holster, a look of cynical satisfaction on his face. He gave another order, his voice a little calmer now, and the men found themselves being ushered back to the cell. The officer had taken his pound of flesh and was once more in charge.

The men returned to the cell, completely drained of emotion, and as Docherty sank down to the cold floor he flippantly remarked, "I have to tell you all, the rest of the day may not be as good." He was like a shining star in a sea of despair!

An hour later the cell door was opened once again. The men were ordered to their feet. They were drained of strength, and shuffled into the corridor. Before they fully understood what was happening they found themselves at the front entrance of the jail, and climbing aboard a truck, destined for the Hong Kong border. The chilly early morning air brought them back to their senses, they were on the way to freedom, but they would not allow themselves to believe it, just in case.

They looked at each other, and Mac grinned at Steve, as much to say, "It's okay, soon be time for a 'San Miguel' and a steak pie!"

As the truck made its way along the stony roads the men talked about the 'mock' execution. The Chinese officer had played his parting 'shot' for losing face, but he had lost the day to higher moral values. Even so, it was not an experience they would like to repeat, Steve could still hear the deafening sound of the 'click' of the triggers!

When the lorry reached the border, the platoon was ordered off the rear of the vehicle. As each man climbed down onto the ground he was handed a copy of the little red book by a junior Chinese officer. The men quickly stuffed the booklets into their trouser pockets and forgot about them. Chairman Mao was not popular, in any shape or form!

Steve looked around him in the early hazy morning light. Not far away was a welcome sight of a trusty 'Bedford'. A captain from the R.M.P. drove up to the Chinese truck in a small open 'cross-country' 'Champ' vehicle. The 'Champ' was the British Army equivalent to the American 'jeep', and served the forces well with a 'Rolls Royce' power unit under the bonnet.

The two officers saluted each other, and the Chinaman handed the captain a sheet of paper, saluted again, said nothing, and returned to the cab of his vehicle. The truck turned sharply, spitting stones in the air as it sped away back across the border. It quickly disappeared, and the men were glad to see the back of it!

The R.M.P. captain looked at his sheet of paper, counted the men, gave them a cursory 'look over' and told them to report to the sergeant waiting at the 'Bedford'. He wasn't exactly friendly, but it was early in the morning for a captain to be out of bed! He climbed into his 'Champ', revved the 'Rolls Royce' engine and raced off down the track ready for his breakfast in the Officers' Mess!

The men felt lost, and a little 'peeved'. It was hardly the welcoming party they had expected. They wandered over to the 'Bedford' seeking the sergeant they had to report to. As they approached the rear of the truck an aroma of sausages and fried onions wafted out from the covered rear of the 'Bedford'. They sniffed the air; it was unbelievable, had they all suddenly gone mad?

The 'Bedford's' tail-gate was down, and Steve peered into the covered wagon. Two 'field stoves' had been set up between the two rows of bench seats. Each stove was being tended by a cook from 'Gillman' camp.

As the men crowded around the rear of the truck one of the cooks looked up and shouted cheerily, "Welcome home, lads, breakfast is served!"

CHAPTER 46

The 'Bedford' duly arrived at 'Gillman' camp, the platoon feeling far better for platefuls of sizzling sausages and fried onions. Breakfast buckets of lukewarm rice were quickly confined to the backs of their minds, and they felt good to be home.

The first stop on entering camp was the medical centre, and a complete check-up by the Medical Officer and his staff. None of the men, by virtue of their ordeal, was in good shape. The M.O. prescribed double rations and extra nutrition until further notice, an order they heartily agreed with. Mac asked the M.O. if the order included free pints of 'San Miguel' in the N.A.A.F.I. The officer, a strict 'tea total', gave Mac a stern look, and said nothing.

The Yorkshireman grinned and said, "Well it was worth a try!"

After the check-up the M.O. ordered that the platoon be stood down from duty until further checks, both physical and mental, pronounced them fit for normal duty. Some were more resilient than others, but they all carried scars of some description. Showers, a change of clothes and more food in the cookhouse followed. They had enjoyed the sausages in the 'Bedford', but their stomachs were far from full. They had two weeks of starvation to make up for, and they set to the task with a vengeance! Steve could almost have enjoyed the cookhouse corporal's meatballs back in Hampshire!

In the afternoon, the platoon was ordered to report to the C.O.'s office for interview and de-briefing. The ambush incident had caused quite a stir in British/Chinese relations, and the diplomatic services on both sides had been kept fully occupied with negotiations. As with all relationships whether they are domestic or political, a compromise had been reached, and both sides felt they had scored a few points before shaking hands.

The platoon's thoughts turned to Charlie Strong, who was languishing in a Chinese military hospital, but still captive nonetheless. They missed the likeable hypochondriac, and the platoon wouldn't be complete until his return. Steve remembered Charlie's use of the brown 'yeast' pills on the assault course during basic training in Hampshire. He wondered if the Chinese doctors were administering the same pills.

In the evening the festivities in the N.A.A.F.I. were completely happy and unfettered. The 'San Miguel' flowed freely, and steak and kidney pies filled the parts that the beer could not. As the evening went by the platoon enjoyed themselves again. They were almost celebrities now, and many a free 'San Miguel' was gladly accepted in return for stories of their capture and confinement. Recollections of their ordeal became more liberal as the evening went by. But it was all in the name of sociability, and 'San Miguel'!

At normal closing time the party was in full swing. 'Paddy', stripped down to his underpants and army boots, was performing a 'reel' on one of the tables, and Docherty, aided vocally by Mac, was giving his impression of 'Al Jolson' to anybody who would listen! The orderly sergeant, responsible for discipline in the camp, opened the main door, studied the situation for a few seconds, then quietly closed the door and went to his bed. The men deserved their celebration. In the morning he would probably have to answer to the orderly officer for not closing the N.A.A.F.I. on time. But tomorrow, was tomorrow!

The men eventually went to their beds, oblivious to the time. Steve sank into the soft mattress and thought about Mai Lee and the 'Star Cafe'; he had to explain to her what had happened. There was no way that she would be a 'Madame Butterfly', nor he a 'Pinkerton'! In the morning, he would seek out the services of the intrepid 'Stirling Moss'. He spared a thought for the lonely wooden planks in the damp dark cell in China. He felt his bare wrist, still automatically looking at it for the time of day. He would eventually buy another watch, but the one from Aunt Maude was irreplaceable. He murmured an expletive in Chinese he had learnt as a captive with the rest of the platoon. It was aimed directly at the greedy Chinaman! It was highly unlikely he would ever see the soldier again to extract his revenge, but the odd derogatory expletive helped to take the frustration from his shoulders, and he was certain that the Chinaman's ears would be 'ringing'. He had already decided not to tell Maude of his ordeal in China, and if she did ask about the watch's whereabouts one day a 'white lie' would have to be thought up! He turned over in his comfortable 'basha' bed, closed his eyes, and moved on.

The men slept beyond the normal first parade time, and were reluctant to leave their comfortable beds, the memory of sleeping on wooden planks still clear in the mind. They were excused routine parades and duties for now, and decided to make the most of it. Incarceration had its compensations, providing one put one's mind to it, and Docherty for one, put his total concentration into it. With great dedication he managed to stay in his bed for three days, except for brief visits to the N.A.A.F.I. for beer and steak pies!

Steve slept well for twelve hours, and after a shower and shave, enjoyed a leisurely breakfast in the cookhouse. He had an insatiable appetite, and ate two full plates of sausages, eggs, bacon, fried bread and baked beans in tomato sauce, followed by mugs of hot coffee. Thankfully the Chinese had not destroyed his sense of humour, and eating the baked beans reminded him of Mac's 'Grandad Joe' and his longevity, with the aid of tinned baked beans in a rich tomato sauce at 3.00am in his mistress's bed! Steve could well imagine Joe's possibly seventy-year-old mistress, sitting up in bed, and complaining that the beans kept sticking to her pink 'flannelette' nightie. Nobody is perfect!

Rebuilt by the welcome breakfast he changed into his best civilian clothes and went to 'Stirling's' departure point. His legs were still stiff from confinement, and he decided to spend some time in the camp gym to loosen the tight joints. The Chinaman was busy as usual supervising the loading of his truck. When Steve appeared, 'Stirling' greeted him like a long lost friend, and talked animatedly, obviously happy to see him. Steve didn't understand a word, but the Chinaman's feelings were clear to see, and partly restored Steve's confidence in the Oriental world.

The journey to Kowloon was quiet and sedate. 'Stirling Moss' was aware of his passenger's fragile state, and was probably also aware of the happenings in China during the last two weeks. The camp was a relatively small community, and news travelled fast. More hair-raising journeys could be enjoyed when his charge was fully restored to health and capable of gripping on to the dashboard!

After arranging the time for the return journey and handing 'Stirling' a dollar in payment, Steve walked along the busy streets towards the 'Star Cafe'. He hoped to buy some flowers or perhaps a small bottle of perfume as a 'peace' offering for Mai Lee. She would be thinking that he had betrayed her, not knowing the actual facts. He looked carefully for a shop or street trader, but there was nothing. In England it would be a simple matter, but he was living in a different world now. The luxuries of life were not readily available in the harsh mysterious east.

He reached the 'Star Cafe' his hands feeling strangely empty. Steve smoothed down his sharkskin shirt, ran his fingers through his hair, took a deep breath and walked into the cafe. The room was empty except for a mature Chinaman sat at a corner table using an abacus. Steve looked across at him; he was probably a trader counting his takings, meagre as they might be! He ignored Steve completely, fully engrossed in his accounting.

Mai Lee appeared from the back room, pushing the beaded string curtain aside. She stopped abruptly as she saw Steve. He smiled sheepishly, and held up his hands in greeting, but didn't know what to say to break the awkward moment. She looked at him sternly, as if to say, 'and where have you been?' She had heard of 'Lieutenant Pinkertons' before. Steve hurriedly explained his story of the previous two weeks, incredible as it must have sounded.

At first Mai Lee was not convinced, but when she took a closer look at him and saw his sunken cheeks and very obvious ill health she knew he was telling the truth. She glanced over at the old man, busy with his abacus in the corner of the room. He was not aware of the drama, or 'Puccini'. Mai Lee turned towards the beaded curtain, and simply said to Steve, "Come!"

In the privacy of the back room she looked closely at him, and tears filled her eyes. She held him in her arms; her 'Lieutenant' had come home! He tried to explain further, but she gently put her finger on his lips. There was no need for more talk. She took his hand, and they walked together up the stairs to her apartment.

In the lounge, they kissed and caressed each other. Steve could tell by the strained look on her face that she too had suffered an anxious two weeks. But the torture was over now, for both of them.

As was traditional, no matter what the circumstances, Mai Lee left to make tea. Steve looked around the room. Nothing had changed, and Chow-Chow, Mai Lee's cat was asleep at one end of the settee.

Steve had grown used to the fact that the cat was unfriendly towards him, and he simply said, "Hello, cat," as he sat at the other end of the settee.

Chow-Chow opened one eye and gave him a distant look, annoyed to have been remotely disturbed from her sleep. But she looked again at the stranger her mistress had befriended, and realised that he was not well. Chow-Chow's animal instincts told her that this was no time for Siamese selfishness.

The cat licked its front paws, jumped onto Steve's lap, made itself comfortable and went to sleep!

Mai Lee came back into the lounge, holding a tray of cups, saucers and teapot. She laughed when she saw the scene and said, "I told you Chow-Chow would be your friend one day."

Steve smiled and stroked the cat, and in reply he said, "Her coat is very healthy, you feed her well."

Mai Lee put the tray onto the small coffee table in front of the settee and said, "Yes, she is spoilt terribly, but we all have our weaknesses."

Chow-Chow nestled deeper into Steve's lap, as if to say, "Thank heaven for weakness!"

Mai Lee sat next to Steve and poured the tea, and Steve continued stroking the cat gently. Mai Lee put her hand on his, aiding his caressing movement. All three were together now, and it felt good.

Steve looked at his goddess, she was happy now, the anxious lines had left her face and she was relaxed. The tea was left in the cups, she held his hand, and took him to her bed. Chow-Chow watched them as they went hand in hand to the bedroom, but this time they left with her feline blessing! In the quietness of the bedroom Mai Lee gave herself as only a woman can. She restored his body and his soul!

Later, Mai Lee made a fresh pot of tea, and prepared a meal for them. After hearing more about Steve's ordeal as a 'guest' of the Chinese Government she purposely omitted rice from the dish. It would be some time before he could face that again. For the foreseeable future, it would be boiled potatoes or chips!

The next day was a 'working day' for Mai Lee, but they arranged to spend the weekend together. He would apply for a twenty-four-hour pass, which would enable him to sleep overnight, outside the confines of the camp, without being registered as 'Absent Without Leave'.

When it was time for Steve to return to camp he and Mai Lee shared a passionate farewell. The old saying was true; absence did make the heart grow fonder! When Chow-Chow realised that Steve was about to depart, she rubbed her shining coat against the side of his leg, cementing their new relationship. Steve had two notable girlfriends at the cafe now!

'Stirling Moss' was on time at the pick-up point, and the journey to 'Gillman' was fairly sedate, but 'Stirling' noticed that his passenger was slightly revitalised. Through force of habit, from time to time, his accelerator foot enthusiastically sought the floorboard!

When they arrived back at the camp Steve went straight to the N.A.A.F.I., having built up a considerable thirst. Most of the platoon was at their usual table, still basking in their notoriety and accepting free beers for recollections of their stay in China. Docherty had enhanced his story as much that now it bore little resemblance to the facts, and his nose seemed to grow longer every day! 'Paddy' O'Driscoll, the new man, was also prone to theatrical 'embellishment', and used his Irish 'blarney' to the full.

'Paddy', a hugely likeable man, was becoming very popular around the camp, with military and civilians alike. Because of his unique story-telling ability, he quickly endeared himself to civilian workers' children, who had free access to the camp with their parents. In the evenings they would gather round him as if he was the 'Pied Piper'. He told them stories of giants, leprechauns, fairies and witches. The majority of the children would speak no English, but that didn't seem to matter, they clung onto his every word, and worshipped him!

The next day Steve made out his application for the twenty-four-hour pass and handed it to the 'Admin' corporal. He looked forward to his next hours with Mai Lee, and was greatly relieved that everything was still okay between them. They had both been through a torrid time, but now it was the future that mattered.

When Steve had handed his application into the office, he made enquiries about Charlie Strong. He was in a civilian hospital in Hong Kong. A bullet had been removed from his right leg, and he was progressing well. The corporal had been advised by the hospital that Charlie would be returning to the regiment in two or three weeks. When he did return Charlie would be spending many hours in the gymnasium, re-building the muscles in his leg. It would be a new experience for him and the P.T.I.'s were rubbing their hands in eagerness.

The next evening, after a few pints of beer in the N.A.A.F.I., Steve left the noisy scene and took a quiet stroll around the camp. He still had much to think about regarding the previous weeks, a lot of it was still a jumbled mess in his head. The working day had finished and the camp was tranquil, the evening air quite still. It was a privilege to breathe the fresh air again after the confines of the cell.

A small patch of land had been set aside for the parking of rickshaws and tri-shaws, used in the everyday working of the camp and surrounding area. As Steve approached it he could hear the voices of children, they were singing 'Danny Boy'!

He quietly made his way towards them, not wanting to disturb their singing. 'Paddy' was sat on one of the rickshaws conducting his choir! The children, more than a dozen, were sat with crossed legs, on the ground in front of him. Steve sat on a nearby rock and listened, completely enraptured by the sound. The children didn't understand the words they were singing, but their voices were totally innocent, beautiful and rare.

After an encore of 'Danny Boy', 'Paddy' began to tell the children a 'bedtime' story. Several people had gathered now on hearing the choir, and listened to the story just as intently as the children. 'Paddy' had a rare gift for communication and story-telling. The people watching could not fail to be moved by the gently touching scene, and there were one or two 'misty' eyes in the audience, Steve's included!

After the story, the children formed a line and individually said goodnight in Chinese to 'Paddy'. He in turn wished them goodnight, using the Chinese that he had recently learnt from So Lo. 'Paddy' made the decision to teach the children English. Another platoon man had found his vocation in life!

As the sun set behind the distant hills, military personnel and civilians alike, retired to their respective beds, leaving the rickshaws to enjoy their rest also, after a long, hard, working day!

CHAPTER 47

After two weeks of suitable 'square' cookhouse meals, pies and beer in the N.A.A.F.I. to nourish their depleted bodies, the platoon reported to the M.O. for further health checks. The men, in the main, had recovered well and were fit to return to normal duties. But Steve was still suffering from the ordeal. He was the only one, after all, who had spent ten days in solitary confinement. The others had all been able to rely on each other.

The Medical Officer suggested that Steve should take a week's 'sick leave', in a different environment, away from the camp.

As Steve was re-buttoning his shirt after the check, the M.O. smiled and said, "Singapore is nice this time of year, plenty of Dragon Festivals, and the temperature is not unpleasant." Steve thanked him, and said he would enjoy Singapore! As he was leaving the surgery the M.O. added, "I suggest that you take somebody with you, Galway, for company. The flights will be free, by R.A.F. Transport command, but you will have to find your own accommodation." Steve knew instantly who he would take, and she wasn't a million miles away.

Steve walked to the N.A.A.F.I. thinking of his previous visit to Singapore. It would be wonderful to go back, and having Mai Lee with him would put the icing on the cake. Or should he say 'rice cake'! The N.A.A.F.I. was full of men enjoying their mid-morning break from duties. A cup of tea and a 'wad' (very basic sandwich) was always welcome to see you through the rest of the morning, with thoughts of a 'San Miguel' later in the day.

Kieron O'Driscoll was enjoying his snack and talking happily to the platoon at the table. 'Paddy's' ambition to teach the children English had come to the attention of the C.O., and had received his full backing. Anything that furthered military/civilian relations helped the smooth running of the camp, and assisted a quiet, pleasant life for the C.O. Army writing paper and pencils were made available to 'Paddy', who set to his task with enthusiasm in the evenings at the rickshaw park. After a few lessons the eager Chinese children started to speak faltering words of English, with a distinctive Irish accent! 'Paddy' in turn learnt a few words of Chinese from his intelligent students. There is a saying that if you are a teacher, by your students you will be taught!

Steve went to his bed excited about the prospect of returning to Singapore. The M.O. knew more about a man than simply repairing broken bones and strained muscles! He dreamt fleetingly about Mai Lee and the 'Gateway to the East'. The nightmares of the damp cell were still with him, but were slowly being washed away. In the morning after a refreshing shower and a filling cookhouse breakfast, he made himself ready and travelled to Kowloon with 'Stirling Moss', his erratic, but understanding chauffeur.

When Steve reached the 'Star Cafe' Mai Lee was neither on duty nor in the apartment. A 'stand-in' waitress was holding the fort in her absence. The Chinese waitress spoke no English, and simply smiled politely at Steve when he tried to communicate. He cursed himself for not learning more Chinese other than 'Good Morning and Goodnight'!

He decided to take the ferry across to Hong Kong Island, and return to the cafe later. He had agreed the return journey with 'Stirling', and had several hours to occupy. Steve felt deflated; he had looked forward to asking Mai Lee to go on a week's holiday to Singapore. Now all his plans and excitement had to be shelved for a while. Then he had a depressing thought that perhaps she wouldn't want to visit Singapore anyway! Was he being presumptuous, and over confident?

He left the cafe, walked across the busy street towards the 'Star Ferry', and to his great surprise bumped into the 'Lawyer'. At his side was the buxom seamstress who had released his sexual potential in the bushes! She was dutifully carrying the 'Lawyer's' expensive camera, and smiled at Steve as he greeted them both. The 'Lawyer' looked 'sheepishly' at Steve. He was hoping to keep the liaison with the seamstress a secret, but it was a small world.

They reached the relative safety of the pavement, having 'dodged' the rickshaws, trishaws and the odd taxi, whose drivers seemed to have no respect for life or limb! They were both equally surprised to see each other, and they talked politely about the colourful local scene. Steve felt it best not to broach the subject of the seamstress; he would talk to the 'Lawyer' about it later, perhaps over a 'San Miguel' in the N.A.A.F.I. it was not Steve's nature to pry anyway.

They stood on the crowded pavement chatting idly, the 'Lawyer' still looking 'sheepish' about his seamstress, but keeping a protective arm around her shoulder. A burly European man staggered towards them through the crowd. He was clearly worse for wear from alcohol, barging people out of his way as he came towards them. He extended an arm, trying to force his way past the surprised seamstress who was still clutching hold of the 'Lawyer's' camera. The 'Lawyer' grabbed the man's arm, twisted his own body into an arc, and threw the burly drunkard expertly over his shoulder and onto the ground. The drunken man staggered to his feet, looked at the resolute serious face of the 'Lawyer' and quickly disappeared into the crowd.

The 'Lawyer' straightened his shoulders, and the seamstress smoothed his sharkskin shirt and tidied his ruffled brown hair. Steve looked on in disbelief. Had he just seen the timid 'Lawyer' throw a man, twice his weight, over his shoulder? The seamstress looked at the 'Lawyer' adoringly. From now on, in the secrecy of the 'Gillman' camp bushes, she would 'sustain' the 'Lawyer' in no uncertain manner, and buttocks would be 'greener' than green! Steve looked at the academic 'Lawyer'; he obviously had hidden talent.

The crowd that had suddenly gathered during the short altercation started to disperse. The scene returned to normality, and the Chinese went about their business as usual.

The 'Lawyer' turned to Steve, and quite nonchalantly said, "By the way, did I tell you I also studied 'Judo' at university, to 'Black Belt' standard?"

Steve nodded blankly. He had not yet recovered from the 'Lawyer's' unexpected, out of character actions.

Steve explained that he was taking the ferry across to Hong Kong, and that he hoped to see the 'Lawyer' in the evening for the traditional 'San Miguel' to end the day. They said their goodbyes and the 'Lawyer' and his seamstress wandered off into the busy street, grateful for a little anonymity and relevant privacy. As they walked away, Steve noticed that the buxom seamstress was 'sneaking' her hand into the 'Lawyer's', her 'hero'! Steve was pleased for them both as he watched them disappear into the crowd, and he hoped they would have the same pleasant relationship that he was nurturing with Mai Lee. The bushes were to be congratulated!

Much the same as Charlie Strong, (who was by all accounts being treated well in the Chinese hospital), the 'Lawyer' was beginning to 'open up' and blossom as a man. It was mainly due to his entering into the army service, mixing with other men, and being placed in a different part of the world. Not to mention the buxom seamstress, and bushes! Steve wondered how other people would see Steve now. Would Aunt Maude see a change in her young charge?

Perhaps the days of having to tell him to pull his socks up and reminding him to clean his teeth were over!

The 'Lawyer' and Steve were both lucky to have met compatible women, the academic, with his seamstress who would continue to open his sexual arteries and Steve's relationship with Mai Lee, which was possibly a deeper longer lasting involvement. Steve smiled to himself as he thought about the romantic situations. The ways of the Far East were certainly mysterious, and not to be taken lightly. Even Docherty had come to understand that there was more to 'joss' sticks than meets the eye!

Steve bought his ferry ticket at the jetty and waited for the boat to arrive. The weather was pleasant, and when talking to the 'Lawyer' he had toyed with the idea of asking to use his camera. But the 'Lawyer' had his own day to enjoy, and no doubt he would be taking photos of his seamstress, and perhaps she of him. He had saved a certain amount of money to buy a camera, but that cash would be used on a holiday in Singapore, so the camera would have to be postponed for a while.

The 'Star Ferry' arrived, and Steve handed his ticket to the sailor on the gangplank who was still sporting his captain's peaked cap with the 'scrambled egg' on the brim. The ferry plied itself across the bay towards Hong Kong, weaving its path around the other boats. He looked around the crowded waters filled with a multitude of assorted craft. Nobody appeared to have 'right of way', and the maritime rules of port and starboard did not seem to apply, but it all worked out smoothly without any serious mishaps. He noticed the old man with the wicker basket of live chickens, remembering him from previous crossings. Transporting poultry from mainland to Hong Kong Island was probably the Chinaman's full-time job. He was well past his 'pensionable' age, but that meant little in the Far East, one worked until one died, and that was that! The old man always occupied the same place on the ferry, as if he had pre-booked it. Steve smiled to himself, and humorously thought, *'Perhaps there is a 'pecking' order that has to be adhered to!* The Chinaman habitually flicked the cage with a red handkerchief, in an effort to ward off the perpetual flies and other insects.

The ferry arrived at the Hong Kong jetty. He watched the old man chatting happily to other passengers as he left with his basket of poultry. He obviously enjoyed his work, and perhaps retirement would not have been a good thing for him anyway. Inactivity did not suit all people.

After a small refreshing beer at a bar near the jetty, Steve walked to the

'Peak' lift and took the short ride to the top. He stood at the same spot he had occupied with Mai Lee on their previous visit. He wondered where she was, and how good it would be to have her next to him now. Absence, indeed, makes the heart grow fonder!

The view from the 'Peak' was as stunning as ever. The workmanlike 'junks' made their majestic way along the narrow waterways, and the sun shone on the green hillsides of the other smaller islands. A party of Japanese tourists came to the viewing point, all happily clicking their expensive cameras, recording the scene to take back to Tokyo or Yokohama and show their relatives over a cup of tea or 'Saki'. The friendly attitude they showed to each other made Steve more aware of his loneliness, and he decided to cut short his visit and return to the 'Star Cafe' in the hope that Mai Lee had returned. As he left and walked past the tourists he was envious of their expensive cameras and opulence. The Japanese were a successful nation, there was no doubt about that, and their technology was second to none. Steve wondered why they had such a talent for technical engineering, was it because of their religion that taught self-control and deep concentration?

He wondered if the 'Lawyer' might be in the 'market' to sell his camera, at a cut price! Steve decided to wait until a week when the 'Lawyer' was suffering from financial 'fatigue' before asking him. It was perhaps a little immoral for him to think that way, but business was business, and Aunt Maude deserved more photos before too long.

He thought about Aunt Maude, and wondered if she was still making her pickles and cheese and onion sandwiches. They had become her trade mark in the village and local area, he couldn't imagine his aunt without thinking about them, and it made him look forward to his next food parcel. He promised himself that he would write again soon. He would tell Maude about Mai Lee in short instalments as the relationship hopefully progressed. But perhaps for now, he would leave out the facts that her father is Italian and owns a luxury yacht, guarded by an armed crew! If he wrote that, Aunt Maude would look at the letter strangely and think he was suffering from a 'touch of eastern sun'! The ordeal in China was best kept a secret from her and remain a personal matter between himself and the C.R.A. Maude was a woman of substance, and had plenty of 'backbone' to deal with unusual circumstances, but his confrontation with China was over, and that was that! The only thing for him to do was to regain his complete state of health. That would take some time, with the aid of Mai Lee, good cookhouse food and plentiful amounts of 'San Miguel'.

The boat was tied up at the jetty taking passengers on board, and Steve quickly bought his ticket and joined them. There was never a shortage of passengers on the ferry, either way. The 'Star Ferry Company' had captured the market and the owner was undoubtedly a very rich person. When it had taken its full quota of people, and a few more, the ferry plodded its way across the bay to Kowloon, and Mai Lee. The diesel engine made a thumping sound below decks as the fuel ignited in the cylinders. Steve listened to the thump, thump, thump of the engine, and his thoughts turned to the engines on the railways in Somerset.

Times were changing on the railways in the U.K. The age of steam was drawing to an end, and the mighty steam locomotive was being replaced by diesel engines and diesel/electric multiple units. The long hauls were soon to be taken over by 'Deltic' powered locomotives, and the famous 'Scot' retired to a museum. It was a far cry for the crews who had spent their working hours thinking about steam, shovelling coal into a firebox, and cooking bacon and eggs on a shovel held into the firebox heat for breakfast!

Steve remembered talking to one of the younger firemen on his last visits to the 'sidings'. The young man, recently married, was aware that change was taking place and had enrolled in evening classes at a college in the nearby town. He learnt about diesel engines and electric motors, and was preparing to put his shovel away, and move on. The more ambitious crews would study and make the transition to modern traction, but others, with not the same leanings or capabilities, would, like the mighty steam locomotive, be assigned to the scrap yard!

The nation's long romance with the majestic steam locomotive would sadly come to an end, and the aroma of superheated steam mixed with lubricating oil would be replaced by choking diesel engine fumes. The march of progress some might say.

The ferry gently 'bumped' into the jetty, disturbing him from his thoughts. He handed his ticket stub to the 'captain' crewman, and with some apprehension, went to the 'Star Cafe'.

CHAPTER 48

When Mai Lee returned to the cafe the other waitress explained about the 'handsome Englishman's' visit. Mai Lee smiled to herself as she noted a hint of jealousy in the other girl's voice. From time to time the Chinese inscrutable veil tended to slip! Mai Lee made a pot of tea for herself and sat at one of the outside tables. She knew that Steve would return, and like many Chinese was extremely patient. She sipped tea from the bone China cup, looked across at the ferry pier, and waited for the arrival of her 'Lieutenant'.

Steve handed in his ticket as he left the boat and made his way to the cafe, dodging the rickshaws and cyclists as he crossed the road. Self-preservation was a constant pastime in the Far East! Mai Lee saw him approach and waved to him in welcome. She looked beautifully serene in a pair of light blue slacks and a crisp white short sleeved blouse. Her hair was neatly brushed as always, and shone in the late afternoon sun. He wanted to hold and kiss her then and there, but he was aware that it would be traditionally incorrect. He had to wait until they were somewhere private. Chinese standards had to be observed at all times, regardless of love and passion! Emotional outbursts were accepted in Somerset, but not in Shanghai!

They went to the apartment and Chow-Chow greeted them with a loud purr as they entered the lounge. Mai Lee made another pot of tea, and they shared a kiss as the kettle boiled.

Mai Lee had been to the yacht to visit her father. She made regular visits to the luxury boat, but it was more from a sense of duty than a pleasing experience, her father's brusque offhand manner would never change, she understood that. He was a businessman from the start of day to finish; he had no time for the lighter side of life.

But as she spoke about her father it was clear by the tone of her voice that she was concerned about Giorgio, and circumstances on the yacht. A few days before her mother had died, Mai Lee promised to 'keep an eye' on her father. But Giorgio was a headstrong man, and his daughter's words would have little effect anyway. Her mother's relationship with Giorgio had not been perfect, but where she was concerned, love knew no boundaries, whatever they were. Giorgio had treated the marriage with Italian respect, but business and making money was his first love. People came second.

While she was sharing lunch with Giorgio at the cocktail lounge in the rear of the yacht a small motor launch had been tied up alongside, and a dozen plywood packing cases had been off-loaded onto the yacht. The crew quickly stowed the cases below deck, and the launch left immediately, without a word being spoken. Mai Lee had asked him what was in the cases, and why there was no paperwork with the cargo. To her eyes it had all been very secretive and clandestine. Giorgio had hurriedly explained that it was cases of tea, and the paperwork was to follow, but he was obviously agitated, and changed the subject before she could ask more questions.

Steve and Mai Lee sat at the small coffee table in the lounge and enjoyed tea and biscuits. Chow-Chow moved along the settee to give them room to sit, but drew the line at actually leaving the comfort of the well upholstered resting place. Steve was learning that cats have a mind of their own, unlike some dogs that he had known in the past. Canines were more liberally minded, providing they were taken for regular walks.

Steve enjoyed the chocolate biscuits that Mai Lee had quickly come to know that he liked, and she kept a constant stock in her kitchen. He had never seen them for sale in Hong Kong, and wondered how she obtained them. Perhaps it was through her father's import/export business?

They both relaxed, and Steve decided to take the plunge and ask Mai Lee to go on a week's holiday to Singapore with him. She was pleasantly surprised by the idea, and went to the kitchen for more chocolate biscuits!

At first she was hesitant about going, it would mean flying for the first time, and she was nervous about that. It would also mean leaving Chow-Chow, who was almost like a dependent child to her. Steve gradually reassured her, explaining that he too was apprehensive when he left Lyneham on the 'Britannia', but there was nothing to be concerned about. Mai Lee soon warmed to the idea, and they talked excitedly about the prospect of spending a week together. Her excitement grew at the thought, and her rapid breathing accentuated the movement of her breasts, held captive in her tight white blouse. It was too much for Steve to bear, and he felt a passion grow within him. He unbuttoned his sharkskin shirt, and said a silent prayer, hoping that 'Stirling Moss' would wait a while!

Chow-Chow watched them walk quickly to the bedroom, discarding clothes as they went, littering the lounge floor. An imaginative person would almost see a feline smile on the cat's face as she made herself comfortable on the warm settee, and went into a contented sleep.

Later, Steve left the apartment, tucking his crumpled shirt into his trousers. He hurried back to the pick-up point with fingers crossed for luck. 'Stirling' was pacing up and down anxiously and looking at his watch as Steve arrived, still tucking his shirt in. When he looked down at his shoes he realised that he had forgotten to put his socks on.

Steve tried to explain why he was late. 'Stirling' looked at his watch again, 'tut tutted' to himself and then stared at Steve's face. He took a grubby white handkerchief from his pocket, rubbed some lipstick from Steve's cheek, and then laughed! He had been a young man himself, and knew the score. They both laughed as they settled themselves in the cab of the truck. They were late, but it did give 'Stirling Moss' the opportunity to exercise his accelerator foot! Steve gritted his teeth and clung onto the dashboard.

They reached 'Gillman' camp, and after paying a little extra to 'Strling' for his friendly consideration, Steve went to the N.A.A.F.I. for a much needed 'San Miguel' and steak pie. He was excited about returning to Singapore, and wanted to tell the others of his plans. But Taff was busy at the table writing fixtures for the forthcoming rugby matches, the 'Lawyer' scribbled in his notebook totally unenthusiastic about Steve's plans, and 'Paddy' was preparing his next English lesson for the children. Steve broodily suggested that the platoon was becoming far too academic and domesticated. The only person who partly shared Steve's excitement was Mac, who listened intently, over several gratuitous pints of 'San Miguel'!

Docherty came into the N.A.A.F.I. and broke the air of 'library quietness' by announcing that it was his birthday. It was time for a N.A.A.F.I. celebration! Books and paper were put away, and they 'pooled' some of their financial resources for beer, but decided that pies would be bought on an individual basis. Priorities had to be adhered to, and 'San Miguel' came first!

Docherty was in a very jocular mood, and soon had the N.A.A.F.I. in 'stitches' with his jokes, most of them for broad-minded adults only! He had an extra cause for celebration. He had conquered the sexual problem with his Chinese girlfriend, using Mac's advice on 'Coitus Interruptus' and all was well in the bedroom. The 'joss' sticks were confined to their box, and only used on rare festive occasions. Mac was congratulated by all for his 'fatherly' advice, and Docherty made the unusual gesture of buying him a beer from his own 'pie pot'. It was a measure of how good things were in the bedroom now!

Later, 'Paddy' O'Driscoll, whose resistance to 'San Miguel' was 'marginal', jumped onto the table to dance an Irish 'jig'. Glasses of beer and bottles were scattered to the floor, and indignant fists began to fly! Call a man's parents unmarried if you wish, but never, ever, spill another man's beer! Anglo/Irish relations were stretched for five minutes, but it was a birthday celebration, and normal relations were soon restored, apart from one or two 'black eyes'.

When they had settled again, 'Paddy' wiped his slightly bleeding nose, took a mouthful of beer and announced loudly in his 'Gaelic' way, "God bless all here!"

Steve looked at him ruefully, and rubbed his own aching jaw!

As the beers followed again and the party progressed, tongues loosened and the 'Lawyer' let it slip that he was 'seeing' the buxom seamstress who had played such an important part in the recent rugby match, especially in the bushes. Docherty who had long finished giving the party his version of Elvis Presley singing 'Blue Suede Shoes', continued in the same American vein and remarked that the seamstress was, 'well stacked'!

Mac replied, slightly offhand and belligerently, "She may be well stacked, but some of her shelves are dangerously overloaded."

The 'Lawyer', in defence of his seamstress replied loudly, "She has good child bearing hips!"

Mac quickly retorted, "With hips like that she could bear a 'Churchill' tank, never mind a child!" Mac was not in his usual 'fatherly' frame of mind, and a visit to his favourite barmaid was long overdue!

Although Mac would not admit it, the ordeal in China had also taken its toll on him, and he would not be the same man the others had known for some time. Everybody had their 'front' that they presented to the world, but the façade could be disturbed from time to time!

Taff, who had recovered from the rendition of 'Blue Suede Shoes', realised that more fisticuffs were in the offing, and decided to change the subject completely. He turned to Mac and asked seriously, "Do you believe in the afterlife?"

Mac, taken slightly aback by the question, took a deep thoughtful swig of his beer and looked closely at Taff. "Taff lad," he said in his fatherly voice, "we live our lives as best we can, and when it's done we hit the fan." Then he added, "Forget Heaven, or coming back to Earth as a zebra."

Steve thought it an overly pessimistic attitude, but then he had never worked down a coal pit, which was perhaps nearer to Hell!

The 'Lawyer', still smarting from the remarks about his seamstress decided to test Mac academically. "So, Mac," he said, as if he had him on a hook, "explain to me your general philosophy on life." The 'Lawyer' sat back in his chair, confident in the knowledge that he had his man.

Mac took another large swig of his 'San Miguel', wiped his lips with the back of his hand, and replied, "Well, it's like my old Grandad Joe always says, 'keep your mouth shut, your bowels open, and you won't go far wrong'!"

The others looked at Mac in disbelief, and took into account his almost non-stop vocal 'advice' in the N.A.A.F.I., and his perpetual flatulence in the 'basha', after his nightly quota of mature beer!

When the deathly silence had ended, he laughed, turned to the 'Lawyer' and said, "Anyway, be careful with that buxom seamstress, she may end up sticking pins into your bare backside!"

The 'slur' on his seamstress was too much for the 'Lawyer' to ignore. He leapt across the table and grabbed Mac by the throat. Mac had pushed him too far, and glasses of beer and bottles flew everywhere. Mac's face reddened as he tried to breath.

Taff and Docherty grabbed their beers and guarded their glasses, regardless of whether Mac was being murdered or not!

Steve grabbed the irate 'Lawyer' from Mac's throat, and Mac slumped forward trying to regain his breath. Steve thought to himself, *If the Yorkshireman had seen the academic deal with the drunkard in Kowloon he would not have taunted the man!*

With the amount of beer that had been consumed, the rest of the men in the N.A.A.F.I. joined in the fracas, regardless of who was right or wrong. Shortly afterwards the camp police were called by the N.A.A.F.I. manager who could see his tables and chairs being destroyed. Order was restored and the N.A.A.F.I. closed for the night. They retired to their respective 'bashas', nursing the cuts and bruises they had acquired at the party. A good time had been enjoyed by one and all, and Docherty had a birthday to remember!

The next day Steve went to the Regimental Administration Office regarding the flight to Singapore. The M.O. had already authorised the flights, and travel warrants were on the 'Admin' corporal's desk ready for collection. The corporal was inquisitive about the platoon's short 'stay' in China, and the two talked for a while before the clerk handed Steve the all-important pieces of paper. As he took the warrants Steve mentioned that he was taking a Chinese girl with him to Singapore who worked as a waitress and owned a red 'Ferrari'.

The corporal looked at him questioningly, and thought to himself, *Either the man's a very lucky bastard, or he is completely looney, perhaps the ordeal in China has shifted something up top.* As Steve left the office the corporal half-jokingly said, "Keep taking the pills!"

The following morning Steve returned to the 'Star Cafe', and he and Mai Lee made plans for the holiday. They would each prepare their own luggage and meet at the airport on the day of departure. Mai Lee was anxious about leaving Chow-Chow for a week, but the second waitress agreed to look after her pet. Chow-Chow had grown accustomed to the waitress, who had befriended the cat on many occasions that Chow-Chow had seen fit to honour the patrons of the cafe with her 'regal' presence! Mai Lee would go to the yacht and tell her father of the trip to Singapore. Theirs was not a close relationship, but she felt it her duty to inform him.

Steve started to prepare his clothes, and instructed his 'Laundry Boy' to wash and iron his shirts and trousers, using a modicum of starch in the wash. He went to the N.A.A.F.I. shop and bought a new bottle of aftershave. A shipment had just arrived from England, and the label on the bottle guaranteed to increase a man's aura and masculinity. When the lady in the shop heard of his proposed holiday she suggested that he should also buy a bar of scented soap that she kept under the counter for special occasions, such as weddings, parties, or perhaps in some cases, funerals!

Like many women, Mai Lee packed and repacked her travel case three times before finally deciding which clothes to take. The population of Singapore was predominantly Chinese, although it was inherently Malayan and traditionally attached to the Malay Peninsula. Traditional Chinese attire would be completely acceptable, but she included some European clothes in her preparation, in keeping with her Chinese/Italian character. Singapore was the furthest she had travelled, and had mixed feelings about it. As a young girl she had visited the island of Macao, but that was only to accompany her father on one of the many business trips he regularly made to the Portuguese owned island. Mai Lee remembered remarking to her mother that his business associates looked sinister and not like businessmen at all!

On the day of the flight Steve and Mai Lee met at the airport as planned. She looked enchanting in a pair of light blue slacks, white blouse and unusually, fairly high heeled shoes. Once again Steve refrained from kissing her in public, but gave her a gentle hug in welcome.

They had arrived in good time, and strolled leisurely to the departure gate. On the travel warrants they were both described as 'military personnel', and as such were afforded a certain amount of 'diplomatic immunity', no customs checks or embarrassing questions for them.

The 'Britannia' was awaiting them on the runway apron, and it brought back memories to Steve of his flight from Lyneham. It seemed like a thousand years ago, so much had happened to him since that journey. The flight N.C.O. showed them to their seats, and they made themselves comfortable. It was far from luxurious, but it was free!

The 'Britannia' left on time, and Kai Tak Airport disappeared into the background. The plane gradually gained height over the bay of Hong Kong, the engines powering the massive 'Britannia' reassuringly. As the plane levelled off and started to break through the cloud, Steve asked Mai Lee if she was okay.

She replied, "Yes," but she wouldn't look out of the window, and held tightly to his hand. She was still also concerned about Chow-Chow, but Steve reassured her by saying the other waitress would probably spoil the cat more than she did! Mai Lee laughed and relaxed a little. He toyed with the idea of relating his experience of the shifting cargo at the island of Gan, but realising how tightly she was gripping onto his hand, he decided not to go down that road!

Steve settled back into his 'War Department' seat, and with his new found friend Chow-Chow in mind, said to himself, "Next stop Singa'purra!"

CHAPTER 49

The weather in Singapore was perfect, and the 'Britannia' made a graceful, almost majestic landing, as if to announce the arrival of the two V.I.P. lovers on board for their first holiday together.

Steve and Mai Lee alighted from the aircraft with the other dozen or so personnel, all military people, including a colonel who had been travelling in a separate compartment of the 'Britannia'. The colonel, unlike some junior officers, was completely self-assured in a quiet way, and conversed with the other passengers as they all left the plane. He noticed that Mai Lee was a civilian, and when Steve explained the circumstances the colonel shook Mai Lee's hand and wished them both a pleasant holiday.

So different to the aloof captain in his 'Champ' on the Chinese border, Steve thought to himself.

On the tarmac they were handed their luggage by one of the cabin crew, and once again were ushered through the V.I.P. exit of the airport. The first priority was to find inexpensive accommodation, as financially cheap as possible. The more money they had for other pleasures the better. Steve hailed a taxi, a modern looking European car, recently cleaned and polished. After many years of colonial rule most of the taxi drivers spoke some English, and could recognise a member of the British armed forces instantly, whether they were in uniform or not.

On his first visit to Singapore, Steve remembered being told about the 'Union Jack Club', which was situated in the centre of town. The club was designed to accommodate military personnel when they were on 'leave' in Singapore. Steve decided to try his luck there, and directed the taxi to the club. The Chinaman didn't need direction, he had delivered military personnel there on many occasions, some sober, the majority slightly less coherent!

The manager of the club was a civilian, who hailed originally from Scotland. He was a pleasant mannered man from Edinburgh, who had served twenty years in the British Army. During his last year of service, he had met a

Singaporean Chinese woman, and decided to marry and settle in Singapore. Like many long serving soldiers, he had lost his ties with the U.K. and felt more at home in the Far East. During his army service in Singapore he had formed a friendship with the 'U.J.' club management, and when a vacancy appeared in the management chain it was a natural step to apply. With his quiet, sociable manner and organising ability he fitted the job perfectly. People from Edinburgh tend to speak better English than the English themselves!

Steve explained the circumstances of the holiday to him, and that Mai Lee was a civilian. The 'Union Jack Club' was designed and legislated to cater for military personnel only, and the manager was at first reticent to allow the rules to be broken, but Mai Lee's smile won the day, and swayed his decision.

The club had a separate small annexe, designed for visiting senior managers of the widespread organisation. Nobody was due to visit, and the Scotsman 'bent' the rules to allow Steve and Mai Lee the use of the annexe for the week, and at a very reasonable price. Their luck was in!

They made themselves comfortable in the annexe. For the nominal fee they had been charged, the apartment was perfect. It was a fairly large room, with an adjoining bathroom. The only drawback was two single beds, but they were soon drawn together, and an early night was taken in a honeymoon like atmosphere.

In the morning Steve and Mai Lee shared an intimate warm shower. They smoothed and caressed each other's bodies using the scented soap that Steve had bought 'under the counter' in the N.A.A.F.I. shop. They both had firm, well-shaped bodies, and it was a joy to touch and rekindle some of the moments they had shared the night before in the makeshift double bed. The scented soap had a strangely 'Freudian' effect on him. The aroma of the N.A.A.F.I. soap, whilst enhancing his romantic urges, also reminded him of 'San Miguel', with just a hint of steak pie and 'Cherry Blossom' shoe polish. Sigmund had a lot to answer for!

Steve was beginning to feel stronger now; the incentive to do so was certainly visible in the confines of the shower cubicle!

They spent the first two days discovering the interesting island together, holding hands, and in a carefree manner. Now that Mai Lee was away from her own 'territory' she became more relaxed, and thoughts of fathers, yachts, cafes and Chow-Chow's welfare sank into the background. It was certainly a honeymoon setting, and Steve soon had thoughts of marriage on his mind! However, matrimony was out of the question, for many reasons.

The army, of course, frowned on such 'liaisons' as a matter of foreign policy. Over the years they had seen many tragic partnerships, formed by lonely servicemen and young women seeking a better life in England or other parts of the U.K. The regiment's Commanding Officer would certainly not allow any legal relationship to take place, and if Steve even suggested it to the C.O. he would quickly find himself posted to another unit, hundreds of miles away!

He, and Mai Lee were from totally different worlds, and he could partly understand the army's policy. But the two lovers spoke the same language, so communication would not be a problem, and Mai Lee was partly European. But the British Army knew no flexibility on such delicate matters. Perhaps he was jumping to conclusions anyway, Mai Lee might not want to live in England, after all, she had had reservations about going to Singapore for a short holiday!

Steve's thoughts moved on to Somerset and Aunt Maude. How would she react to seeing Mai Lee on his arm, sporting a wedding ring? It was a fleeting doubt, Aunt Maude was not a bigot or racist in any way, she bought Spanish onions after all! Thinking of England his mind turned to the memory of 'Joy' in Somerset, and Lorraine in Hampshire. Both of the relationships had ended unhappily. Perhaps he would be foolish to try again! Possibly he was destined to be a bachelor for the rest of his life. He dismissed the idea, thinking maybe third time lucky. He decided to put his cares away, and employ an amount of fatalism in the future. 'Whatever will be will be!' 'Qué sera, sera', as the Spanish onion seller might say in his French accent. Or as Aunt Maude always said, 'Don't worry, it'll all come out in the wash!'

The weather in Singapore continued to please. Sandals, shorts and singlets were the order of the day, for both of them. Mai Lee could wear anything and still look ravishing. Steve was not a jealous man, but when male passers-by gave her an admiring glance, his blood tended to boil. He realised it was an emotion he needed to come to terms with.

They walked, talked, and were happy in each other's company. In the night they created a physical and spiritual love that no Hollywood film director could hope to imagine in his wildest dreams. In the morning the scented soap was put to good romantic use in the warm shower, and Steve wished he had bought two tablets from 'under the counter'!

He thought humorously to himself, *The soap must contain a magical N.A.A.F.I. potency.*

It was probably manufactured using a top secret War Office formula, involving the subtle mixing of mature 'San Miguel', steak and kidney pies and

'Cherry Blossom'! Whatever the formula, the scented soap certainly worked wonders in cubicles!

On the third morning they slept late. The travelling from Hong Kong and taking their first sightseeing excursions discovering Singapore had exhausted them. A certain amount of battery recharging was required. A large plateful of tinned baked beans in a rich tomato sauce would not have gone amiss, but Mr. Heinz had not yet put Singapore on his delivery list. Tinned baked beans were not compatible with 'bird's nest' soup!

The club did not provide any chambermaid service, and Steve was glad of that. There was no need to vacate the room early for cleaning purposes, and Mai Lee would keep the apartment spotless using the meagre but practical utensils provided. When bed sheets or bathroom towels needed changing an order was placed at the lounge bar in the morning, and clean sheets and towels collected later in the day. The system worked well, and reduced the running costs of the club.

After a relaxed sleep, and a very late 'continental' breakfast, the young 'tourists' felt eager to continue their 'soirees' around the island. Singapore, especially the seafront, was a lively bustling place. It had been aptly named the 'Gateway to the East'. Merchant ships from all parts of the world anchored off-shore, and 'junks' and smaller boats of all descriptions were kept busy from first light to darkness unloading and loading cargo. The Singapore River proved a useful inland waterway, and was equally as busy. The seamen and river-men, mostly Chinese, toiled ceaselessly, and the ever increasing trade swelled the economy, initiated by Sir Stamford Raffles at the start of the island's colonial period.

Steve thought about his first visit to the island, and Bugis Street. He wished he could return to the unique place, and if he was travelling alone would certainly have done so. But Bugis Street was a man's domain, where basic male emotions were given vent. It was no place for a lady regardless of how broad-minded she was! It was also possible the street stall holders would still remember him. The thought of he and Mai Lee being chased by knife wielding stall holders did not appeal to him. Perhaps it was time for a more sedate holiday, and a visit one day to an 'army' club similar to the N.A.A.F.I. What could possibly go wrong in a military controlled establishment? But that would be another day. They needed to continue sightseeing in order to get a better feel of the interesting island.

Steve and Mai Lee found the tourists' favourite shopping haunt of 'Change

Alley', situated near the seafront. It was a quaint, unusual place with a character all of its own. Wide enough for pedestrians only, with stalls and small shops on either side it was ideal for pleasant browsing. The stalls and shops, mostly Indian owned, sold silks, beautifully embroidered cottons, highly ornamental music boxes and all kinds of other gifts suited to the tourist trade.

Several of the shops sold 'bone china' tea sets, at a very reasonable price, which included transportation to a foreign country. Steve immediately thought of Aunt Maude, she would love to own such a set. After discussing the price with the Indian shop owner a suitable deal was agreed upon. Steve wrote Maude's address on a sheet of paper, and after an assurance that the tea set would be properly packed against breakage he handed over the Singapore dollars. The parcel would be transported by a well-known shipping line, the P&O, (Peninsula and Orient), and would take about six weeks to arrive in Somerset. Steve was doubtful that any fragile commodity could travel so far and still be intact. He could only hope for the best and hope the stevedores were not heavy handed! He calculated that the package would arrive about the time of Aunt Maude's birthday, a pleasant surprise for her.

Having completed the transaction, the two 'tourists' strolled further down the interesting 'Alley'. The tiny street was crowded with shoppers, mostly European. Nobody seemed to be in a hurry to leave, it was a pleasant place to be, and any haggling over prices was carried out in a jovial manner, there was no 'hard sell' here! Mai Lee was enjoying the shopping experience; it was a pleasant change from 'waiting' on customers in the 'Star Cafe'. She picked up a beautiful Indian silk shawl from one of the stalls. The stallholder draped it expertly over her elegant shoulders. She smiled at Steve. He put his hand into his pocket!

After an interesting day of sightseeing and shopping the lovers walked to a nearby open air Chinese restaurant on the seafront. Mai Lee's new silk shawl went well with Steve's sharkskin shirt, and they made a picturesque couple as they enjoyed the balmy evening air. They ate their fill of 'bird's nest' soup, followed by chicken chop suey, with lychees in a thick cream as dessert. The setting in the open air restaurant was perfect, and Steve considered with a smile that even the cookhouse corporal's meat balls at 'Morval' barracks would have tasted like the best caviar. Mai Lee looked at him enquiringly as she saw the smile on his face, but it was difficult to explain about English 'meat balls', so he merely leant forward and kissed her. That was explanation enough for her and she smiled back!

They walked slowly back to the 'Union Jack Club', enjoying the evening air and allowing the meal to digest naturally before a good night's sleep. From time to time as they strolled hand in hand Steve stroked Mai Lee's silk shawl, thinking of the beautiful slender shoulders it covered.

They had shared a good day together, and relaxed on the apartment bed reminiscing on the day's events. Mai Lee had taken her blouse off to gain the cooler air of the evening. Steve kissed her and stroked the shoulders he had longed to touch earlier. He kissed her more firmly, and removed the white 'bra' from her taut breasts. The rest of her body was warm from the heat of the day, but her breasts were cool, almost cold. It was nature's way of controlling the temperature of a mother's milk, awaiting an expectant infant into the bosom of life!

He stroked her breasts; they were 'silkier' than the Indian shawl. He gently bit her nipples and she stroked his brown hair, drawing his face against her. The raw passion that he had built up during the day simply from being with her, suddenly erupted. Their arms and legs entwined in a frenzy of activity, but suddenly the two single beds slid apart on the polished floor and the lovers found themselves firmly on the apartment floor, literally brought back to Earth!

After the initial shock they laughed until their sides ached, and then they made love on the solid floor, under the 'protection' of the coiled bed springs. Later the bed legs were tied together using four of Steve's cotton handkerchiefs to prevent any further romantic tragedies, and normal service was resumed in a sensual vein, on a more suitable plane!

CHAPTER 50

The next day the weather was much warmer and humid. The 'tourists' decided to take a bus ride for a morning's sightseeing, to save their legs, and shoe leather. Steve explained about the buses being second-hand, and from England. It was a far from comfortable ride, but they were both young, and in a strange way the lumps and bumps in the road made the sightseeing more entertaining and enjoyable. Mai Lee was 'sold' on anything English anyway, new or second-hand!

They went to the north of the island, and visited Changi jail, as Steve had promised himself he would. As a soldier he was interested in the history of the jail, especially during the Japanese occupation of the island and the notorious use they made of the prison, and the ill treatment of the many civilians who were left stranded when Singapore fell, unable to return to their home countries. But the jail, and the desolate surrounding area was a depressing place, and they stayed only a short while before moving on. Steve decided to study the Japanese invasion more closely later, but he could sense that Mai Lee was becoming anxious because of the jail and its intimidating presence. The holiday was meant for lighter things, and they left the jail to its haunted memories.

When they returned to the south of the island it was late afternoon, and shadows were casting over the old, Governor's residence near the seafront. The very colonial building had housed many British Governors, the latest being William Goode who served until June 1959, when Lee Kuan Yew, Singapore's first Prime Minister, took over the reins. The bus passed the 'Padang', a large grassed area in front of the residence. People were resting on the grass after the heat of day, but they would return to their toil later; it was almost a Spanish siesta, governed by the climate. The 'Padang' itself had played host to many relaxing games of cricket, mostly between a Governor's eleven, and another aspiring team of young colonialists.

The dusty, bus journey had made their throats dry, and Steve suggested they go to the 'Britannia Club' for a refreshing drink. The 'Britannia Club', or 'Brit Club' as it was generally known as, was situated near the seafront on a corner of the Stamford Road, directly opposite the Raffles Hotel. Steve explained to Mai Lee that he had visited the club once before with Mac and Taff (the Three Musketeers) during the previous twenty-four-hour stopover.

The 'Brit Club' was designed to cater for military personnel in their off duty hours, much the same as the 'Union Jack Club', but it was a far more modern building with a sea-view and a large open plan lounge area, suitable for the more discerning drinkers! The club wasn't exactly strewn with roses and perfume; it was more the aroma of 'Tiger' and 'Anchor' beer. But Mai Lee was fairly broad-minded, and Steve was certain she would enjoy the Western experience. It would be a big change from cocktails on her father's luxury yacht!

A short trishaw ride from the bus station saw them walking up the steps to the main lounge doors. The lounge was well patronised by military personnel from the three armed services, mostly men, although a small number of women were also enjoying the social atmosphere. Mai Lee would not feel out of place in the club, and to Steve's relief she, and he, relaxed.

They found vacant chairs and a table at one of the spacious windows which allowed a good view of Stamford Road. Steve looked across the road to the Raffles Hotel on the opposite corner. Two more different settings could hardly be imagined, the 'Britannia Club' with its rowdy soldiers and sailors and beer swilled floor, the 'Raffles' set in well-kept gardens and palm trees. The hotel was iconic, and frequented by well-heeled people visiting the island. The 'Brit Club' was probably a 'thorn in the side' of the wealthy American owners.

Steve was interested in the colonial-style 'Raffles', and had read some of its history in a magazine at the U.J. Club. Apparently, the last wild tiger was shot dead at the hotel. It seemed hard to believe, but the management claimed that the animal was killed in the now famous 'Long Bar', where, in the early 1900's one of the barmen, who went by the name of Ngiam Jong Boon, invented the renowned cocktail, 'Singapore Sling'. Perhaps the barman was inspired by the sudden presence of the tiger! In order to back up their claim, the management stated that the shooting happened on 13th August 1902.

With a smile on her face Mai Lee asked Steve if he was certain that there were no more tigers on the island. He laughed and assured her by saying, the only thing there now relating to tigers was the beer! Talking about beer reminded Steve how dry his throat was. As it was a special week he felt that a special drink was in order; the 'San Miguel' could wait for his return to Hong Kong. He explained his thoughts to Mai Lee, and asked if she too would like a different drink to celebrate the holiday. She pondered the question for a moment. Mai Lee didn't normally drink alcohol, but she had heard of an English drink called 'Babycham', and because of the importance of the week decided to try one.

Steve went to the bar, which was already beginning to fill with the evening's drinkers. The barman, a middle-aged Chinaman, spoke fairly good English, and had been employed at the club for many years. Steve explained the 'holiday' situation and asked the barman if he could suggest a suitable celebration drink. The barman grinned, showing several gold fillings in his teeth, a sign of middle class success in Singapore. He looked Steve 'up and down', assessing his possible drinking capability. For a second Steve thought he was about to suggest a 'Singapore Sling', but that was probably 'out of order' for one reason or another! The barman suggested that he try a 'Singapore Screwdriver', a cocktail consisting of vodka and orange juice, with sliced fruits, but with two secret ingredients. It sounded as mysterious as the 'Singapore Sling'. Steve took his good advice and bought a 'Screwdriver', plus a 'Babycham' for Mai Lee.

He made his way through the increasing crowd of drinkers, and back to the window seats. As he sat down he glanced across at the Raffles Hotel again, and remarked to Mai Lee that it would have been wonderful to stay there, but the cost was totally prohibitive.

Mai Lee looked at the 'Screwdriver' in surprise. It was a very different drink to her 'Lieutenant's' usual refreshment. She sipped on her 'Babycham' carefully, deep in thought. The cocktail tasted good, but Steve was used to drinking beer not dainty mouthfuls with sliced fruit, and the small glass was quickly emptied. He went to the bar and ordered another 'Screwdriver'. The barman was surprised to see him so soon, but supplied him with another cocktail. As Steve walked back to the window seat he wondered why the drink was called a 'Screwdriver'; he was to discover the reason later!

The general noise in the lounge became louder as the number of clients increased, one trying to be heard above another. A 'Petty Officer' from the Royal Navy started to play an old upright piano situated in a corner of the bar area. He played the popular tunes of the day, and from time to time, inter-mixed with the tunes, gave his interpretations of some popular classics. Steve could detect the strains of 'Swan Lake' and 'Beethoven's 5th Symphony' intermingled with 'As time goes by' and 'Roll out the Barrel'. A steady supply of free beer was placed on top of the 'upright', in order to keep his artistic fingers supple. A person with pianistic talent was always welcome at any social gathering.

After listening to, and joining in with the general sing-a-long selection of perennial favourite songs, Steve went to the bar and ordered another 'Screwdriver' for himself and a second 'Babycham' for Mai Lee. She was more conservative in her drinking, and although interested in the music, spent most of her time staring at the 'Raffles' across the road. She too was fascinated by the colonial hotel, and tigers in the 'Long Bar'!

Steve carefully picked his way through the crowded lounge, and blinked his eyes, trying to focus them. His feet felt as if they were being 'screwed' to the floor, and he said to himself, "The orange juice in the cocktails is stronger than I thought!" When he reached the bar he became aware that he was not completely sober!

There were several Australian sailors at the bar, and Steve found a small gap between them. He hailed his gold toothed 'custodian of the cocktails', placed his order, and prepared his cash with some focal difficulty for payment.

An 'Aussie' sailor was sat next to him on a bar stool, and said in a friendly manner, "G'day!"

Steve returned the compliment with an English 'hello!'

The barman was preparing the drinks and trying to serve other people at the same time and to pass the time Steve entered into conversation with the 'Aussie' sailor. They talked about Singapore in general, and Bugis Street, a place almost every serviceman was conversant with, but before long the talk turned to cricket and the 'Ashes' series that was currently being played in Australia.

After discussing the matches in a friendly way for a while the sailor's attitude changed, and he became sarcastic and unfriendly. He took a mouthful of his beer and said to Steve, "You Poms can't play cricket, do you know that?"

Steve wanted to keep the conversation pleasant, and jokingly said, "Well, Freddie Trueman has skittled a few of your people out!"

The 'Aussie' had a 'chip' on his shoulder, probably from being cooped up on a ship for several months. He took a large swig of his beer and said in an aggressive voice, "Trueman is a Pommy bastard!" and pushed Steve heavily in the chest, sending him reeling backwards against the other drinkers at the bar. They were 'skittled'. Precious beer had been spilt, and fists had to fly!

Steve unwittingly found himself in the middle of the fray and was forced to swing his arms and fists in self-defence. The beer spilt on the floor made a liquid 'ice rink', and several of the drinkers found themselves on the wet, foamy surface. Some were eager to return to the fray others content to stay on the floor, out of harm's way! Steve lashed out at any jaw or body that was within range. His main aim was survival, but gradually he began to enjoy the encounter, and with every punch landed on somebody's jaw he felt as if a giant weight was being lifted from his shoulders. He was off-loading the anger and frustration he had built up whilst being a prisoner of the Chinese Republican Army. Perhaps he wasn't so different to the 'Aussie' sailor after all!

Somebody threw a 'lucky' punch that landed squarely on Steve's right eye, but the cocktail 'sedation' lessened the effect of the blow and he carried on regardless.

The musical Petty Officer closed the piano lid. He was tired of tickling the ivories, and felt the urge to 'tickle' somebody's jaw! Perhaps there was another 'score' to settle! He flexed his knuckles, and entered the fray with the air of a composer about to create an unforgettable concierto! A bottle flew across the bar and completely smashed a bottle of whisky; the barman slammed the counter steel shutters down; drinking was done for the day.

The main lounge doors burst open, and six burly military policemen made a dramatic entrance, swinging their truncheons menacingly. They were never far from the 'Britannia Club'. Their sudden presence was normally enough to stop any brawl, but the drinkers were not to be denied, and the fighting continued. One of the 'Aussies' poured a pint of beer over an M.P.'s head. The policeman's complexion turned into a deep red, and with the red cap perched on his head, resembled a soggy 'Strawberry Sundae'!

But enough was enough, the M.P.'s drew their loaded side-arms, and the revellers stopped in their tracks. Truncheons were one thing, but loaded guns another. A good time had been had by one and all, but it was time to leave. Mai Lee pushed her new Indian shawl into the top of her skirt, left the comparative safety of the window seat and dashed into the melee. She grabbed Steve's arm and dragged him to the exit door. The police made no attempt to stop them. The fewer arrests they had to make the less paperwork there was later.

Steve and Mai Lee almost ran to the 'Union Jack Club'. Adrenalin was flowing through their bodies, and the distance did not matter, and within minutes Steve felt completely sober. In the apartment he took off his beer soaked shirt and trousers. Mai Lee went to the bathroom, soaked a small towel in cold water and bathed Steve's right eye. It was swelling rapidly; in the morning he would have a 'shiner'. After bathing the eye, she applied 'Tiger Balm' ointment, the Chinese 'cure all', to Steve's cheek and eyelid. When the nursing duty was completed she went to the bed, took a pillow and blanket, and placed them on the settee. She looked at him sternly, kissed him very lightly on top of his head, went to the bed and switched the room light off. Steve was in the 'dog house'!

Two hours later she switched the light on and called his name, he was forgiven. He dragged his aching body from the settee, and went to the luxury of the bed. They held each other without saying a word. It was not an overly passionate embrace, but more of a mature understanding of each other's values. Mai Lee was aware of his principles of fair play, whether it be in sport or life in general. He in turn was grateful for her understanding and ability to show compassion.

They felt relaxed in each other's arms, away from the cares of the world. The single beds held together in a display of solidarity. They understood the importance of the two lovers needing to be together, and the handkerchiefs knotted more tightly as Steve began to kiss and caress his precious treasure.

Mai Lee was feeling an extra passion, from the animal excitement at the 'Brit Club' and possibly the effects of the two 'Babychams'. Alcohol can have an additional 'kick' when one is not used to it! She slid her hand into Steve's underpants and stroked him, her slender fingers almost playing a tune on his body. His manhood swelled, an internal force being released from its inner source. She too felt her loins grow warm and soft. They both felt equally sexual, which was unusual in two people; they were both aggressive and animal like. She yanked off his underpants and caressed him, with an urgency within her that would not be denied. Steve was glad he was not wearing his sharkskin shirt; it would have stood little chance of survival under such sexual circumstances. (Moira Theodopolis had little to offer when opposed by a Chinese/Italian)!

Steve's manhood grew under the aggressive physical attack, and an uncontrollable urge overtook his mind and body. Her white panties were flimsy, and his erection so strong that he simply forced himself past them, brushing aside the fragile cotton like a petal being blown from a flower! She urged him on, all inhibitions put to one side in the basic need to have her man take control of her being. The ordeal in China was at last completely forgotten by both of them, and as their love juices came together they were again as one. The two single beds gave a sigh of relief! Their job was done.

Much later, in the cool tranquillity of the small hours, Steve and Mai Lee rested their heads on the single white warm pillow. Their bodies and minds melted together. There was no need for the second cold pillow on the settee!

CHAPTER 51

The next morning they shared another warm shower, using the last of the scented soap. The N.A.A.F.I. was to be congratulated on their achievement, and Steve hoped to buy more of the 'scented soapy sensual stimulant', from under the counter!

Mai Lee applied more 'Tiger Balm' ointment to Steve's upper cheek and eyebrow. He had a notable 'black eye', and looked like a boxer who had been forced to retire in the tenth round of a very gruelling fight! Steve glanced at his knuckles, they too were slightly swollen, but he decided not to mention it in case of unpalatable criticism, from certain quarters!

He went into the bathroom to 'survey' the damage to his face. It looked worse than it felt, and he smiled to himself remembering the night before in the 'Brit Club'. In a strange way he had enjoyed the fight, but in the same breath hoped he had not caused anybody real harm. But Australians are a tough breed, and he was worrying unduly!

Looking at his 'black eye' Steve was reminded of boxing, and 'Smoky' Funnell, the punch-drunk boxer at 'Morval' barracks in Hampshire. He hoped the authorities had stopped 'Smoky' entering the ring for his own good. He was a likeable man, and deserved better.

On the lighter side of boxing, it reminded Steve of a joke he had heard on the radio in Somerset. Two well-known American comedians (Bud Abbott and Lou Costello) were playing the parts of a news reporter and a punch-drunk fighter. The reporter, (Budd Abbott), interviewing the boxer, said, "Champ, you've had two hundred and sixty-five fights, and you've won two hundred and sixty-five! Now how do you account for that?"

The punch-drunk boxer looked perplexed, thought for a while, and then replied, "Well, ya can't win 'em all!'

Steve looked at his 'black eye' once more in the mirror, laughed and thought, how strange the world of fisticuffs was. He decided to use the past tense; enough was enough, no more 'Brit Club Brawls'.

When Steve returned to the lounge Mai Lee looked at his eye and asked why the fight had started. He replied that it was about cricket, and the 'Ashes'. She went to the bathroom to moisten another towel for his eye, thinking to herself, *It must be very important this cricket thing!*

The pungent aroma of the ointment reminded Steve that the 'Tiger Balm' gardens, another tourist attraction, was not too far away from the club and would be well worth a visit. Mai Lee would enjoy the Chinese architecture and the fresh air would be good for both of them after the smoky atmosphere of the 'Britannia Club' the previous day.

After a light 'continental' breakfast, they took a quite leisurely rickshaw ride to the gardens. The rickshaws, Steve noticed, were very light and delicately balanced. He wondered how an obese passenger and a small slim rickshaw man would disturb the equilibrium when engaged in transportation. With the many pot holes in the roads Steve could easily imagine a rickshaw man being suddenly shot into the air, clutching onto the staves of his fragile vehicle for dear life!

Being of modest stature and weight, the two lovers arrived at the gardens safely. The weather was almost perfect, with just the occasional 'fluffy' white cloud in the blue sky. The temperature was also pleasant and conducive to wearing sharkskin shirts and white cotton blouses.

They strolled through the very Oriental gardens, holding hands and stopping now and then to admire the well planned scenery. It was not a 'garden' in the English sense of the word. There was little grass or other greenery, and Steve was aware of the absence of trees, something he had taken for granted in England, that 'green and pleasant land'! The 'gardens' were mostly white stone and alabaster designed to withstand the extreme heat of the summer months with the minimum of maintenance.

The Chinese were a very practical race! The landscape was enchanting in its own Eastern way, dotted with statues of mythical Gods, symbolic animals such as dragons, lions and serpents. Small pagodas were dotted around the gardens, and allowed shelter from the sun and the rainstorm.

As they walked, Mai Lee occasionally glanced at Steve's 'black eye', and thought about the previous day. She regretted placing him in the 'dog house' for two hours, but she felt it her female duty to 'advise' him against fisticuffs! She began to understand the intricacies of the game of cricket, full tosses, leg before wicket and overs, but the 'Ashes' remained a mystery to her, and she would ask him to explain more fully one day.

The 'Tiger Balm' gardens were very ornate, and the designers had made good use of the alabaster in making the statues and ornaments. The atmosphere created had a tranquil effect on the whole area, and sightseers walking around the narrow winding pathways spoke in lowered voices, as if in an effort not to break the spell. The designers had succeeded in transferring the magical soothing formula of 'Tiger Balm' ointment to the gardens! Decorative red and white Chinese lanterns were abundant, and tiny chimes and bells that hung from them created a soft oriental symphony in the light afternoon breeze.

They went to one of the small pagodas, to rest their feet and legs. Steve was used to trekking, but Mai Lee was starting to tire from the miles they had covered since arriving in Singapore. They climbed the dozen white marble steps that led to the ornamental pillars and red slanting roof and its tinkling lanterns.

An old Chinese woman was sat on one of the solid marble bench seats. She looked distraught, and was wringing her hands in her anxiety. Mai Lee went up to her talking for a while and then explained to Steve that the woman had just lost her husband after fifty years of married life. Her two children had died at a fairly early age, which was not uncommon in the Far East. She was completely alone, and had come to the gardens to find tranquillity and hopefully spiritual guidance.

They stayed with the old lady as long as they could, Mai Lee putting a comforting arm around her shoulder. When they left, Mai Lee gave the woman her new Indian silk shawl, a very caring gesture that brought a lump to Steve's throat. He handed the old lady some of the dollars from his pocket. As he gave her the money she smiled warmly, and he could see the grateful look on her face. They had given her hope for tomorrow, and there was a lot to be said for that! They left the lady, clutching her new Indian shawl, and no longer wringing her hands.

As they left the gardens Steve thought of Aunt Maude. She too had lost her husband, but in the added drama of a world war. After his death Maude was equally as vulnerable and alone as the forlorn Chinese woman, but Aunt Maude had the 'Welfare State' to turn to for practical help and assistance. The Chinese widow had nothing!

Steve looked at his watch; they had spent nearly five hours in the gardens. After a cold orange drink at a street cafe and watching the 'world' go by for a while, they strolled back to the centre of Singapore City, still thinking of the old lady. It had been a thought provoking experience for both of them.

In the early evening they were both feeling hungry, and Steve suggested a visit to a restaurant he had noticed near the Raffles Hotel on Stamford Road. The small restaurant, aptly named 'The Stamford', served mostly Chinese food, but they did offer a 'European Mixed Grill' on the menu. Steve quickly availed himself of one. It had been some time since he had enjoyed a mixed grill, whether it was cooked in Somerset or Singapore!

The food was delicious, but he drank only water with it, perhaps as a penance for his 'activities' at the 'Britannia Club'. Mai Lee chose a simple dish, which was much lighter than the grill, and she too drank only water!

Steve could tell that Mai Lee liked the clean restaurant. She glanced approvingly around her, and smoothed down the white crisp tablecloth with her slender fingers, almost in a caressing way. As the waiter walked past the table she smiled at him and said a few words in Chinese. The waiter's face beamed, and he bowed courtly. It was as if she had just bestowed a knighthood on him, such was her regal presence.

After coffee and a Chinese liqueur served in a tiny glass, they left the restaurant and walked out onto Stamford Road. Sir Stamford was well remembered in the area! Their legs had recovered from the day's walking, and Steve suggested that some 'liquid refreshment' at the 'Britannia Club' might be nice. Mai Lee looked at him, straight faced. She was not convinced that it would be a good idea. She pointed out that the lounge floor may not be quite 'dry' yet, and a quiet stroll along the seafront would be better for all concerned. He smiled at her and took her slender hand; she was becoming his 'Guardian Angel'.

After a slow pleasant walk, they returned to the apartment and showered the dust of the day from their bodies. They had spent another enjoyable day together, and both were tired and needing sleep, but it was a contented, relaxed tiredness. Mai Lee inspected Steve's 'black eye'. Her partial anger at his fighting had gone now, and she enjoyed playing the nurse and ministering to his needs. More 'Tiger Balm' was applied with the occasional kiss, on the other cheek.

They talked about the enchanting gardens, and the tragic old lady in the pagoda. Steve had passing thoughts about old age and its subsequent problems. But old age was many years away for him, and he put thoughts of becoming a pensioner to one side. He explained to Mai Lee about Aunt Maude losing her husband because of the world war. However, she could not understand why it was called a 'World' war when she and her kind, who lived on the same planet, knew nothing of it and had not experienced the slaughter that had taken place in Europe.

Steve tried to explain about Adolf Hitler, his hatred of the Jewish people, and insane pursuance of power. But Steve had problems understanding it himself, and was unable to explain fully. Mai Lee said she preferred to try and understand the complexities of cricket, and googlies! They rested on the welcome bed and enjoyed its luxury; it had been a long day, albeit an enjoyable one. Before sleep, the two lovers said a prayer for the old Chinese lady, and as they held each other, hoped that she too would find somebody to cling to, whether it be a physical or spiritual relationship.

The next day, after a warm shower with no scented soap, they realised that they were nearing the end of the holiday. Time had passed quickly, and there was no way to slow the clock. Steve still had ambitions about the Raffles Hotel, and the possibility of staying there, if only for a few fleeting hours. Mai Lee was of the same mind, the colonial hotel had a strange magnetic fascination, and she felt drawn to it, possibly the European side of her character coming to the fore again.

They decided to 'pool' all of the cash left, and stay at the 'Raffles' for one luxurious night. The following morning, they would take a cheap bus ride to the airport, and hopefully the awaiting 'Britannia'!

They packed their cases, and Steve untied his handkerchiefs from the bed legs. They laughed about the night the single beds had parted, and wondered if they would have the same problem at the 'Raffles'. They remembered making love under the protection of the coiled bed springs. If the Raffles Hotel had much the same to offer, perhaps with potpourri and extra scented soap in the shower, it would be a luxury to look forward to! They ended their stay by making love on one of the single beds, and afterwards said a fond farewell to the apartment that had served them so well.

The 'Union Jack Club's' Scots manager wished them well on their departure, and was good enough to reimburse them for the final night's change of plan. As they left he jokingly hoped the service at the 'Raffles' would be as good as his!

They hired a trishaw for the short journey, and rested the suitcases on their knees. The trishaw man was not pleased. The extra weight was not good for the fragile wheels and tyres, but at the end of the ride Steve gave him a few extra cents that compensated for his anxiety!

The Raffles Hotel was colonial luxury at its best. The floors were highly polished, and expensive bamboo furniture, with soft cushions, adorned the entrance lobby and lounge areas. There seemed to be at least two waiters for every guest in the hotel. The waiting staff all male, were mostly Malay and dressed in white trousers and tunics. Highly polished brass buttons held the tight fitting tunics, and a black pillbox hat, immaculate white gloves and highly polished black shoes completed the uniform. It was a colonialist's dream of paradise!

After paying for the night's stay in advance, Steve's pockets felt decidedly empty, and the waiter received a small tip for carrying the cases and showing them to their room. But the waiter had been taught well to show appreciation whatever the amount.

The spacious bedroom had the luxury of two ceiling fans, and the new guests looked at the opulence of their surroundings. They stared at the bed in amazement. It was a double, four-poster, with rose pink mosquito netting hanging from its upper structure. Mai Lee pressed her hand into the soft mattress, and her slender fingers disappeared into the 'Eider' down. She looked around the room and smiled approvingly; it could be a very pleasant stay and looked forward to a night in the luxurious bed with her 'Lieutenant'. She could quite easily have been a colonialist! Steve sat on the double bed; there would be no need for handkerchiefs and no 'Single Bed Syndrome' that night!

After 'sampling' the bed with Mai Lee, Steve looked around the room. On a bamboo, glass topped table was a 'Gideon' Bible, a copy of 'Tatler', and several ancient copies of 'Punch' and 'Horse and Hounds'. When he opened the wardrobe door he detected a slight aroma of moth balls. Directly alongside the four-poster bed was a 'room service' bell. Steve toyed with the idea of ordering a bottle of wine, then felt in his pocket.

Later in the afternoon, they entered into the spirit of the very English hotel and 'took' tea and cucumber sandwiches with the other guests at 4 o'clock. The only sound to be heard in the lounge was the tinkling of tea spoons and the odd 'plop' of sugar lumps being dropped into tea cups from highly polished silver tongs. A waiter, immaculately dressed, stood at a discreet distance with a white linen cloth draped over his forearm, in readiness to wipe up any drop of tea accidentally spilt onto the ornate tea tables. Steve felt like spilling some of his tea just to see what the waiter's reaction time might be. Steve grinned at Mai Lee and shared his mischievous thoughts with her. She quickly admonished him, and jokingly said that if he did so she would make his other eye black!

In the evening they bought a small bag of mixed fruit from a street stall.

They wandered along the seafront filling themselves with the pleasant evening air, rambutan, bananas and ripe lychee. Fruit had never tasted so good!

When they returned to the hotel, they looked across the road to the 'Britannia Club's' open windows. The musical Petty Officer was giving his rendition of 'Roll out the Barrel' intermingled with the instantly recognisable notes of Beethoven's 5th Symphony. It was business as usual at the 'Brit Club'!

They went into the hotel lounge, where the waiters were 'fussing' around with their silver trays, taking orders for glasses of 'Madeira' from ex-military colonels, pots of tea for foreign diplomats, and whisky with dry ginger for businessmen and their long gloved 'ladies'!

Steve smiled to himself, and thought, *The Petty Officer would be hard put to find an appreciative audience here.*

They said goodnight to the other guests they had passed the time of day with earlier at tea and went to their room. They had paid dearly for the use of the four-poster and intended to get their money's worth! After a shower they rested naked on the luxurious bed. Steve regretted not buying more of the N.A.A.F.I. scented soap. There was something magical about its formula of 'San Miguel', hot pies and 'Cherry Blossom', it was irreplaceable.

The room was warm and Steve switched the two ceiling fans to 'maximum', increasing the air circulation around the luxurious bed. It was not the season to be troubled by mosquitoes, but they lowered the rose pink netting around the bed, and felt like two children playing in a secluded tent, lost in their own little world.

They rested naked on the bed, and between kisses, talked about the week they had spent together. Much had happened in the few short days; it had been memorable for both of them.

The wonderful seafront came to mind, and the hospitality of the 'Union Jack Club'. They remembered their friends, the two single beds, who had clung together at a most important time. The 'Britannia Club' and Beethoven's 5th Symphony played by the flexible fingered Petty Officer and the tragic old lady in the 'Tiger Balm' gardens. All of those memories came flooding back to them as they relaxed in each other's arms. But most of all they realised that they had discovered a wonderful, lasting love for each other. Singapore had been the catalyst of their absolute coming together. Steve knew that whatever happened in the future, he would never say goodbye to Mai Lee! Time had passed so quickly but any thoughts of tomorrow and Hong Kong were put firmly aside. They nestled into each other's arms, and let the world go by. They felt strangely guilty about making love in the luxurious, expensive bed and their highly respectable surroundings.

Their bodies enjoyed each other. The cool shower had made their skin like silk, and they ran their fingers over each other, the sensation awakening desires for sex in both of them. They began to make love in the seclusion of the pink 'tent'. They discovered a love that went beyond lust or passion, it was a blending of physical and spiritual well-being, and their bodies and minds melted together. Sir Stamford, and his hotel, would not have been offended!

At the height of their lovemaking Steve unknowingly hit the 'room service' button with his arm, and as the lovers were reaching a climax in their sexual activity they looked up to see a smartly dressed waiter peering down on them through the pink netting, silver tray in hand, awaiting their order!

When the two startled lovers had regained their composure they ordered two, very cold, 'Singapore Slings'!

The Malay waiter returned with the drinks, a broad grin on his face. They sipped the ice cold 'Slings' on the continued comfort of the now fairly 'warm' bed, and laughed about the 'cheeky' faced waiter staring down at their naked bodies. When they had finished the potent 'Singapore Slings' they both felt the urge to repeat the sexual performance on a grander scale. Steve made certain his arm was clear of the 'button', and they re-melted into each other's arms.

In the morning the 'cheeky' waiter came to collect the travel cases. They blushed at his knowing grin; he had seen more of them than they of him! So to speak. In the hotel lobby he handed the lovers their cases, and with a cheerful smile wished them 'Salamat'. They blushed slightly again, but this time in a happy, contented way. They walked to the bus stop, laughing and giggling as they went. Sir Stamford had served them well, and they too in turn would not be forgotten, but it would be some time before they could take tea again without blushing to their roots!

CHAPTER 52

The flight back to Hong Kong was uneventful, and the two exhausted lovers engaged mainly in their own quiet thoughts and memories of the week in Singapore. It had been an unforgettable time for both of them. The 'Britannia Club' had played a big part in the week, and Mai Lee looked at Steve's still partly swollen cheek as the aircraft flew across the South China Sea to Kai Tak. But Mai Lee said nothing about the fight with the Australian sailor. She would learn more about the cricket and the all-important 'Ashes' as time went by.

The reliable 'Britannia' aircraft delivered them safely to Kai Tak Airport, and after a short bus ride and ferry across the bay they were glad to reach Mai Lee's apartment. After they had showered they realised that they had not eaten for twenty-four hours, and Mai Lee made a light meal after a 'raid' on the cafe's kitchen below. Steve looked at Chow-Chow, who had greeted them with a loud purr and affectionate rub of her body on their legs as they entered the lounge. The other waitress had looked after Chow-Chow well, and Steve remarked that the cat had 'put on' a few ounces in weight during their absence. Mai Lee smilingly agreed, her 'paternal' anxiety had been for nothing, but it was natural.

They sat on the settee and enjoyed the much needed meal. Chow-Chow had gained weight during the holiday, but with the exercise and eating slightly less, the tourists had lost a few pounds! After the food and coffee, Chow-Chow settled onto Steve's lap and was soon asleep; it was good to be home!

However, time was marching on, and Steve's week-long pass was due to expire at midnight. Mai Lee suggested she drive him to 'Gillman' camp in the 'Ferrari', it would be a fitting end to the holiday. They decided to go well before darkness fell, it was not good to drive at night, regardless of which sex you were. The road to camp was isolated, and when darkness fell, the villains awoke!

The 'Ferrari' purred along the dusty road, glad to be released from its week in the garage. Mai Lee had removed her shoes as usual to drive the sophisticated machine, and a pink silk scarf held her hair in place as the breeze brushed over the open sports car. Steve glanced down at Mai Lee's legs as the intruding breeze gradually forced the light skirt she was wearing up towards her thighs. She was aware of the situation, and smiled to herself, and returned Steve's glances from time to time. It was a far more pleasant journey for Steve to his normal hair-raising, white knuckle experiences with 'Stirling Moss'. And Mai Lee had far better legs!

When they reached the camp gates Mai Lee was not allowed to drive into the camp, not having the required security pass. The occupants of the guardroom stared out of the windows, not believing what they were seeing; one of their own arriving in a very expensive 'Ferrari' sports car, and being driven by a beautiful Eurasian girl.

Steve said goodbye to Mai Lee, and she surprisingly kissed him in public, the Italian extrovert side of her character coming to the fore again. She revved the engine slightly more than usual, took off her silk scarf, and sped off down the road to Kowloon. Steve hoped that she had not contracted a contagious accelerator virus on the road, from 'Stirling Moss'! Steve walked past the staring eyes in the guardroom with a smug look on his face. Tomorrow, tales of the 'Ferrari' and its passengers would be rife!

The dusty road had made Steve's throat dry. It was time to reacquaint himself with 'San Miguel' instead of 'Singapore Slings' and 'Screwdrivers'. In the N.A.A.F.I. the platoon was enjoying the usual beer before bed. It was time for Steve to plead insolvency; he had just five cents in his pocket. The other men 'pooled' some of their resources onto the table for his beers and a pie. Tomorrow it was, thankfully, 'pay parade' and he would be a 'rich' man again. Holidays are great, but they cost!

The men were curious to know about Steve's still recognisable 'black eye'. He explained quite theatrically, the fracas at the 'Britannia Club' and his Australian 'friends'. The 'Lawyer' listened carefully as the tale evolved and scribbled in his notebook. Later, after conversation about the fight had subsided, he handed Steve the book. The 'Lawyer' had again waxed lyrical and had written: -

Camy a friend, tarry a foe
Let others weep.
We'll drink a toast to 'San Miguel'
Then to our beds for sleep!

The 'Lawyer's' 'Olde English' poetry was beyond the platoon, and Mac, who had been listening half-heartedly, grabbed the notebook and added in his raw Yorkshire style: -

Forget the people who laugh or weep,
Let's drink a toast to 'Barmaids Lusty',
Then to their beds for sleep!

Steve laughed, and bought them both a beer from the 'pool'. He suggested they apply for the post of 'Gillman' camp poet!

The conversation turned to food, something always close to their hearts. The Medical Officer had convinced the cookhouse corporal that garlic was good for the men's health, and the 'Lawyer' said that he could definitely taste the 'continental' breath taking bulb in his baked beans.

He added, "Perhaps a 'clove' a day keeps the doctor away?"

"Aye," replied Mac, reverting to his strong Dewsbury accent, "one clove of garlic keeps the doctor away, but two cloves a day on the breath keeps every bugger away!" He raised his eyebrows to accentuate the statement.

They immediately thought of their love lives. Grandad Joe's tinned baked beans in a rich tomato sauce were recommended for longevity and satisfactory sexual activity, but English beans mixed with French garlic was another matter, and could result in serious malfunction in the bedroom! After much discussion over more 'San Miguels' Steve agreed, as platoon leader, to have a quiet word with the cookhouse corporal. The general opinion was that the standard of cooking was decreasing and needed to be addressed. Steve reluctantly agreed to include it into his talk with the cookhouse corporal, but a certain amount of diplomacy would be in order, otherwise they could end up with meatballs!

Mac said the cookhouse should use Joe's maxim for cooking - 'when it's brown it's done, when it's black it's buggered, go to the fish and chip shop!'

Docherty came into the N.A.A.F.I. and changed the subject by trying out his latest joke on the platoon, he said,

"A young boy asked his mother, 'Mummy, what's a schizophrenic?'
His mother looked at him sternly and said,
'Be quiet, and eat both of your meals'!"

Steve said he preferred the joke about the actress, and the bishop and the one-legged jockey!

When the N.A.A.F.I. closed its doors for the night Steve went to the 'basha' and prepared for sleep, exhaustion had suddenly overtaken him. He went to his bed and felt his injured cheek. The swelling was almost gone, but his memories of the week in Singapore would live on, and on.

He wished that Mai Lee was with him in his lonely bed. He clutched hold of the pillow as if he was holding her; he kissed the soft pillow and went to sleep thinking of many things, including single beds tied together, the 'Raffles' and Malayan waiters, 'Screwdrivers' and 'Singapore Slings'! But most of all, simply, her!

In the morning, after 'pay parade', Steve caught up with all of the news and happenings that had accrued whilst he was in Singapore. Taff had been promoted to Lance Corporal, (acting, unpaid). The C.O. had taken note of the Welshman's organising ability and leadership in rugby matters. The C.O. had obviously forgotten Taff's derogatory remarks when the C.O. was acting as referee during the first rugby match against the 'Boot Boys'! Taff had remembered to salute the C.O. before the delivery of his tirade on the field of play, and on the more serious side it was considered that with his quiet resolute character, he would make a good N.C.O. (non-commissioned officer).

'Geordie' had returned to the regiment's central depot in the U.K., and Steve was to assume leadership of the platoon, 'acting unpaid'. If all went well for the next three months he would receive his second stripe and the extra remuneration for carrying rank. Taff would become his second-in-command.

Time went by and routine duties, including border patrols continued. Diplomatic relations between the two countries had become more amicable, and the border incident was forgotten. Drug smugglers were once again the main problem for the patrols and police alike who joined forces on the treks.

Charlie Strong had been returned by the authorities in China, and was making a gradual recovery from his bullet wound. In the Chinese hospital he had apparently spent many hours instructing the nurses on the correct way to administer pills, medicines and potions. The doctors and surgeons also came under his scrutiny, and he regretted being 'asleep' during the operation to remove the bullet from his leg! He considered that his advice during that period would have been invaluable to the surgeon. It was 'hinted' that the Chinese had not re-patriated Charlie for practical reasons; they simply wanted to be rid of him!

Under the watchful eye of the P.T.I.'s Charlie spent most days in the camp gymnasium, slowly rebuilding the muscles in his leg and at the same time enhancing the rest of his body. He had become a hero since returning from China, and would show his bullet scar to anybody at the drop of a hat, or more specifically, his trousers! Charlie was a changed man now, far removed from the fragile hypochondriac that Steve had first met at the training camp in Hampshire. He had served his country, and the army was serving him well in return.

As a matter of routine the platoon went to the firing ranges on a refresher course with their Sterlings; weapon drill was one thing, but practical use with 'live' rounds was essential from time to time. In the evening the men went to the N.A.A.F.I. for the usual relaxation after a busy day. Charlie went to the serving counter and joined the queue for beer. He had spent most of the day in the gym, and it was time for relaxation with the rest of the platoon. He was growing strong now but the muscles around the bullet wound were 'pulling' after the exercise.

The queue 'jostled' along, the men anxious to 'wet' their appetites. A private from a different platoon nudged against Charlie's injured leg, making him wince.

Charlie turned to the private and said, "Watch it!"

The private looked at Charlie and replied, "You're a pleasant soul aren't you?"

Charlie rubbed his leg to soothe the pain, and said, "Yes, and you're an 'ah soul'."

The men in the queue waited for the usual flare of fists, but the two stared each other down for a few seconds and it went no further. The private picked up his beer and hurried off. You didn't 'mess' with Charlie now, the China incident had sealed his new character. No more pills or potions for Charlie Strong!

The Medical Officer decided that Charlie should return to the U.K. to complete his rehabilitation before finishing his two years National Service and returning to civilian life.

On the day of his departure Steve and the padre watched him leave 'Gillman' camp, his kitbag slung jauntily over his shoulder. He walked with an air of confidence and strength now. His surname was no longer a source of ridicule, but used in admiration.

As they watched him stride down the road towards the camp gates, the padre turned to Steve and said smilingly, "Blessed are the meek for they shall inherit the Earth!"

Steve nodded in agreement at the padre's biblical words. Charlie knew that they were watching him, and without turning, waved an arm in farewell! Steve and the padre retired to the N.A.A.F.I. and shared a beer together. They drank a toast to Charlie Strong, the hypochondriac who had turned into a hero!

Life in the camp continued with its normal routine, and people went about their business. Taff planned another rugby match between the consortium of 'Boot Boys', 'Laundry Boys' and seamstresses, versus the platoon, but the 'Lawyer' made it clear that his seamstress would not be available for selection. Taff said he was being selfish and over protective. The buxom seamstress had been a big crowd drawer in the previous encounter. But the 'Lawyer' was adamant; his seamstress was not to be molested or bruised in any way.

In Kowloon Steve continued his ever blossoming romance with Mai Lee and Chow-Chow, to Mai Lee's surprise, presented her with a litter of kittens.

It explained Steve's observation that the cat had 'put on' several ounces in weight when they arrived back from Singapore.

Steve took one of the male kittens to the camp, secreting it under his shirt as he passed the guardroom. The cat quickly matured and became the 'basha' mascot, deterring mice and other small animals from the 'basha', including small snakes that frequented the long grass that surrounded the living quarters. The platoon named their new recruit Chow-Chow two, and it received the honorary rank of sergeant (acting, unpaid).

The platoon had completed yet another border patrol, and was placed on 'stand down' for the normal routine of three days. Steve obtained a forty-eight-hour pass and made his way to Kowloon with the intrepid 'Stirling Moss'.

When he arrived at the 'Star Cafe' Mai Lee was in her apartment tending to Chow-Chow and the two remaining young cats that she had yet to find homes for. Mai Lee was toying with the idea of keeping them for herself. But when Siamese cats matured they tended to become jealous and spiteful of each other, and increasingly territorial. Cute as Chow-Chow was, one spoilt child in the apartment was enough, and on Steve's advice Mai Lee continued looking for suitable homes. But finding homes for cats in a country that is not exactly pet orientated was difficult, to say the least.

CHAPTER 53

The weather was fine and warm, and after tea and a biscuit in the apartment Mai Lee suggested to Steve that they drive along the coast road to a floating restaurant, and after a meal, take the 'Ferrari' further along the picturesque coast and pay a surprise visit to her father on the yacht.

Steve was quite happy about the restaurant idea as it sounded a very pleasant place to eat, but the thought of seeing Giorgio again did not sit well with him. He disliked the man and his arrogant ways. But he was Mai Lee's father, and Steve told a 'white lie' saying he looked forward to seeing him again. On the bright side there might be a few palatable cocktails as a consolation. Steve could tell Mai Lee was still inwardly concerned about her father. It was no longer acceptable to her not to question his 'business' activities, she had closed her eyes too much in the past in 'blind' faith.

It was a pleasure to ride in the 'Ferrari' as always and the floating restaurant was in a perfect setting: anchored some fifty yards from the shore, and connected by a hand-railed wooden walkway. The weather was perfect for dining in the open air, and several other customers were already enjoying a meal in the pleasant atmosphere. As they were shown to their table Steve looked around him. To the left was coastline scenery, to the right the open sea with the sun glinting on the blue water.

After a first course of octopus soup, they ordered plates of mixed seafood and a basket of Chinese bread. They talked briefly about the holiday in Singapore. It was like a distant memory now, but one they would never forget. They could laugh about the fight with the Australians in the 'Britannia Club' now, and it prompted Mai Lee to ask more about cricket, and the 'Ashes'. She was interested in anything English, and wanted to integrate with her 'Lieutenant' as much as possible.

Steve tried to explain that the 'Ashes' was the trophy the teams played for, and were in fact the burnt remains of the set of bails used during the first test match between England and Australia. Mai Lee found it difficult to understand, and when Steve thought about it he too found it incredulous. How could anybody play for an urn full of burnt ashes? But that was cricket, and it symbolised the meaning of sport and 'the game thing'! The only way to fully explain the game would be to take Mai Lee to a cricket match, but where?

After the satisfying meal the waiter presented them with the bill, together with two small glasses of the restaurant's special liqueur. As they left the floating restaurant and walked along the wooden walkway towards 'terra firma', Steve reminded himself to write to Aunt Maude again. He could imagine the look on her face when she read he had eaten octopus and squid!

They returned to the 'Ferrari' and drove on down the coast towards the yacht, and Mai Lee's father, Giorgio. The ferry boatman took them to the yacht, weaving his tiny boat around the carefully placed 'junks' that created Giorgio's privacy and secrecy. It seemed a fruitless plan to Steve, if the boatman knew of the secluded yacht, then so did other people, including the police. But some Italians were well known for their eccentric ways.

The yacht was as immaculate as ever. The crew seemed to do little else than clean and polish the boat, keeping it in showroom condition. The permanent rope and aluminium ladder was equally smart, the ropes covered with a white 'Blanco' that Steve was familiar with regarding his own military kit. When they reached the varnished deck Steve remembered to take off his shoes and socks in order to placate Giorgio and his unusual fetish for maritime cleanliness. Steve's feet were hot anyway, and it was a relief to go barefoot, regardless of Giorgio's idiosyncrasy!

The armed crewman was waiting at the top of the ladder as usual, and was equally unsmiling. Being a member of Giorgio's crew he probably had little to smile about! After greeting Mai Lee in Chinese and giving Steve a suspicious sideways glance he walked quickly away in the direction of Giorgio's cabin.

Steve and Mai Lee walked gingerly barefoot to the stern of the yacht and the open spaced cocktail lounge. A white gloved steward was stood, almost to attention, waiting to serve. Steve looked at the well-stocked bar, and began to 'warm' to Giorgio slightly. Perhaps he wasn't such a bad chap after all!

Giorgio duly appeared, smartly dressed as always with his black straight hair held in place by a thick scented cream.

Steve thought to himself, *It's probably 'Brylcream' with an added perfume!*

Giorgio's manner was abrupt and 'clip' tongued; he was not pleased to see them. Steve began to wonder what Mai Lee's mother had found attracting in him, but sometimes there was no explaining love. The hunchback of Notre Dame had his admirer after all!

Giorgio explained that some of his business associates were due, and he would return to the cocktail lounge as soon as possible. Mai Lee's probing questions would have to wait! Giorgio curtly invited them to help themselves to any drinks and food they required, and then left as abruptly as he had arrived, unnecessarily smoothing his black hair as he went. The bar steward pulled his white gloves tighter over his fingers and awaited their instructions, but Steve had the feeling that he was been 'spied' on rather than waited on! As Giorgio had walked away Steve could sense that the Italian was more tense than usual. Perhaps it was a more than usually important meeting with his business associates!

They made themselves comfortable on the luxurious armchairs and ordered drinks. It was a strange unreal setting, and Steve could not visualise the boat ever being used for a sea voyage; the tables, chairs and accessories would simply disappear over the side in the slightest 'swell'. It was difficult to tell, but the crew did not look like competent sailors.

The steward made a cocktail for Steve and fresh orange juice with fruit for Mai Lee. Steve went to the boat's handrail and looked around the area. The yacht was surrounded by Giorgio's 'armada' of 'junks', completely blotting out the scenic coastline. There was an isolated quietness, a strange setting indeed.

Steve noticed a spear fishing gun on one of the chairs and picked it up, curious about its design. The trigger mechanism was very similar to the military weapons he was used to. He asked Mai Lee if Giorgio was a water sportsman. She laughed and said her father was a non-swimmer, but he demanded fresh fish on his table, and the crew used spear guns to catch fish from the surrounding waters.

After three large cocktails Steve felt the need to visit the toilet, or 'head' as it was known in maritime terms. Mai Lee explained that it was at the front of the boat, on the lower deck. Steve kissed her before leaving, and the steward politely looked away, readjusting his gloves nervously, such familiarity was 'foreign' to him.

Steve went barefoot along the port side of the yacht. The varnished deck was hot underfoot and he wished that the soles of his feet were as tough as the crew's obviously were. Their skin had become toughened, generation after generation. Two of the crew were polishing the brass handrail, and talking animatedly. They too looked tense and nervous, and as Steve approached they stopped talking and lowered their heads until he had passed.

He went down a set of steep stairs and onto the lower deck. A narrow corridor separated the cabins on either side. The light was not good after the direct sunlight of the upper deck, and some of the doors had been recently varnished obliterating any previous signs. Eventually, near the bows of the yacht he came to a door marked 'heads'. Giorgio was as nautically correct as he was on maritime 'spit and polish'. Steve opened the door slowly, not knowing if the facility was occupied or not. The 'smallest room on the boat' was empty and Steve gratefully closed the door and availed himself of the amenities. The toilet and washroom space was as immaculate as the rest of the yacht, with highly polished brass taps and toilet paper of the highest quality.

After freshening himself up, he returned to the narrow corridor. His eyes had become adjusted to the different light, and he started back down the corridor towards the stern. He came to a cabin door that was slightly ajar and curiosity overtook him. He entered a small storeroom, and stacked against one bulkhead was six large plywood tea packing cases. Tea was not an unusual commodity for a businessman to be dealing in, but Steve was still curious. One of the cases had been slightly set apart, and the lid loosened. Steve carefully lifted the plywood lid to reveal hundreds of small white neatly folded packets; he had seen many similar sachets on border anti-smuggling patrols with the Hong Kong Police. He opened one of the sachets carefully to reveal a small amount of powder, wetted a finger and put the white finely ground powder to his lips. It was heroin!

Steve winced at the taste, and thought, *So this is what Giorgio is exporting.* Suddenly many questions were answered; the luxury yacht and its secrecy, Giorgio's expensive lifestyle, his ownership of the cafe, and lastly, but not least, the 'Ferrari'. But Steve was certain that Mai Lee was not entangled with the criminal gang, and she would be as surprised as Steve at the heroin discovery.

The other 'tea' chests were also full of sachets; there were thousands of them in the storeroom. It was a large yacht, and the existence of more storerooms was quite possible! The contents of the storeroom were worth a fortune on the world drug market, but at what cost for the people who would be taking the drugs, and destroying their lives?

A sudden sound behind him made Steve turn sharply. One of the crewmen stood in the open doorway. He was dressed the same as the other men, in white trousers and shirt, and of course barefoot, but he had the additional 'uniform' of a wide leather brown belt, and a brown sheath that carried a long knife. He was obviously a senior member of the crew, perhaps the bosun. The Chinaman looked at Steve, and then at the open 'tea' chest. The bosun grinned menacingly, stepped into the cabin and closed the door firmly behind him, he wanted no witnesses! He drew the knife from its sheath and grasped it professionally. The long blade looked extremely lethal; it certainly wasn't designed for whittling wood. Steve glanced around him without taking his eyes completely off the knife, there was no escape, and he was trapped!

The Chinaman grinned again, he knew he had the upper hand, and passed the knife from hand to hand with the manner of a man well used to causing fatal injury. Steve felt strangely naked, and wished he had a loaded Sterling in his hands. The bosun taunted Steve with his knife, sadistically enjoying every moment, the Englishman had discovered the Italian's cache of drugs, and if the intruder was to die, Giorgio would ask no questions!

Steve started to panic and sweat broke out on his hands and face. He retreated, his back towards the rear bulkhead. He glanced down at the open 'tea' chest in desperation, and in his panic considered throwing the light plywood chest at the Chinaman. Then, from behind the 'tea' chest he noticed the pointed arrow of a loaded spear gun looking up at him!

Steve grabbed the gun with the grateful air of a man being thrown a lifeline at sea after a shipwreck. The Chinaman stopped grinning, but there was a look of deep hatred in his eyes, and his mind was set on one thing, killing! He disregarded the fact that Steve was holding the spear gun and started to advance.

Steve, without being aware of it, squeezed the trigger of the 'hair' action gun. The spear left the gun, creating a strange whooshing noise as it parted the air in the front of it. The steel spear entered the Chinaman's neck, throwing him back against the closed door. The knife dropped to the floor and blood started to stream from the crewman's neck. Steve looked disbelievingly at the unmoving man, and then at the spear gun. It had all happened in an instant, and he could hardly recall grabbing the gun and using it.

Steve looked more closely at the Chinaman. Blood was pumping from his neck; the spear had severed the jugular vein. He couldn't understand why the Chinaman was still stood against the door. Steve took a pace closer to the motionless figure, and saw that the steel spear had passed directly through the man's neck, and had pinned him to the wooden door. He looked again at the man's face and eyes. Blood had ceased to pump from his neck, he was dead!

Steve felt cold, and tried to collect his thoughts. All he had wanted was to use the toilet. He put two of the sachets into his pocket to remind himself that it wasn't a terrible nightmare and perhaps evidence for the police in the future. He looked at the cabin door, it was the only way out, and the dead Chinaman was hung on it. He gingerly edged the door open, and the man swung with it. The Chinaman's face was ashen now in death, a stark contrast to his red blood soaked shirt and trousers. Steve made a supreme physical effort not to be sick, and staggered out of the room, still clutching the spear gun.

CHAPTER 54

Steve walked slowly along the narrow corridor towards the stern of the yacht. The general temperature was warm, but he felt cold and clammy. His legs almost refused to carry his weight as he climbed the stairway to the deck. As he walked to the lounge area his first instinct was to grab Mai Lee's hand and run, but run where? The small ferry boat was not in sight, and the yacht's ladder was covered by an armed guard, and nobody left the yacht without Giorgio's consent, including Mai Lee. Steve felt as if he was still trapped in the damp dark cell in China.

When he arrived at the cocktail lounge Mai Lee was reading a fashion magazine, completely unaware of the drama below deck.

She noticed the spear gun in Steve's hand and laughingly said, "I see you have been fishing, did you catch a big one?"

Steve's mind was numb now, and he simply replied, "Yes, but I left it pinned to one of the cabin doors."

She looked quizzically at him, smilingly shook her head, and returned to her magazine.

The bar steward was not tending to his numerous bottles and glasses, for some reason he had deserted his post. Steve went to the bar and poured himself a large whisky. He was not a great lover of the strong Scotch drink since Sgt. McNiff's birthday party in Scotland, but this was much needed for 'medicinal' purposes! He had just killed a man, albeit in self-defence, and the reaction was starting to take effect. He was trained to kill an enemy on the field of battle, not civilians on luxury yachts. His hands were shaking as he poured the precious liquid, and he spilt a measure of it, McNiff would not have been pleased!

After his second glass of whisky Steve's nerves started to settle down and his hands stopped shaking. But his mind was racing, his suspicions of Giorgio had proved to be correct. Mai Lee would have to be told eventually, even if she didn't already know. Perhaps she was aware of his criminal activities, but could not accept the facts? She would have seen the pathetic drug addicts on the back streets of Hong Kong. To think that her father might be in some way responsible for their demise was not a pleasant thought.

After Steve had sufficiently composed himself he sat opposite Mai Lee, took one of the heroin sachets from his pocket and tossed it onto the fashion magazine she was resting on her lap.

She picked it up and looked questioningly at Steve. "What is it?" she asked.

Steve hoped that he was doing the right thing by being dramatic and to the point, but she had to know the facts sometime, and now was as good a time as any. He said bluntly, "It's heroin, your father is a drug smuggler!"

It was a short sentence, but one that would change Mai Lee's life for ever. She looked at the sachet, and then at Steve. He could see the sudden shock on her face, and she threw the packet of drugs to the floor as if it was red hot. He went to the bar and poured her a large whisky; she too required 'medicinal' sustenance!

After they had finished their drinks, and replenished them, Steve told Mai Lee about the dramatic few minutes in the storeroom, but omitted some of the gory details, they were not for a woman's ears. When she realised how close she had come to losing her 'Lieutenant' she clutched hold of his hand in a sudden panic, and silently wished she had not decided to visit the yacht to question her father about his business dealings. But the questions had all been answered, and she had not spoken a word on the subject! She had been denying the truth for some time, but now it had literally been dropped onto her lap.

Steve looked at the spear gun, and angrily threw it over the side of the yacht. It sank into the waters, buried at sea. The gun had saved his life, but he had killed a man with it, and wanted no further part of it. He wondered how his mind would have reacted if he had killed the Chinaman on a normal field of battle, soldier against soldier. That would have been a very different scenario, and more logical to deal with. A soldier is a soldier, and a civilian a civilian, ne're the 'twain' should meet!

Steve looked along the starboard side of the yacht; a small power driven boat was approaching, and it was fully laden with 'tea' chests! Mai Lee joined Steve at the handrail and they watched anxiously as the crew threw lines to the boat, and the off-loading of the plywood 'tea' chests began in earnest. The crew, including the bar steward, passed the cases quickly for storage below as if they were too hot to handle. It was certain now that the dead bosun would be discovered in the storeroom, and when that happened all Hell would break loose! The two crewmen who had seen Steve go below deck would put 'two and two' together, and the end result was not to be thought about. Regardless of his daughter's feelings, Giorgio had to protect his 'empire', and one missing British soldier was not important.

One hundred yards away a modern motor launch quietly nosed its way through the armada of 'junks'. On its white painted hull was written, in bold black letters, 'Police'!

When the cargo off-loading was almost complete the police launch emerged from the stationary armada, and its engines burst into full power, the propellers churning the water as it quickly gathered speed. Pandemonium immediately broke out on the yacht. The lines to the small boat were hastily cast off, and the three remaining 'tea' chests on the boat were ditched into the water. The small boat sped off in the opposite direction to the fast approaching police launch.

The luxurious yacht's powerful super-charged engines burst into life sending plumes of black diesel smoke from the stern of the boat. Giorgio shouted from the bridge, and two crewmen jettisoned the rope/aluminium ladder. The yacht was obviously on permanent 'standby' for such situations, and within seconds was underway. In a matter of minutes, the scene had been transformed from one of controlled tranquillity to complete chaos.

The yacht gained speed rapidly and smashed its way between two of the fragile 'junks', shattering one of the 'junk's' wooden stern as it powered through the gap. The stricken boat immediately listed onto its port side and began to sink. Giorgio had breached his own defences!

Steve and Mai Lee grabbed the stern handrail in an effort not to be thrown overboard as the yacht swerved violently. They looked at each other in disbelief as the police launch pursued them through the gap. Giorgio headed the yacht towards the South China Sea, the island of Macao, and freedom! The yacht's engines were on full power now, and the engine's super-chargers screamed as they were given full vent to their turbine power!

The police launch was equipped with a fixed machine gun, mounted on the bow, and the crewmen commenced firing across the bow of the escaping yacht, in an effort to slow it down and possibly force it to surrender. The police were now convinced that Giorgio was their quarry, and he was their prey in the fight against the drug smuggling 'Barons' of Hong Kong.

Giorgio and one of the crew hurled hand grenades at the police launch; the grenades had been kept on the bridge for just such circumstances as these. A smuggler's life was always fraught with possible danger! The police launch 'weaved' from side to side, and Giorgio's actions were hopelessly out of range and fuelled by anger and hatred rather than logic. He was a criminal, and the police his enemy! The grenades either burst in the air or sank below the water's surface before exploding, causing a volcanic like eruption in the water. Giorgio was obviously insane, and shouted angrily at the police. Who were they to invade his secret domain?

The police realised that their tactics were not working, and started firing directly at the yacht's bridge. Giorgio disappeared from sight, shouting expletives at the police and shaking a fist in defiance. At first the gun fire seemed to have little effect, but after a few minutes, black smoke started to billow from the open windows. Deep red flames began to engulf the entire bridge, and the fire was quickly spread by the stiff afternoon breeze. Steve looked at the increasing inferno and saw that the situation was becoming more desperate by the minute. Mai Lee clung on to him, bewildered by the speed of the dramatic events. Thoughts of her father's criminality raced through her mind, and her emotions were torn apart. She was glad that her mother was not alive to witness the terrible day!

The police launch was content to 'track' the progress of the yacht. They knew that sooner or later the vessel would falter in its course. The yacht's powerful diesel engines suddenly stopped, the fire on the bridge had destroyed the engine remote controls, and the fuel 'racks' in the engine room had automatically shut down; the police had their man!

Without power the yacht quickly came to a standstill. Steve and Mai Lee let go of the handrail and were grateful to collapse onto the lounge chairs that by some miracle were still on board. They tried to calm themselves and take stock of the situation. The police had obviously been 'tipped off' regarding the delivery of the cargo. It was quite possible that Giorgio had competitive enemies in the drug trade!

Steve looked along the length of the yacht. The fire was spreading rapidly, and as he watched, three of the crew dived into the water and swam for their lives. As Steve peered over the handrail he said to himself, "Rats leaving a sinking ship!" He wondered if the crewman he had killed was still 'hanging' around on the cabin door. Under the circumstances he had little sympathy for the Chinaman.

Mai Lee was shivering, more in shock than anything else. The wind was fresh but not cold, and Steve held her to him in comfort. The police boat was 'standing off' waiting for Giorgio to give himself up, they simply had to wait.

Giorgio was trapped in a corner, his powerful engines had been silenced, and his 'empire' was on fire.

Steve heard the whirring noise of a large electric motor. He looked over the rear of the yacht. The flat transom stern was opening like a giant garage door! Steve and Mai Lee watched in open mouthed amazement as a small speed boat emerged from the open stern. At the wheel was Giorgio, dressed in a black roll-neck sweater and black trousers. His dark greasy hair was dishevelled, and he hunched over the steering wheel like a madman.

Attached to the rear of the tiny boat was a massive outboard motor. Giorgio pressed the starter button on the dashboard, and the engine roared into life. The police were taken by surprise, and had put their engines on standby such was their confidence that they had captured their prey. But Giorgio was not a man to be taken lightly. The speedboat made a swift manoeuvre to evade the police launch, and Giorgio the drug 'Baron' pointed the bow of his escape boat towards the open sea. The police put their engines on full power, but they had lost the initiative and the propellers struggled in vain. Providing Giorgio's engine did not falter he would make it to the criminals' sanctuary of Macao. The Hong Kong Police had no jurisdiction on the Portuguese owned island. The best that they could hope for was to track his course in the future and wait for a more favourable day to bring the 'Italian Baron' to face justice in the courts of Hong Kong.

The yacht's stern door remained open, and water lapped into the boat. The fire on the bridge was spreading rapidly. Steve looked at Mai Lee, they had to leave the yacht, and quickly. In his earlier search for the toilet he had seen an inflated rubber dinghy strapped to one of the outside bulkheads. Mai Lee was in a dazed shock and Steve took her hand. They cautiously made their way along the deck. The heat from the fire was making the heavy coats of varnish soft, and it stuck to their bare feet. Steve cursed Giorgio and his strange maritime regulations. Smoke from the fire made them cough and their eyes water, and the crackle of expanding burning wood was everywhere.

They reached the dinghy, and Steve noticed there were two wooden paddles attached to the rubber boat. He unstrapped the dinghy from the bulkhead and dropped the light boat over the handrail into the water. There was no time for preparation, he told Mai Lee to jump into the water as close to the dinghy as possible. He didn't even know if she could swim, and decided to ask her later, as they had only one option at the moment, and that was to get off the fire stricken yacht.

Steve followed Mai Lee into the water. The rubber dinghy had landed upright and they grabbed the hand ropes to haul themselves into the tiny boat; for the moment they were safe. They both gasped for breath after swallowing sea water, but were grateful to be off the yacht which was now almost totally in flames. Steve unstrapped one of the paddles and they moved away from the burning yacht.

Mai Lee was holding her left shoulder. She had slipped when jumping from the yacht and injured herself on one of the handrails' stainless steel uprights. Steve gently unbuttoned the top of her blouse and looked at the shoulder. Blood was oozing from a two-inch gash at the front of her shoulder. He took off his shirt folded it into a pad and pressed it onto the wound. Mai Lee held the pad in place, and Steve continued to put a safe distance between them and the yacht, which was now entirely engulfed in flames.

Steve heard the sound of small explosions on the yacht, which was probably weapon ammunition being ignited by the intense heat. He looked around the area, Giorgio's tiny escape boat and the police launch had disappeared over the horizon. He held Mai Lee to him and gently kissed her forehead, she was still in shock, and her injured shoulder was causing obvious pain. He took stock of himself; he had just killed a man, and the thought made his stomach churn. His sharkskin shirt would probably never be used again, but at least it was being put to good use. They were both going through a dramatic time, but they were still alive.

Suddenly a huge explosion ripped through the hull of the yacht, lifting it momentarily clear of the water. A mushroom of dense smoke and flames rose into the air, and debris showered down onto and around the small rubber dinghy. Steve held Mai Lee closer to him, protecting her as best he could. Either Giorgio had set a 'scuttling' charge before leaving the yacht, or the engine fuel tanks had ignited from the intense heat of the fire.

As the mushroom of black smoke began to clear, a huge vulture-like bird emerged, as if appearing from nowhere. The bird circled the dinghy, looking for somewhere to land. Steve looked up at the massive bird; its wingspan was at least five to six feet. Steve turned to where the yacht had lain. The vessel had disappeared, only small pieces of debris remained bobbing about on the disturbed water's surface. He looked at Mai Lee's shoulder and saw that his once white shirt was now bright red. He held her shivering body closely to him, and she grasped his arm.

The dinghy, although mainly inflated rubber, had a wooden stern, suitable for clamping an outboard motor to. The vulture gradually reduced the height of its encircling, and landed on the wooden stern plank. Steve and Mai Lee were half lying, half sitting, in the bow of the dinghy. Steve, still barefoot, kicked out at the massive vulture, trying not to disturb Mai Lee who was only half conscious. The bird moved to one side of the stern, flexed its huge wings and dug its claws into the stern plank. The vulture was going nowhere!

Steve looked more closely at the bird. Its feathers were jet black and it appeared to have escaped the mushroom of flame and smoke unscathed, it was a 'survivor' in life! Its claws, which were digging deep into the stern plank, looked gnarled and capable of picking up a sizable prey. It had the large hooked beak of a meat eater and black beady eyes that fixed Steve with an unblinking stare; he had his next meal! Like the police, all he had to do was wait! Steve assumed that the bird had belonged to one of the crew, or perhaps even Giorgio Busetti. He was the type of man who would enjoy a certain perverse satisfaction from owning such a huge predator.

Steve looked at the water's surface. Debris was everywhere, and he could also see many small white packets amongst the pieces of yacht. They gradually absorbed the sea water, and sank into the water's bed and mother Earth. For Steve, it was a symbolic act. The drugs were returned from 'whence they came', without harming man or beast!

Steve looked at the horizon; there was nothing to be seen. The once turbulent waters were suddenly very still and the yacht's remains did not move. There was an eerie silence. It was as if somebody had switched the world to 'off!' They were completely alone. Steve licked his sun dried lips and tasted the sea salt. He wondered if the vulture preferred salt or pepper with his evening meal. Through all of the drama he still held on to his sense of humour – just! The vulture shifted its position on the stern, and blinked its eyes at Steve!

Steve ignored the bird's eyes and held Mai Lee closer to him. He carefully checked her shoulder. The bleeding had stopped, and she was no longer shivering. The shock had left her; she would be all right now.

Steve looked at the vulture, and said loudly, "Well this is it, bird; it's time for the cavalry to arrive!"

CHAPTER 55

It was the year 1962, and springtime in England. The trees and hedgerows were starting to bear new greenery, and the land was waking from its frosty sleep.

Steve Galway stared out of the 3rd class railway carriage window. He was surprised how clean it was, and that the 3rd had been newly painted. He looked forward to seeing Aunt Maude again, and savouring her cheese and pickled onion sandwiches once more. Steve closed his eyes and sank back against the green upholstery; an inner feeling of contentment filled his mind and body.

Mai Lee looked at Steve from the seat opposite. She smiled lovingly at him; her 'Lieutenant' had come home! She looked at the wedding ring on her finger, glanced out of the window at the passing scenery of Somerset, and then returned to her book about the Queen of England, Buckingham Palace, and garden parties!

End of Story